The mafia in power!

THE SICILIAN SPECIALIST

A novel that explodes with terrifying truths about U.S. Intelligence and organized crime on an international level, a suspense story that swings from Sicily to Massachusetts, to Cuba, the Everglades, Guatemala, Mexico—and ultimately to Dallas, Texas for the most shockingly real climax of all!

BOOKS BY NORMAN LEWIS

Fiction

Nonfiction

THE
Sicilian
Specialist

Norman Lewis

BALLANTINE BOOKS • NEW YORK

Library of Congress Catalog Card Number: 74-9057

SBN 345-24759-0-195

This edition published by arrangement with Random House, Inc.

First Printing: November, 1975

Printed in the United States of America

BALLANTINE BOOKS
A Division of Random House, Inc.
201 East 50th Street, New York, N.Y. 10022

To Kiki and Gawaine

Part

One

1

Three weeks after the Allies invaded Sicily in 1943, a small contingent of Moors with the Anglo-Canadian army advancing up the coast murdered their officer and deserted. Having seized, and decamped in, four jeeps, the Moors took an island road away from the battle and began a marauding expedition into western Sicily. When their gas gave out at Campamaro, they made the village their stronghold and base for forays into the surrounding countryside. Racing up out of the darkness, jillaba skirts caught up at their knees, pigtails flying, knives in teeth, they fell on isolated farms, looted, burned, beheaded resisters and raped men, women, and children: whooping and giggling, they scampered back to Campamaro, carrying their booty and wearing a collection of rings, wrenched or cut from fingers. Sometimes they dragged a girl or a boy or two with them, and after they had done with them, and their bleeding and lacerated victims had dragged themselves away, they banged their drums and danced the night through.

On the night of the third day of their occupation, seventeen-year-old Marco Riccione, who had hidden with his mother and young sister in an old oil cellar as soon as the Moors appeared, escaped and crossed the mountains to reach the farm of the nearest man of honor, Tagliaferri of San Stefano.

2

Tagliaferri, a small sun-wizened countryman who had spent many years in America, sent for his three subordinates in the association and they concocted a plot. Realizing they were too few to resist the Moors by force of arms, and uncertain even whether such resistance might not be punished when the main body of the Allied forces arrived, they planned a classic solution to the difficulty. Marco Riccione described the conditions in the Campamaro area: the Moors were famished; there was no bread, the only animals the peasants hadn't slaughtered and eaten themselves were pigs, forbidden to the Muslims by their religion. A search through the farms of San Stefano produced nine chickens, and these were killed and injected with white arsenic. Riccione then agreed to take the chickens to Campamaro. He was given a bicycle, and on this he pedaled back over the mountain road to his village, the dead chickens dangling from the crossbar. As soon as he rode into the village street, the Moors pounced on him, yelping like dogs. Riccione's thumbs were tied together and he was dragged to a hut to be abused sexually by the sergeant-chief and any others, in order of rank and seniority, who felt in the mood. After that the chickens were grilled on a spit and eaten. It was half an hour or more before the venom began its paralyzing work, spreading through tissue, nerves, blood, bone, until it burst through the walls of the ultimate cell in the last strand of wiry Moorish hair. As their intestines boiled, the Moors ran screeching in all directions, tearing at their flesh with their fingernails, vomiting bile and squirting a bloody flux. The dying process was slow, and one Moor crawled a half-mile from the village to the spot where, chewing a cud of earth, he sucked in his last breath eight hours later.

By the end of the day it was all over, and the village of Campamaro had eleven Moroccan corpses on its hands. Their presence was embarrassing because Allied advance guards were reported in the vicinity. A way out of the difficulty was suggested by the resourceful Riccione, who produced an abandoned German submachine gun and with it fired scores of bullets

into the bodies, after posing them in the attitudes
of men who had fallen, gun in hand, their faces to
the enemy.

Cunning was admired even more than bravery in
Campamaro, and Riccione was given a hero's treatment in the village. The priest, Don Emilio Cardona,
waited before mass to embrace him publicly on the
steps of the church. Don Carlo Magna, the landowner,
let it be known that he would not oppose a betrothal
with his daughter, who was weak in the head but
had the largest dowry of any girl in the province.
An exclusive circle of old men who played cards
endlessly and in absolute silence in the village tavern
invited him to join them. It was more than a week
before the first Allied tanks reached Campamaro,
and by that time the corpses of the Moors, who had
been left where they lay, had suffered from the hot
weather and the hooded crows abounding in the area.
The Allies showed no interest, so the bodies were
dragged away at night for burial where they could
improve the soil of garden plots.

With the conclusion of this episode Campamaro's
involvement in the world conflict was at an end, but
the part played by Marco Riccione in the village's
salvation had been noted elsewhere, and commented
on. The qualities Riccione had displayed were too
rare to be wasted. Mussolini's attack on the association
of men of honor had left it weakened and depleted,
and its terrible powers were now wielded by a constantly shrinking number of old men. Many of these
believed that the emergency justified some slackening
of the severity of its standards, and a search for new
blood.

Within the month a rare and impressive ceremony
took place behind shuttered windows in a house at
San Stefano, where Tagliaferri and his three other
men of honor gathered to admit Riccione to membership. All five, dressed in stiff, dark suits as if for
a wedding, took their places around a table; then,
grasping a kitchen knife that had to serve as the ritual
dagger, they sawed in turn at the balls of their thumbs
until blood came. This was allowed to drip and mingle

on a paper scrawled with signs copied from the Book of St. Cyprian, a country handbook of magic always to be found in such backward mountain villages. Tagliaferri held the paper in the flame of a candle until it burned away, and the ceremony was at an end. No one spoke. The five men rose to embrace each other.

To Marco Riccione the experience was a soul-piercing one. From this moment onwards the old loyalties were sheared away, and he was manacled to new ones. He was no longer subservient to the law, or answerable even to the commandments of religion, because the secret and silent men who had taken him into their protection dictated the law to the lawgivers and offered their own form of absolution. All that was demanded of him was devotion to the iron code, and to those who followed it—who, since wealth and standing were of slight importance in the association, could be shepherds or princes, and were instantly identifiable among the mass by that quiet gaze, that sinister tranquillity bred of a sense of their power and invulnerability.

2

Outside, the midday calm of the great and glorious city, clothed in saffron under its many cupolas; within, a watchful lassitude among the rusted palm fronds of the Albergo Sole, each palm in its small desert fog. Marco had been sent off on the almost hopeless search for martinis in a town that offered little but Marsala, often horribly streaked with yolk of egg. Bradley was left to defend himself against Locatelli's criticisms.

"I break out in a sweat every time I think about it," Locatelli said. "He isn't even a grown man. A kid of twenty-two."

Bradley broke off an indulgent humming of *Nun ti scorda' di me,* a tune saturated with the nostalgia

that had fallen upon them all at the war's end. "Ages
don't mean the same here," he said. "These kids
grow up quick. They're grown men with a grown
man's responsibilities by the time they're out of their
teens. He may look like a kid, but he's a serious married man."

"Do you know how old his wife is?"

"Fourteen. What does it matter? It's the local tradition."

"This is the biggest assignment we've ever had."

"Or ever likely to have."

"It'll cost us our jobs if anything goes wrong."

"Nothing will go wrong. This man is Don C.'s
representative, and that's enough for me. Don C.
is less of a fool than any man I've ever met. Our
friend will carry out whatever his orders are. Efficiently."

Bradley wrapped up the rest of Locatelli's objections in a complex gesture involving both hands, before
pushing them aside. He was a man conscious of a
certain leaden quality in his blood, of a mind slowed
and clogged with calculation, doing what he could
to remedy it; he had gathered together a repertoire
of meaningful gesticulations picked up from the
Italians, as well as a range of spurious vocal expression.
At this moment his eyes twinkled unnecessarily, while
the austere and beetle-browed Locatelli, who rarely
used his hands except to eat, nursed his fears and
mumbled his warnings. "We're going to save Europe,"
he said, "and this unexciting-looking young man is
going to help us save it. He's about to have greatness
thrust upon him."

"Not this way, we aren't," Locatelli said. "If we
play this Don C.'s way, all we're going to do is create
a bunch of martyrs. If we fuck up we're finished in
this country. Out."

Watching him, Bradley shook his head. Locatelli
sat with his head hunched between his shoulders in
a way that reminded him of a vulture. He fought
back his exasperation. This man who had once been
an enormous asset was becoming a liability, if for
no other reason than because pessimism was in-

fectious. He was a founder-member of the organization in the old pre-Pearl Harbor days of the COI, and had enthusiastically transferred himself to its offshoot, the admired and derided OSS—already referred to by West Pointers as Donovan's Dragoons. Locatelli had charged with Byronic fury and fervor into every venture; no exploit behind the lines in Norway or in occupied France was too wild to deter him. But his biggest near-success had been his secret visit in 1943 to Mussolini, leading to an arrangement by which the dictator had almost stayed on as head of the Italian state, perfectly prepared to cooperate with the victors and to discipline his people in a way that the Allies were ill-equipped to do. The agreement had been frustrated by the intervention of the Churchillian warmongers, and with its collapse Locatelli's career had eased into the shadows. With the demise of the OSS, the Agency had inherited him, with, it now seemed to Bradley, much of the deadwood of the old organization. Now in his late thirties, Locatelli seemed to have been pushed suddenly to the threshold of old age, with furrowed brow and humbled lackluster eyes.

Bradley glanced up and saw Marco coming through the palm fronds toward them, treading silently in his rubber-soled American officer's boots. "Here come the drinks," he said. "Do your best not to let him see that you don't have much confidence in him. He's sensitive behind that poker face." He called to Marco, "How did you make out?"

"I got them," Marco said. "And I told him they must be very dry." He walked with flatfooted care over the polished floor tiles, eyes focused on the two glasses on the tray, face perpetually stiffened as if for an occasion: a face dehumanized by a wedding photographer or creator of graduation portraits.

"Real dry martinis," Bradley said. "Fantastic, huh? How did you manage it?"

"The barman is from my part of the country. Caltanissetta," Marco said. For the first time in the week that they had known him, he smiled.

They drove five miles out of town along the Sagana road in the command car, and parked in a disused limestone quarry cut into a mountainside. It was a desolate, crystalline place under the sun at noon, with a smell of sagebrush and desert, and small daggers of reflected light pointed at them from all directions. A track took them out of sight of the road. In places, chalky mud seeped through the grass, and Bradley noticed the care with which Marco avoided dirtying his boots. Locatelli had drawn apart slightly from the other two.

"Everything go off as you hoped?" Bradley asked.

"Everything is fine," Marco told him. "The big meeting will be held at Collo on June 1. Cremona has agreed to be there, which means that all the provincial party leaders will come. This is what we hoped for."

"I'm glad to hear it. We'll still want all the details of the action you propose. This is no time for evasion and mystery. It isn't enough to tell us that such and such a person will be removed from the scene; we have to know how you propose to set about it."

Bradley sensed Marco's embarrassment. He was like a prude being pressed for details of a sexual encounter.

"It will be arranged for them to go," he answered. "There is no problem. They will simply vanish from sight." A quiet and composed young man, with little that was emphatic in his manner, he allowed himself a rare gesture, one of finality: an invisible pen held between his fingers as he drew a conclusive stroke across the bottom of a page.

"You're still not telling me anything," Bradley said.

Locatelli's eyes were narrowed in anguished concentration, preparing himself for what he did not want to hear.

"They will be attacked by bandits," Marco said.

"My, oh, my. Bandits, huh? Surely not our old friend Attilio Messina once again?"

"Attilio is the only bandit left with the force to carry out such an operation."

"Well, what d'ya know. It certainly takes some thinking about. And has he actually agreed to oblige?"

"He will be given an order, and he will carry it out."

Was there pride in the soft, even voice? Bradley couldn't be sure. If any other human being he knew had made such a claim, he would not have bothered himself to laugh at its absurdity. Voiced by Marco, it had a staggering validity.

"Who'll be giving the order?"

"A certain person."

"By which you mean Don C."

Marco didn't reply to the remark, which Bradley already regretted as an indiscretion.

"What d'ya say to that, John? Isn't that something? All our problems are going to be solved by Attilio. How about that?"

Locatelli's head was turned away. "I prefer to withhold comment."

A weight around his neck, Bradley thought. Sometimes he wondered whether headquarters had intentionally encumbered him with this man. In their fear of audacity, in their distrust of vision and strength, could they have entrusted Locatelli with the secret mission of keeping him in check?

Marco had paused to scuffle with the side of his boot on a tuft of coarse grass. He tore a leaf from a bush to wipe away a gob of chalk that still stuck to the polished leather.

"The whole C.P. of Sicily eliminated at one fell swoop," Bradley said. "Simply by setting the bandits on them. The magnificent simplicity of it. In any other country in the world it would be the sheerest fantasy."

"It's sheer fantasy here," Locatelli said.

"We should eliminate only the leaders," Marco pointed out. "Only a handful—those whose influence is most dangerous to the peasants."

"And it would start the biggest rumpus since Katyn," Locatelli said. "Worse."

"Yes," Bradley said. "I'm afraid you're right there, John. Can you imagine the outcry?"

"Any public resentment would be against the bandits," Marco said. "The bandits would be acting on orders, but this would never be known."

"You're saying that the true story would never leak out?" Locatelli asked.

"I am sure," Marco said.

"What makes you so sure?"

"There are means of ensuring this."

"No mystery or evasion, please," Bradley said.

"Apart from us, only the bandits will know the true story, and they also will be removed from the scene. As soon as it is decided that the bandits serve no useful purpose any more they will be eliminated."

Eliminated. Removed from the scene. Bradley's private colloquy was spoken aloud. "Extraordinary world we live in. I suppose these euphemisms must perform some protective function . . . isolate the imagination from damaging realities."

At his side, Locatelli had moved closer to scold him in a dry, clucking ventriloquist voice. ". . . and have you ever paused to consider what the general's likely to say about this?"

"The general," Bradley said. "Wasn't it Nelson who held the telescope to his blind eye? The general? Well, why don't we cross that bridge when we get to it, John?" He was staring down at the three dwarf shadows thrown ahead of them by the high sun. "What did you say the name of that place is, Marco? Where the bandits would knock off the Reds?"

"Collo. Near Lecara Friddi."

"Never heard of the place. It lends itself to the operation?"

"The meeting will be held in an open space at the top of a pass, with mountains all around. A natural amphitheater of rock."

"That's rather well put," Bradley said. "Descriptive."

"Several thousand villagers will attend from the villages on both sides of the pass. At a given moment the roads can be cut so that they will be in a trap.

The whole area can be dominated by machine guns and mortars."

"They're using mortars these days, huh?"

"Bazookas, too," Marco said. "The latest field telephones, radio transmitters—everything. Your army gave them all they asked for with the exception of mountain artillery."

Bradley raised his eyebrows and widened his eyes to indicate his surprise. "Where'd they get all that hardware from?"

"The last general," Marco said.

"Yeah, of course, I was forgetting. The time they had that beautiful platonic thing going with the separatist state. And a great pity nothing came of it. Satisfy my curiosity: just where will the police and anti-bandit forces be when all this is taking place?"

"Somewhere else."

"Just somewhere else. Marco, you never cease to amaze me. One other point: could this thing get out of hand?"

"I don't follow you, Mr. Bradley."

"How many people besides Cremona are you planning to take out?"

"Thirty at the most. This would include the majority of the provincial party leaders."

"It's out of the question," Locatelli said. "It's not even to be thought about."

"Thirty is okay," Bradley said. "A hundred might be too many."

Locatelli, warped and anguished, yet imprisoned by decorum in Marco's presence, scrabbled desperately with his hands.

"Deft political surgery at the right time and place," Bradley said. "A small price to pay for freedom."

"A massacre's a massacre whatever you call it. Cremona is regarded as a hero," Locatelli said.

"Was," Bradley said. "Partisans are a thing of the past now. How long did it take the crowd at Jerusalem to forget Jesus Christ? These bandits of yours," he said to Marco, "even allowing for the fact that, mistakenly or not, we supplied them with arms, have been consistently outnumbered—about thirty to one—by your security forces. How come they're still in business?"

"There are some things one cannot look into too closely," Marco said. "Perhaps the time had not come for them to go."

Some country, huh? Some country. Bradley addressed himself with a kind of dazed enthusiasm to the landscape, the ravaged quarry walls and the sky with its lackadaisical crows. A horsefly bit through the crackling skin on his forearm, and was squashed flat with an instant slap.

Marco continued with the standard summation given sooner or later by any Sicilian to any outsider prepared to listen. "The centuries have taught us many lessons. We have learned how to settle our problems in our own way. A foreigner cannot always be expected to understand."

"I guess not, Marco. I guess no foreigner possibly could. When do we have to make up our minds about this beautifully simple plan of yours?"

"We must know soon," Marco said. "The meeting is only two weeks away, and such an opportunity may never be offered to us again."

Locatelli's ventriloquist's voice rasped in Bradley's ear. "The general's on leave for another week. Be at least a week before you can contact him."

"Whoever said anything about contacting him?" Bradley said. "We'll tell him when it's all over."

They dropped Marco off at the Quattro Canti, and saw his precise somber figure diluted, then lost in the swirling of the crowd. Bradley turned off into the Via Maqueda. The gas shortage was still keeping the cars off the street, but there were a few painted carts and many pedestrians, their faces still whitened by the famines of the past, strolling ten abreast down the street toward favorite bars, where they would line up for their coffee substitute before going home for the siesta.

Once again, Locatelli moved to the attack. "This isn't Italy, and Sicilians aren't Italians."

"So you've said before, John. Maybe there is a difference, but so what? You can't expect me to share your prejudices."

"For God's sake, what do we know about this man?"

"Apart from the fact he's from Don C., he's passed a double-A security check. He worked for the British for two years at Catania, and after that for another two years at the Caltanissetta base. I checked with the C.O. there and he couldn't have been more enthusiastic. He said he's the only Sicilian they've employed who never stole. He's also reputed to be a member of the Honored Society."

"If it exists," Locatelli said.

"If it exists."

"So what are you going to do?" Locatelli asked.

"Go ahead," Bradley said.

"It's the worst piece of insanity I've ever heard of."

"It's the logical thing. It sounds wild, but when you think about it, it isn't. The Sicilians were going to do it in any case."

"Then why not leave it to them?"

"Because if we have a hand in it, things won't get out of control. I want to know just what goes on." Also because, Bradley told himself, of his feeling for history and his own personal involvement with it, and because he loved this country and felt called to its defense.

"Tell the general about it and see what he has to say."

"He's a plain soldier; he'd be out of his depth. Anyway, there isn't time. The boss has a simple heart, God bless him. Once a soldier, always a soldier."

They had been slowed to a walking pace over a terrible piece of road where the bomb craters of four years before had been filled in with rubble and earth, but the surface never replaced.

"This scheme is free-lancing at its worst," Locatelli said.

"I'd have said free-lancing on a magnificent scale."

"When I think of what's at stake it makes me shiver."

Bradley wanted to say, This is a great new adventure, and we're in it together. What do the generals and the politicians matter? *We're* the new men. *We're* going to call the tune. But all he said was, "You need a drink."

They were now in the Ruggiero Settimo Square, beyond which the town offered nothing of pleasure, but in it was located the only bar in Palermo outside that of the Albergo Sole where a real dry martini might occasionally be found. Here they would pass a half-hour, and the chances were that Locatelli would take out the signed photograph he always carried of the vanquished Duce—wearing an extraordinary bowler hat—and shake his head over it. "The hope of our times," he would say. "The most original political philosopher since Plato," and Bradley would politely agree with him.

He pulled into the curb, switched off the engine and slapped Locatelli jovially on his bony thigh. "Cheer up, John. I might even be able to arrange for you to have some sick leave home, if that would interest you—but after the big event, of course. It would have to be after the event."

Marco walked as quickly as the crowd would let him up the Corso Vittorio Emanuele and went into the Birreria Venezia, standing a little apart from the other customers who were drinking a concoction made from roasted nuts. He was served with a minute cup of genuine coffee by a barman who knew little of him, but who was responsive to the whole range of human vibrations. The glass counter contained rows of little cakes made from marzipan and egg yolk; he took one, bit at it twice, and swallowed, carefully wiping the tips of his fingers on the paper napkin supplied. The barman hovered with a respectful arching of the eyebrows, ready to produce more of the privileged coffee, but Marco shook his head. He had nothing to say to the sleekly servile young man behind the counter. For Marco, the man and his chattering customers hardly existed, though they were solid indeed by comparison with such foreigners as Bradley and Locatelli, who were part of the furniture of a phantom world, the depthless stage scenery of his own private universe which would cease to exist when he ceased to exist.

As he left the *birreria* one of the two customers turned to watch him go. He walked quickly the hundred yards to the Vico Marrotta where he lived, and where the body of his young wife awaited him. Excitement and anticipation stirred his blood as he turned off the main street into the narrow entry to the *vico,* a sly, mean alley he and Teresa had lived in since their marriage. Here a selection of the city's cheapest and most bedraggled whores occupied the dark street-level *bassi,* half-starved government servants had crowded into the upper floors and the tatters of Mussolini posters still flapped in the wind out of reach. Passing a jeep filled with *carabinieri* of the new anti-bandit squad, squatting like pied fledglings on the edge of their nest while their sergeant enjoyed a clandestine cigarette, he turned into a doorway and went up to his third-floor flat.

He heard the shuffle of Teresa's slippered feet on the bare hallway. The door opened a couple of inches to show the small, cautious triangle of her face, then she slipped off the chain to let him in. She put her arms around his neck, and he flattened her lips with his, and felt his teeth on hers, and the pressure of her breasts and pregnant belly, and smelled the raw scent of her flesh. She was naked under her frock, as any Sicilian housewife always was about the house in summer, and he lifted her dress to her waist to caress her buttocks, then picked her up, two fingers of his right hand in her vagina, to carry her across the hallway to the shuttered room behind which contained only half-darkness, a table and a bed.

Marco put his wife down on the bed and forced his way into her, triumphantly aggressive and encouraged by her shrieks, which might have been either from pain or pleasure. As big as an African, his mother had boasted of him to all her friends. In such villages

as Campamaro and San Stefano, the old custom
persisted at child-betrothals of displaying the boy's
genitalia to close relatives of the girl, in token of
what was to be expected of him when the time came.
He would stay with her, driven as much by custom
as desire, for an hour or more, as long as orgasm
could be delayed, after which, in the trough of exhaustion, they would eat together a mouthful of pasta
before he went off to what was left of the day's work.
In this way the siesta went every day, and at night
it was early to bed so that the relentless thrusting could
be resumed with as little as possible loss of time.
Every man worthy of respect inflicted these daily
penances upon his wife and himself.

Withdrawing for the last time, Marco made the
alarming discovery that there was blood on his member
and on the sheets.

"I must have hurt you."

"You didn't."

"You're sure."

"Of course I'm sure."

He explored with his finger, then inspected the
unmistakable smear.

"I went too high."

"No."

"I'm afraid for the baby. We must get Dr. Bellometti."

"I won't let him come near me. I'll keep my legs
up. I'll put a pillow under my feet."

It had been the remedy, he remembered, for the
terrible bleeding of the wedding night. "I'm going
for Dr. Bellometti," he said.

"I won't see him. Get Bruna if you can." Bruna
was the midwife, a toothless, cackling witch, a dis-
penser of fearsome potions, called in by all the old-
fashioned husbands who debarred male doctors in
gynecological matters.

But Marco went for Bellometti, showing himself
by this decision as capable of breaking with tradition
when the emergency was real enough. "There's been
some bleeding all along since the first night," he explained to the doctor. "Not much. Once in a while."

Bellometti, born in an encampment of Arab-style hovels on Mt. Cammarata, where no nubile woman was ever seen in the street after six A.M., and where he could still remember the bloodstained sheets displayed in triumph at the windows of nuptial chambers, looked at Marco with new respect. Times had changed, anl largely for the worse, but there were still a few stallions about.

"And there's these pains . . ."

"Do you want me to look at her?"

"Yes, Doctor. Don't be angry, but please wash your hands first. If you need some penicillin, I can get some."

"I believe in providence, clean bandages and fresh air," Bellometti said. "You're afraid of sunshine —that's half the trouble. You keep the shutters closed, and the place becomes a breeding ground for germs."

They were peasants living in the city, Bellometti thought, but still peasants at heart, oppressed by the terrible monotony of the peasant existence and seeking relief from it in violence of any kind—of which that of the bed was simply the most accessible. He was reminded of a *contadino,* who could afford nothing but maize gruel, shoving raw peppers into his mouth and chewing until his eyes spurted tears. In some villages, he knew, the newspaper sellers could get a lira more for a front-page picture where the blood streaming from vendetta victims had been colored in by hand.

Bellometti put Teresa on her side, knees drawn up, and made his investigation, while Marco, his back turned, listened uneasily to the increased rate of her breathing. Bellometti was the only other man to have seen or touched her body. It was a kind of second defloration, and the more he tried to think of the doctor as detached and impersonal in this task he had performed so many hundred times, the more Bellometti's obstinate humanity asserted itself in his imagination. Teresa's beauty—the thick, dark hair framing the full lips and fine eyes characteristic of the classic South, the narrow waist, the abundant breasts and hips—was of the kind that turned every

male head in the street, and it was hard to believe
that this exposure of her sexual parts and exploration
of her body could fail to provoke an erection in any
man, even the custom-hardened doctor.

A silence punctuated by faint gasps from his wife
was climaxed by a single suppressed cry as Bellometti
inserted a speculum and opened it to its full extent.
A moment later the examination was at an end, and
the doctor announced that there was nothing serious
to report. Marco relieved his suspicious fears by a
quick glance down at the profile of the doctor's trousers as the two men strolled in the hallway toward the
door. Bellometti, fumbling with his bag, reduced his
voice to a pacific whisper. "A day or two's rest, that's
all. Reasonable precautions at this stage. Don't throw
your full weight on her. Support yourself on your
elbows. She's young but well-formed. I'll look back
again next week if you like."

He left, turning at the door to remind Marco once
again that nature was the great healer, and that in
fact to die was as natural as to live, but nothing in
his visit had reassured Marco. That afternoon he was
afraid to leave Teresa; afraid that she had merely
not wished to admit to being in pain; afraid that the
bleeding might return. He was still convinced that
should a dangerous hemorrhage happen in his absence,
it would be the hour of the neighborhood crones,
with their secret remedies and the terrible infections
they might carry.

3

Two days later Marco drove with Bradley and
Locatelli to the bandit village of Montelupo. He had
advised against their presence, but given in to Bradley's
insistence. Bradley had borrowed a Fiat *millecento*
for the occasion with Palermo plates, and both
Americans were dressed as commercial travelers
might have been, in meagerly cut suits of a local dark

gray material. Locatelli had also been in favor of
Marco's visiting the bandits unaccompanied, arguing that the risk of kidnapping was too great, and
his depression deepened as Marco pointed out the
spots on the lonely mountain road where the bandits
had staged bloody ambushes, and the roadside crosses,
with their bunches of withered flowers, put up by
bereaved relatives. Bradley drove the way he spoke
and moved, with a determined flamboyance.

"What line are we going to take if they actually
grab us?" Locatelli said.

Bradley noted that Locatelli's increasing squeamishness and moral sensitivity were accompanied by a
slackening of courage. Danger, a phantom once to
be exorcised by laughter, had become a real presence.
Gripping the edges of his car seat, Locatelli worried
about armed men in hiding among the rocks, and also
about their speed on a road with many hairpin bends
and precipices.

"It won't happen," Bradley said. "There isn't a
chance of it."

"Why not?"

"Because if there's one thing we know about these
guys it's that their intelligence is perfect. Their quar-
rel is with the police and the army, not us."

"What about all those civilians who've been held
for ransom?"

"Italians, not Americans. So far there hasn't been
a single case of interference with Allied personnel."

"If we're ordered to stop, we stop immediately,"
Marco said. "We make no attempt to resist or escape.
When we explain who we are, they will let us go."

"How many do you suppose there are in this particular area?"

Bradley was concentrating on the hairpin bend
ahead. He took it fast and wide on a downhill gradient
a little steeper than one in ten, cutting in at the apex
of the curve to skate gravel gouged by the rear tire
at the frail barrier of hemlock and convolvulus screen-
ing a hundred-foot drop. The car lurched and slewed
and the enormous triangles of the landscape shifted
suddenly. Locatelli saw a limestone cliff above, and

knew that it continued into the abyss across the edge of the road to his right. He gritted his teeth. An army could have hidden in the dense scrub growing in all the flat places.

Marco answered. "A hundred or two—perhaps less at this moment. Some of the bandits go to the mountains only in their spare time. On weekends when they have nothing to do, or when they can find no work on the farms."

Locatelli grimaced. "Do you know what I'm going to do when I get off that ship?" he said to Bradley. "I'm going to kneel down and kiss the earth."

"You'll miss all this when you're away from it," Bradley said. "You'll find you can't do without the tension."

Montelupo came into sight, a cluster of gray, scabby buildings among the rocks.

"Well, there it is," Bradley said. "Kinda romantic in its way, isn't it?" He slowed to enjoy the savagery of the village's setting. This was what was called being in one's element, he thought: these great white rocks, poised as if by design, one on the other; the glaciers and remote snowfields of crystalline chalk; a pine here and there, wonderfully knotted by the wind; water crashing in a gorge beneath them; an Arcadian shepherd on a hilltop who probably dug up a gun and went off with the Messina band whenever called upon. In all, a place still under its delicate pagan spell, and he loved everything about it.

A narrow, broken track wound up from the main road to the village, and they drove several hundred yards up it and parked in the shade of a fig tree. Here Marco left them to go off to his meeting. Twenty feet away a windowless hutment with an open stable door held the dark, superimposed shapes of humans and goats. A mangy she-ass straightened its tail to let go a yellow stream in their direction. Insects clicked in the scaly branches all around.

"What I can't understand is why several thousand soldiers and police are combing the island for this fellow," Locatelli said, "when he's right here in his own village."

"And living in some comfort at that," Bradley said. "Fourteen *carabinieri* died in ambushes last week, but Chief Inspector What'shisname comes up here to drink a bottle of wine with him."

"What's the answer?" Locatelli asked.

"They need him around."

"If you ever put this in a book, nobody would believe you."

"The book wouldn't get published anyway."

"Twenty or thirty yards from where we're sitting right now, a bunch of bandits are hiding out. The toughest collection in history."

"And yet you're as safe as you would be on West 93rd Street. Probably safer."

"This shouldn't have happened," Locatelli said. "It could all have been avoided." A large and glittering horsefly buzzed into the car, and he drove it out and wound up the window hastily.

"What could have been avoided?"

"All this mess. If only we'd have been ready to play ball with Mussolini, none of these problems would have come up."

"I know," Bradley said. "You've told me so often. But we weren't. That's just the trouble; we weren't."

Marco went to the village bar where Cavaliere Santo Flores was waiting for him. The Cavaliere was the man of honor who ruled over a large but vague area to the northeast of Palermo, a gray, waddling shapeless man in his early sixties, enfeebled by his great bulk and poor lungs, who had to be supported wherever he went by two henchmen who walked at his side, half dragging and half lifting him along. A slow procession followed to Attilio Messina's headquarters in a village back street, Santo Flores grunting and wheezing with asthma as his two men hauled him over the cobbles, and Marco keeping respectfully to the rear. The street was empty and shuttered. They passed the tiny square where Messina had ordered the public execution of police informers and those charged with oppressing the poor, and turned into an alleyway where the bandit lived in his mother's house when not in action in the mountains.

Here Santo Flores, a man who had been honored by the king of Italy, and an intimate friend of several dukes, was shoved, along with his escorts, without ceremony into a tiny waiting room, while Marco was shown into Attilio Messina's presence. The great bandit came as a surprise. It was hard to believe that this fussily dressed young man in a green silk shirt, with chubby fingers and sleekly brushed hair, could have killed so many. He made an actor's entrance into the room, spreading the aroma of eau de cologne through the tightly packed peasant furniture. He had been one of the great guerrilla captains of all time, and had defeated all the troops sent against him, while cultivating the Robin Hood image that greatly delighted the ballad singers. The English, and then the Americans, had supplied him with weapons, both in the delirious belief that they could somehow detach Sicily from the Italian mainland as a separate puppet regime—a colony, or even a U.S. state—with Messina as its head. But by now the bubble had burst, the Allies wanted to thrust him out of their memory, and to the secret men who had gathered the reins of power into their own hands he was no more than a nuisance. His destruction had been ordered, but before he passed into oblivion they had prepared a final mission for him to perform.

Marco handed Messina the letter from Don C. which he knew contained the order to go into action against the Reds at Collo. In return there was a guarantee, given by the man who had come to control, in one way or another, the destinies of all Sicilians, that the bandits would be permitted to emigrate and settle in Brazil.

Messina, who had not spoken, tore open the envelope and took out the letter. He read it slowly, his lips forming the words silently in the way of any semiliterate peasant. His expression kept pace with his thoughts, ranging from frowning doubt to a final smirk of satisfaction. Marco noted with contempt this inability to mask feelings; it was all that was to be expected of a bandit.

Messina went to the door and called, and a moment later his cousin and second-in-command of the band, Annibale Sardi, came into the room. Weasel-faced, with huge black eyes set closely together and dressed in an American officer's uniform grotesquely worn with polished black top boots, Sardi made an even worse impression on Marco. The mutual dislike felt by the bandits and the men of honor was a matter of tradition. The men of honor despised the bandits as undisciplined, temperamental and lacking in firmness of purpose, and the bandits in turn were contemptuous of men who seemed devoid of manly courage, and who gained their ends in underhand fashion. Too often the men of honor had been their executioners, when in the bad times the bandits, having been recruited as the private armies of the great landowners, got above themselves and had to be destroyed.

Messina and Sardi went to look at a map pinned on the wall in a corner of the room. Messina found Collo and pointed it out to his cousin, and the two men talked in low tones. Meanwhile, Marco was kept standing. The coolness of his reception was insulting; by local usage he should have been asked to sit down and given a glass of wine, and a second chair should have been found for his hat to be placed upon, whether he wore one or not. It was no more than Marco had anticipated. The Messina bandits had dared to insult and threaten men of the caliber and prestige of Santo Flores, and the men of honor had swallowed their insults without the slightest gesture of anger, simply noting faces, names, times and places, and committing them to the implacable archives of their memory. For Marco the experience was a form of spiritual exercise. It offered him an opportunity to practice the art of indifference. Indifference was the armor of the men of honor, who strove incessantly for a detachment that in the end touched the confines of selflessness, in preparation for cool and efficient action. He stood and watched, hands slipped into the pockets of his jacket, compelling himself to feel nothing for these men whose orders he had just brought.

A few minutes later he was dismissed wordlessly, with the kind of nod given an importunate beggar. Outside, Santo Flores sprawled in a chair, his men grim-faced on either side. Twenty years before, he too would have remained unperturbed at the offense, but as strength and nervous force had slowly drained from him, he had lost as well a little of his self-control, and now he was purple-faced and shaking.

4

On the eve of June 1 all the participants in the drama to be staged the next day were taking up their positions. The bandits, trudging across the mountains to the point where they would set up their ambush, were glum and limp in their jaunty new uniforms. By now the rank and file were convinced that somewhere ahead doom awaited them, and that it had come closer. The shepherd auxiliaries recruited for the operation, whose job it was to carry the heavy equipment, showed reluctance and hostility, and several of them had been forced from their homes at pistol point to join the expedition. Just before the band began its march, Messina learned that Sardi had arranged an alibi with a Palermo chest specialist, who would be prepared if necessary to support his statement that he had been under observation at his clinic on May 1.

A thousand or more peasants from half a dozen villages in the area had gathered in the small town of Miera under the mountain pass of Collo, where the great political meeting was to take place on the next day. They had filled the inns and all the spare rooms in private houses, and the overflow were now comfortably and cheerfully camping out in the streets. This was to be the biggest public demonstration of its kind in western Sicily since the days before the Fascist dictatorship, but more people had come for the festa, the cattle fair and the sideshows than for the politics. A moonless and grass-scented night had fallen when Bradley, Locatelli and Marco in the old *millecento* rattled into town. For some time Locatelli had held out against being included in this expedition, but in the end, after Bradley consented to radical changes in the program, he agreed to come along. When none of Bradley's arguments in favor of what he called the "economy of terror" had succeeded, he had given in to his compatriot's suggestions, unable to face the prospect of going it alone. Cremona and the provincial party heads would not be assassinated but kidnapped and removed from the political scene until after the elections.

But Locatelli's fears of involvement with Don C. were dismissed. "I don't see why that guy has to come into it at all. Can you explain to me why he has to do anything for us?"

"He owes us favors," Bradley said. "It also suits him if we're in this together."

"Why?"

"Why? Well, we cover up for each other."

"I don't ever want to have to cover up for that man."

Rooms had been reserved for them at the *locanda*. Bradley and Locatelli went off to see the sights, and Marco left them to go to a meeting with an emissary of the bandits. They watched him disappear in the drift of the holiday crowds through the flare-lit street.

"Ever thought about precognition?" Bradley asked.

"Can't say I have."

"Sometimes I wonder. Through a glass darkly," Bradley said. "That young man gives me a strange feeling—something I can't describe. I believe he's capable of great things outside the scope of this present operation. I have plans for him."

"He has no morality," Locatelli said.

"On the contrary, he has a very rigid morality. It just happens to differ from ours."

"I've had a number of interesting chats with him,"

Locatelli said. "He's concerned with one thing only: his immediate family. Nothing else exists for him, and that includes you and me. This is what you have to remember about him."

"I wouldn't say that at all."

"It's a mentality you only find in Sicily. They look after their own. Anybody outside the family has no importance."

"He'd be very useful to us—apart from the present operation, I mean," Bradley said. "He's the kind of guy I'd like to have around."

Marco met his man in a bar on the town's outskirts. He was conspicuously dressed in a white city raincoat with padded shoulders, and made a display of a calendar watch and a couple of heavy gold rings. His name was Cucinelli, a nineteen-year-old, pink-faced farmer's boy who was the best-natured and at the same time the most ferocious of the bandits, with eighteen homicides to his credit. Marco pulled him away from the bar and they went outside, Cucinelli filling the night with his pointless laughter. He had been chosen for this mission by Messina because he knew that if cornered by the *carabinieri,* Cucinelli would never allow himself to be taken alive and thereafter tortured into giving away the plans for the ambuscade. Cucinelli told Marco that the bandits had already taken up positions in the mountains overlooking the open space where the meeting was to be held, and that they would attack promptly at nine in the morning. In turn, Marco told him that the orders were now changed and that Cremona and his friends were to be taken alive. Cucinelli tittered his agreement, subjected Marco to a parting hug, and gave him two American cigars, which Marco accepted politely but threw away as soon as Cucinelli was out of sight.

Next, Marco visited a part-time bandit who was a harness-maker when he could get enough work to feed his family, gave him an envelope containing twenty thousand lire, and told him to take a couple of friends and go to the village of Fermagosta, ten miles away to the east, and carry out a fake grenade attack on the police post there at dawn, sustaining the attack for as long as possible. Despite the high-level orders removing the public security police from the area so as to give the bandits absolute freedom of action, through some bungling thirty-two men of the anti-bandit squad had remained in their Miera headquarters, and in this way Marco expected to draw them off.

Bradley and Locatelli wandered from group to group, observing the families squatting like covens of witches of all sizes and shapes around the cauldrons where the supper tripe was boiling; the puppeteer's audience of children bloodthirstily cheering a slaughter of Saracens by Crusaders; a crowd attracted by a ballad singer's promise to defy police prohibition and sing to them of the exploits of Attilio Messina.

Locatelli scratched miserably at the nervous itch he had developed in his jaw and neck. More than ever he felt exposed and defenseless since Marco had left them. "Where do you think Riccione is?" he asked Bradley.

"He said something about looking up a friend. Probably an excuse to be on his own."

"He seemed quieter than usual today."

"You're more sensitive to atmosphere than I am."

"This business could be getting on his nerves."

"Not Marco. He's a tough customer. It could be trouble at home. His wife's got something wrong with her. He didn't give me the details."

"Surprising he mentioned it at all."

"He didn't have much choice. She doesn't trust their doctor, so she's been going to a midwife. He thinks she may have an infection."

"Does it sound bad?"

"It doesn't sound good. On the village midwife level this country's about the same as Africa. They stuff the vagina with boiled herbs to stop a hemorrhage. The one thing that's always taboo is soap and water."

"What made him come to you?"

"He wanted to know if we had any service gynecologists."

"And do we?"

"There's one at every general hospital—probably has to look after the nurses. Anyway, I've arranged a visit for him as soon as we get back."

"Tomorrow, I hope," Locatelli said.

"Sure, tomorrow. Don't worry, John, this thing won't last more than a couple of hours."

Locatelli scratched at his neck again. A child straying from the flickering aurora of a cooking fire collided with his legs and let out a howl, and he groped unsuccessfully in his pockets for the remains of an O'Henry bar with which to silence him. "I'm still unhappy about this, Ronald."

"I know you are, John. It's the way you're made. You gotta quit worrying and accept the fact that at this stage there's nothing we can do about it."

"I think we've embarked on a course that's extremely dangerous, as well as potentially inhuman. Just look at all these kids; the place is full of them."

"They'll be all right. Nobody's going to get hurt."

"And mortars won't be used. You're quite certain of that?"

"Absolutely certain."

"Because there's no such thing as accurate mortar fire—not in my experience."

"Mortars are out," Bradley said. "The whole idea, as we've agreed, is to fire a few shots in the air, stampede the crowd and rush in and grab the Reds. It's timed for nine A.M. They're going to have a mule race and a parade of carts going on at that time, and the kids will be watching that. This place is twice as big as a football field. They have all the sideshows and the candy stalls at one end of it, and the political meeting at the other. The people having themselves a good time up at the fairground won't even know what's going on. Happy now?"

"No, I'm not happy," Locatelli said, "because these things have a habit of going wrong. I've seen too many typical military fuck-ups. I'll be happy when it's over."

"This isn't going to be a military fuck-up because the kind of brains who've worked it all out don't happen to be the military variety. Ten minutes is all this little operation is going to take, and then we can all go home."

"I wish I could believe that," Locatelli said. "I truly do."

They slept badly through the night of distant laughter, horseplay and barrel-organ music echoing up and down the cavernous streets. At breakfast Locatelli tasted the mess of bread soaked in goat's whey and pushed it away. "Seen anything of Marco?" he asked.

"He's up on the roof with his binoculars," Bradley said. All things considered, he felt wonderfully relaxed.

"Where do you think the police went off to in such a hurry?"

"I can tell you that: Fermagosta. There was an attack on the *carabinieri* barracks early this morning."

"Far from here?"

"No, but they'll be out of harm's way for the rest of the morning. They'll have to go up there on foot to avoid the risk of an ambush."

"Coincidence."

"I wouldn't think so," Bradley said. He allowed himself a knowing, complacent smile, then gave a quick cautious glance around the small bare room furnished in the good taste of poverty. Two peasants in thick holiday clothes and wearing their hats sat in silence over their maize gruel in a far corner. A Madonna above an offering of a wax chrysanthemum, and clutching a typical monkey-faced child of the local slums to her breast, looked down on the scene with disenchanted eyes. "Everything's going to be fine," he said. "The politicians went off with the band half an hour ago, and there are still five or six hundred of the rank and file down in the square waiting to be formed up."

"It's bigger than I thought it was going to be," Locatelli said. His hand went up to the nervous rash which had now spread to his throat.

"Marco estimates that about a thousand are going

from Miera. Supposed to be twice that number coming up from the other side."

"Three thousand. How will they get them all in?"

"It's going to be a tight squeeze," Bradley said.

"There are too many people. Something has to go wrong."

"No, it doesn't. Why should it?"

"There's going to be shooting. You yourself said the idea was to start a stampede. Kids are going to get trodden underfoot. People will be crushed to death in the panic."

"We hope not," Bradley said.

"You *hope* not. That isn't enough."

"Accidents can happen. We have to be ready to accept a few casualties. We have to weigh them against the huge positive benefits likely to result from a small preventive action. The Nazis stampeded the crowds on the roads of France. It was a good idea because battles didn't have to be fought. People have to be frightened off the Reds. This could have the effect of putting an end to civil strife on this island for a decade to come."

"Terror doesn't work," Locatelli said.

"The trouble is, it does."

"You have to persuade people, not terrorize them. If this turned out to be a massacre, it would only make everything a hundred times worse."

"Half a dozen cases of broken bones don't make a massacre," Bradley said. "Don't let's lose our sense of perspective."

The last of the barrel organs in the procession was being trundled past on its donkey cart and had started to play the old favorite, *Mamma sono tanto felice*. Locatelli felt the tears gather in his eyes. Despite his contempt and mistrust for Sicilians, he was touched. "Can you imagine any other people who would want to go on serenading their mothers for all these years?"

"They voted Red to a man at the primaries last month," Bradley said. He put his spoon down to smile at Locatelli with conciliation. He had been a man Bradley greatly admired, a man who had once possessed the strength to flout all the rules and disregard the odds. But over the years, with the loss of his bodily cells, the valor had leaked from him. Now he saw two sides to every question. With a drying up of the semen he had been invaded by a fatal compassion that only half masked weakness and nervous fatigue. It would have been far better not to have included him in this venture. When he next saw the general, Bradley proposed to broach the matter of a replacement as tactfully as he could—"ideally, by someone who sees things more in terms of black and white. A tougher personality. Perhaps even, dare I say, a touch of cynicism in the make-up?" A quotation from Lorca, whom the general had once confessed to admiring, occurred to him: ". . . a man with a mouth full of flints."

"You don't really want to pull out now, John?" he asked quietly. "You don't really want to quit and leave me to fight this on my own?"

In an hour the town was empty; listening through the window for the faint toneless clatter of barrel organs, Locatelli heard only the twitter of sparrows. The mountains covered with their flaking rust stood over Miera, but even through Bradley's binoculars there was no movement to be seen on them.

Marco came with the car, and Locatelli went down to him first.

"You seem kind of quiet. *Perchè stai zitto?* Anything on your mind?"

"Nothing, Mr. Locatelli."

"Everything going to be all right, you think?"

"Everything's going to be okay."

"They're all up there by now?"

"Most of them. The meeting's already started."

"What about our friends?"

"They're all ready to go. I spoke to a fellow they sent down last night."

"Do you think they're to be relied upon?"

The smooth, empty bridegroom's face was enlivened by an instant of malice. "These are poor, stupid people, Mr. Locatelli, but they must obey their orders."

Bradley clattered down the *locanda* stairs, eyes shining, face tightened by excitement. A cheerful foresight stirred in his blood, assuring him that this moment called him to the climax of his career. He grinned at Locatelli and clapped Marco in a light embrace. "How long is it going to take us to get up there, Marco?"

"Ten minutes. Maybe less if the road's clear."

"Well, whaddaya say? Better a few minutes too soon than arriving too late for the show."

They climbed into the Fiat, Bradley at the wheel, and started off. Five miles of winding rutted dirt road took them close to the pass. A few straggling families with sheep and donkeys slowed them down. It was a day when the peasants waved at strangers, and sometimes gestured with their bottles to offer wine. Marco leaned forward to pluck at Bradley's arm. "You could have a good view from here, if you want to stop."

Bradley pulled the car off the road, rushed a low bank and cut the engine. They got out and climbed a slope to take in the scene. About two miles away the mountain of Pizzuta, where the main body of bandits would be lying in ambush, thrust its weird teat into the sky; across the plateau, mirages sliced into the step-pyramid peak of Cumeta, where the shepherd auxiliaries waited under the menace of the bandits' guns, ready to take the peasant crowd in the rear. Collo lay between the two mountains, among colossal boulders strewn there by the cataclysms of prehistory.

"A lunar landscape," Bradley said, greeting the view with wide gestures of astonishment and delight. The scene was printed on his retina a little out of register, with ghost outlines in prismatic colors, and the sullen rock masses crested with hallucinatory light. The wind among the razor-edged rocks whistled delicately, like swifts in the sky. A few hundred yards off, a group of peasants had found a shortcut to their destination over the mountain flanks, and in the mangling perspectives they appeared strangely crabbed and Breughelesque. Little could be seen of the crowd at Collo but a termite movement in the grain of the distance. "We have to get closer."

Marco was cautious. "You want to drive right into Collo, Mr. Bradley?"

"Why not? You can't see anything from here."

"We may not find anywhere to park in safety."

"Why don't we take a chance on that?"

They climbed back into the Fiat and drove on, turning under the shoulder of Pizzuta into Collo, where they wedged the car into a disorderly tangle of peasant carts and pushed their way on foot into the noise and bustle of the crowd. Here the quiet Sicilians were transformed by raucous holiday glee. People screamed to be heard above the children's toy trumpets and whistles, the barrel organs clanging out *Mamma* and *Mala spina,* and the fairground barkers advertising their gambling games and displays of human freaks. Young farmers raced around on mules over which they pretended to have little control. A crowd odor arose of hides, cows' sweat, rope soles and wood fires. Bradley noticed many suckling mothers, and wondered if the red paper hats worn by most of the boys had any political significance.

They went in search of the rally and found it centered around an enormous flat-topped rock, from the summit of which the speaker addressed the crowd. Cremona had begun his speech. He was the partisan hero of three engagements with the German troops in the Udine area, where he lost a hand, was captured and then tortured by the Gestapo in the barracks at Palmanova before escaping to take over again the command of his Garibaldini brigade. He stood with eight of his supporters under the red banner, his false hand stuck in his jacket pocket, gesturing constantly to the crowd with his undamaged arm in a way that reminded Locatelli of a man trying to rid himself of a persistent mosquito. The distance made it impossible to distinguish the hero's thin, high-pitched voice. Waiting for the action to begin, Locatelli's nerves were getting the better of him, advertising their revolt by cramps of the stomach. He farted carefully, afraid that the wind might be followed by diarrhea.

It was now nine-fifteen, with the attack fifteen minutes overdue. Bradley glanced continually at his watch, worried that at any moment Cremona might finish what he had to say, climb down from his platform and vanish from sight.

"What's holding things up?" he whispered to Marco.

"I think they have not calculated how long it takes to come down from the mountain."

"Where do you suppose our friends are right now?"

"They could be in this crowd making their way closer to the speaker."

"Trouble is, he's going to stop speaking any minute. What's going to happen then?"

"He will talk for another hour at least. These speeches are very long. He is only now talking about his adventures in the war. That always takes half an hour."

Locatelli was out of earshot. Bradley gave Marco his practiced Machiavellian smile. "It's clearly understood that if they can't grab him, he's to be taken out, however they do it?"

"That is clearly understood."

At this moment Marco's feelings were only of impatience to get the operation over and done with; otherwise he was indifferent—provided of course, that the outcome was seen as satisfactory by his superiors. He could think of little but the trouble with Teresa. The night before she had complained again of pain. Now in his imagination he saw her on the bed in the dark inner room as the pains became rhythmic and sharp, too shy to call for the neighbor's help, out of reach of the midwife, who had to be brought in Marco's car, screaming with agony and fear as the water broke and the bloody fetus was expelled from her womb. These images were followed by others of uncontrollable hemorrhage, sepsis and putrefaction.

When Bradley spoke again, he seemed to be echoing

Marco's own inner misgivings. "Let's only hope that nothing's gone wrong."

"Let's hope so, Mr. Bradley."

"Did you hear that?" Locatelli said.

"What?" Bradley asked.

"That popping sound. It sounds like gunfire."

Bradley listened. "Fireworks," he said. "Rockets. They always set off fireworks at these festas."

Just as the bandits were used and dominated by the men of honor, they in turn used and dominated the wretched shepherds in their area—many of whom were prepared in hard times to engage in a little banditry on their own account, but who on the whole preferred to be left alone to look after their animals. In a press-gang operation the bandits had rounded up fifty-three shepherds for service at Collo, but three had escaped on the way, one of them shot and wounded, but still able to drag himself out of range of the bandits' fire. Though each shepherd had been given an Italian Army light carbine, the six regular bandits who had taken them in charge mistrustfully carried the ammunition themselves. They also carried a radio transmitter, to be operated by one of the bandits, with which they were to keep in contact with the main force. The shepherds and their guardians took up positions on the slopes of the step-pyramid mountain Cumeta just before dark. The plan was that next morning, at a signal radioed from Messina, they would come down the mountainside ready to take the holiday crowd in the rear and capture—or in case of necessity shoot—such political personalities who might attempt to escape from the main attack delivered by Messina. To prevent more shepherd desertions, the bandits, already exhausted by their long march across the mountains, were obliged to mount guard over them all night.

A rumor that they were being led into a trap, and that their leaders were preparing to abandon them, had shattered bandit morale. They felt in need of the protection of the shepherds' numbers, but could not risk supplying them with ammunition before zero hour; after a sleepless night their nerves were beginning to play tricks, so that normally unimaginative men began to be obsessed with signs and omens, and grazing sheep could be taken for human forms crouching among the rocks. The establishment of radio contact with Messina on Pizzuta had a calming effect, but then, with only a matter of minutes to go before they went into action, an extraordinary circumstance threw everything into confusion. Two lads from Miera looking for a quiet place to tryst with an itinerant prostitute stumbled on their hiding place, and all three were immediately seized and tied up. One of the boys turned out to be a cousin of the radio operator, and from him the bandit learned that his uncle and aunt were in the crowd at Collo. Certain that a massacre was not to be avoided, the radio operator suddenly ducked behind a rock and ran away. Two of his comrades went in chase and, profiting from the diversion, five more shepherds deserted; there was an exchange of shots between the bandits and the deserters, although no one was hit. Thereafter, with the radio transmitter out of action, all contact between the two bandit forces ceased.

This radio silence provoked black pessimism on Pizzuta, where demoralization had also spread like a creeping paralysis. These men, whose natural intelligence had never been dulled by education, who retained the refined and apprehensive instincts of animals, could detect the proximity of death almost as a physical odor. Rumors were transmitted as if by thought transference among the isolated groups on the slopes of Pizzuta. A panicky theory shared by all was that the public security police and *carabinieri* had agreed to sink their notorious and traditional differences and unite to destroy them. Some claimed to have heard the sound of shooting from the direction of Cumeta, and this could best be explained as a surprise attack by the temporarily united police.

The main body of bandits had been split into three groups, each equipped with a Breda machine gun, and one of the three-inch mortars, which, though now banned, had been brought along to be on the safe side. Shortly after nine, when tension was at

its maximum, and within fifteen minutes of the loss
of contact with Cumeta, a lookout posted on the higher
slopes of Pizzuta reported that a body of some thirty
men were approaching the bandits' position from
the rear and were within half a mile. There was
a surge of panic around Messina, which he felt
necessary to quell by drawing his pistol. He doubted
whether the appearance of these unidentified strangers
represented any new danger: they were more likely
to be peasants on their way to the meeting than police
in plain clothes charged with the implementation of
a betrayal. However, there was no time to investigate;
the original plan had collapsed with the silence from
Cumeta, and the trap so artfully prepared had ceased
to exist. If Messina now gave his men the order to
go in and seize Cremona and the rest of the political
leaders, there would be no one in the rear to prevent
their escape. There was no time to concoct a new
strategy, no certainty that he would be able to keep
the band in control for many more minutes. Bandits
were temperamentally unfit for waiting; they were at
their best in action. Messina signaled to his machine
gunners the order to open fire.

Giuseppe Cremona, leader of the Sicilian Com-
munist Party, was under no illusion as to the nature
and origin of the faint popping sounds which caused
some members of his audience to scan the sky for
exploding rockets. He was a survivor of many engagements and ambushes, and could identify the heavy
Breda machine guns by their slow, steady rate of
fire. He screamed warnings and started to wave his
arms up and down like a heavy bird trying to launch
itself into flight, but though little local pockets of
agitation had appeared in the crowd where bullets
smashed into flesh and bone, it was impossible to
make his audience realize what was happening. Eight
provincial party secretaries sat solemnly on a row
of chairs behind Cremona, and at its third burst
Messina's Breda toppled four of them in a scrambling,
blood-spurting heap. One of the wounded got up and
rushed to show Cremona his hand, from which three

ngers were hanging on shreds of skin, but at that moment, as Cremona turned to clasp and console him, a bullet shattered his windpipe, and he stood for a moment, swaying and sucking in breath through a hole in his throat, then fell over backwards.

Like Cremona, Bradley had been surprised at the sluggishness of the crowd's first reaction, at the gestures and cries of bewilderment rather than fear. Their first impulse, when they understood the sound of distant gunfire above the uproar they themselves had created, and when the first bloodied victims began to fall, was to draw together rather than escape—to become a herd. Seen from a distance by Messina's machine gunners, the compact peasant mass flinched under the impact of the bullets in the way that a horse troubled by insects ripples its hide. Soon all the machine guns were firing, and the bandits armed only with rifles blazed away in a frenzy, no longer bothering to take aim. Under this punishment the crowd opened up, and a panic-stricken group broke away, still not realizing where the shooting was coming from, and began to run for shelter in the direction of Pizzuta. This provided the excuse for the bandits, who had quite lost their heads, to open fire with their mortars. The firing was unpracticed and wild, the shells falling haphazardly in and around the crowd, some causing no damage at all, others great slaughter.

Fear, thought Bradley, was a contagious and dangerous emotion, a tiger to be fixed and dominated by the power of the eye. It was pointless to run or duck or move a muscle of the face as the motar shells whooshed overhead. A man in a jaunty peasant imitation of a city suit had wandered toward them, his face a bloody membrane in which little but the hole of his mouth was distinguishable. Beyond him, a prancing frieze of mules rose up, and one, cantering way, released an enormous blue bundle of guts from a rent that had opened beneath the rectum. Children too old for the protection of their mothers' skirts ran like rabbits, bouncing back as if from the snarer's nets at each new shell burst ahead.

Locatelli too had faced the jaguar fear, rediscovering in the emergency his icy imperturbability of old. He held himself tautly; there was nothing to be done except stand one's ground. Unnecessarily he took Marco's arm in a comforting grip as a nearby shell burst hammered his ears and threw up a fleecy fountain of pulverized rock. Ricocheting bullets wailed and droned everywhere, and the mortar shells digested stone and spat it out as obsidian lancets and razors. He wiped a crystalline sediment from his skin and awaited the moment of reorganization for action and healing, when there was a place of safety to which mutilated children could be carried, when this distraught multitude could be calmed and its losses counted.

Bradley sucked cordite smoke and chalk dust into his lungs, and raising his hand out of habit to mask a cough, found something like a red slug sticking to its back. Before flicking it disgustedly away, he imagined it for a moment as a sliver of lip. A nearby shell blast had puffed rags and debris into the air which might have been the result of a direct hit on a living body. A strange quirk of human behavior distracted him from speculation: the spectacle of a woman moaning with horror not so much because she was bleeding, but because the blood had ruined her holiday dress.

Now the frantic hubbub had sudsided, and Bradley found himself alone. He was calm and yet short of breath, as if he had just run up a flight of steps. A few shots spluttered in the distance against the shouting that was dying down. The peasants who surrounded him moved in dreamy, exhausted fashion. Somewhere close behind him a querulous old voice complained continually of some injury. The agony and fear of Collo had been compressed into fifteen minutes.

At this moment, after a brief skirmish with the shepherds on Cumeta, the bandits there had taken flight, carrying one of their number who was bleeding to death. On Pizzuta, Messina had ordered a withdrawal, though one of the detached groups he had been unable to reach still sprayed their bullets at the crowd in aimless and desultory fashion, in an effort to keep up their courage. Bradley felt a sudden sense of deflation, of anticlimax. Something had drained from his body, leaving a melancholy void—just as if he had been with a woman, he realized.

Marco rematerialized, patting the dust from his dark suit. There was nothing to be read on his face.

"Something sure went wrong, huh?" Bradley said.

"Too much shooting," Marco said. "Cremona is dead," he added hastily, assured by his instinct that this piece of news would be accepted in partial compensation for the collapse of the original plan.

Bradley tried to match Marco's deadpan expression. "How about those guys who were with him?"

Marco was ready with the current acceptable euphemism. "I guess they were taken out as well, Mr. Bradley."

"The whole bunch of them? Holy cow! Messina must have gone crazy."

"He was always crazy," Marco said. "But now he is crazy and alone. Now he will have no friends left anywhere."

His intuition told him that Bradley was not displeased at the way things had gone. Marco had never believed that Bradley intended his last-minute orders curtailing the scope of the bandits' action to be taken seriously. A special look, a current of understanding and complicity, had passed between them. "We wouldn't want to have a shambles on our hands," Bradley had said, adding almost in the same breath with which he urged caution and moderation, "but personally I wouldn't feel too unhappy if certain persons could be taught a small lesson."

Bradley's unspoken but hinted-at views had coincided with those of Marco's superiors. The time was at hand for the bandits' elimination, and it was long overdue for the peasants to be taught a lesson. It was Marco himself who had put forward the suggestion, through his old friend Tagliaferri, that two birds might be killed with one stone. Certainly the peasants would never forget the massacre inflicted on them this day, and soon they would know who the authors of the massacre had been. The bandits could never have existed without the peasants' surreptitious backing: their secret offerings of food and shelter, the information they brought to the bandits' hideouts of the whereabouts of the troops and those against them. Now the peasants would turn on them, leaving them at the mercy of the men of honor, who had decided on their destruction.

"Where's Locatelli?" Bradley asked.

"He's back there helping fix up the wounded."

"Let's go and give a hand," Bradley said. "We have to do what we can for these people."

5

Two trouble-free months slipped by. Marco went on working as head of civilian contracts at the Caltanissetta base depot. The remaining handful of troops on the island were supplied through him with the ripest and juiciest grapes and the most unblemished tomatoes at prices that undercut those of the cheapest suppliers in the wholesale market of Palermo. The colonel raised his salary and gave him a command car of his own. He ate in the officers' mess, but remained correct, silent and aloof, and did not drink in the bar. When the colonel, who was beginning to suspect from occasional absences sanctioned by GHQ that Marco might be more than he seemed, decided one day to invite him to dine at the fashionable La Palomina restaurant, Marco extricated himself gracefully from the obligation.

His family affairs progressed in spite of the strong headwinds of the times. The alarming symptoms manifested by Teresa at the time of Collo had subsided by the time he got back to Palermo, and never recurred. For a week there was no love-making but thereafter abstinence was forgotten and their encounters in bed were as violent as ever. Despite his incessant fussing—the homeopathic doses, quack remedies, in-

jections and excess of vitamins he forced on her—
Teresa's health was unimpaired.

Marco sent regular sums of money to his mother
and his elder brother, Paolo, who had never fully
recovered from the war and the two years spent in
a British POW camp. His sister, Cristina, who had
decamped in 1943 with an Allied officer, had finally
been tracked down in Catania, where she was working
as a call girl. Marco sent a priest to induce her to
change her way of life, and provided a dowry of
100,000 lire; she hoped soon to marry a foreman
of a plastics factory. He constantly urged both his
mother and Paolo to come and live with them in
Palermo, but they seemed happy where they were
in their mountain village, and put him off with excuses.

In mid-August, a message left with the colonel
at the depot called Marco at a meeting with Bradley
in the Parco della Favorita. He went with some reluctance, instantly sensing trouble ahead. Bradley, whom
he had not seen since June, gave him a crushing hand-
shake and an actor's smile, and thanked him twice
for coming. They sat together under the palms on
a splendid old Victorian wrought-iron bench, and
Marco waited a long time for the American to come
to the point.

"And when are you expecting the child?"

"In two months."

"Wonderful," Bradley said. "You must be very
excited."

"We are."

"Having it at home?"

"At the Sant'Angelo hospital."

"I don't know of a better place. They tell me the
equipment's very up to date. They'll look after her."

"I've been given an introduction to the head gynecologist," Marco said.

"Marvelous. Nothing like having friends at court.
Any plans for the immediate future?"

"We're hoping to take a vacation as soon as Teresa
can travel. To the lakes. Sirmione."

"You'll enjoy it. Especially at this time of the year.

Get away from the heat. And you'll like Sirmione. Unpretentious but good. I know it well."

"Is there any news of Mr. Locatelli?" Marco asked.

"I've had no communication from him," Bradley said. "As you know, he's back in the States." His face, padded here and there with the indulgence of approaching middle age, had become taut, redrawn in the vigorous squares and triangles of a cubist master. He glanced around quickly out of a habit of prudence, but this was a quiet place with small chance of interlopers. Twenty yards away an old municipal employee, too stiff to bend, was using a pointed stick to spear up leaves from an exotic tree that shed its coarse foliage in summer, giving a snort of pleasure as he transfixed each leaf. Farther off a nursemaid in a uniform designed at the end of the century, with lace cap, starched cuffs and cotton gloves, sat under a parasol watching two children.

"We have a severe problem, Marco," Bradley said. "The Collo thing's backfired on us."

"I don't understand you, Mr. Bradley."

"Someone has talked to a crazy senator back home and supplied him with a memo giving all the details. With, by the way, the true casualty figures."

"Even though they were never published in this country?"

"Despite that fact. What's more, all the names involved seem to have been mentioned—certainly mine."

"Have you any idea who could have passed on this information?"

"Yes, I have, but it's only a hunch and I don't want to say any more. You probably know who I have in mind."

"Only five people knew all the facts about Collo, Mr. Bradley. Including Mr. Locatelli. Mr. Locatelli seemed very unhappy about what happened."

"Sure, he was unhappy. Also he was starting to drink too much. I said I don't want to say any more about it; let it go at that. The thing is, all hell could break loose. So far it hasn't hit the newspapers, but if it really blows up it could be used as an election weapon. The President's opponents wouldn't stop at anything to discredit the administration. It's not impossible that a congressional committee could be sent out here."

"What would its purpose be?"

"To collect evidence and examine witnesses."

"In Sicily it is unusual for witnesses to be forthcoming."

"Yeah, well of course that's always a help." Bradley's smile of appreciation was stretched as if by elastic, which suddenly snapped. "How about those bandits who set up the thing? How come they're still in circulation? If any interested person succeeds in getting to them at this stage, we're going to be looking at big trouble."

A brown leaf floated down past them, rocking on hinges of air, and the old gardener, ready with his sharpened stick, waited like a duelist on guard. Behind him, the nursemaid from the last century had crumpled demurely into sleep.

"There have been certain unavoidable delays," Marco said. Increasingly his conversational style was influenced by the many letters he dictated about the base depot's business. "However, we think the matter will be resolved within days," he added.

"I'm relieved to hear that. There's been very little mention of them in the newspapers lately. It's been hard to guess what's cooking."

"The leaders, Messina and Sardi, have been separated from their men," Marco said. "Without leadership the rest of them are like a body without a head. They can be eliminated at any moment."

"Well, that's a relief," Bradley said. "How about Messina and Sardi themselves? Is it going to be as easy to finish them off as you appear to think?"

"We do not think that there will be any difficulty. Sardi is ready to betray Messina when the right moment comes."

"Betray him to whom?"

"To the police."

"But haven't the police always backed Messina?"

"The colonels and generals, Mr. Bradley. The ordinary policeman always hated him. He murdered too many of them."

"Sorry, Marco, I didn't understand. I've been living among you people all these years, but I'm still a babe in arms when it comes to some things. The big shots think he's a useful guy to have around, but the underlings don't see it that way. Incidentally, when it comes to finishing the small-time bandits, who's going to do the dirty work? The men of honor?"

"I'm sorry, Mr. Bradley?"

"The friends, if you like. You're what they call a friend, aren't you?"

"I try to be a friend to my friends."

"Quit side-stepping," Bradley said. He laughed. "Okay, let it ride. The main thing is that I have your assurance that we don't have to lose any more sleep over the bandits, whatever happens."

"Nobody has to lose any more sleep over the bandits."

"Is Don C. in on whatever final solution you have planned?"

"Don C., Mr. Bradley?"

"Don Claudio Villalba. I suppose you've never heard of him?"

"By reputation, of course. More than that I can't say."

"Listen, Marco. Who's trying to kid whom? Would it amaze you to know that we've been in touch with Don C. ever since before the invasion? Would that surprise you, Marco?"

Marco's eyes looked back into Bradley's with no more expression in them than one of those enormous, vacant mosaic faces that watched the worshipers from the walls of the Cathedral of Monreale. This studied emptiness of gaze and inertia of the features were described by the Sicilians as serenity, which was much admired, but it was purely Oriental and negative, having little to do with the Western understanding of the word. Bradley sometimes suspected that it involved a technique actually suspending thought.

For a moment he was irritated. The guy knows

I know, so what's the point of all this? Why doesn't he level with me once in a while? "Does it ever occur to you," he said, "that this secrecy thing can be carried too far? I'm well aware that it's the local tradition, and I admire and respect it as such, but when two people like us—let's face it—are working for the same objectives, it can lead to confusion and a loss of effectiveness." Shall I tell him? he asked himself. Yes, I may as well. "We know who Don C. is and we know who you are. We also know that Don C. sent you to us in the first place, that you're supposed to be his bright-eyed boy. That being so, how about a reasonable exchange of information from now on? It would make life much easier."

Marco smiled as he did when he was embarrassed. "Mr. Bradley, I assure you you're very much mistaken. In this country things can get exaggerated. Too many people say the first thing that comes into their head. I work eight hours a day in the base depot, as anyone will tell you. This doesn't leave me any time to interfere in things that don't concern me. You could say I have a few connections—friends, if you like—that's all. I try to help; it's only natural."

Grinning, Bradley listened to the habitual smoke screen of words and excuses. The Oriental inheritance. Never bind them down to a straight yes or no; it was a waste of time to try. "Yeah, yeah, I know," he said. "Okay, Marco. You play it your way."

The meeting to discuss Marco's plan for the bandits' elimination, presented to Don C. through Tagliaferri, was held in the Archbishop's villa at Monreale and was attended by the heads of eleven families of the Honored Society, each one of whom as he came into Don C.'s presence bent over to kiss his ring. At this time Don C. was in his early fifties, a man of heavy features, exhausted expression and solemn eyes. He was famous for his slovenly attire, his habit of wearing carpet slippers at all times, the coarseness of his language, the faint whiff about him of the byres of his farm, his pretense of going to sleep in the middle of any conversation that bored him, and his seemingly hypnotic control over the island's natural rulers: the princes, the dukes, the barons, the Archbishop himself. He was the subject of innumerable legends, one being that at the time of the Allied landings he had simply picked up the telephone, asked to be put through to the German field marshal in Rome, and instructed him to withdraw his troops. From the fact that the troops were mysteriously withdrawn, that western Sicily fell to the Allies without a shot being fired, and that the Allies in due course showered honors and favors on Don C., it was reasonable to believe there was something to the legend. The war at an end, he had let it be known that his goal was the establishment of domestic peace and social order in Sicily, at a time when thirty-two bands of outlaws were still at large in the mountains, a separatist army secretly armed by the Allies was skirmishing ineffectually in the east of the island, and the trade unions had resurrected themselves to make the lives of the landlords miserable and startle them with the specter of the class war.

Marco was called to Monreale in case it was decided necessary to question him on the details of his plan, but he spent the hours kicking his heels in a barn with the bodyguards who had come with their masters, all of them men famous for their silence. On the few occasions when any mention of Don C. was made, he was referred to reverently as "a certain person." The meeting had been set for seven A.M., and at midday Marco's protector, Tagliaferri, came out, clapped him on the shoulder and nodded in a way that indicated matters had gone well. They drove off together in Tagliaferri's car.

Marco's plan, praised by all the men of honor for its simple practicality, hinged on the expedient of luring the bandits after they had been separated from their leaders out of the mountains, where they were in their element, into the unfamiliar plains where they could be trapped without refuge and slaughtered at ease. The plan commended itself all the more to Don C. in that it gave him the opportunity to designate as executioner the only man of honor who threatened his position as the head of the Society. This was Benedetto Gentile of Monreale, who had started life as a goat boy and had retained a passion for his animals that induced him to live like a primitive nomad in a series of shacks built along the grazing trails of his now enormous herds. Gentile, who harbored a grudge against the bandits for their habit of rustling his animals, accepted with satisfaction the charge laid on him. He was signing his own death warrant, Don C. believed, because it only had to become known that Gentile had caused a bandit's killing for him to be involved in a vendetta with the man's family. Not even the powerful Gentile could survive a dozen or more vendettas fought by men who would put aside every other occupation in their lives to work, over a span of years if necessary, for the day of vengeance.

In accordance with Marco's plan, instructions were given to the chiefs of police to move all their forces from Monreale and concentrate them in the mountains of the Trapani area. Here the bandits were holding out while awaiting news of Messina and Sardi, who were supposedly arranging safe conduct and passports for their emigration to South America. In the usual way, a police spy working with them kept them informed of the police's intentions and movements, and within hours of the arrival of the anti-bandit squads in the Trapani mountains, a forged letter purported to have been written by Messina was delivered. This ordered the band to move in small groups at two-day intervals to Monreale for the purpose of reporting to Gentile, who would shelter them and pass them on.

The procedure was perfectly normal. In their endless migrations, the bandits always traveled in threes and fours to avoid drawing attention to themselves, and when they slept under a roof it was always to a man of honor that they went. Gentile was taken by surprise at the arrival of the first party of four bandits, who covered the journey across the mountains in half the time he had expected, and so they had to be received in amicable fashion, their ever-present suspicions calmed, their bandit sensitivity to atmosphere soothed and dismantled before they could be induced to drink the drugged wine, tied up and handed over to the police. The experience was a dangerous and embarrassing one for Gentile, who forthwith ringed his farm with armed men who shot the next contingent from ambush. A sole survivor, fired on from ditches and from behind walls, escaped to the Palermo highway, where he was chased and run down by a car.

The third and fourth parties—alerted by no more than instinct, by the sudden increase in pressure of the sense of doom from which they had suffered for so long—changed their minds and the direction of their eastward trek. But they were lost. Without the further instructions from Messina that they were supposedly to pick up from Gentile, the march turned into an aimless wandering in a landscape filled with traps. In a moment of confusion and despair, the police spy deserted his friends, walked into a *carabinieri* station and announced who he was, producing a secret police identity card he carried concealed in a tube in his anus. The *carabinieri* sergeant telephoned his HQ at Palermo for instructions, received them, came back whistling, drew his pistol and with the greatest of composure shot the man twice through the head.

The few bandits who remained at liberty lost their nerve completely and began to run in all directions like frightened sheep who hear the howling of the wolf. Several of these were captured by the shepherds they had so often tyrannized in the past, and, in accordance with the Bronze Age custom of the region, were roped up and thrown alive into deep crevices in the earth where their remains would never be discovered, to prevent relatives of the murdered men from swearing a vendetta "in the presence of the body." It was a time when any stranger acting in a suspicious manner was likely to be taken for a bandit on the run and, to be on the safe side, quickly and quietly disposed of. Two men who presented themselves at the hospital of Monreale, with bullet wounds and no satisfactory account of how they came by them, were secretly transferred to the clinic at Corleone run by the famous Dr. Di Stefano, a man of honor, and both expired under the anesthetic. Another man of honor received a night visit by the handsome and dauntless Cucinelli, who, Tommy gun in hand but in the friendliest manner, asked for a car, money and food; all this was immediately provided, but Cucinelli had hardly covered ten miles when a twenty-pound charge of dynamite blew him and the car to smithereens, so that only one hand and a pair of blood-soaked boots could eventually be forwarded to his parents for burial.

Those who died by the hands of implacable enemies were lucky indeed, for the men whom Gentile had drugged and surrendered to the law, as well as a few stragglers picked up by the police on their own account, were thrashed on the testicles as part of the interrogation, which—if the police thought they showed signs of arrogance—commenced with their mouths being forced open with an iron spoon and crammed with human excrement.

Almost all the bandits had begun as young peasants of courage and resolution, too bold to submit to the abuses and calamities of the war. In the mountains they had fought with intelligence, and often with chivalry, but gradually, under crushing pressure, courage had degenerated into animal ferocity, and their eventual destruction was accomplished by any means, however cruel. A last desperate trio, holed up for three weeks by their pursuers in the uncharted caves of Strasetta, killed and ate the thighs and buttocks of a *carabinieri* corporal they had taken with them as hostage. For their crime, when captured, their legs were hobbled and they were doused with gasoline, then encouraged to do their best to escape; a short while later their captors went after them, throwing lighted matches.

Messina, who knew nothing of these events, had been sent by Inspector General Mancuso to Castelve-trano to await a military plane that would use the airstrip there to fly him out of the country. The day before this was to happen Mancuso drove fifty miles from Palermo to say goodbye. He took with him a pretty prostitute from the best house in the city, and a hamper of provisions, and that night the three feasted on thrushes grilled on a skewer, Parma ham and Orvieto wine. After dinner the two men shared the prostitute. Weeping with emotion, Mancuso told Messina that he loved him more than his own son, and although this was not quite true, he had formed a real attachment for the bandit during the two years he had commanded the thousand security police who had been occupied by their hopeless chase in the mountains. When Mancuso left at two in the morning, Messina was very drunk, and an hour later, when Sardi arrived to do the work for which he was to be so well paid, he was asleep in his chair.

Arrested despite all the promises made to him, Sardi died in prison shortly thereafter. His death surprised no one, but it called for painstaking organization. The bandit had freely admitted his intention when brought to trial of telling all he knew, and fearing that an attempt would be made to silence him, he took extraordinary precautions before eating any food brought to his cell; he would taste nothing before testing its effects on a kitten he was allowed to keep. The opportunity came for those who waited and watched when Sardi's chest began to trouble him again. The doctor prescribed a well-known proprietary medicine. When the bottle arrived, Sardi examined it closely, then broke the seal and swallowed the contents. Instantly he fell screaming to the ground, and half an hour later he was dead.

On the same day, Inspector General Mancuso, shortly after leaving the Birreria Venezia, where he had drunk a thimbleful of black coffee and eaten two small almond cakes, suffered a heart attack on the Via Maqueda and died in the ambulance on the way to Sant'Angelo. At the inquest the coroner expressed surprise that the ambulance had taken an hour to reach the hospital—a trip that normally occupied no more than ten minutes. When Colonel Fosca of the *carabinieri* anti-bandit squad, who had often collaborated with Mancuso, fell in front of a streetcar a week later, he was found to have suffered a stroke. In the bars and coffeehouses of Palermo where these things were commented on, people found it strange that such a young and vigorous man had died in this way, but they soon forgot. During this period leaves of absence for Marco from his duties at the base depot were granted more frequently than usual.

There remained the key figure of the formidable Gentile, who in his whole life had left his farm perhaps half a dozen times, but who was now tempted to visit Miera by news of the enforced sale of a herd of goats belonging to the widow of a man killed in the massacre at Collo. It was a moment when no one seemed to be able to lay his hands on money and prices were low; in addition, Gentile counted on the fact that the news that he would be there, spread in advance by his agent, would discourage other potential buyers from bothering to attend. Gentile inspected the goats, placed his bid and then sat down in the shade at one of the tables in the little square, where a few weeks before the peasants had assembled under their banners before setting out for Collo. Some yards away, children were bobbing up and down on the horses of a hand-cranked merry-go-round, and there was a distant view of the misted and fateful shape of Pizzuta. Here, within sight of at least a hundred people, Gentile was approached by a stranger who, after turning aside to compare his appearance with a photograph he carried, pulled a heavy-caliber revolver out of his pocket and shot him five times in the face and body. The police could find no one who had seen or even heard the shots fired, a fact on which the newspapers commented with weary sarcasm. There were newspaper photographs of the body, a blanket spread over it, and the rivulets of blood on the cobblestones. Two days later Gentile's funeral was reported: the mile of cars, the million lire's worth of flowers, the oration by a deputy. After that the matter faded from the public mind. These days, it was the kind of thing that happened once a week.

The process of liquidation was rapid and smooth, and by the end of September, hardly a month after Marco's encounter with Bradley, it had been satisfactorily completed. Don C. expressed his gratitude in typical fashion for Marco's share in the successful operation. Marco, who never expected rewards, received a visit from Tagliaferri to congratulate him and to pass on the good wishes and thanks of a certain person. At the same time Tagliaferri advised him to buy as much land as he could pick up in an area adjacent to one of Palermo's southern suburbs. Much of this district consisted of old municipal rubbish dumps and was regarded as worthless for any purpose, but a week after Marco had paid a deposit on 10,000 square meters, bought at a bargain price, the city council announced that the area had been designated for priority industrial development. Marco sold out the day after the announcement for fifteen times the price paid. He donated one tenth of his profit to the Degli Eremiti Orphanage because this was the way a man of honor behaved, giving little thought to the certainty that his action would be reported back to Don C., with the consequent increase of his standing.

A celebration was called for, and Marco took Teresa on an excursion to the small seaside town of Mondello, where he had booked a table for lunch at Zu Tanu's restaurant. Zu Tanu's was a piece of Sicilian Victoriana, half castle, half mosque, built among the tamarisks at the end of a shell of beach, a comfortable hour by coach from Palermo in the golden days when princes and dukes had driven out with their courtesans to inflame themselves with lobster and champagne before making love in one of Zu Tanu's *chambres privées*. An atmosphere of severe discretion lingered among the plush, the marble cupids and tarnished gilt. Patrons of Zu Tanu kept to themselves, conversed in low tones, in the deep alcoves in which they were seated, and never saw more than they were intended to. The establishment was a favorite resort of the men of honor when in a romantic frame of mind.

A specialty of Zu Tanu's was its bathing cabins, dating from the invention of sea-bathing. These had once been drawn by horses into a foot of water, to allow the occupants to climb down a few steps from what was in effect a sumptuously furnished room and dip their extremities in total privacy in the sea. The horses had been gone since the early twenties, but a few of the cabins, most of them in early stages of decay, still remained and were popular with couples, who hired them for a few hours at a time with a single purpose in mind.

The hire of one of Zu Tanu's cabins was almost an obligatory feature of a sentimental anniversary, and when Marco made it clear to the waiter with an instantly recognized sign what it was that they wanted, he was disappointed to find that all the better cabins had been taken; only a small one, somewhat in need of redecoration, was to be had. It was narrow, cramped and dark, and equipped with a settee whose springs had been ruined by a century of enthusiastic abuse. Teresa was in the last month of her pregnancy, her navel leveled in her enormously distended stomach, her movements slow and cumbered, and intercourse, particularly with Dr. Bellometti's warnings in Marco's ears, could only be achieved in an awkward and undignified posture. But the seedy surroundings, physical difficulties and sense of adventure added to their excitement, and as she first lay on her side and then knelt on the ridiculous settee, there was no mistaking the spontaneity of her movements or the reality of her cries, and there was no repressing the immediacy of his own climax, almost as soon as he had penetrated her from the rear.

Later, when reconsidering all the circumstances of that day, Marco came to the conclusion that these were the hours when suddenly, her fifteenth birthday hardly behind her, Teresa had turned her back on her childhood and accepted the preoccupations of a mature woman. He had mentioned in the most casual way that something had happened out of the blue, as a result of which their future and that of their child seemed assured. They would shortly be leaving the small flat in the *vico,* he told her, to begin another kind of life, and unquestioningly Teresa began to plan the structure of her future in this new dimension.

Like all the peasants of the stony desert of Sicily in which they had been born, they were victims of a kind of psychosis, an obsessive dread of weakness and isolation, which they fought against continually with whatever weapons they could find. Browbeaten by a dubious present and a dreadful past, peasants fled their mountain villages as soon as they could, to any small township where they were no longer at the mercy of every bully, always living in hope of a further move to Palermo itself, with its indestructible crowds and its three kinds of police. Every man like Marco who remained a peasant at core, carrying the genes of hopeless subservience in his blood, was constantly in the market for affection and loyalty, and maneuvered incessantly to create as many ties as possible; to surround himself with faithful friends and those who owed him obligations; to be a godparent when he could; to arrange political marriages for his children. Every woman like Teresa who had learned fear at her mother's knee, and had witnessed the sufferings of the vulnerable, wanted to breed invulnerable sons who would become lawyers, politicians and priests. In a dogfight over famished land, the acknowledged victor was the man who could raise a rampart around his family and defend them against the rest. Such men were not only strong but good—the words for goodness and strength being identical in the dialect. Thus Don C., who was the strongest, was also the best; the wearer of an iron halo of power. Weakness and evil were words that were practically interchangeable. Given any choice in the matter a woman married a man as any African tribeswoman did, not for his looks but for his ability to fight for her and her family. Teresa had instinctively discerned

Marco's obsidian peasant hardness, and she would have married him, rather than a handsome weakling unable to defend the future of his family, had he been a dwarf.

6

In the month that followed, the foundations of success were solidly laid. The Ricciones moved to a flat in the select residential area of Acquasanta acquired through Tagliaferri at two-thirds the asking price. It was in a new block with a marble-floored entrance hall, elevator, spittoons like baptismal fonts on the landings, enormous windows, a swimming pool, a children's playground, and a concierge dressed in something like an admiral's uniform, who addressed all the tenants in the polite third-person singular—a custom reintroduced with the departure of Mussolini. There were two spare rooms, and they agreed that as soon as the baby was born more attempts should be made to induce both their widowed mothers to come and live with them. Marco had an especially soft spot for his mother-in-law, who still spent her days crouched over a lacemaking frame in her native village of Pioppo. Hearing that his brother Paolo wanted to buy a garage in Campamaro, he sent him a gift of 200,000 lire. He joined three social clubs and two local charitable organizations. He bought a Lancia Augusta with a special Farina body and spent his spare time tuning its engine. At the end of the month their first child was born in the Sant'Angelo Hospital.

Two days later Bradley telephoned to ask for another meeting. "First of all, heartiest congratulations, Marco. Wonderful news. A son, eh? Marvelous. Both doing well, I hope?"

"They're fine, Mr. Bradley. No trouble of any kind. It was all over in a couple of hours."

"Splendid. What are you calling him?"

"Amedeo."

"That's a pretty name. Unusual. I like Amedeo. Wonderful news, Marco. I'm very happy for you both."

It was another corner of the Parco della Favorita. They sat in a forgotten arbor by a fountain that no longer worked, where the water, flowing out of sight, filled the air with an odor of hothouse plants.

"The news is, I'm finally pulling out," Bradley said. "I'll be leaving for the States next week. I wanted to see you and say goodbye."

"We'll be seeing you again, won't we, Mr. Bradley?"

"Well, I don't know about that, Marco. I don't suppose that I'll be coming back here. There's nothing for me to do; this isn't where the action is any longer."

"It's been a very pleasant association. You'll be missed."

"Thank you, Marco. I want to ask you a straight question. How are you making out nowadays? I hear the base closed down. How are you utilizing those remarkable talents of yours?"

"I expect to be joining a real estate company."

"D'ya suppose you'll be satisfied with that?" Bradley's expression, on the verge of a smile of mockery, challenged Marco to deny the mediocrity of the occupation.

"It's a change. It's all experience."

"It's kind of quiet here these days," Bradley said. "This place has turned into a backwater—thanks, by the way, largely to you, Marco. Gone are the old days when you couldn't open a newspaper without reading that somebody had been kidnapped, or that Messina had shot up a police station somewhere. You did a fantastic job."

"The part I played was a very small one."

"Well, I happen to know better. Maybe I know more about what happened than you suspect. All those shenanigans behind closed doors in the villa of a certain man of God. Who'd better be nameless, Marco, who'd better be nameless. Still, why should we worry? You got the results."

"That trouble you mentioned back home . . . Some senator who was asking questions, wasn't it? Did anything come of it after all?"

"Nothing whatever. It died a natural death. As I knew it would, if things went the way we hoped."

"I'm glad of that. That must be a great relief."

"Relief, huh? You're not kidding. That was a bad moment, I don't mind admitting." Abruptly, Bradley screwed up his features in mock anguish and wrung his right hand as if the fingertips had been scalded in boiling water. Like so many of the gestures he had picked up, it was not quite appropriate—in this case because it was Neapolitan, and alien in the Sicilian context. "Still, that's water under the bridge," he said. "We have the future to think about now, and it's going to be an exciting one, Marco. Tough, too; make no mistake about that. I don't mean in Sicily any more—that's old hat. I'm talking about Berlin, Latin America. Sooner or later the Far East."

"Let them get on with it, so long as they leave me in peace."

"I don't know whether that's the right attitude, Marco. For an old man, maybe yes, but a young man has to be involved. I'm talking about the future of civilization. Aren't you ever concerned about the threat to our Western culture and heritage?"

"If you want me to be frank—no, I'm not. Mr. Bradley, I'm too small to worry about these things. I leave them to other people."

Suddenly Bradley took him by the arm in what was supposed to be an impulsive manner. Once again the gesture was out of place with a Sicilian, who never expected to be touched by another male except in certain formalized conditions. "Marco, you're lost here. Wasted."

"I'm sorry you see it that way, Mr. Bradley. I don't know what I can do about it."

"How would you feel about coming to the States?"

"You're joking, Mr. Bradley."

"Not this time. You're never likely to hear anything

further from a joke than this particular proposition. I'd like you to join my organization."

"It would be out of the question. I'm sorry. All my life is here, my family."

"I don't want you to decide right now. I don't want you to say yes or no; just think about it. The cash inducement wouldn't be substantial, but most people find living in the States pretty nice these days after the shortages here. I can say this: your wife would like it. You'd be able to afford to send your boy to a good school when the time came. Why don't you talk it over with Teresa and see how she feels about the idea? Maybe the three of us could meet for a chat?"

"What I don't understand, Mr. Bradley, is what use I can be to you? I've been studying law in the evenings, but it will be years before I qualify—if I ever do. And in the U.S. the system is different. I'd have to start all over again."

"Marco, we need your special aptitudes, and you know as well as I do what I mean. Before turning this down I want you to ponder over it very carefully. There's time for further conversations on the subject before I take off. You have to ask yourself whether you want to spend the rest of your life in an office in a quiet town like this, or whether you want to be where the action is."

"I'll certainly think about it," Marco said, "and I'll talk to Teresa, but I don't think there is any chance of making such a move. She has her mother, and I have mine, to say nothing of a brother and sister. We couldn't leave them behind. I've just bought a new flat in Acquasanta. We have many friends and relations to think of. I think I can say now that it's out of the question."

"Please give it a day or two just the same," Bradley said. "I'll be in touch later in the week."

Bradley went straight from this meeting with Marco to his old headquarters in the Via Isidoro Carini, where his replacement Alistair Ferguson, in the space of a single week, had revolutionized his office. This was the tougher kind of recruit the general had promised: a young man with a "realistic" outlook. Everything about Ferguson, who had never been in Europe before, was fresh and new, including a brisk young cynicism, straight from the training center, worn like a Brooks Brothers suit. He was clean-shaven, with the latest New England face—cheek-bones high as a Mongol's, exuberant pale eyebrows, eyes crinkled with geniality, and cheeks that bore the bloom and polish of youth. Though an Italian soldier was permanently on guard at the entrance to the *palazzo* and visitors' passes had to be shown at a barrier on the ground floor, he had insisted on fitting a combination lock to his door, and the wondrous new electric filing system occupying one-third of the room space was also secured by a lock.

"He wouldn't buy it," Bradley said. "As I expected."

"What was the objection?"

"The objection was that he's perfectly happy as is. Young wife, child, fairly affluent, some social position. Why should he want to turn it all in for a life which, we may as well face it, offers less-than-average security?"

"Why indeed?"

"Money interests him less than most of us. He's already got what most people are looking for in life," Bradley said.

"Or more."

"And strange as it seems, Sicilians are unadventurous."

Bradley stroked the surface of Ferguson's newly imported desk that filled the room with its smell of imitation leather. Half a generation, yet a lifetime apart, he thought. Americans were becoming continually more American, and this young man would only proclaim his race and motives by mingling with the Palermitan crowd dressed in what he naïvely assumed was an inconspicuous Italian civilian suit of poor cloth and meager cut. The days after Ferguson's arrival Bradley had subjected him to a test, with what he saw as satisfactory results. "The *carabinieri* have a suspect," he had said casually. "They're going to break his balls on the *cassetta*."

"Literally, you mean?"

"Literally. I thought you might want to go along. They're supposed to be able to get a confession in about ten seconds flat. We may have something to learn from them. I don't know; this world isn't getting any better. We face tough times ahead."

They attended the brief ceremony together, and the confession was obtained. It was not a spectacle that Bradley cared for, but by an effort of will power he was able to close his ears and withdraw his mind. Afterwards, Ferguson might have been slightly paler than usual, but his composure remained unbreached.

"Information obtained in time may save a hundred or thousand innocent lives," Bradley said. "I've always been a practicing Christian myself. If I have a single personal reservation, it's that evil cannot be fought with good."

"Will that guy recover?" Ferguson asked in a commendably offhand voice.

"Oh, I imagine so. Even if he's never quite the same man again."

"Is Riccione indispensable to us?" Ferguson asked now.

"Sooner or later we're going to need him. This guy's a truly great tactician. When it comes to planning an operation, he's in a class by himself. The way he handled the Messina thing was brilliant. No detail overlooked."

"But could this somewhat special brand of usefulness operate in the U.S.? I mean, in an unfamiliar environment."

"The U.S. unfamiliar to a Sicilian? You're kidding. He'd be like a fish in its element."

"What are you going to do?" Ferguson asked.

"I don't know. I have to think about it. I'd still like to get him if I could find a way. Don C. might be able to help."

"And would he oblige?"

"He'd have to if I put it strongly enough."

"What's Riccione going to say about being pulled out whether he likes it or not?" Ferguson asked.

"We'll worry about that when it happens—if it ever happens."

Slightly embarrassed by his lack of command of up-to-date euphemisms, Ferguson searched for an acceptable one. "Do you think he—ah—suppressed Gentile?"

"Not in person; of course not. We're talking about a man of some sophistication. What he did—and I can tell you this as a fact—was to tip off one of Messina's people that Gentile was responsible for their famous relative's sticky end."

"Despite the fact that Gentile was one of the boys, and therefore in theory untouchable?"

"Untouchable under normal circumstances, possibly, but he'd been getting too big for his britches. There may have been some sort of trial, and he had to go."

Stabbing out nervously with a finger, Ferguson managed to press a button on his filing cabinet. A drawer slid open, an electrical mechanism whirred briefly, and a subsection of file holders slid into view. He was saddened by the knowledge that they contained nothing. "Where do you manage to dig up all this stuff?" he asked.

"Contacts. I've been seeing a famous personality, late of Dannemora Penitentiary."

"Spina, in fact?"

"None other. He was invited by Don C. to be present at the famous meeting at Monreale when the decisions were made."

"Why does he have to do anything for us? Surely when we sprung him we were quits. He doesn't have anything to thank us for."

"Not at the moment, but he hopes he will."

"Am I allowed to know more?"

"Very little. I'm in agreement with that old service adage that the less anybody knows about anything, the better. He seems to think we might be able to help him one of these days. Does that satisfy your curiosity?"

"I'd like to meet him," Ferguson said.

Bradley shook his head. "No can do. He's an engaging man, but very reticent. We have a coffee together, and a quiet chat occasionally. He makes an exception in my case because we're old friends, but on the whole he likes to keep to himself."

"John Locatelli was in on this with you, wasn't he?"

"We worked together for a short while."

"What do you suppose made him do what he did?"

"I guess his nerves were going."

"Do you feel it's the act of a coward to take your own life?"

"No," Bradley said. "I've never held that view. He was getting old for the kind of existence he was obliged to lead. His nerves probably wouldn't stand up to the stress and strain. Certain things he couldn't face up to, maybe. Who are we to judge?"

"He was a nice fellow. I met him at the Center. He came down to give us a lecture."

"One of the very best," Bradley said. "Sensitive—perhaps too sensitive for his job. You probably heard of the big deal with Mussolini he nearly pulled off. We were all great admirers of John Locatelli. My view is that his nerves were in bad shape."

"He kept his idealism to the end," Ferguson said, and then winced. A word from a world he had renounced had slipped in under his guard. "He was kind of sincere," he said in correction.

"Locatelli allowed himself the luxury of a private conscience," Bradley said. "It involved him in something of a tightrope act. Far better to put your conscience in the care of the nation." Both men laughed.

"I suppose that double cross of Gentile would have worried him," Ferguson said.

"You're probably right. He was a plain soldier who lived with the myths of the past."

"They tell you about things like this at the Center."

"About *what* things?"

"Like this Gentile business."

"Are we still talking about that?"

"The fairy tales of our times," Ferguson said. "You

listen to them and put them out of your mind because you don't really believe them. Then suddenly you find yourself in a place like this, and it's reality. I've been going over some of these cases you gave me. These vendettas. It's incredible. That fourteen-year-old boy they shot the other day for something his father did before he was born. How can Sicilians be like this?"

"Because they're different."

"I'm here because they wouldn't give me Paris," Ferguson said.

"I know."

"You actually like it, don't you?"

"Yes."

"What do you see in it? If I may ask."

"What do I see in it? I don't know." How could one ever explain this amalgam of undefined sensations? This response to the lapis lazuli of the great city, the marble griffins, the breasted angels, the palm skies, the straw faces, the displays of virgins' blood, the scent of hidden water, Christ's face over the shoulder of the Archbishop's intelligent smile. "The things we understand started here just as much as in Athens." And I helped to save it, he assured himself; I helped to defend it. "You ought to go to Syracuse," he said.

"I'd like to; this whole town smells of shit," Ferguson said.

"We were talking about how Sicilians are different," Bradley said. "They have a religion of their own, even if it's not Christianity. They stick to the rules. Their loyalties are narrower than ours, but stronger. If they're on your side, they're on your side. That's why I want to keep Riccione. I can think of situations where he'd be indispensable."

Ferguson tried to interpret Bradley's smile. He's a schemer, they had warned him back in the States. A bit too wild. So far it's always come off, but some-day he's going to fuck up in a big way. Ferguson felt himself to be on the brink of involvement in one of those ruthlessly grandiose maneuvers on which the

Bradley legend had been founded. "If you felt you had to go to Don C., what do you suppose he'd do?"

"Exert pressure," Bradley said, clearly relishing the euphemism. "I don't say for a moment it would be done this way, but the true facts of the way Gentile was put on the spot could be leaked to his people. If so, how long do you think Marco would be able to stay on this island?"

Ferguson's eyes widened in admiration and delight. Here was the pure essence of betrayal: the grand deception, a triple cross as cold and romantic as a polar ice peak.

"I see what you mean," he said.

7

Sicily settled down to the enjoyment of the years of peace, prosperity and brotherly love. A docile and incredibly industrious peasantry went back to work, putting in twelve-, fourteen- and even sixteen-hour days without complaint; trade union leaders who tried to make trouble were first warned off, then quickly and quietly disposed of if they persisted. The men of honor looked after the marketing of the peasants' produce, and saw to it that they all got more or less fair shares of water from the wells and aqueducts under their control, at prices they could somehow or other manage to pay. The churches were full. Petty criminality came to an end: a tourist leaving a handbag on a café table could expect to find it still there the next day. Shopkeepers returned to honest dealing. The prostitutes of the lean postwar days had long since been reclaimed. There were religious processions with free handouts of macaroni on all the feast days. Everybody voted Christian Democrat, and people went about eagerly looking for something to do for a friend.

For Marco and Teresa it was a period of calm and fulfillment in which the word *hope* ceased to have any meaning in lives that could hardly be improved. A year after the birth of Amedeo, a girl arrived and was given the name Lucia. The Ricciones sent to Campamaro for a nurse, who dressed in the still-fashionable late Victorian style, and wearing white cotton gloves and carrying a lace-edged parasol took her charges daily to the nearby Parco della Favorita. All the attempts to induce their mothers to leave their hill villages and come to live with them in Palermo had been unsuccessful, so on alternate weekends they made excursions to Campamaro or Pioppo. They were as much in love with each other as ever, and Marco never ceased to fuss over Teresa's health. The children were constantly visited by Dr. Bellometti for imaginary ailments, and at Marco's insistence injected with vitamins which were quite superfluous in view of their excellent health. On his sixth birthday Amedeo was admitted to a nursery school run by nuns. The school was largely subsidized by funds his father provided.

Marco worked for his old sponsor Tagliaferri, who, financed by Don C., had set himself up in the real estate business in the Via Cavour, and within a few years did so well that he bought a construction company to put up the houses and factories on the land he had often been able to secure at giveaway prices on the city outskirts. Tagliaferri looked after his friends, and his friends' friends. His next venture was a trucking company, kept fully occupied by carting builders' materials to his many developments. It would have been easy and convenient for him to have had the trucks serviced in Palermo itself, but instead, those requiring an overhaul were sent thirty miles to Paolo's garage in Campamaro.

Managing the real estate office was a job suited to Marco's temperament. It was essential to be on good terms with everybody in city hall; to be able to do a favor for the mayor and any of the councilmen who mattered; to remember the saint's days of children and well-placed wives; to know how to bestow a gift gracefully, in such a way that a man of standing and sensibility would not be likely to take offense; to carry out one's side of any bargain with extreme scrupulousness. In the ordinary course of his duty he met and inevitably made a favorable impression on every citizen of Palermo who held a key position of any kind. He had been given the opportunity to kneel and kiss the ring of the Archbishop's finger. The chiefs of both the *carabinieri* and the *pubblica sicurezza* were entertained at dinner in his elegantly furnished flat in the Acquasanta. The seal was set on his success when, at the christening party given for their daughter, attended by the Archbishop's secretary and a number of barons, two unkempt strangers suddenly appeared among the crowd. They were Don C. and his gardener-driver. Don C. stayed five minutes, left an envelope containing fifty thousand-lire notes, mumbled an incomprehensible sentence in Marco's ear, and departed, but Marco knew that power had flowed from the old man's body into his, and that every guest present had witnessed this apotheosis. These were the days when it seemed that the sun would shine forever from a faultless sky.

Then the two brothers Johnny and Pete La Barbera arrived in Palermo, having been deported as undesirables from the United States. Now back in their native country, they formed the advance party of what the newspapers were to call *La Mafia Nuova*—the New Mafia. Johnny was forty-three and Pete forty; they had left Sicily in early childhood and made several fortunes in loan-sharking and on the New York waterfront before someone decided that since they had never bothered to acquire U.S. citizenship, there was no reason why they should not be sent away.

Johnny and Pete were conspicuous against the background of Palermo. They brought with them their white Cadillacs and a taste for display unfamiliar in the reticent island atmosphere. Neither man spoke more than a few words of Italian. They frequented such restaurants as the Caprice and the Olympic, where they conducted noisy parties in the company of the city's most expensive courtesans and a few local hangers-on. At first the Sicilians felt obliged to accept them, but they did so with reserve. A man of honor compelled for any reason to cross the Atlantic could always be certain of a hospitable reception on the other side, and he knew that if he decided to stay, a place would be made for him. Therefore an effort was made to tolerate the brashness of the American brothers.

Three months after their arrival in Palermo, the La Barberas bought an old army camp on the Boccadifalco road, just outside the city, converted the main building into a laboratory, surrounded the whole site with an electrified fence, and began processing morphine imported from Beirut into pure heroin. Next they took over a small fruit-packaging and exporting firm, and for several months every case of lemons exported to the U.S. contained at least one plastic imitation fruit filled with heroin. When, through a tip-off to the New York police by a right-minded docker who discovered a heroin-filled lemon in a case he had stolen, the system came to an end, the three million dollars the La Barberas had made in narcotics was reinvested in the construction business.

A number of firms were engaged in building the expanding city's new roads, bridges, residential suburbs, office blocks and hotels, and men of honor with a financial stake were to be found in all of them. It was a time when nests were being happily feathered, and such minor coercions as existed were disguised under nicely spun hypocrisies, but with the appearance in the field of the La Barberas the mellow dictum of live and let live was at an end. It had always been customary on the island to give an enemy one single warning, but those who fell afoul of the La Barberas by refusing to sell out to them or take them into partnership were slaughtered forthwith in ambushes, run down by speeding cars, or even taken out to sea, knocked on the head and dumped into the water. To the horror of the tradition-bound men of honor, resisters were killed in the presence of their families, and for the first time in Sicilian history, a woman was kidnapped to compel her husband's compliance. The La Barberas surrounded themselves with a force of local criminals—*straccie,* trash, as the men of honor called them—stiffened by an elite of gunmen imported from the U.S. Within a year they had gained control of central Palermo. Emissaries from Don C. who presented themselves at Johnny La Barbera's headquarters in the Via Maqueda, with the mandate of preventing the outbreak of war, were taken by the *straccie* in attendance and thrown down the stairs.

A few days later, in the autumn of 1953, Johnny La Barbera kicked open the door of Tagliaferri's office, pushed aside a secretary who tried to intercept him, walked into the inner room, dropped into a chair and put his feet up on Tagliaferri's desk.

Tagliaferri was reading through a letter the secretary had just brought in. He went on reading. La Barbera took out a large cigar, trimmed the end of it and put it back in his breast pocket. Tagliaferri read on, made some notes on the letter in his small, slow, careful handwriting, and put it aside.

"You're Tagliaferri, aren't you?" La Barbera said. A large man, he had the squeaky voice of a dwarf.

Tagliaferri looked up. "That's right."

"I'm Johnny La Barbera."

"I know. I've seen you before."

"Hey, you speak English pretty good. How come?"

"I spent twelve years in the States. What's on your mind?"

"Tagliaferri, we're competing with each other. You're jacking up my prices and I'm jacking up yours. Neither of us can afford it."

"I'm not complaining," Tagliaferri said.

"No? I had the impression that things weren't going too good with you these last few months. It could be a crock of shit, but there's a story going around that the bid you put in for the new Sagana bridge was turned down."

Tagliaferri examined the big-boned face carefully, searching for the ingredients of weakness and vanity which would give a clue to how the attack on this citadel must be mounted.

"I still don't see them taking yours."

"Why do you say that?"

"Rossi's still in this."

La Barbera grinned hugely, his cheeks dimpled like a child's. "Dinja read this morning's paper? The poor guy's no longer with us. He got dead. Somebody blew his head off at that night club, what's-its-name, out at Mondello."

"I'm sorry to hear that," Tagliaferri said. "Rossi was a good friend of mine."

"Yeah, he was a nice guy. There was just one thing wrong with him: he was pigheaded. He wouldn't move with the times."

"You were out for a piece of his business, weren't you?"

"Was I? Who told you that?"

"These things get around."

"I wouldn't put it that way. Maybe I offered him a deal like I'm prepared to offer you one. This thing of yours is on the skids, and the way it's going in another month it'll be out of existence. In the last weeks you've had to lay off half your men. They tell me work's stopped on the Crispi building since those two guys got killed in that accident with the scaffolding over there."

Tagliaferri had been staring down at his clenched monkey's paw. The interview had sent his blood pressure up and started a slight thumping behind his eyes. He was a man who suffered from tensions that could find no relief in a normal man's anger.

"What are you asking for?" he said.

"A half-interest," La Barbera said. "I'll pay for it at the present value. If you keep me waiting, it's gonna be a lot less."

"Nothing doing," Tagliaferri said.

"Think about it. Take your time and think it over."

"I don't need to think it over."

"Right now you got something to sell. You got assets. The stock and equipment could be listed at cost price in the books. I'm gonna be fair with you, Tagliaferri; I like to give everybody an even chance."

"I said no."

La Barbera got up. "Sorry you feel that way. I figure if we were in this business together it could still go places. You know where to find me if you change your mind."

Tagliaferri followed him to the door, and saw waiting for his visitor on the landing the two smirking jailbirds who provided the La Barbera muscle and had come up the stairs behind him. One of them saluted him impudently, and as much as La Barbera's visit it was this man's impertinence that convinced Tagliaferri the whole edifice of respect built up so carefully over the generations was beginning to crumble; at last something must be done.

He called Marco to his house near the Orto Botanico for a conference on possible remedies, and Marco suggested a plan to be submitted for Don C.'s approval. "He won't like it," Tagliaferri said. Both men knew that with the passage of the years their chief had become more and more the advocate of peaceful solutions.

But in the early morning two days later, the garage of Tagliaferri's trucking company with five trucks inside was burned to the ground. Tagliaferri telephoned Marco. "I've been in touch with a certain person again about the new boy, and he's given us the green light."

Marco called Johnny La Barbera, purporting to be an employee of the Agenzia Immobiliare Garibaldi, where, he had discovered, La Barbera had once asked about a house advertised for sale.

"Mr. La Barbera, we have your name on our books for a house in a central location. Are you still interested?"

"If it's what I'm looking for," La Barbera squeaked, "and the price is right."

"I think you'd like this one. It's considerably larger than the other you inquired about, and it's centrally located—in the Piazza Caracciolo. Seven beds and three reception rooms on three floors. I would say it's a particularly charming house, and it offers the great advantage of a courtyard, so if you happen to have a car it eliminates the parking problem. Houses with courtyards are few and far between in our experience."

"I'll come by and look it over," La Barbera said.

The house on offer was charming indeed. It had been built in the Spanish style for a mistress of the last of the viceroys. Even La Barbera was impressed by the magnificence of its architecture, especially because here, in the very heart of this teeming city, there was room for both his and his brother's white Cadillacs. La Barbera paid the asking price without demur, ordered several million lire worth of furniture, and within a week he and Pete moved in.

Three days later they each took a girl friend and drove out in Johnny's car to Zu Tanu's restaurant at Mondello. Through a whim of Johnny's, the table where Rossi had been sitting when he met his end had been reserved for them. They dined excellently on the lobsters which were the specialty of the house, turned down the waiter's suggestion that they might want to retire after dinner to a couple of the restaurant's celebrated bathing cabins, and instead drove straight home to the house in the Piazza Caracciolo.

It was late at night by the time they got there. Johnny rang the bell on the wrought-iron courtyard gates, but when after a few minutes the porter did not appear and he began to rattle the handle impatiently, he discovered that the gates were not locked. Followed by the others, he entered the courtyard, switched on the light and found that a strange car had been parked behind Pete's Cadillac, and that it would have to be moved before he could drive his own car in off the street. When La Barbera angrily opened the door of the intrusive Alfa Romeo, there was an explosion that illuminated the whole piazza with a greenish flash, broke windows a quarter of a mile away and caused several midnight strollers to fall to their knees in the belief that the end of the world had come. No identifiable bodily parts of the four victims were found, but the next day a few pieces of flesh taken at random were placed in four coffins. Two of these, through a mild conspiracy between the police and the undertaker, were stated to contain the girls' remains and therefore were decorated with white sashes symbolizing purity and

virginity. Both of the girls' families later received
an anonymous present of two hundred thousand
lire.

The circumstances of this episode, which touched
off a small civil war in the city of Palermo during
the autumn of 1953, were probed with mechanical
thoroughness by Alistair Ferguson and reported on
at some length to his superiors in Washington. Within
a few days, Bradley, who had been absent from Sicily
for over six years, flew in to confer with him. He
was met by Ferguson at the airport, and on the way
back they stopped for sentimental reasons for a drink
at the Albergo Sole.

"It hasn't changed," Bradley said. But it had, and
he felt a moment of sadness. Could the years ever
fail to tarnish memory? This kernel of the once magnificent Palermo had shriveled within a shrinking city.
Or could it be that his own eyes spread this lackluster
film over once familiar beauty?

"It has character," Ferguson said. He too had
changed, to the point where Bradley hardly recognized
the naïve enthusiast of the past. Now he wore sandals
and a massive gold ring engraved with what appeared
to be cabalistic signs, and moved with the sleepy
calculation of an opium smoker. He ordered Marsala,
with egg yolk in a separate glass, then poured the
yolk into the wine and stirred carefully with a spoon.
So this, Bradley thought, was what had become of
the hard man the general had provided, the champion
of the new realism, the young fellow of promise who
had been left to defend what had remained of their
hard-won spheres of influence in this country. He
clutched at a straw of hope. Could it be some subtle
disguise Ferguson had assumed, the better to carry
out his secret duties?

"I gather you changed your mind about Sicily,
since you applied for a second tour of duty," Bradley
said.

"The fact is, I've gone more or less native," Ferguson
said, raising a finger to remove a filament of egg yolk
from his lip. He was soldiering on, protected so far
by the regularity and verbosity of his reports. He col-

lected rumors, uncovered or invented plots, discovered security risks in the scandalous conduct of trivial politicians. Back in Washington they were satisfied, but Bradley's visit had taken him by surprise. He watched his visitor cautiously, warily preparing his defenses. In the years since he last saw Bradley he had heard a great deal about him, and nothing that he had heard made him wish for closer contact with the man. One of the wild ones, they had always said, a chronic free lance, a man who believed that the guiding hand of destiny lay heavily on his shoulder.

"If it suits you, why not?" Bradley said. "Let's go, shall we?"

Absent of expression and driving his black Alfa like a maniac, Ferguson conveyed them back to Bradley's old headquarters, where all the complicated locks had gone. They were greeted by the specially imported desk of old, now piled high with papers. Illustrated magazines were stacked around the floor and a collection of gesticulating theater puppets hung from the walls.

"You've arrived at an exciting moment," Ferguson said. "Two more cars blew up yesterday. Thirteen or fourteen killed. I forgot how many were knocked off the day before."

"I've just been looking at the pictures in the *Giornale*," Bradley said. "Very gory. Who's winning at the moment?"

"The old firm," Ferguson said. "The new boys didn't stand a chance when your friend Marco took out the La Barberas. Johnny was the brains of the organization. When he went, they were like a lot of sheep. They're fighting some kind of rearguard action, but it's only a matter of time. They don't have a strategy."

"I read your last report," Bradley said. "Just how do you know that Marco was really responsible for that explosion at the Villa Medina?"

"How do I know? How can I explain it? I've lived here for nearly seven years. The time comes when you can pick these things out of the air. I guess it's a kind of knack. In this place fact and rumor are mixed up together. In the end you develop an instinct, and somehow or other you can pick out the truth. The funny thing is that Palermo isn't really a secret place at all when you get to know it. You can almost say that everybody knows everything that goes on. The only thing is that nobody can ever *prove* anything. It's like a sixth sense"—he tapped his head, closing his eyes—"a kind of flair, I suppose."

"How do you imagine that he found out that La Barbera was looking for a house?"

"It was just a logical guess. Everybody in this town wants a house, but ninety-nine percent of the population have to live in apartments with the neighbors breathing down their necks. There are only about two hundred private houses in the whole city, and you can wait for years for one. All they had to do was offer a house with a courtyard and they couldn't go wrong. Anybody would take it like a shot."

"Simple when you think about it, but the simplicity of genius, huh? You ever run into Marco these days?"

"Once in a while. I know where he lives down in Acquasanta. You want to see him?"

"No," Bradley said. "He's the last person I want to see. You remember when I told you that the time might come when I needed him? Well, it looks as if the time may be pretty near. The person I have to see is Don C. I've done him a few favors in the past, and I can't believe he'll say no when I ask him to do one for me now."

Marco was surprised but not alarmed by the summons to Don C.'s presence in his farmhouse at the foot of the Cammarata mountains. Only the most favored of the men of honor, those who had been marked as worthy to fill positions of responsibility and trust, were received by the great man in his home, but from the time when Don C. had honored him at Lucia's christening party, he had allowed himself to believe that he was in high esteem.

There was a protocol to be followed on such occasions. Don C. would receive his visitor seated in the

shade of a fig tree in his courtyard. Normally he was
a man of extraordinary silences, preferring to com-
municate through gestures which themselves were
few and restrained: a backward jerk of the head suggested negatives of every degree of emphasis; the
fluttering of his fingers signified doubt; an eyelid pulled
down by the index finger expressed disbelief. At these
audiences, however, he would make a special effort,
putting a large number of questions in his weak and
husky voice. The questions were banal—of the kind
asked on government forms—and in any case Don
C., who asked them as an empty politeness, and because something had to be said in the intervals of
sipping camomile tea brought by the housekeeper,
knew all the answers in advance. He was believed
to know, down to the most trivial detail, the life story
of every man of honor. In this remote farmhouse
among the sun-scalded silent fields, with its stink
of pig's dung and whining flies, nothing escaped his
scrutiny, and no one was beyond the reach of his
power.

Tagliaferri had given Marco a few pointers on the
way to behave. "He's human, so show respect, but
don't exaggerate. Don't go down on your knees. He
doesn't enjoy being toadied to. Times have changed."

His sponsor had made a further suggestion. Don
C. notoriously disliked ostentation, and Marco was
overdressed for the visit. His second suit, produced
for inspection, was considered equally inappropriate
and Tagliaferri advised him to buy something more
acceptable from a secondhand clothing shop. It should
be ill-fitting, though not grotesquely so, and if possible
neatly patched. The old Fiat with rattling pistons
and battered wings would do; the newer Lancia
Augusta would be out of place.

Don Claudio rose in the summer at about three-
thirty A.M., before dawn, and liked to conduct his inter-
views before breakfast, so Marco was instructed to appear by seven. It was a two-hour journey on a good
road reinforced by the Allies as far as Lercara Friddi,
after that a rutted track to the village of Cammarata
and beyond. Don C. owned several thousand acres

of parchment-colored land at the end of the valley under the shoulder of Mt. Cammarata, and grew wheat on it by methods calling for the maximum amount of labor to produce the minimum yield. It was a part of the world where one ate donkey flesh at festas, where a witch had been burned to death in 1852, and where peasants addressed a prosperous-looking stranger as "Your excellency," and sometimes sold off a nubile daughter to the highest bidder when food prices rose at the beginning of the winter.

In the sallow morning light Don C.'s farmhouse looked like a mud casbah in the High Atlas, its walls pierced with tiny square windows behind ramparts of gray prickly pear. Black crones working among the corncobs ripening on the flat roof drew rags, Arab style, across their features as they straightened to watch Marco. A bunch of thin peppers hanging from a window looked like bloodied knives. Half a dozen cars, all of them in battered condition, had been shoved into what shade could be found among the cactus, and Marco noted among them Don Claudio's famous Bianchi, vintage 1928, peach-colored with rust, its near-sided door tied up with string. He knew now that some sort of general meeting had been convened, that the ancient cars had been borrowed for the occasion by the provincial heads of the association, and that at this moment their drivers, who had come dressed like street cleaners and gamekeepers, were conferring with their chief on some matter of high policy on which their opinion had been sought.

The steward waiting for him at the gate was one of those leather-faced countrymen in corduroy and black breeches who had wheedled a house and a few acres of stony soil out of Don C. in exchange for doing odd jobs, and for serving as bodyguard whenever his chief had to make the trip into Palermo or Monreale. He showed Marco into a room as bare as a prison cell, containing a low bench and a tap dripping into a basin in an angle on the wall. The first thing anyone was expected to do who came into such a farmhouse out of the dust-clogged landscape was wash himself, and Marco rinsed his hands under the tap and dried them on a square of grubby cloth hanging on a nail nearby. Then he went and sat down on the bench, at the other end of which now sprawled the youth who had followed him into the room, which he filled with the stench of sheep. When Marco looked in his direction the boy jerked his head away to stare at the wall ahead, but when he got up to look out the barred window he felt the vacant shepherd's eyes swivel in his direction.

Through the window he saw a corner of the courtyard, a wall displaying its scar tissue of flaking plaster, a broken cartwheel, harness covered with dust and bird droppings, and a lean cat tapping the earth with its paws like a young child testing the keys of a piano. A group of three men of respect came into sight, walking thoughtfully, heads together. The heavy, brooding faces conferred by success in rural Sicily seemed to Marco to have been sharpened and drawn into aquiline shapes by some emergency, and as they came nearer, hunched a little as if under the weight of the long cloaks still worn in these country parts, he recognized one of the heads of the Gentile clan and his own protector Tagliaferri. At this moment Tagliaferri looked up and their eyes met. Marco made the slightest nod of recognition, but Tagliaferri instantly looked away and the three men passed on out of sight.

He went and sat down on the bench again. The young shepherd was staring down at his weatherbruised hands and occasionally cracking his finger joints. Something had gone wrong, Marco knew; he also knew that in the association there were no fluctuations of fortune. Stars only rose and set.

A half-hour passed. The shepherd, who Marco was now beginning to fear might be his guard, cracked his fingers and fidgeted constantly, stirring up odors of sheep urine and byres; a bluebottle whined in a slant of sunbeams to lasso him with a lariat of whining sound; one of Don C.'s bantam cocks produced a sound nearer a whimper than a crow. Through the window Marco watched the men of honor come and go, pushing or dragging their shadows grudgingly.

In this interlude he said a stoic farewell to many hopes. Something had gone wrong. Death might already lie in wait somewhere on the lonely road back to Palermo.

Finally, quick footsteps slapped on the flagstones outside, the door flew open and a small, neat man bounced into the room. He was dressed in the most splendid suit Marco had ever seen, though something about him gave the impression that he was shrinking slightly in his clothes, which flapped as if in a slight breeze about his arms and shins. In the bucolic silence he moved with an energetic thrust of the joints and a quick squeak of shoes.

"*Salutami gli amici,*" the man said in a bad Italian accent, and then in English, "You're Riccione, aren't you? I'm Spina. Glad to know you."

Marco took the small hand with embarrassment, not knowing whether or not to kiss it, and was relieved when the man drew it away. He knew of Spina as a remote and legendary figure, the man who, from a cell in a maximum security prison in the United States, had plotted with Don C. the overthrow of the Axis powers in Sicily, and as a reward had been paroled and deported. Rumor and fable as well as the facts themselves had contributed to an image of awe-inspiring power. Spina had been Don C.'s counterpart in the United States, a Caesar who ruled absolutely and who swept aside all opposition to his plans for the reorganization of the families along the most effective military lines. It was hard to believe that this concentrated, bustling, smiling, shrunken man one April day back in 1931 had murmured the order for the elimination of his old chief, the terrible Giuseppe Masseria, and forty of his key supporters, stipulating that no man was to be executed in the presence of his wife or children, and instructing almost in the next breath that $20,000 worth of flowers be distributed among the various funerals.

Indeed, Spina's reputation had been almost too great for the Sicilian men of honor to bear. Where they dealt in tracts of primitive land and whatever it produced, Spina had managed an empire of guilty pleasures; where they commanded a hundred men, Spina controlled ten thousand. Basically the Sicilian men of honor remained farmers at heart, whereas Spina had been a financial manipulator, politician and general all rolled into one until his temporary eclipse. For this reason, when compelled to return to his native land, Spina had been received with wary reserve, but this he had overcome with his charm. He smiled, cajoled and flattered, and in the end the Sicilians conceded and almost forgave the enormous gangster car and diamond rings. The men of honor consoled themselves with the knowledge that there was nothing Sicily had to offer that was big enough to keep Spina among them for more than a short time. He was too brilliant, too flamboyant. Nor could they understand the brash democracy of his manner, which made them uncomfortable, as it had Marco, because it left them unable to show respect in proper form, and this was as necessary to their well-being and peace of mind as the respect that they in turn expected to receive.

"I've been talking to the old man about you, Riccione," Spina said. "He had some nice things to say, and it's a pity it had to be like this."

Marco felt another moment of embarrassment. It would have been best to address Spina by his first name, prefixing it with Don, but he couldn't remember the name and he knew that the more he tried to the less hope there was. "Mr. Spina, I'm afraid I don't understand what's going on here."

The lithe muscles of Spina's face twisted his mouth and eyes instantly into an expression of amazement. "Don't tell me nobody put you wise, Riccione. It's one of those trials they used to put on in the old days—way back in Don Vito Ferrer's time, and before. I guess these boys back here in the sticks still believe in ghosts. Twenty witnesses or more to be heard. This could go on for the rest of the day. You wouldn't believe it, but there's actually an old guy out there in sheepskins." He laughed, uncovering as he did so his back teeth in a way that increased the skull-like appearance of his face. The pupils of his dark eyes glittered genially in the stained whites. "A guy in sheepskins, and nobody batted an eye."

"Some of the country people are very backward, Mr. Spina," Marco said. Spina's mockery had startled him. Men who wore sheepskins did so because they had turned their backs on the corruption of life in towns, and had retired to the mountains where they were respected as the guardians and upholders of the ancient law. Spina's irreverence was typical of the new men who had returned from overseas after the peace, and who were ready to challenge all the institutions. He felt weakened by Spina's easy-going contempt. For him the association had become father, mother, brother and sister. It had stretched out its hand and raised him up from the death of life in Campamaro. It had canceled the servile, peasant inheritance in his blood, and charged his being with that cold but brimming self-confidence which enforced the respect of all who had dealings with him. But he felt bound to accept his share of Spina's scorn, and it wounded him at the same time as it infected him with the beginnings of criticism and doubt.

"And you hadn't any idea why they sent for you?"

"None at all, sir."

"I been hearing you're a stand-up guy. They tell me you have balls. You aren't going to whine even if your luck's run out. They sent for you because you're on the spot. Any idea why some of these guys want to fry your ass?"

"No sir."

"I'll tell you. You're accused of putting the finger on a certain Benedetto Gentile who passed away in tragic circumstances some years back. Let me lay it right on you: if you're found guilty, you know what to expect."

Running his tongue across the inside of his lips, Marco felt a tiny scale of loose skin and bit it away. Fear, which can appear in as many guises as love, had touched him with its cold fingertips. In this case it showed itself as an agonized unreadiness for death. Back in his youth, in his encounter with the Moors, he had not felt this unreadiness; then he had seen his life as something that was simple and shapeless, without a defined beginning and end. Now his life was enmeshed with that of his wife and children, and it could not be destroyed without dismembering their lives too. Their precious beings were grafted on his. He had to have time to disentangle the soft tendrils of dependence and prepare them to live without his protection. He was not ready to go.

"Feeling a little depressed?"

"I'm thinking about things, Mr. Spina. Just thinking."

"Well, don't let it bug you too much. As it happens, you won't be found guilty. There had to be a trial because the Gentile outfit wanted it that way. You'll be found not guilty by eleven votes to one—that's assuming the old man abstains."

The cold shadow of death had drawn away. Marco shook himself free of the vision of the lonely road to Palermo marked with crosses of so many forgotten ambushes. That night Teresa would wait for him and he would come.

"But you still got your cock caught in the zipper," Spina said. "This Gentile outfit is going to put the hammer on you whatever happens, and there's too many of them. Besides, the old man has to have peace. The way I see it from where I sit, you'll have to leave the country."

Marco nodded, waiting.

"How do you feel about that?"

"I've got a wife and two children."

"You're both young. Your wife will enjoy a change."

"We bought a new place last month, Mr. Spina."

"Don't bleed on me, Riccione. You bought it cheap; I heard about it. You can sell out and make a profit right now."

The emergency had jogged Marco's brain into remembering Spina's first name. "I'd be happy to go along with anything you suggest, Don Salvatore."

"You're lucky, Riccione, even if you don't know it. Okay, so you've got some weight here, but not much. You're going to be fifty-five years old with kidney stones before these guys will be kissing your ring. This is always going to be a small setup. You know something? This two-bit island depresses the hell out of me. A guy like you could really hit the big time over in the States. Buy yourself a Lincoln Connie in a year, maybe own a split-level house and a beach-front vacation home on Long Island."

Why Spina? Marco was thinking. Why was he being told of Don C.'s decision by the great Spina, when until now it had always been Tagliaferri, his sponsor, through whom commands were passed down?

"How soon does it have to be, Don Salvatore?" Marco asked.

"The move? Pretty soon, Riccione. This thing is urgent. Don C. could fix up an arrangement with the opposition for you to stick around for a week, no more. After that there'll be about fifty Gentile boys looking for you with twelve-gauge pump guns loaded with buckshot. You wouldn't have a prayer."

Spina gestured delicately, three fingertips and thumb pressed together and a rhythmic oscillation of the wrist. It could mean anything according to the context, but in this case it promised annihilation. The long, tooth-revealing smile stretched the skin over his cheek and jawbone. Marco accepted the avengers with the pump guns as a piece of theater. Reality was more likely to be the slow and wary passage of the years until one day a bright-looking young Gentile who had changed his name and obscured his past might come to him for a job; or a Gentile who had made it his life's work to study his movements had himself taken on in the bar where Marco went to drink his coffee; or a mechanic with secret allegiances in the garage where they serviced his car found a way to do a little tinkering of his own.

"Would this be for long, Don Salvatore?"

"Ten years, maybe. Your friends would like you to stay alive. That nice young wife of yours is kind of young to be a widow."

"I'm not sure I can get rid of the apartment and the furniture in a week, Don Salvatore."

"No sweat. Tagliaferri can take care of that and

have the money transferred. That settle the problem?"

"I guess it does, Don Salvatore."

"That's the attitude, Riccione. The right philosophical approach. Everybody knows you ran a good race here. You'll be looked after when you get to the other side. You'll be connected and given every chance to move into the big time."

"I'd like to thank you for the interest you've taken, Don Salvatore."

"That's okay, Riccione. That's okay. I've taken a personal interest in your case because you're a guy with prospects. I have a hunch you're going places. I'm sending you somewhere where you can expand your lungs and take in air. You ever heard of Salisbury, Massachusetts? No, I guess not. Well, I have a good friend who has all the business locked up there—a partner of mine from way back when I was an alcohol cooker. He's a good man, and he has a piece of everything. That's where I'm sending you, Riccione."

"I want to thank you again, Don Salvatore. I wish I could describe the gratitude I feel in my heart."

"Don't think about it, Riccione. And try not to talk like a Guinea. When you're connected, this is how it's gotta be. All friends together, and each working for the other. Sooner or later I'll be coming to you for a favor, and I know you'll come through for me."

"Just give me the chance, Don Salvatore. That's all I ask."

"Let's get down to details," Spina said. "The *Principe di Piemonte* leaves from Genoa for New York on Monday, the eighth. That's exactly a week off. I had a hunch the way things might go, so a first-class cabin's been reserved for you and your family. Somebody whose name we needn't mention is picking up the tab for the tickets. Do me a favor and cut out the thanks."

We'll be all right, Marco was thinking, Teresa and the children and myself, but what about the others? How will they manage? The two lonely mothers with old age over the horizon? Cristina whose bourgeois husband sooner or later might throw the facts of her past in her face as an excuse for deserting her? Paolo with his new garage, his Agip agency and his Fiat service franchise, but with worsening asthma putting increasing strain on his weak heart? The legion of cousins, three, four or more times removed, who had appeared at the whisper of his prosperity, with their claims on his protection and love; doles of money for the needy; Christmas turkeys; Epiphany dolls; advice on marriage and lawsuits over land—all of them responsibilities he had accepted with eagerness, almost with gratitude. What would they all do? To whom would they turn for succor and support when he was gone?

"Well, what do you say?" Spina asked. "How do you feel about the future now?"

Part

Two

1

He was taken in hand by Andrew Cobbold, once Andrea Coppola.

"Your name is no longer Marco Riccione," Cobbold said. "Try to forget that it ever was. It is now Mark Richards. You'll be given a responsible position in the Stevens organization, and you're going to live on Champlain Avenue, which is considered a good address. Try to live up to it."

"I'll do my best, sir."

"And don't call me sir. This is a democratic country."

Cobbold sat watching him through sleepy eyes. He was a young, balding man with a thick compensatory growth of black hair about the ears and the creamy white skin of a young girl. His expression was one of scorn alternating with conciliation, and when he got up Mark was once again taken by surprise that he was so short. Cobbold was a lawyer, the head of the Vincent Stevens legal department, and believed by many in the organization—which lived on rumor rather than fact—to be next in line of succession to the Stevens empire, of which Don Vincente Di Stefano was the founder. According to these rumors, he had supplanted the natural heir, Don Vincente's son.

"Now, take me," said Cobbold expansively. "Where do you think I come from?"

Mark knew that Cobbold was a second-generation American who had inherited a small beer fortune made during Prohibition and had been to Harvard Law School. He shook his head.

"I was born in Mulberry Bend," Cobbold said. "Elizabeth Street. But you wouldn't know where that was, would you?"

"I haven't been in the States long enough," Mark said.

"No, of course you haven't. Mulberry Bend was the Italian ghetto. My father started with a storefront bank. What I'm trying to say, Richards, is that none of us have to go through life with our pasts hanging around our necks. This is 1956. You're finished with Sicily now, and I hope to turn you into an American. Where did you pick up that accent, by the way?"

"I worked for two years as an interpreter with the British before I was taken on by the American base depot at Caltanissetta, Mr. Cobbold."

"It's the best thing about you," Cobbold said. "Otherwise—I may as well be perfectly frank—you look like a greaseball. What do you drink, Richards? At home, I mean."

"We drink wine sometimes."

"I thought so. Well, you'll have to get to like whiskey. I suppose you eat a lot of pasta?"

"Not too much," Mark said. "Once or twice a week, maybe."

"Don't eat it in public. It marks you down for what you are. The whole thing is not to stand out, to be as inconspicuous as possible. Above all, no kissing between men."

Cobbold drummed his beautifully manicured hands softly on the desk top. The hair in full retreat from his scalp grew exuberantly elsewhere, furring fingers and wrists. Behind him on the wall Moulin Rouge dancers whirled in a Toulouse-Lautrec poster.

"When did you last take Mrs. Richards out on the town?"

"A week or so ago, Mr. Cobbold."

"I'd like you to make a regular thing of it. Nobody's going to think it's strange to see you in the company of your wife. Just the opposite. We have a different attitude toward women in this country. You have absolutely nothing to fear; nobody's going to pinch her ass in a public place. I want to see you fit in. You'll be living in a district that has class. Emulate your neighbors. Mow the lawn on Sundays. Join the Racquet Club. I don't want to see you wearing those clothes after today. Buy yourself a couple of custom-made suits, and wear tweeds on the weekend. Get that hair cut. Sorry to have to talk to you like this, Richards, but there's no place for Mustache Petes in the Stevens organization."

"That's all right, Mr. Cobbold. I quite understand."

"Good. Now we're going to run over to the country club together, have a drink and discuss some of the finer points. What will you be ordering?"

"A whiskey," Mark said.

"It doesn't have to be whiskey. It can be a gin and tonic, or maybe a vodka martini. Do you order cake with it?"

"No, not cake."

"Splendid. Cake is out. We're making progress."

The waiter had white hair and a withdrawn, patrician expression: a human stage-prop of this room with exposed timbers and English sporting prints on the walls.

"My friend will have malt whiskey with ice," Cobbold said. "Glen Livet or Glen Grant if you have it. Bring me the same. It's very pleasant here," he went on. "Quiet. Particularly in the summer. Always a nice breeze blowing. Don Vincente will put you up for membership. They kept him out of this place when he first came here, so he bought it."

Stealthy as an assassin on the thick carpet, the waiter came with the drinks and disappeared.

"There're some things you have to know," Cobbold said. "You'll be seeing Don Vincente himself in a few days or weeks, but I'll fill you in about the organization. It was set up to be a family business but it didn't turn out that way. The two older sons lost interest and moved out. As for the youngest boy—well, you'll be able to judge for yourself. You must have heard of some of his escapades."

"They tell me he goes for girls and fast cars," Mark said.

"We own several factories, a bank, both of this town's hotels, its three restaurants and this place. The thing is, Don Vincente can't last forever, and I can't imagine Victor carrying on when the time comes. You'll probably agree when you see him." He lowered his voice, though they were the only occupants of the room, and his expression of languid mockery sharpened. "We're also interested in a number of places of entertainment, though our investment here is declining. Some of them aren't strictly legitimate, even if the law winks an eye at them. The trend is to pull out of these . . . shall we say borderline activities, and reinvest elsewhere. Right now Don Vincente is buying hotels in Havana, which is supposed to become the playtime capital of the future. But since you're in the real estate division, you must know all about this."

"The overseas section could handle that," Mark said. "My office deals mostly with our business in and around town."

Cobbold settled in his armchair, crossed his legs and threw back his head. "I understand you saw something of the legendary Spina shortly before you left home."

"I was with him for about an hour in all."

"Was there anything extraordinary about him?"

Mark thought about it. "Yes, there was. He wasn't what you expected. I would have thought he'd be a big tough guy. He was small—pleasant, too. You felt you could get along with him. He had a face like a monkey."

"He's killed a lot of men in his time," Cobbold said. "He and Don Vincente were in business together way back. They ran the Italian lottery down in Lower Manhattan. That was before their ways separated. As you know, Spina was sent to prison for compulsory prostitution. I understand that he and Don Vincente were born in the same village and emigrated together.

Alcamo Marina, if I remember right. The last of the old-timers, huh? He was deported as soon as they let him out of Dannemora. They tell me he's based in Naples these days."

"He's leaving Italy," Mark said. "Maybe he's already gone."

"Are you sure?"

"Unless he was kidding. He came down to the ship at Palermo to say goodbye, and said he hoped I'd look him up in Havana someday if I ever happened to be in Cuba."

"He said that? So he's going to Havana after all. And you liked him? You fell for that famous charm of his?"

"He was an easy man to like."

"Have you ever heard of the Castellammarese War they had over here way back in the thirties?"

"I've heard of it."

"He had forty men gunned down in one night. A killer, Richards. Just a killer. A man out of date in this day and age."

Mark didn't reply. He was indifferent to such bloody legends. Spina had come to his aid in Sicily, had helped him and his family leave the country in safety, and had arranged for Don Vincente to take him under his protection. Whatever the man had done to his enemies was of no concern; he would always remain in Spina's debt.

Mark also knew that Cobbold had lost his father in the Castellammarese War.

2

For the first six months in Salisbury, Teresa was bewildered. The cities of the United States which she had often imagined had in the two weeks before their arrival been Palermos with wider avenues, higher *palazzi,* vaster squares and more dangerously charging traffic: places where the intimacies of the city had been developed on a grander scale, and where the silence, isolation and boredom of the country—so detested by people of peasant origin—had been erased. Nothing could have been more unlike the Salisbury of her imagination than the reality. The majority of its houses were of wood, a depressing material for the peasant who craves the solidity and protection of stone; still worse, in all the better residential streets, such as Champlain Avenue, they had been built in isolation from each other on wide plots of lawn. Sicilians dreaded open space. Whether in Sciacca, Agrigento or Palermo, they lived crowded together at tightly as possible in apartment houses, with their neighbors on the staircases, landings, passageways, the balconies all around and the street below. A constant and vociferous human presence protected them from the memory of the marauders of the past, and at the same time endlessly reminded them that all human life basically flowed in the same direction.

For six months Teresa sat tight, struggled with loneliness, comforted herself with her children, and examined and assessed the new world around her with growing curiosity. Then the change began to take place. She was a good linguist, better than Mark, with a prodigious memory, extraordinary powers of mimicry and a genuine respect for words. She spoke English whenever she could: to the clerks in stores, the delivery men, the cleaning woman, to Mark at home and finally, when her confidence was complete, to the neighbors. By the time a year had gone by, she spoke it perfectly, and with an authentic Salisbury accent unencumbered by the trailing vowels at the end of words that so often betrayed the immigrant Italian. From being a typical young Sicilian woman who hardly left her home except to go to Mass, she now spent as much time as she could out of the house wandering through supermarkets, window-shopping, attending coffee mornings and bridge afternoons. She arranged her baby-sitting with precision—by this time they had decided that Amedeo would in future be called Martin and Lucia, Lucy—and found time to join the St. Vincent de Paul and Christ Child societies. Mark bought her a Volkswagen, which she learned to drive in less than a month.

Contact with new friends stimulated her thinking and widened her interests. In Sicily young wives together talked about little but their children or their sexual experiences with their husbands, which they dressed up with wild fantasy. Here, conversation was impersonal. When it came up, sex was discussed at a secondhand level—like something in a television serial, and of little more importance than ceramics, basket-weaving or Republican politics.

In Teresa Mark saw a new restlessness, a new reserve, and a new and almost unfeminine curiosity, and with it there was a change in her physical appearance: a loss of weight, of the gentle, indulgent fat of thigh and bosom, an increase in physical liveliness—even, he suspected, an increase in height.

Moreover, the constant volcano of their sexual life had cooled slightly. The iron routine of the bed imposed by Sicilian custom had been broken by the fact that no one took siestas in Salisbury. For males in Mark's position as assistant manager of the Stevens real estate office, they were replaced by prolonged business lunches. On days when he was free, he went home and they went to bed. It was the only time they spoke Italian together, using the vulgar words for which they had found no satisfying substitute in English.

" 'Sta minchia," she would cry. "Quant'è grossa. Me fa male."

She had taken to wearing panties. At first he was scandalized; back in the old country the only young women who wore them were prostitutes in brothels who employed them as an erotic stimulant. But he soon resigned himself, and learned to take a delight in removing them. There was a lot to be said for some American customs.

For all such Italians and ex-Italians, the first priority was to become impeccably American as soon as they could. The Italians had moved into the area roughly twenty-five years before, elbowing aside the original Dutch and German ethnic groups, to place themselves under the paternal umbrella of the all-powerful young Vincente Di Stefano.

Cobbold described the beginnings of this racial movement to Mark. "He ran everything. He had all the politicians in his pocket. And he was good to his own people. If you came from Naples or Sicily, you got a job. If you were from anywhere around Castellammare you got a *good* job. Things have changed since those days." They were at the country club, where Cobbold had just had a sauna and a manicure. "How's the whiskey?" he asked.

"It's okay," Mark said.

Cobbold sniffed his glass with pleasure. "This is not just wine. This is vintage claret, which is also permissible."

"What happened?" asked Mark.

"What happened? Well, my diagnosis is that they had it too good for too long. Read your history. No empire lasts forever. The sons weren't interested in the business. He sent them to Princeton, and as soon as they graduated they went off. I'm sure you're familiar with the proverb, 'Don't make your children better than yourself.' There was a time when I would have described him as the *Capo dei Capi,* if ever such a person existed in this country. There wasn't a boss in the United States who didn't send a greeting card on his saint's day. Of course, this town is still wide open but the underpinning has disappeared. What we have now is a king without his army." He sipped his claret, holding it in his mouth till the bouquet vanished before swallowing. "I suppose you might consider me an illustration of the process that's taken place," he went on. "My father distilled poisonous liquors which provided the wherewithal to send me to college. I drink Mouton Rothschild. Can you imagine me carrying a gun?"

"How do you see the future of the organization?"

"The future? Well, since you ask me, it seems obscure. I feel cautiously optimistic about the Cuba setup because there we'll be moving into totally legitimate businesses. Here, I'm not so sure. With our momentum we can carry on awhile; a time; after that I wouldn't dare guess. This business was founded on the principle of direct and personal authority, which if necessary had to be enforced, but now it can no longer be enforced because enforcers are a vanishing breed." He put down his glass and laughed. "Mark, I've known you for nearly a year now, and I'm going to tell you something that's going to amuse you. When you first appeared on the scene I couldn't help wondering what you were doing here—why the old man should have been so anxious to import you. You didn't appear to have any qualifications other than what used to be called muscle. Was the old man going abroad to find the kind of talent that was no longer produced in this country?"

He laughed again, and Mark joined in. "The only reason I came here," he said, "is because Salvatore Spina arranged it."

Cobbold was thoughtful again, his face yellowed and melancholy in the club's discreet lighting. "Which in itself could have been suspect," he said. "You probably didn't know the whole truth about Spina. Wheels within wheels. A maze of plotting and intrigue. And of course I remember in my original investigation discovering that there was a certain Bradley involved in this somewhere. Either Spina was working for Bradley, or Bradley for Spina. I never found out."

"I used to see a bit of Bradley back in the old days in Palermo," Mark said. "He was an army officer. I never heard that he was mixed up with Spina in any way. But you never can tell; Bradley knew some funny people."

"Something tells me that he's going to turn up here before long," Cobbold said. "And from what I learned from my spies, he's bad news. That, by the way, goes for Spina, too. And remember, Mark, Spina came through for you, so sooner or later he's going to ask you to settle the debt."

3

Fourteen months after his arrival in the States, Mark was summoned to Don Vincente's presence. The old man lived in a large, ramshackle house hidden away two miles out of town in its own woodlands and park, which he had rebuilt in part to resemble an Orsini castle that had much impressed him on a visit back to Italy in his late twenties.

Mark drove up a twisting drive through unkempt rhododendrons until the huge, sallow building barred the way. Here the third of the house that had become a castle displayed its battlements and machicolations of yellow brick, its gatehouse defended by embrasures for cannon, and a fake drawbridge over a ditch littered with broken Chianti bottles. At the time of his visit to the home country, somebody had pointed out to Don Vincente the equestrian statue of Marcus Aurelius on the Campidoglio, and one of his sycophants had promptly suggested that he had a physical resemblance to the emperor, as well as the obvious comparison in matters of power and prestige. Don Vincente had pondered this, and on his return had had statues of himself and his family made in the Roman style by a local funerary mason. These had been clustered around the gateway: Don Vincente attired for a triumph, his brow wreathed in laurels, scowled down at Mark from the back of an enormously fat horse; Donna Carlotta, his wife, as a Roman empress, reclined smirkingly on a moss-covered stone divan. Mario and Claudio, the two older boys, dressed as young senators, had been added at a later date. Victor, the unsatisfactory son, had not been born at the time.

Mark was shown by an elderly man he would have taken for a gardener into an interior that was totally familiar to him; it could have been any middle-class Sicilian home of the last generation, with dusty plaster saints, a religious picture in each room, and a faint sweet smell given off by the very walls themselves—of flowers wilting in the family shrine, of incense and garlic. Don Vincente received him in an overstuffed Victorian drawing room: a sad-faced man, almost as untidy as Don C., with a tremendous hooked nose, small, reddened eyes, and a turkey's wattle of red skin stuffed into the neck of his open shirt. In his early days he would have passed for an American of the second or third generation, but as he put on weight the lean and lively face of youth took on flesh and then grossness, and now Mark was astonished to see that in his reversion to type he had actually grown each of the nails of his little fingers enormously long, in the old-fashioned Sicilian style.

Don Vincente's manner was kindly and informal. When Mark bent to kiss his ring, he dropped a flabby claw on his shoulder and kissed his cheek. Behind them, arising like a tower from the clutter of marquetry and ormolu, a grandfather clock imported from Italy with a garishly painted face ticked with somber precision, and a canary shrilled in its cage and scattered seed and grit on the carpet.

"Richards, how long have you been in the States, now?"

"Just over a year, Don Vincente."

"It's a shame we didn't meet before. I've been kinda busy. How they been treating you meanwhile?"

"Very well, Don Vincente. Nothing to complain of."

"I been hearing a lot about you. They tell me you work well. Still living down on Champlain Avenue? That's a nice place. I'd kinda like to live there myself if I didn't live here. It's a pretty nice neighborhood. How are you getting along with the neighbors?"

"Pretty good. They're a nice crowd."

"That's great. Living in a small town like Salisbury is different from a big city. You have to make an effort so people will like you. What social organizations did you join?"

"The Kiwanis and the Cristoforo Colombo Society, and I've just been elected to the Racquet Club."

Don Vincente raised the smooth arcs of skin where his eyebrows had once been. His expression became one of wild, macaw-like speculation. "I don't know how you made it, Richards. It's very discriminating."

"You sponsored me, Don Vincente."

"I did, huh? Well, I suppose that accounts for it. I'm glad you joined. Means you're drinking at the same watering hole with some of the biggest guys in the country. Another thing you ought to do is get yourself picked for marshal of the parade on San Rocco's Day."

"They don't hold the parade anymore, Don Vincente."

"Don't they, now? That's too bad. Well, I guess it's another sign of the times. I hear your wife's active in charity. That's a good thing, too. She should apply to be a Gray Lady sometime. I guess she's too young now, but when she's older maybe."

A young man in riding breeches appeared in the doorway and coughed for attention. It was Don Vincente's problem child, Victor, who despite the impetigo that disfigured his face, a weak chin and an evasive, petulant expression, was instantly identifiable as his father's son.

"The Bird died on me again, Pop. Can I take yours?"

"Sure you can take it. You know you can take it. But please don't bust in and interrupt when you know I'm having a private conversation."

"Crazy about cars," he explained to Mark when Victor had left. "What he doesn't know is that I know he ran the Bird into a tree last night. Totaled it." He wheezed an indulgent laugh. Then suddenly the familiar, paternal manner changed and Mark felt a distance between them. "Richards, I want to ask you something. You saw a good deal of Cobbold, didn't you?"

"Only in the way of business, Don Vincente. Outside that he keeps pretty much to himself."

"Yeah, I know he was exclusive. Anyhow, from what

you saw of him, were you able to form any opinion?"

"He's a clever man, Don Vincente. There's no doubt about that. He's had a good education, and it shows."

"You're not telling me anything," Don Vincente said with a touch of severity.

"And he's devoted to your service." Mark had been warned by those who still studied and deferred to Don Vincente's whims that it was better to be the bringer of good news to their chief than the reverse. Don Vincente wanted to hear that his dependents served him well.

"I gave him a big job to do out of the country. Did you know that?"

"I heard he's in Cuba."

"That's right. Havana. I have big business interests down there right now, and he's been down there straightening out the local politicians. Doing a good job." The canary, suddenly in vigorous action on the bottom of its cage, sprinkled them with its seed. "I don't remember ever having been given cause to beef about Cobbold as a worker. The trouble is, it turns out he's a *carogna*. He's gone to the Narcotics Bureau. There's a big setup in junk down in Havana, and he's blown the whistle."

"I don't believe that, Don Vincente."

"Shut up and listen. Nobody's asking you to believe anything; you're being told. I don't allow, and never have allowed fooling with junk. But what friends of mine want to do is their own business. Cobbold's done his best to turn in a friend of mine, and you know what that means." The sun, shifting from behind a cloud, glared at them through a high stained-glass window, and Don Vincente's skin turned old and waxen in the yellow light. "Luckily we still have connections on the other side. One of the guys down there knows you, by the way, from way back in Palermo. I've forgotten his name."

"Bradley?" Mark asked.

"Could have been. He said you'd worked together. Said he'd stop by and say hello one of these days. It's a good thing to have a connection at a time like this, Richards. When a guy tries to turn a friend of mine in, I feel the same as if he's done it to me. The guy he blew the whistle on happens to be a friend of yours too."

Spina, Mark thought. It adds up. In his meetings with Cobbold at the country club for a working lunch or a discussion over drinks of the legal aspects of some new land deal, the subject had inevitably cropped up: Spina and his move to Havana, his involvement in the narcotics business, his probable ambitions. Trying to recruit Mark's sympathy, or at least to neutralize him as a partisan, Cobbold had hinted freely at Spina's suspected intentions. Don Vincente's health was failing, and the time had already passed when, back in Sicily, by iron custom he would have been deposed. Though only a few years younger than Don Vincente, Spina was a relatively fit man, and saw himself—since Don Vincente had no son clever and strong enough to take over—as the rightful successor. But as Spina had been debarred from entry to the States since his deportation, he had persuaded Don Vincente to transfer his assets and operation to Havana, where, when the time came, a smooth takeover would be arranged. Mark did not agree with Cobbold's unhappiness over the present and future situation, and now, by his attempt to use the authorities as the cat's-paw for his own ambitions and revenge, he had evidently committed the unforgivable crime.

"I heard you had a great reputation for setting a case up, Richards, so I'm going to ask you to do something for me."

"Anything I can, Don Vincente."

"I hate a *carogna*, and I guess you do too. This guy ate at my table every Sunday. That big house of his on the Ridgeway, I gave it to him when he got married. Anyone will tell you I treated him better than my own son. He knows all my plans. It's a great betrayal." Emotion had produced a shivering pearl at the end of Don Vincente's enormous nose. He pulled out a handkerchief and trumpeted loudly. "You'd do me a great favor, Richards, if you made a trip down to Havana and settled this thing for me."

"When you say settle it, Don Vincente—"

"I mean *settle* it. I don't want to hear of Mr. Cobbold ever again."

The request—in reality an order—called for instant compliance. It would have been fatal even to feel reluctance, because any hesitation would have been immediately detected. "When do you want me to leave, Don Vincente?"

"As soon as we've figured out how to handle it. I'll be bankrolling you. The rest has to be your baby. I know you have no direct personal experience as a *sicario*. You'll be expected to set it up—and let me lay it right on you, it isn't going to be easy. This may turn out to be the trickiest assignment you've handled so far. This guy Cobbold is a lot smarter than Gentile."

Gentile, Mark thought; he knows about Gentile. Sits up here in this dump in the sticks, never shows himself, but knows everything that goes on. His admiration for Don Vincente increased.

"Cobbold is smart. He must have some idea of what's in the wind. He lives in a plushy hotel and never moves out anywhere without a couple of bodyguards. I just got a report on the situation. They sleep in his apartment. They even wait outside when he goes to the can. You can hire all the button men you want in Cuba, but you won't be able to get near him. I nearly forgot to mention that he's a great buddy of the local chief of police."

"Whoever worked on this—"

"That's you," Don Vincente said.

"—would have to arrange to take him when the bodyguards weren't around."

"Sure you would. And when would that be?"

"When he was with a woman."

"He goes for the dames, doesn't he?" Don Vincente said.

"So they say."

"Even though he's got a nice little wife of his own. Jewish girl."

"I didn't know he was married, Don Vincente."

"He doesn't talk about her, and he keeps her out

of sight. I'd have liked to keep women out of this, but if it's the only way . . ." Don Vincente was notorious for his puritanism, his dislike of prostitution, his readiness to turn away business rather than allow obscene burlesque shows or cabaret acts in his places of entertainment. Women, even if they were not Sicilians, were potential mothers.

"Maybe it won't be necessary to bring one in, Don Vincente. Maybe those bodyguards aren't around all the time. Anyone would have to see for themselves. They'd have to go down there and spend a day or two studying his movements to see what could be done."

"He was a guy you never saw outside business hours without a dame in tow," Don Vincente said. "I should have known he wasn't to be trusted."

"Our old friend, Cobbold," Mark asked his assistant, Di Santis, "what sort of girls did he go for?"

"Blondies," Di Santis said. "The icy showpiece type. Like every other Guinea."

"Just a minute, you're a Guinea yourself."

Di Santis was straight out of Brown, where he had majored in economics. He had a second-generation sense of humor. "Sure I am, but I try to avoid the ethnic vices."

"Where do you go to look for blond bombshells?"

"Anywhere. This town is full of the kind of broad who appeals to a guy who wears Adler Elevators like Cobbold. Has been ever since television put the skids under Hollywood and California lost its lure. Right now we have twelve burlesque shows on Dwight Street."

This was true. Their style and range varied from the Flamingo—where on Saturday nights they featured all thirty-two positions from the *Kamasutra* and strippers prowled among the tables ready to pounce on a likely male and rub his face between their breasts—to the Bavarian Manor—now offering a blues singer whose principal asset was a thin, sweet voice and who only stripped down to her pants.

Linda Watts, originally from South Bend, Indiana,

was a basically serious girl who had once been a competent secretary but had had the misfortune to win a small-town beauty contest. Thereafter she had felt obliged to take up photograph modeling, then gravitated to sporadic employment in burlesque. She could neither sing nor dance very well, but she moved gracefully and possessed a precarious beauty based on her perishable coloring and complexion.

Mark went to see her in her dressing room after her act. Don Vincente had once owned the Bavarian Manor, and though he had sold it along with all his other interests on Dwight Street, his name still carried weight there.

"I hear things aren't too good, Linda. How would you like to make a quick ten thousand?"

"Ten thousand! What would I have to do, rob a bank?" Her laugh was unpleasant. It was part of the equipment of a girl who has been forced to construct some protective semblance of worldly wisdom and hardness. For the same reason, the kindness in her face was beginning to fade. But she was redeemed by those features that never lost their novelty and attraction for a Southerner: blue eyes and hair that was like a close-fitting helmet of pale gold silk.

"You'd have to be pleasant to a friend of mine."

"We ought to get this straight. I sing for a living—at the moment, anyway."

"You're finishing here, aren't you?"

"Next week. I flopped—the biggest frost in history."

"You don't have to put yourself down. You were too good for a dump like this." He really meant it.

"Thanks, pal, for that kind remark; I needed it. Anyway, it's unemployment checks for me again. What was that sum of money you mentioned?"

"Ten thousand."

"I wondered if I'd heard right. What's wrong with your friend—he's suffering from leprosy?"

"So far as I know, there's nothing wrong with him."

"I heard of an oil sheik who had to break chickens' legs when he had a girl. Is it something like that?"

"My friend is young, handsome, charming and well-heeled. I'd be very surprised if he had any perversions. You'd have to spend two or three days in his company at most."

"And nights, naturally."

"Perhaps; I don't know. If you were asked to, yes. When the assignment was over you'd suffer from total loss of memory."

This last sentence disposed of the self-protective banter. Linda's expression became thoughtful and intelligent, and small lines suddenly appeared at the corners of the mouth and nose, immediately rescuing her face from insipidity. "Why?" she asked, in a voice that was crisper and pitched a tone lower.

Mark tasted without pleasure the bourbon on the rocks she had insisted on sending for. He preferred the dumb sweetness of a moment before. Linda's face was now too coolly masculine. "Because you would be receiving a bundle, and you're strapped for money."

"That's not what I asked you. I would have to know more about this. How could you expect me to say yes to a proposition like this without knowing what it's all about?"

"There's a couple of hundred nice girls around this town who would go to bed with this guy for a hundred bucks," Mark said. "The difference is that you know how to use your head. I've looked up your record, and from what I've read you have brains. Hence the offer of ten thousand. All I'm prepared to tell you is that the deal's a legitimate one. You wouldn't be fooling with the law."

"Young, handsome and well-heeled, huh? Where would all this take place? Here in Salisbury?"

"No. It would be in a vacation resort, somewhere down South. As soon as you finish your contract here. My friend's down there now. You'd go down there and stay with him for a few days, be around him for a while and then go home."

"I wouldn't come back here?"

"No, you'd go home. That's part of the deal."

"You mean stay there?"

"Stay there. Until you were told anything different."

"I don't get it. You're going to have to tell me more about it."

"There's nothing more to tell. This is a guy who's lonely. He likes girls, particularly your kind of girl. Where he is right now, you don't see your type of girl around, so we're sending you to him. Perhaps I should say taking you, because I'd be coming along."

"An expensive present, in other words." She put all the bitterness she could into her voice. "You're an Italian, aren't you?"

"What makes you think that?"

"Everything about you except the way you talk. Everything in this town is run by Italians. I happen to know that this dump belongs to one."

"Used to," he corrected her. "I don't see how that comes into it."

"Something tells me you work for the same man."

"It's unimportant what I am and who I work for. I happen to know you want to get out of this business, and what I'm offering is the chance to break away. Do the folks back home know what you're doing here in Salisbury?"

"What do you think?" she said. "I come from a solid Presbyterian family. My father was a deacon."

"You ought to go home," he said. "You're a very pretty girl. You should go right back to South Bend, marry someone in the insurance business and have some kids. I mean that; this is no life for you. You'd go back looking as if you'd hit the big time, and nobody would know any better. You could forget that any of this happened."

"I'll have to think about it," she said. "I'll think about it and let you know."

"Sorry; this has to be a snap decision. What's to stop you making your mind right now?"

The strain of indecision had aged her slightly with a temporary penciling that would soon become permanent under the eyes. "Shall I tell you? Because I'm afraid."

"Of what?"

"Of this whole thing. It seems kind of weird."

He cupped his hands on her shoulder. "Baby, what did you figure me for a few minutes ago?"

"An Italian."

"Now, let's just suppose I happened to be one. You must have heard of their reputation?"

"Only too well," she said. "Only too well."

"Whatever they may have told you, one thing is generally agreed. Guineas don't make trouble for pretty girls. Ask any of your friends. Besides which, I have a hunch we'd get along well together."

"But it isn't going to be you. It's going to be somebody else."

"I'd be there. I'd be around to look after you until it was time to go home."

She nodded as if in gratitude, and the small frown smoothed away. "You see, the thing is, I scare easily," she said. "I don't like to be alone."

4

Two days later, on the eve of departure, Mark ran into complications at home.

A variety of social activities had been planned for the week ahead, and Teresa, who had never before raised objections to his comings and goings, seemed put out by the news of his trip. "Couldn't you have given me any warning?"

"I didn't know myself until today."

"But why Cuba?"

"Because the company wants to increase its investment there."

"You don't speak Spanish."

"I don't have to speak Spanish. I have to be able to put a value on a building."

"How long will you be away?"

"Possibly a week. Probably less."

"I'm going to have to cancel everything. I don't see why we can't come with you. The sunshine would do the children good."

"Sorry. It can't be done."

"But why not?"

It was the first time in their married life that she had questioned his absolute authority. Back in Sicily he would have turned his back on her and walked away instantly without replying, and later in the day or in bed that night she would have made what atonement she could for her insubordination. Now he said mildly, "Because there isn't time to make all the necessary arrangements."

"It doesn't take much time to book three extra tickets."

"This is a business trip," he said, level-voiced but with an attempt at finality. "I'll be on the move all the time."

"Couldn't you leave us in a hotel down by the beach somewhere while you're doing your business?"

"I couldn't do that either." He put it down to the ladies' lunch club, and the company of socially aware and responsible girls who had been to Vassar. Her photographs assured him that she had remained the same, yet for him her beauty had faded like the fragrance of a too-familiar perfume. He did not demand stupidity from a woman, but he believed that intellect should be subordinated to the special feminine intelligence that was a woman's endowment. The friends Teresa had been able to make in Salisbury thought more but felt less than the women he was attracted to. "If you think the children should have a holiday, what's wrong with Miami? You'd get all the sun you want, plus hygiene, and the kind of food they're used to."

"I'm tired of Miami," she said. "That's what's wrong with it. Why don't you ever take us with you when you go anywhere?"

"Because the places I visit aren't family places. Right now Cuba's in the middle of a revolution; people are being shot down in the streets. You don't take your wife and family to a place like that. I'll probably be going again, and if the revolution's over by then I'll fix it for you to go along. That's a promise."

But Teresa was not mollified, and her resentment

showed in a silence that lasted the rest of the day. For the first time, it was he who had to coax back her good humor, rather than the reverse which had always been the case in their few tiffs of the past.

Mark had left a ticket to New York for Linda at the check-in counter and when he boarded the plane she was already in her seat. He did not look in her direction. When the hostess passed with an armful of magazines he took a *Newsweek* and put his head in it. Glancing back some minutes later, he noted that she had already entered into an animated discussion with the man sitting next to her, who was leaning over her, eager and attentive. Mark thought her white linen costume suited her better than the lamé dress of the Bavarian Manor. It had seemed quite reasonable to her that he did not wish them to be seen traveling together. On the Miami flight from La Guardia, they again sat separately. This time she was seated ahead of him in the second row. She seemed happy and relaxed, ordering two drinks in rapid succession, then pressing the bell for the steward and discussed something with him, employing the delicate hand gestures of a Balinese dancer. Later, fragrant and aloof, the target of side glances from every male, she passed on her way to a prolonged visit to the ladies' room.

At Miami, immigration formalities made it necessary for him to take her in charge.

"What's this?" she asked.

"A tourist card. You need it for Cuba."

"You didn't say we were going abroad."

"You can't call Havana abroad. It's the U.S. in the tropics. They speak English."

"That's fine with me," she said. "I once saw an old film about it. Alice Faye, wasn't it? I've always wanted to go to Havana."

At ten thousand feet Cuba was a skin of vegetation stretched over a land saturated with brilliant light. The plane bounced down through bulging cumulus and the air currents of the early evening to deposit them at Rancho Boyeros. They were plunged into milk-warm fresh air, greenish light sifted through palms and a crowd of absurd, maracas-shaking, straw-hatted tourists. Now they were firmly together, Mark steering Linda with his hand on her forearm, a growing possessiveness stoked by the admiration blatantly, almost brutally displayed by thickset men with marvelously laundered shirts, who moved reluctantly to let them pass and turned to follow her with glittering eyes. They took a limousine downtown, where Mark booked Linda into the Lincoln, a sedate hotel on the Avenida Italia, and went on himself to the Sevilla, where he had learned that Cobbold was staying.

He checked in and was given a fourth-floor room over a narrow street raging with traffic. The hotel itself was noisy, with bare, tiled floors and slamming doors, and the sealed-in heat of the day had not yet been absorbed by the cooling walls. He took a shower, changed into a cotton suit and then tried to call Cobbold, but the desk clerk reported that he could not be found. Under the pretense of dissatisfaction with his own room, he went down to reception and was shown a plan of the hotel. Cobbold had taken a penthouse suite on the eighth floor consisting of a sitting room and, beyond it, a bedroom which—since the suite was located at a corner of the building—drew any breeze from two directions.

Mark spent the next hour in a quick reconnaissance of the hotel and its surroundings. The Sevilla had been conceived in the grandiose mood of the past, with an open-handed use of space squandered everywhere in patios, passageways and landings. The elevators could be operated only by attendants, and were slow to come. The main entrance was from the Calle Cuarteles, a one-way street coagulated with traffic moving toward the Paseo de Martí, where it was obliged to turn right. A secondary entrance was through a shopping arcade from the Paseo. Due to the official state of alarm and occasional shooting in the streets, both entrances were guarded by a soldier armed with a submachine gun.

In a quick glance through the Havana *Post,* an

English-language newspaper he bought at the cigar stall, Mark read that five corpses had been picked up that morning off the streets, after the battles or executions of the night before. Going out into the Calle Cuarteles and turning against the traffic to the right, he found himself immediately in a small square in which half a dozen police cars were parked, with machine-gun-armed police in readiness to be driven to any emergency. It was clear that the vicinity of the Sevilla was quite impractical for Cobbold's elimination.

The service entrance to the hotel was equally ill-suited for a quick getaway following the operation, the basement being reachable only by elevator, which took an average of three minutes to respond to a summons, or through a door at the bottom of a staircase which seemed to be kept locked.

Mark had retired to the bar to consider these points over a coffee when he was called by a page to the phone. It was Linda.

"I asked you not to phone," he said.

"I'm sorry. I was lonely. Were you able to see your friend?"

"Not yet."

"I don't know what to do with myself."

"Why not go out and look at the sights?"

"In a place like this? It's impossible. They won't even leave me in peace in the lounge; I had to come up to my room. Couldn't I come over and have a drink with you?"

"No, you better stay where you are. I'll give my friend another hour, and if he doesn't show up by then I'll come over and we can go out and eat."

By nine there was no sign of Cobbold, so Mark took a cab over to the Lincoln, picked Linda up and had them driven to a restaurant, El Bohío, that he had seen advertised as "typical" in the Havana *Post*. It had been built in the style of a peasant's hut with a thatched roof, to appeal to tourists, and they ate in the gardens, under trees strung with colored lights and full of the canary-twitterings of disturbed birds. Night had drawn all the sun-rotted color out of Havana and transformed it into an image carved in pale ivory. The buildings around them were softly luminous, as if a tiny remnant of the day's fierce solar refulgence had survived in the surfaces of stone, and the bustle of the restaurant was soon absorbed in a vast surrounding tranquillity.

As Mark and Linda drew the city's bland breath into their lungs and were soothed by its mellow sounds, they both underwent change. Her romantic soul, buried under the recent layers of indifference, took courage, and the poses she had trained herself with such perseverence to adopt, slackened and lost their conviction. Mark, an addict of all things tangible and measurable, was touched by the transformation. He noticed the smoothing of Linda's voice and the disappearance of the harsh little laugh so often used as a defense. Now she was a secretary on holiday again, frank and careless, and with nothing to lose.

Between the small gourds hanging from a trellised plant, they could see the Morro Channel, along which a ghost schooner, sails set and masts creaking, was being moved by the scene-shifters of the night toward the open sea. Three fishermen stood motionless in its bows, holding lanterns on poles.

"How beautiful," she said.

"This is a pretty nice town when they quit shooting at each other for an hour or two."

"It's wonderful. I'd like to stay right here and not go home at all. Why don't we do just that?"

He supposed that she was advertising her availability, of which he had never been in serious doubt. Preferring not to lose sight of the business arrangement, he took the envelope containing ten one-hundred-dollar bills out of his pocket and shoved it toward her. "I nearly forgot," he said. "Here's the agreed advance."

"Not now," she said.

"A deal's a deal. Take it."

She shook her head again, so he picked up her handbag, opened it and put the envelope inside.

"Why did you have to remind me?"

"You make it sound like an ordeal."

"It is."

"Listen, Linda, please don't take this personally, but I know what it's like in show business. You've been around. You had to."

"Do you believe I've ever done anything like this before?"

"Probably not, but I still don't see what you find so awful."

"There's something terribly cold-blooded about it. Listen, seriously, could I pull out at this stage?"

"No," he said. "You couldn't. It's too late to have cold feet."

"How long do I have to stay with this friend of yours?"

"Two or three days, I expect. As I told you."

"Could it be less?"

"I don't know. It might be; it might be more. At this stage we can't even be sure that he'll want to fall into line."

"You mean he may not want to sleep with me when he sees me?"

Mark shrugged his shoulders.

"What happens if he doesn't?"

"In that case the deal's off, but you keep the thousand dollars."

"I hope that's the way it goes," she said.

"I don't think there's a chance. My friend's got good taste in women. I have a feeling he'll fall for you in a big way."

"You're married, aren't you?"

"Yes."

"Are you in love with your wife?"

"I am."

"Is she good in bed? Most Italian women are, aren't they?"

"They say so. Personally, I've never had any cause for complaint."

"You don't like me," Linda said.

"You're wrong there."

"I mean, I don't have any physical attraction for you."

"Why do you say that?"

"Because if I did, you wouldn't have admitted what you just did about your wife."

"Most of the time I tell the truth. I can't help it."

"It's a pity you feel the way you do about her—speaking selfishly, of course. Do you think you could do something for me?"

"It depends. The circumstances being what they are, it has to."

"Don't worry, I wouldn't ask you to stick your neck out. All I'd like is for us to stay on here for a day or two when this is all over. Not necessarily right here in the city, but maybe by some nice beach where we could swim and lie in the sun and relax. If you find me attractive, it shouldn't be any great hardship."

"I can't promise anything," Mark said. "I'll see what can be done."

"This is a lovely place," she said. "And afterwards it's going to be South Bend for me, so I don't have much to look forward to."

They strolled six blocks back to the Lincoln under the gray, night-spangled walls of the old city. Linda was delighted by the families assembled decorously behind the iron-grilled windows of street-level living rooms, by the city squares forested with palms and the carriages drawn by lively skeletons of horses that kicked fire from the stones. Mark speculated on the presence of the many yellow military-security cars at the street intersections, reaching into the darkness with revolving beams.

A block from the Lincoln a small crowd had gathered to stare down in silence at something in the gutter. Mark laid his hand on Linda's arm. "Wait here a moment," he said.

He pushed his way to the front of the crowd. A young man lay spread-eagled, his limbs in ungainly, broken postures, his head on the curb. Blood had dribbled from vacant eye sockets and dried and caked on the cheeks.

"*Muerto,*" a voice confided softly in his ear. "*Estudiante. Policía. Se han extraído los ojos.*"

He went back to Linda and hurried her away.

"What was it?" she asked.

"Some kid knocked off by the police," he said. "Looks like they're pretty rough in this part of the world."

At the hotel she said, "Come up," and then, minutes later, "Please don't go."

He had been excited by the certainty that her body awaited him, and that with its little endowment of mystery was his to take, without preamble or preliminaries of any kind. He felt a trace of his childhood anticipatory joy, when on the morning of the Feast of Epiphany he and his brother and sister had been awakened to receive their gifts wrapped up in parcels that offered no clue to what they contained. But in the hotel bedroom with its odor of Flit, its gargling pipes and the tingling bluish light of its old-fashioned fluorescent tubes, the mundane facts of life greeted him. She had shaved off her pubic hair.

"Why?" he asked. "Why?"

"I was in this Oriental extravaganza thing at the Baghdad before I moved to the Bavarian Manor," she said, "and the management insisted on it. Does it matter so much?"

"It seems kind of funny, that's all."

"You don't have to look at me there."

In a mild way he was a hair fetishist, like most Sicilians from the backwoods whose first experience as young boys of twelve or thirteen had invariably been with middle-aged prostitutes, dark and hirsute, whose custom it was to go up into the mountain villages with the charcoal-sellers before a festa. Bold at the prospect, but then often shy and reluctant, the youngsters could usually be brought up to scratch by a surprise revelation of what lay in wait, and judicious manual stimulation. In the lamplit gloom of the charcoal-seller's caravan, the aging whore would say archly, "Don't be nervous dear, I've got something to show you." The aftermath of this shocking moment was never quite erased.

He did his best, but was further discouraged by the matter-of-fact roll and thrust of Linda's hips that began as soon as he entered her. His climax slipped away beyond his reach, and with the loss of force his other senses sharpened. He smelled the alcohol on her breath, and a flavor of stale beer was in her mouth.

"Do you make love to your wife like this?" she asked.

He withdrew immediately, got up and walked over to the window. All the stars had fallen, leaving the sky pale and empty, and beyond the city an obscure moon had turned Havana Bay to steel. He began to dress, beginning to think of what he had to do the next day.

5

Cobbold called him in his room from the hotel's coffee shop before eight A.M., and Mark dressed quickly and went down. He found Cobbold alone at the counter, spruce in a seersucker suit that reproved the limpness of Havana's humidity. Two coffee-skinned men with low foreheads were slumped despondently at a neighboring table like bored chimpanzees at a zoo tea party, and Mark took these to be bodyguards. He sat down on a stool next to Cobbold, who turned a cool look on him. "This *is* an unexpected pleasure," he said in a voice that contained no satisfaction.

"I called you a couple of times," Mark said. "I didn't get in until late."

"So I heard," Cobbold said. "As a matter of fact, I saw you last night at El Bohío. Rather bogus, perhaps, but charming all the same. What brings you to Havana?"

"A property the company's interested in."

"For use as what?"

"A casino."

"Oh, my God. Not again. Not another casino." Sternness and disbelief showed on his face. "In any case, why you?"

"You'd better ask Teddy Maclean, who handles the overseas business," Mark said.

"Casinos here are a thing of the past—at least the way things are right now."

"I don't make the policy."

A morose black man in the top half of a hussar's uniform shuffled into sight behind the bar. "Coffee?" Cobbold asked.

"Thanks."

"*Tráigame dos cafés,*" Cobbold said to the bartender. "You want toast?" he asked Mark.

"Just coffee."

"*Y un tostado para mí.*"

The bartender went off, and the sun that had been lying in wait somewhere behind the gray-profiled buildings across the street sent a sword thrust of intolerable light between them. Cobbold pouted silently while ten seconds ticked away. "This property of yours," he asked suddenly in a sharp, schoolmasterish voice. "Where is it?"

"Avenida de Maceo, 264-66." Mark had prepared himself for questioning.

"By that, of course, you mean the Malecón; the sea front. We don't call it Maceo any more." He brightened a little, perhaps soothed by the opportunity to put Mark in his place as an outsider. "It's been on all the agents' books for years. The whole sea front has become one enormous shithouse. You can pick up a place on the Malecón for anything you want. How much are they asking for it these days?"

"Three hundred thousand."

"Three hundred thousand, huh? That's a hundred thousand less than it was last month. Next month you'll be able to buy it for two hundred thousand—if it's still on the market. If anything's on the market. Let me tell you something, Richards. If the company buys this property, they'll be throwing their money down the drain. What I can't understand is why they sent you when all they had to do was ring me up."

"It looks cheap in comparison with anything else they've bought here," Mark said. "I guess the reason Don Vincente wanted me to come down was that buying property happens to be my particular line of country."

The bartender came with the coffee and toast, and they shared his stricken glance. "The trouble with this organization," Cobbold said, "is that half the time the right hand doesn't know what the left is doing. If I've told Don Vincente once, I've told him a dozen times—this is no time to buy property in Havana. I know you're a political innocent, Richards, but has anybody told you that there's a revolution going on in this country? Did you hear the shooting last night?"

"I saw a kid who could have been dumped from a police car. Somebody had gouged his eyes out."

"That's routine," Cobbold said. "Bring more butter," he called after the bartender. *"Tráigame más mantequilla.* There was a battle in the streets about three A.M.," he said. "Twenty or thirty students killed. What I've got to try to make you understand is that these guys—I mean the students—are winning. The government is on its way out. Therefore it doesn't make any sense to buy property now. If you want to make a deal of any kind it has to be with the new boys. Anything you buy now you may lose. If you buy this property in the Malecón, you'll lose it. If I negotiated a purchase with the incoming government, it would be different. They'll honor it. That's why I say you're wasting your time."

An early morning drunk floated in, oscillating gently like a drowned man in the swing of the tide, with a blurred underwater face that the eels would soon nibble at. One of the two low-browed men at the table got up, took him by the arm and steered him quickly out of sight.

"Why the gorillas?" Mark asked.

"In this place you don't always know who your enemies are," Cobbold said. "It seems stupid to take risks. These two guys, by the way, are policemen on duty. Can you imagine any other town where for a small fee the local police chief will arrange to look after you?"

"I understand Salvatore Spina's in town," Mark said. "How does he view the future?"

"Salva and I don't meet. The situation here is that he pulls in one direction and I pull in the other. Spina's in junk. They tell me he sold five million dollars' worth only last month. I also hear that the president's cut came to nearly a million. Which means Spina's behind the president, and the president's behind Spina. Well, as soon as the new government's in, Spina's out. We're in legitimate business, so we'll be staying on. Spina cuts the president in on the junk, and we make a liberal contribution to the rebels' war chest. Why shouldn't we? We're backing a sure thing."

"It sounds a little dangerous to me."

"Only for a week or two more. Next month a very good friend of ours will be in the hot seat over at the Palacio Presidencial."

While Cobbold talked on with the occasional soft, plastic hand gestures and expressive elevations of the eyebrows that he had inherited from his father, Mark busied himself mentally with the complex technical problems of the elimination. The bodyguards seemed alert and efficient. Another tourist had come in, safer this time but touched by the temporary insanity that Havana inflicted on so many of its visitors, grinning inanely and swinging in one hand a stuffed baby alligator bought in the souvenir shop. He was moving genially toward them, but the bodyguard headed him off. Cuba was a country, Mark suspected, where the technique of protection had been developed to match any peril that might present itself. The ratio of police to the civil population, he had learned, was six times higher than in the U.S.A. No free lance, he knew perfectly well, would be persuaded to take on a contract with little hope of coming through it alive, whatever the reward.

"The one thing I don't understand," Cobbold was saying, "is where this man Bradley comes into this. You remember we discussed him before. I can't get over the feeling that he's at the back of Spina. But why? My spies tell me he showed up in Havana last week. Any theories?"

"About Bradley? None at all."

"There's something about him that gives me a funny feeling in my gut," Cobbold said. "It's the same feeling you used to give me when you first arrived. I couldn't quite figure out what you were doing in the States. I've gotten to know you better since then, and I've come to realize you're on the level. I don't much care for mysteries. Anyway, let's forget our troubles. How long will you be staying?"

"No longer than I can help," Mark said. "I have to see this property and make a report, and then I'll be pulling out."

"Why be in a hurry? You ought to stay a few days. I'd be happy to show you around—I mean the kind of things a man like you appreciates, that tourists don't see. This town has a lot to offer. Take this hotel. Can you tell me of any other first-class hotel in the world where if you ask the bellboy for a woman he brings up a selection? Can you beat that? And what they're offering is not streetwalking hustlers, but really good-looking broads."

"So you like the place?"

"Very much. I'd recommend it to anyone who didn't object to caramel-ass. If you want one, ask for *prieta*. That's what they call them here; it's the polite way of saying a black girl." He laughed thickly, as if with food in his mouth. "In the night, as they say, all cats are gray."

There must be a way, Mark was thinking. For example, if Cobbold happened to have a car, it might be possible to fly in the expert from Palermo who had wired up the car parked in the courtyard of the La Barberas' house in the Piazza Caracciolo.

"One thing you'll never see," Cobbold was droning on, "is goose pimples. The skin has this silken quality you rarely find in whites. I personally don't subscribe to the view that they have an unpleasant smell, and I would describe myself as fairly fastidious about things like that. By the way—if you'll forgive my curiosity—where did you find that radiant creature you were with last night? Surely she isn't a local acquisition."

"She's a girl from back home who wanted to come along. Do you want to meet her?"

"If you haven't signed up any exclusive rights," Cobbold said.

"None whatever. It turned out not to be such a good idea. I think she wanted to see Havana more than to spend a weekend with me."

"Marvelous—I mean from my point of view," Cobbold said. "Why don't we all have dinner tonight? Somewhere like El Paradiso? It's supposed to be the best night club in the world."

"I'll ask her."

"Do you think she'll come?"

"I don't see why not. I'll call her later and let you know."

"Do that. I'll keep the evening free. Let's leave it that if I don't hear from you, I'll assume it's okay and pick you up in the lobby tonight at eight o'clock."

When Cobbold slipped down from his stool, the bodyguards pushed back their chairs and moved toward him, one on each side. "Be seeing you, then," he said, and he turned and went through the doors with the two men close behind.

So far, Mark thought, nothing—in accordance with his original plan—could have been easier. It was strange to him that this man, so wise in his way, so sensitive, so intelligent and so powerful that he had even begun, it was said, to challenge the authority of Don Vincente himself, could have carried nothing in the blood inherited from his ancestors to warn him that death had moved closer.

Just near enough to the sea front to offer a glimpse of the bay, while just far enough away to avoid the odor of excrement whenever a breeze blew from the beach, El Paradiso had been acclaimed as the most glamorous night club on earth. Normally the huge circular building ringed with a diadem of light was open to the sky, but it was famous for a system by which, at the throwing of a switch, 22,000 square

feet of roof slid silently into position to replace the
real stars, veiled with rain, by the even brighter firma-
ment of a thousand artificial ones, each twinkling
in realistic fashion in a rosette of blue-sprayed, ano-
dized aluminum.

They were shown to the corner table that Cobbold
had reserved. He sat in the angle of the walls, placed
in such a way that he could see everything that went
on, and anyone who had dealings with him would
have to pass the two bodyguards, now in dark-blue
silk suits brooding over their daiquiris at the next
table.

The presence of Linda had wrought a transformation in Cobbold's manner and even appearance. In
the soggy morning atmosphere of the Sevilla, Mark
had found him gross, but now a certain dignity was
apparent.

All the charming falseness of Havana conspired
in their surroundings to create a romantic mood.
Beautifully simulated tropical trees, with real orchid
plants glued to their branches, trailed plastic lianas
over the tables, and fake moonlight was dispensed
by cunningly concealed lamps. Everything about El
Paradiso was above reproach. The food was excellent,
the service rapid and the champagne real. Two dance
bands alternated rock and roll with the stunning
percussion of dance rhythms imported from the
African jungle.

To Linda, Cobbold was charming, attentive and
deferential; it was clear that she liked him, and that
he was totally captivated by her. The occasion
displayed her beauty to perfection: her splendid hair,
hoar-frosted with El Paradiso's expensive moonlight;
her expression childlike; her eyes devoid of speculation; no line or crease, however faint, threatening
the perfection of her skin.

Safe in his corner, Cobbold made reference to an
ankle injury that prevented him from dancing, and
Mark and Linda took the floor.

"Well, what do you say?" Mark asked.

"He's not too bad," she said. "Better than I'd expected."

"Andrew's okay. I told you you'd like him."

"What happens next?"

"Well, I get the impression he likes you too. So let nature take its course. It just happens that I can feel a bad headache developing. When we leave, I'll probably get him to drop me off at the Sevilla, and then run you around to your hotel."

"And then?"

"And then? Well, it all depends. The thing is, I want our friend to see as much as possible of you in the next few days. I leave it to you how that's best achieved."

"Do you want me to go to bed with him right away?"

"You're expected to use your head. When I call you up tomorrow morning, what I'd like to hear is that he's asked you out for tomorrow night. If he wants to make it the night after that too, better still."

"You want me to see all I can of him."

"Exactly. I want you to spend all the time with him you can."

The rhythm changed to a complicated Latin-American beat that confined them to a corner of the floor, and their bodies separated to keep time as best they could. Through El Paradiso's make-believe jungle, Mark could see the small, pale oval of Cobbold's face, always pointed in their direction.

"Please tell me what this is all about," Linda said.

"It's something involving a business deal. I'd like to know where he is, as much of the time as possible. At least I'll know when he's with you."

"When the cat's away the mice will play, huh?"

"Could be."

"Who are those two Cuban guys with him?"

"Bodyguards," he said. "The country's in an unsettled state. They provide them for anyone who's here on important business."

"I see," Linda said. "Why don't they give you bodyguards, too?"

"I'm not important enough. I only want to buy a rundown building on the sea front."

"What am I to say if he asks me about myself?"

"Tell him as much of the truth as you have to. Don't romance."

"What if he found out about our arrangement?" she asked.

"That would be fatal," Mark said. "I can't imagine anything likelier to have more unpleasant consequences."

"I wonder if I'm afraid of you," she said. "I suppose I really am."

"There's nothing whatever to be afraid of," Mark said. He spoke more slowly. "I know you're going to stick to your side of the bargain. To the letter."

"I'm beginning to like you less," she said.

"That's a pity. I'm beginning to like you more."

"Can we sit down now?"

"When the band stops playing," he said. "And remember Cobbold's got his eye on us. Don't look at him. Just try to relax and act as though you're really enjoying this."

Mark phoned Linda early next morning from his room.

"How are things?"

"Fine," she said. "I guess so, anyway. I just woke up."

"Sorry I had to drag myself away last night. I had black spots in front of my eyes. Otherwise a pretty good evening, wouldn't you say? I knew you'd enjoy meeting Andrew Cobbold. How'd it go?"

"It was fine," she said. "Andrew was charming."

"What's happening today? Any special plans?"

"I've got news for you. We're having lunch. I think we're going to another place with stars in the roof tonight. Happy?"

"Yes."

"I thought you would be."

"Anything on tomorrow?"

"Well, as a matter of fact, yes. Tomorrow we're driving out to a beach someplace and having a picnic."

"Which beach?"

"I wasn't told."

"I'd like to see you sometime today," Mark said.

"It's up to you. I suppose I'll be in most of the afternoon."

"I'll call you around five or six," he said. "See how things shape up. Maybe we can have a drink."

Experience had taught Mark that telephone calls can be monitored, meetings reported on, details of supposed business negotiations checked. Everything had to tally, so he went scrupulously with a man from the real estate agent's to view the property of the Malecón. The three adjacent houses had been built by a millionaire driven mad by his sugar profits; they were weird seaside palaces, hideously painted, that had striven after gaiety, but displayed mania and terror. Conscientiously he climbed staircases of gilt and marble; inspected Bluebeards' chambers where the odor of doom hung on the air; crossed sagging floors to peer through brine-smeared windows overlooking the sea. A mile out, the waves came in under a freshening norther, crested and the color of cornflowers, to fall pale and limp inshore, tainted by the floods discharged from the town's sewers. Almost immediately below, the tide fumbled with nicotine-stained fingers among black rocks, and placed with the premeditation of mantelpiece ornaments, natives squatted in their dozens to defecate.

Straight-faced, Mark checked all the physical particulars and arranged to be supplied with photostat copies of leases. The embassy supplied a list of surveyors, not a single one of whom they could agree to recommend. "Venal to a man," the commercial attaché told him.

He called his office back in Salisbury and spoke to Maclean, in charge of overseas development, assuming there was a secret ear somewhere on the line. "Do you want to go ahead with the survey?"

"Do as you please," Maclean said. "If you think it's worth it."

"I had a word with Andrew Cobbold. He's not impressed."

"Andrew Cobbold, huh? What's he doing down there?"

"Fixing up some deal with the government. I'm not allowed to know."

"Pretty nice fellow, Cobbold."

"One of the best."

"And you say he's not sold on the idea."

"He says we should wait, that we can do better."

"Supposing somebody else snaps it up?"

"Andrew says they won't. He says the property's been on the market for years. But in any case, something's coming up. Maybe we shouldn't have bought those other hotels when we did. I think we should hold our fire."

"You're on the spot, Mark. You have to do what you think best."

"There are a number of aspects to this deal I ought to discuss with you before we make a move."

"Anyway, find out their rock-bottom price as it stands. There's no harm in that."

"What about the survey?"

"Why not have it done anyway? What does it cost?"

"Things move slowly here. I could be holed up until Thursday. Don't you want me to get back?"

"There's no hurry for a day or two. You could look around and see if there's anything else available that might be of interest."

"Okay, I'll do that."

"And say hello to Andrew for me if you see him again."

"I will."

"And tell him I hope he makes his deal, whatever it is."

6

Don Vincente had given him an address at 10th and 27th streets, Vedado, which turned out to be a solitary office block under the wall of the Columbus Cemetery. There was a Cuban sentry at the door, and another soldier prowling near the desk inside, where a civilian whom Mark took to be an American questioned him about the reason for his visit, then spoke to someone on the telephone before he was allowed up in the elevator. This delivered him to the fourth floor, where a third Cuban soldier escorted him down a corridor to an office where Salvatore Spina awaited him.

"Surprised, Richards?"

"I guess I am, Don Salvatore."

"Nobody would think so," Spina said. "Nothing ever shows on that mug of yours. Anybody ever tell you you look like a sphinx?"

Mark took the small brown hand and leaned over it without actually touching it with his lips. Spina had aged in the interval since their last meeting, and his sun-dried skin, already parchment, would soon be leather. But the genial marmoset's eye exploring the emptiness of Mark's features was as lively as ever.

"I heard you were in Napoli, Don Salvatore."

The remark was a diplomatic one. It was tactful not to let Spina know it was unlikely that a single member of the Vincent Stevens organization, or of any other of the groups with which it was in loose association throughout the United States, had not heard of Spina's move to Cuba, and the reason for it. It was common knowledge even among well-informed sections of the ordinary public that Spina had assumed control of the international traffic in narcotics, which in future would be directed from Havana. A few also knew that immense quantities of heroin and cocaine were now being shipped direct from the Mediterranean to Cuba, where it was landed, free of any customs interference, and thereafter passed on through well-tested and trouble-free channels to the States.

"I decided to make Havana my home eighteen months back," Spina said. "It's a pretty nice place. A good climate, and I like to be near the sea. How about that view, Richards? Isn't it something?"

Mark glanced out obediently at Havana under a

windy sky. A mile away at sea, the fishing boats were dancing harborwards. Below, the prospect was of the cemetery itself: the streets of a metropolis of tombs, even in the high surrounding walls themselves, where ten thousand Cubans had been filed in the neat archives of the dead. "That's a very fine view you have, Don Salvatore. Peaceful."

"It gives me a feeling of light and space," Spina said, "and that's what I want. Havana is a fine city. Shame you came now, just when a bunch of students are giving trouble. There was an attack on the palace last night, as I guess you've heard. All the guys who did it were killed, so maybe things will quiet down for a bit. This president happens to be a very good friend of ours, and the next one might not be as easy to do business with. How long are you figuring on staying?"

"As long as I have to, Don Salvatore."

"And no longer, huh? What's the matter? Don't you like Havana?"

"I've got a wife and a couple of kids back in the States."

"Yeah, of course, I know. You're a family man, Richards. Well, we won't keep you any longer than we have to. I may as well tell you right now that I know why you're here and what you have to do. This contract is going to be a tricky one. We have a problem with this guy Cobbold; he's smart, and he's spread a lot of money in the right places. I guess you've heard all this?"

"Don Vincente told me how it was."

"A *'ncarugnutu,* as we say. A man who breaks his oath. There's only one remedy in a case like this, Richards. *Livarisi la pietra dalla scarpa*—take the stone out of the shoe. You've heard the expression before? You know what I mean?"

"Only too well, Don Salvatore. I can't see any other way out."

"How long have you been here?"

"Two days."

"Which means you haven't had much time to study the setup as it stands."

"Only that he seems to have a hunch he may be hit. He never moves anywhere without a couple of Cuban cops."

"They tell me you arrived here with some broad. Does she figure in this?"

"We had a report Cobbold liked girls. The idea was that he might take a liking to this one, so that she could keep tabs on his movements."

"And did he?"

"It looks that way, Don Salvatore. He's seeing her twice today and once tomorrow."

"The thing is whether he leaves the cops at home, Richards."

"We'll know the answer in a few hours, Don Salvatore."

"Because if he doesn't, I don't see what's to be done. To take Cobbold we have to use a Cuban free lance, and we won't find one willing to take it on unless we can get the cops out of the way. They'd want to use an MG, and they'd be afraid of hitting a cop by mistake. There was a guy who killed a cop last month; they picked him up, tied him to the bumper of a squad car and dragged him all the way from Vedado to the precinct house downtown. There wasn't enough flesh left on his bones to feed a hungry dog."

Mark could see that the episode had shocked Spina, who was known for a certain squeamishness, an aversion to the sight of blood and a dislike of unnecessary violence. In the days when his old chief Masseria and those who had remained faithful to him had to go, he liked to hear of a life terminated cleanly with a single shot through the brain.

"You're the expert, Richards. What's the solution?"

"If we could get him away from the gorillas, a marksman could take him. But could we find one?"

"Sure we could. This is the homeland of marksmen. Getting hold of one presents no difficulty. But what I've got to be able to do is guarantee his safety. It could be done through a very special friend as a favor to me, so if anything went wrong, my ass would be caught in the gears. I couldn't afford to take a failure on this deal. How are we going to get him on his own is what I want to know before I talk to my friend."

"He's planning to take this girl out to a beach picnic someplace tomorrow."

"I don't see how that helps us. I guess you haven't seen any of the beaches around here. If they go anywhere, it will be to the Jaimanitas or the Yacht Club. The Yacht Club has a ten-foot high fence around it to keep out the riffraff. At Jaimanitas they have a beach guard about every ten yards and waiters in swimsuits so that the customers won't have to get out of the water to fetch their drinks. We've got about as much chance of hitting our friend on those beaches as you have of walking into the palace and knocking off the president."

"Something tells me that this is going to be a quiet beach, Don Salvatore. The picnic idea doesn't go with the kind of spot you describe. My view of Cobbold is that he's going to want a place where he can be intimate with this girl, so he'll be looking for some spot where they can get away from the crowd."

"You may have something there. Not too many people want to go to the Jaimanitas or the Yacht Club for a quiet picnic with a broad."

"Could we find a marksman good enough to take him out when he was with a girl?"

Spina's lively expression was infused by scandalized surprise. "It all depends what you mean by that. D'ya mean when they were in a clinch?" Although he had spent several years in Dannemora for organizing the prostitution of New York, he had tender feelings for women in general and did not care to hear of one suffering violence.

"No, I mean when they were close together. Maybe a yard or two apart."

"I see. Well, speaking personally, I wouldn't want to take any chances. That's why if we employed anyone, it would have to be a perfectionist. I know of one guy who is supposed to be able to take a man out of a crowd with a clean head shot at two hundred yards."

"Right here in Cuba, Don Salvatore?"

"As a matter of fact, he's doing a life rap for multiple homicide and arson on the Island of Pines. I might be able to borrow him for a day."

"You mean they'd let him out of the can here to take a contract?"

"If you know the right people and you can pay enough, anything goes. This fellow is a psycho, a nut case. He has to kill because he hears bells ringing in his head or something. They tell me he never misses. The story is that the last time they let him out it was to knock off some Mexican politician in Nogales who wanted to rat on a concession for a casino. Some guys from Phoenix had lost a bundle on it. They found out that this Mexican was crazy about horses and rodeos, so they went down to see him in Nogales and put on a rodeo in his honor. The problem was to get him away from all the other guys who were with him, so what they did was shove a lot of booze into him and sit him on a horse and send him out into the ring. This Cuban psycho got him through the head with his first shot at a hundred and fifty yards. *And* while the horse was bucking about. Whaddaya think of that?"

"I find it kind of hard to believe."

"What, that he could kill the Mex on a bucking horse at a hundred and fifty yards?"

"Not so much that, but the idea that in any civilized country you can arrange to spring a man from jail for a job like this."

"Who said this was a civilized country? It cost twenty thousand to get him out to do the Mexican job. I think we could get him for less. In any case, you don't have to worry; I'd be picking up the tab."

"If you think it can be arranged, it sounds like the answer."

"I'll talk to my friend in the government on the subject, and let you know as soon as there is any news. Where'll you be?"

"Back at the Sevilla tonight. Right now I want to see the girl in case anything's turned up."

"You'll be interested to hear that his real passion

is photography," Linda said. "He wants to take photographs of me—that's why the beach trip."

"What sort of photographs?"

"Artistic ones, I suppose." She made a face.

He had slipped into the Lincoln for ten minutes, and they were in the patio sipping tropical fruit drinks with a muffled flavor of strawberries and cream, followed by an unpleasant aftertaste. Mark found it impossible, with his Sicilian admiration for dignity, not to appreciate Linda's adaptation to the formality of the surroundings. Even in repose something advertised her grace. It was hard to imagine this cool, blond Proserpine standing before a moronic audience to strip off her clothes to music. No wonder Cobbold showed promising signs of infatuation.

"I wonder why he didn't stay last night?" he asked.

"Probably because he had those men with him."

"Having bodyguards can't help his love life."

"Is this turning out the way you hoped it would?" she asked.

"We'll keep trying," he said. "How was the lunch?"

"Nice. We went to a fisherman's restaurant down by the docks. Real fishermen were eating there, not just tourists."

"With the bodyguards right at the next table?"

"Right. In cream sharkskin outfits this time."

"What did you talk about?"

"This and that. He's good company—amusing. He's very considerate and easy to like."

"Don't forget you're working for me," Mark said.

"I'm not about to forget it. It's never out of my mind."

"This is like selling real estate or life insurance. Personal feelings about the customer don't come into it."

"I realize that only too well. Perhaps I ought to add to what's been said that I still like you better than him."

"That's a nice compliment," he said. "I hope you mean it."

"Of course I mean it. I hope you've thought about

what I asked you—I mean about our staying on here for a day or two after this is all over."

"I haven't thought it out yet, but I will. Those bodyguards—"

"This *is* strictly a business call, isn't it. Go on."

"I imagine they were in the car when he called for you?"

"Always. One sat with him in front, and one with me."

"Do you happen to know if it's his car?"

"No. He rents it from Hertz. A Cadillac. Chauffeur-driven."

"Did he tell you what he's doing this afternoon?"

"He said something about a meeting with a politician. He's picking me up at eight. We're going to the Sans Souci for dinner, and tomorrow it's going to be the beach and photography."

"Any idea where?"

"No. We're taking a picnic, that's all he said, and we'll be swimming if this wind dies down."

"I'll probably call you in the morning," Mark said.

He called Spina from a phone booth. "Is it okay to talk?"

"Where are you calling from?"

"A booth near the Lincoln."

"This place is free of bugs," Spina said. "But you can never be sure. Watch what you say, and before we go any further I have news. The guy we're interested in could be made available."

"That's great. I have news, too. Our friend is making this beach trip tomorrow with photography in mind."

"In the buff, you mean?"

"I get that impression."

"That's a useful piece of information. Sounds like this beach has to be really peaceful. Somewhere like Santa Fe or Baracoa. They're about the only two places I know within fifty miles of the city where you could have that kind of picnic without much chance of being disturbed. You got a map?"

"I can get one."

"It has to be one of these places. Maybe you should get down there right away and give the area the once-over. See how it could be set up if it turns out we're right."

"I'll do that," Mark said.

"And I'd like to see you here as soon as you get back."

A call to Cobbold narrowed the choice. "I'm just going out," he said. "Otherwise I could have shown you the best places on the map. We're suffering from a plague of stinging jellyfish at the moment, so if it's just for a swim you'd be better off going to one of the clubs. They can fix you up with a membership here at the desk."

"I'd like to get away from the piped music. Somewhere I can undress on the beach."

"In that case, anywhere past the Club Miramar. Tell them to drive you west of the city. There's nothing at all to the east. Baracoa's not bad, but you get sharks and barracudas on the far side of the reef, so keep in shallow water. Are you going to hire a car?"

"I'll probably rent a Hertz."

"If you park, don't go too far away. They'll take the wheels off it in five minutes."

Mark drove the car a few hundred yards up a path and parked in the shade of a wind-stripped palm, where the tracks of cars that had been driven down to the beach before were filling in with sand. When he switched off the engine and sat for a minute, small, pink landcrabs came out of their holes all around. Back on the highway he timed the passing of the occasional farm truck: roughly one every three or four minutes. A plane dragging a banner advertising Cristal beer circled low over the Miramar, then flew off, leaving behind a throb of engines to be absorbed by sand and water. A short distance away, a shelter had been built of spars and driftwood, thatched with palm, and outside it were piled a dozen or more conch shells. It was one of a number of such shacks he had seen on the beach—put up, he supposed, by Negro vagrants, who slept rough. He got out of the car, and walked to the water's edge, where a line of bright jellyfish straight from blancmange molds had been deposited, and a varnished tide lay over the half-submerged coral. A passing brown pelican dived suddenly on a fish, vanishing momentarily in an opaque geyser of foam, to break the surface again twenty yards further on. Halfway to the horizon a speedboat passed through the nearest channel, making for the Miramar. Mark waved, but there was no reply from the boat, and he concluded that to all intents and purposes he was out of sight.

After about an hour a conch fisherman appeared suddenly from behind a rock, carrying an armful of shells he had fished out of shallow water. A short distance from the shelter he began the process of extracting the meat from the shells. Anywhere else, he would simply have used a machete to slice the top off the shell, but here, near the beach clubs, the shells themselves were valuable as souvenirs when polished. To remove its contents, he held the conch high over his head, then hurled it down with all his force on the wet sand. After twenty or thirty times, the stunned and dying shellfish finally released its hold. The conch fisherman, a long-limbed Negro with enormous hands and feet and hair strangely hennaed by the sun and salt, made a ballet of this operation, scampering and dancing about the sand and throwing his head back with a loud invocatory shout at the instant he threw down the shell. He seemed not to notice Mark's presence. Mark viewed his caperings with contempt; he was a half-human creature from the murky shadows of an alien world, a man driven half-crazy by poverty and solitude.

He waited until the sun collided with the fiery western horizon, bounced back slightly before penetrating it and was swallowed up, then started back for Havana and Spina's office behind the Columbus Cemetery.

"Well, we have the guy," Spina said. "It's all been fixed. We can have him on the same terms as they made for the Mexican deal: twenty G's a day, or fifty for a week. He's flying in on the morning plane tomorrow from Nueva Gerona."

"Do they send a screw with him?"

"Nothing's been said about it."

"Don Salvatore, how can they be sure they're going to get him back once he gets out?"

"My friend says he has a kid son they hold till he shows up again."

"It's crazy."

"Sure it's crazy. It's anything you like. Anyway, we're getting him. The thing is can we use him? Any more ideas? What about that beach?"

"If it's anywhere, it will be this side of Baracoa."

"That's what I figured."

"If he has to have a quiet place, it's about the only one."

"No one about, huh? You checked?"

"Beachcombers."

"How about the traffic on the road?"

"Trucks going to farms once in a while. Not many. The area looks as if it had been hit by a hurricane."

"And no police?"

"None that I saw."

"They have plenty to keep them busy in the city without going around looking for it in the country."

"It was very quiet. Only twenty miles from the city, but you could have been anywhere."

"A perfect setup," Spina said. "D'ya know something? It's almost too good to be true." He smiled almost wistfully, as if in private reminiscence. "A hit never happens that way. A nice clean hit is the hardest thing in the world to bring off. Something always has to go wrong."

"They'll probably change their minds and not go to a beach at all, Don Salvatore. Maybe there'll be a hurricane tomorrow."

"Sure there'll be a hurricane tomorrow, if we're going to have any more of them this season. All the same, I guess we have to make plans, just in case there isn't a hurricane."

7

Bonachea Leon was one of the most insignificant-looking human beings Mark had ever seen. They had driven out just before eleven to Marianao and had pulled the car in to wait in the parking lot of a restaurant just beyond the junction with the Avenida del Golfo, at a point which every car traveling westwards would have to pass. They sat under a Coca-Cola umbrella fifty yards back from the road, a bluish stripe bordered by equidistant shade palms. The restaurant was one of the many in the outer suburbs of Havana that catered in the evening to white men with colored mistresses, and each car could be parked separately for curb service, in an almost encircling bay of bamboo screens to shut out the eyes of the world. At midday Mark and Bonachea were the only customers. The sun scorched the countryside to silence, and hardly any cars passed. The driver, an authentic button man from Kansas City, supplied by Spina along with the car, sat at the wheel sipping a 7-Up. He was a film gangster from the thirties who wore a fedora at all times and actually talked out of the corner of his mouth. All three of them had been supplied with official *ordenes de misión* that guaranteed them freedom from police interference, and in addition Bonachea had been given a special safe conduct signed by the secretary of the Minister of the Interior.

Bonachea was eating a hamburger with the concentration of a man listening to noble music. He was one of those Cubans with a deprived and negligible body that one day would take on fat and come into its own. His shoulders hunched, he sat munching thoughtfully, his shirt hanging loosely away from a caved-in-chest. His waxen skin was that of a man close to tuberculosis and gave no evidence of the blood beneath. The eyes under a bland, domed forehead were sleepy and almond-shaped, suggesting

Chinese immigrant labor somewhere in the family tree, as did the smooth unshaven upper lip and the few fine hairs at the corners of the mouth. Nothing whatever had been said about the mission, though Bonachea, who had learned English in prison, was happy to talk about his career as a painter. "You like to paint, mister?" he asked Mark.

"Sure I like to paint," Mark said, his face turned away.

"What you paint, mister?" Bonachea insisted.

"Anything, I guess. The back porch. The walls. What the hell, anything."

"I paint pictures," Bonachea said. He took out a pocketful of newspaper clippings about a one-man show in Nueva Gerona of the paintings he had done in jail. Mark glanced at them and handed them back. Even to touch them while they were in Bonachea's hands disgusted him. He shifted his chair slightly to avoid contact with the other man's, but seconds later Bonachea moved too, avid for any form of contact.

From the little Spina had been able to find out about Bonachea, he had been a cowhand in Alta Gracia, in the province of Camaguey, who had been recruited at the age of sixteen into a force of irregulars formed by a Cuban dictator to deal with his enemies. On the way home by train from a routine massacre, Bonachea had shot and killed a peasant driving a bullock cart on the road running parallel with the railway, and in due course was sentenced to life imprisonment. He told the psychiatrist that he'd had no reason to shoot the peasant, but mentioned that he had had an erection at the time. A feature of the case that did not escape the attention of certain observers at the trial was that Bonachea had been able to shoot a man clean through the brain from a train moving at approximately forty miles per hour.

Mark drank his beer, and his body changed it instantly to sweat. The tension of waiting tightened his stomach muscles as if in preparation for some physical effort, and he felt unable to get enough air into the lungs. As he stared down the blue, flickering road, the sweat from his eyelids misted his vision. Bonachea was tugging at his sleeve. Now he had family snapshots to show: a thick-lipped mulatto wife and a crinkly-haired, bright-eyed boy in a sailor suit. This was the son they held as a hostage. His wedding had been celebrated in the parish church of Nueva Gerona and attended by the prison's deputy governor. "He lives like he's in the Waldorf," Spina said. "His wife comes in and he can lay her whenever he wants. He's a valuable piece of property."

Bonachea called for another hamburger, lifted the top half of the bun to sniff at the meat and began to chew again. He groped with a tiny nicotine-dyed finger in a cavity of his mouth, removing what might have been a shred of gristle and examining it with interest before flicking it away. Compelled to watch, Mark felt a nausea so overpowering that it forced the tension of waiting into the background. In the Sicily of old, a man compelled to take this kind of employment would at least have known how to maintain a decorous aloofness and silence. The service of death demanded a minimum of dignity, but here there was nothing but contempt. A huge mouthful had distorted Bonachea's servile grin; then with a sudden convulsion of the throat he swallowed, gasping for a moment before he signaled to the waiter again.

Mark looked away into a landscape that breathed shimmering air from all its pores. The heat had laid its drab camouflage over the colors, and a sallow lagoon that stretched between the restaurant and the sea had begun to float. An advertising truck appeared, to bray into the baked empty spaces in praise of the painkiller Mejoral, and from the opposite direction a priest on a Vespa droned past, blackness leaking from his soutane into the ashen air. His passing emptied all life from the scene apart from a disjointed cow standing in a swamp, an egret on its back.

The gangster in the car bleeped softly once on the horn, and Mark, looking toward Havana, saw the chocolate Cadillac hired from Hertz coming crisply out of the spongy distances. He got up and slipped behind a bamboo screen, through which he could still see the road, while the man from Kansas City lay down across the front seat of the car and pretended to go to sleep. Cobbold's Cadillac came up, slowed, then turned sharply with a rasp of gravel into the parking lot. One of the bodyguards sat in the front with the driver, and Cobbold sat between the other bodyguard and Linda, in white, in the back. The bodyguard in front went into the restaurant, and came out again carrying a number of cardboard cartons and a blue plastic bag. These he put in the trunk, and then they drove off, heading westwards as before. Mark waited with Bonachea until the Cadillac was out of sight; then both men got into their own car and moved off after the Cadillac, but at hardly more than a walking pace. Five miles further on they saw the car parked just where Mark had hoped it would be. They pulled off the road into a palmetto thicket. Bonachea got the gun in its brown canvas fishing-rod case out of the trunk and, leaving the driver, they crossed over to the beach and began to walk along it.

The hurricane of the year before had poured colored sands together and mixed them with its stick. Palms festooned with sea shells stood in pools of rotting sea water, and here and there the sand spouted bamboo like tufts of hair growing from warts on an otherwise clean cheek. With his fishing case, Bonachea immediately became part of the landscape: a beach-combing nondescript on his way to fish for bass wherever a likely surf could be found. Mark signaled to him to draw back while he went on ahead; alone, he was better prepared for a chance encounter, for coming across the picnicking party unexpectedly under the shelter of a dune. ("Thought I might find you somewhere along here, Andrew. Don't think I want to butt in. Seen any place where I could get a bare-ass swim?")

Luckily, he saw Cobbold and his party from the top of a low bank formed where sand had piled up in the lee of palmetto. It was a scene full of animation. A beach umbrella had been set up over a picnic table and several chairs, and Linda and the driver were unpacking picnic boxes; Cobbold and his bodyguards had wandered down to the water's edge to watch the activities of two lines of fishermen, each tugging on the end of the ropes attached to a shallow-water net that was slowly being dragged inshore.

Cobbold began to take photographs: group shots and close-ups of the fishermen, and using up a whole film on the splashing fish concentrated in the last pocket of net. When the catch was finally on the beach he took a number of photographs of the fish, then still more of the fishermen holding up the fish. A discussion ensued between one of the bodyguards and the fishermen, after which Cobbold made a selection from the catch and money changed hands. The next stage was the collection of driftwood and the making of a fire over which the fish was to be grilled. Under the beach umbrella, bottles were being opened and glasses already emptied. The fishermen mixed sociably with Cobbold's party, and accepted food and drink. No one was in a hurry, Cobbold repeatedly lifting his camera for more pictures. Linda posed with the fishermen while Cobbold squatted, trying this angle and that as she laughed into the sun through the golden curtain of her hair, backed by the dark torsos and ivory smiles of a dozen Cuban Sinbads.

Mark and Bonachea crouched in the tattered shade of the palmetto while the mosquitoes curled like smoke from the decaying vegetation and fed on them. Bonachea had found a reserve of hamburger and was chewing with an eager swarm of flies at his lips. Down on the beach, Cobbold had moved slightly away from the rest to crouch down and change the film in his camera in his own shade. Mark heard the rasping of metal projections on stiff canvas as the gun came out of its sheath, then seconds later felt the sly repellent caress of Bonachea's fingers on his forearm—as much a sexual advance as an attempt to draw his attention. *"Ahora?"* Bonachea whispered. "Now?"

"No. For Christ's sake, wait till I say. How much noise does that thing make?"

"Leetle. *No mucho.*"

The setup was only fair at best, Mark thought. There had never been any chance of conducting this operation in clean and classic style. The true professional aimed at a mystery that could never be solved, a sensation for the morning editions which, in this country with its daily harvest of violence, would be forgotten overnight. If there were witnesses, none should be left to tell what they had seen. But here this ideal was beyond reach. There were too many people on the beach: fishermen who showed no signs of leaving, the driver, the two bodyguards who would come running like bloodhounds to the scent of cordite the moment a shot was fired. Above all, there was a woman Mark happened to like, and who, in any case, by the iron laws of custom had to be spared.

He watched and waited for the right moment. However unpromising the circumstances might be, no better opportunity was likely to offer itself than this outing. Down on the beach, where the grayness of the tropics at high noon had swallowed up all color but the scarlet of the beach umbrella and the orange of Linda's bikini, the animation was dying down. Some of the fishermen finally collected up the catch and went off in single file—staccato, shadowless figures bound for their invisible village. The few who remained, unable to fight off sleep, had crammed themselves into a knife blade of shade under the belly of a beached boat. Linda came back from splashing her ankles in the water and now lay stretched out, face downward, under the umbrella, while Cobbold lowered himself to the sand at her side. The driver and bodyguards occupied the chairs, and one of them had drowsed off, head fallen sideways, chin on chest, arms hanging so that his knuckles rested on the sand. With Linda gone from the water, sea birds planed out of the glassy sky and settled in roosting attitudes where the tide had left little patches of spittle on the sand. The plane advertising cigarettes made another pass over the distant Miramar, droning hypnotically before plunging back into the coarse-textured silence of the sky.

The wakeful bodyguard got up and began a slow

trudge toward a feathered hedge of bamboo topping a shallow cliff which marked the maximum advance of the sea at the time of the September storms. He pushed his way through the bamboo and, out of sight of the others on the beach, unbuttoned his fly and urinated. A stone or shell took his attention; picked it up, examined it, then threw it away. He spent a few more minutes kicking around sand and picking up more stones, pocketing some and discarding the others before making his way back.

Bonachea was on his knees and elbows, shifting his position with a faint scrunching of sand for a better aim. Precise metal facets and edges lisped in their greased channels as the rifle's bolt was drawn back. *"Ahora?"* he whispered again.

"No. Wait, I said."

A long, measureless pause followed, while a weight under Mark's ribs took shape and became an expanding ball, and then Cobbold suddenly folded into a sitting position, pulled himself to his feet and held out his hand to help Linda to hers. A bodyguard who came out of his chair to join them as they moved away together was waved back. Hand in hand they began to plod toward the bamboo, the pallor of their city bodies darkened by the terrific whiteness of the sand. Cobbold's shape overlapped Linda's; his camera hanging from a neck strap bounced lightly on the thick fur of his chest. Held back by the sand, he walked as though wading in water up to the knees, his hands stretched out to grab a purchase on the air.

They passed through the bamboo hedge into the refuge of their supposed invisibility. *Now,* Mark thought. His mouth brimmed with saliva that he was unable to swallow. A bad time, and a bad thing. An order carried out in a way it never should have been, in breach of unwritten laws. He lifted his hand as a signal to Bonachea. Linda had taken off her bikini. Cobbold held her in his arms for a moment and then backed away, his camera raised to his eye.

At Mark's side, Bonachea was snuffling like a dog. A side glance showed Mark a face transfigured by mania. Suddenly he noticed the sharp, catlike smell of his sweat. *"Ahora?"*

"Yeah. *Ahora!"*

The noise of the gun was hardly more than a hiccup, a fart, a contemptuous expulsion of air through compressed lips, but through it flicked the viper's tongue of sound left by the departing bullet. It was hard to believe that this popgun explosion could be followed by any dramatic effect, yet instantly the crouching figure with the camera, already half-lynched by the heat haze, seemed to shatter. Linda, on her knees, wavering in mirage, was the source of a thin, seagull mewing. A bird at the tide's edge had bounced a foot into the air and dropped back on the same spot. A fisherman rolling from the shade of the upturned boat stood face toward them, shading his eyes with his hand. One of the bodyguards pointed, shouting, and reached for his hip.

Mark and Bonachea turned, hunched together under the dune's skyline, and began the scramble down the slope. Hardly thirty yards away they saw coming at them the Negro conch fisherman of the day before, his ebony skin bleached in the hard midday sunshine to a leprous gray. He had been mooching along the shore with an armful of shells and a small octopus roping down from a hook, and curiosity and the hope of selling the octopus made him change direction to come capering toward them. As he recognized Mark, his lips drew from his teeth in a foolish grin.

Giggling and dribbling, Bonachea raised the gun, and the man stopped, the white gap of his smile twisted shapeless by bewilderment. He threw down his shells and the octopus and raised his hands to shield his face, then dropped them as Bonachea pressed the trigger and the gun hiccupped. The bullet struck below the nose, producing a hardly visible entry hole, boring a clean tunnel through the brain to exit with a spurt of bone splinters, brain cells and blood through the base of the skull. The Negro cavorted wildly in a last frantic escapade of nerves and muscles before crashing down to the sand. Bonachea wiped his mouth and shoved his gun back into its case. Back on the road, the driver had spotted them; as they ran toward him, he spat out his cigar butt and started the engine.

They met the first of the city taxis in the suburb of Almandares, and as soon as they saw a call box Mark told the driver to stop.

"Take this man over to the airport," he said. "Domestic lines." He went into the box and dialed Spina's number. "I thought you might want to hear from me."

"How'd it go?" Spina asked.

"It was okay."

"Sure you got what you were after?"

"As sure as anybody can be. I didn't stop to check, but it looked good from where I stood. If the man's all he's said to be."

"Was it what I'd call clean? You know what I mean?"

"Maybe not as clean as it might have been. We had a small complication."

"That's a pity. Anything we have to worry about?"

"No. It could have been less complicated, that's all."

"What's happening to that important guy?"

"He's taking off. There's a plane this evening."

"Back where he came from, to the comfort and privacy of his personal suite. Some country, huh? Some country. How about the broad?"

"If everything goes as we hope, she could be on her way tomorrow."

"It might take longer than that," Spina said. "They might want to ask a few questions for form's sake. It could take longer. You be going with her?"

"I thought that would be best," Mark said. "Just to make sure she doesn't get into any trouble."

"That's a sensible precaution. Listen, it's important to handle this right. I don't have to tell you that. It doesn't matter what she says right now, because nobody's going to listen anyway, and anything can be fixed. What's important is what she says later. It's nothing to me; I'm thinking of you. It could put you in line for bad trouble later. You could find yourself in a box."

"Thanks for the warning. I'll take all the necessary steps."

"You gotta do that. She has to be made to understand that if she talks she's going to step on her tongue. Listen, you figuring on coming over here before you push off?"

"It's hard to say. I'd like to, but I'd better see how things go. I have a feeling I might be kind of busy in the next few hours."

"Well, if I don't see you, have a nice trip, and don't forget to look me up whenever you're in town. We have a big thing going here, and it's going to get a lot bigger, so I expect you'll be back again."

"I expect so too."

"And give my love to all the fellers back home. Tell them I'd like to come up and see them, but they know how it is."

He took a taxi to the Sevilla. There were no messages for him. He went into the bar, and for the first time in his life ordered a double brandy. Then he went up to his room, undressed, closed the shutters and got into bed. He lay for an hour wondering why it was that he felt as he did, trying to come to terms with an unidentifiable disquiet, a nagging uneasiness that he was feeling for the first time and that any other man would have instantly recognized as shame. Mark had been a conformist all his life, content to abide by the rules, holding himself strictly answerable to his clan morality. Now, for the first time, he had violated the spirit of his own code. He remembered that even Spina had been shocked at the proposal that Cobbold be executed while in the company of a woman.

When the telephone rang, his impulse was not to answer it. Finally he picked up the receiver, knowing it would be Linda on the line.

"I'm at the Miraflores Hospital. Something horrible's happened." There was a pause. It might have been a faulty line, or she could have been struggling to speak.

"I can't hear you," he said. "Go on. What is it? What's the matter?"

"Andrew's been terribly injured. He's been shot, and I think he's dying. The police are here now, and I can't understand what they're saying. He's just lying there and nobody's looking after him or even trying to do anything for him."

"Hasn't a doctor seen him?"

"He just came and looked at him and went away. It's horrible. They're leaving him to die."

"I'll be over there right away," Mark said.

The Miraflores Hospital was across town in Buena Vista, near the airport, and by the time he had pulled his clothes on, caught a taxi and crossed the city, more than half an hour had gone. He found Linda in a casualty reception room. A nun sat muttering prayers over a sheet-covered form on a stretcher resting on a trolley. There was a terrible stench of ether and, underlying it, a faint slaughterhouse whiff. A cripple in a grubby hospital tunic was sweeping up cigarettes and bloodstained scraps of cotton wool.

Linda came up, accompanied by a nurse who went away and left them together. "He's dead," she said. "I had to sign a paper." He was astonished by the matter-of-factness of her voice, contrasting strangely with her distraught appearance. "All they were interested in was making sure I signed the right form. They did nothing. Looked at him, that's all."

"Probably nothing they could do. Was he conscious at all?"

"I don't think so. He never moved. He was quiet until the last minutes, when he was dying. Then he made a terrible noise."

"He didn't feel anything," Mark said. "It must have been some sort of nervous reaction."

"I hope so," she said. "He had a terrible wound." She raised her face that was smudged and reshaped in the plainness of grief. "I knew he was going to die."

The nun got up, dropped her rosary into a pocket

in her skirt, picked up an enormous straw shopping bag full of packets of soap powder, toilet paper and biscuits, and shuffled away. Under the sheet Cobbold showed little bulk. His corpse might have been that of a child.

"The police were here a few minutes ago, and they want to see me again," she said. "They took my tourist card away. I have to go to some office tomorrow morning."

"Tell me what happened," Mark said.

"We were on the beach and somebody shot him."

"Who shot him?"

"I never saw. He was talking to me, and then all of a sudden he fell over. He just lay there on the sand with half his face shot away. I heard a shot and he fell down; that's all there was to it."

"Were you by yourselves?"

She looked at him with a sort of dazed curiosity. "Why are you asking me questions? Maybe I'm crazy, but I have a feeling you know all the answers. Anyway, the answer is no. Those two men who were always with him were there, and the driver. They've all gone off with the police."

"You need a drink, and so do I," Mark said. "Let's get out of here and go somewhere else to talk."

In a bar in the next block where Cuban workmen played dominoes, a parrot screeched in Spanish and a cat was asleep on the counter, he ordered two brandies.

"He could have been shot by the revolutionaries," he said.

The suggestion seemed to arouse her. The muscles of her face tightened, and her eyes fixed on his were in focus. "Don't insult my intelligence," she said.

"I said *could* have. A lot of people are getting killed in this country right now. There was a police notice in the *Post* only this morning warning people about driving out into the country."

"Why should revolutionaries have wanted to shoot Andrew?" she said. "If they were going to shoot anybody, it would have been the Cubans who were with us. Andrew had nothing to do with them."

"You could be wrong about that."

"Where do you come into this, and where do I? Why did you bring me here in the first place? Why did you give me money to keep tabs on Andrew?"

"I've told you."

"But you never convinced me. I know I'm dumb, but I'm not that dumb."

"You were told all I could tell you. In your own interests, it wouldn't have been advisable for you to know more."

"Tomorrow the police are going to talk to me again. Some English-speaking police captain is going to ask me a lot of questions. He's going to ask me why I came here."

"The answer is you came here on vacation."

"With you?"

"Certainly. Why not? If they ask you."

"Do I say that you and Andrew knew each other?"

"If you're asked."

"I tell them we went to that night club together?"

"Tell them everything. There's no point in holding anything back."

"Including our deal?"

"No, that you don't mention."

"I thought you wouldn't want that brought up," she said.

"It was made clear from the start that you were being paid to use your intelligence," Mark said.

"All right, but now I want the truth."

"Very well, here it is. The real story is that Andrew was messing with power politics. In this thing that's going on he made a deal with the other side, and he was paid off the hard way. It was inevitable."

"And where do you come into this?"

"We were both employed by the same firm. It was my firm's money he was using. We had to know where it was going and who his contacts were."

"And did you find out?" she asked.

"I didn't have enough time."

"I want to tell you something," she said. "I got to like Andrew. He was a pretty nice guy. He's dead now, and I don't think I've ever felt sorrier about anything in my life. If I were the weeping type, I'd cry my eyes out."

"He was a nice guy," Mark said, "but he had to gamble. He took crazy chances." He put his arm around her shoulder to stroke her cheek. A boy came in selling the early evening edition of *El Sol,* and he bought a copy and read in the headlines of the last day's crop of death.

"How soon can we get out of this dreadful place?" Linda was asking. "Can we leave tomorrow?"

"I hope so," he said. "If the police let you go, we can take the afternoon plane."

8

Experience had taught Spina that the main problem in bribing Latin-American politicians was in finding the right intermediary through whom the bribes should be paid. In Havana the position was simple, and was generally known. One went straight to the tax office at the Municipio, paid a deposit on one's estimated income tax for the year, and there and then asked for an interview with the secretary of whichever minister one wished to bribe. As such deposits were only made by those with corruption in mind, there were no misunderstandings. At the Municipio, Spina was fascinated to observe that the gray little employee put the envelope containing the fifty hundred-dollar bills he gave him into a child's money box before going off with it into a back room, from which there came shortly the tinkle of a telephone receiver being lifted.

From the Municipio, Spina took a taxi to the Ministry of the Interior, where the Minister's secretary, a sibilant Latin whose three years of law school at Penn had left no mark on his personality, awaited him. The secretary wore one of those faultlessly laundered Cuban shirts with many unnecessary pleats and buttons, and a huge wedding ring on his dimpled hand; gold winked in the corners of his mouth when he smiled. "Our interests clearly coincide," he said. "The last thing we wish to encourage is the impression that the lives and property of foreigners are not properly safeguarded in this country."

Spina felt a huge contempt for the man. Having paid for cooperation, he saw no reason why he should not dictate his terms. "A full report has to appear in the press as soon as possible," he said. "After that it can be dropped and forgotten, but I want to see a draft of the report before it appears."

The scent of coffee intruded on a womanly odor of skin creams as a waiter from the café across the road entered with a tray and two cups. Spina rejected the sugar, and the secretary raised his cup to his lips, his nostrils quivering sensitively like a rabbit testing fresh lettuce.

"It is precisely because these young men realize they are at the end of their tether," the secretary said, "that they commit these desperate and foolish acts. In this case a full confession has been made, and a number of other persons have been incriminated."

Spina offered an ironic smile. "You certainly move fast," he said. "Has the murder weapon been found?"

"Not so far. I think not."

"Well, tell them to find it," Spina said. "By tomorrow, if possible. Have a ballistic expert's report published in the newspapers."

"On the front page?"

"No, no, somewhere at the back. A small paragraph. This thing has to be played down."

"Of course," the secretary said. "Of course. Leave it to me. I think I know exactly what is required." He spoke in the calm and reassuring voice of a tailor discussing the details of a custom-made coat. The secretary was a man with iron control of his nerves. He was generally thought by Cubans, who viewed with wry resignation the defalcations of those who ruled them, to divert 50,000 dollars of the public funds to his pocket in a single year, while his superior, the Minister, accounted for a quarter of a million. "Do you think your ambassador will be satisfied?" he asked.

"Why shouldn't he be? He should be impressed with the speed with which the arrests have been made."

The secretary got up to shake hands. "Mr. Spina, believe me when I say I'm most grateful. You've been very kind." An appropriate hollowness entered his flexible voice. "I was almost forgetting. What arrangements do you wish to make for the body? Do you desire burial in Cuba? If so, I presume your embassy will contact us with their instructions."

Spina was astonished. "Burial in Cuba, did you say? Certainly not. This guy was important. He rates the biggest funeral his hometown can put on. We'll be chartering a plane to fly him home. A coupla thousand of his fellow citizens are going to want to walk behind that coffin, Mr. Secretary."

Bradley arranged to meet Alistair Ferguson in an outdoor café in the Parque Central. Another bright morning had emptied its jubilation into the open spaces of the city, and all around them Cubans streamed on errands that seemed to lead to nowhere in the ivory and cinnamon of Havana.

"How are you making out? Getting used to it yet?" Bradley asked.

Ferguson picked up the frothy pineapple drink that had been placed in front of him, sniffed at it and put it down. "I suppose I *will*," he said dubiously. "A lot of things still came as a surprise."

"That's how you used to feel about Palermo," Bradley said. "You probably forget. In the end we practically had to dynamite you out. Don't worry, you can always fall back on me. I'll be passing through at least once a month."

Ferguson made a depressed face, and Bradley clapped him on the shoulder. He hoped Ferguson would measure up to what was expected of him in Cuba. Sicily had never given him the chance to show what he could do, to fulfill the promise of toughness and resolution that had won favorable mention from his superiors back in his training days. If ever a place offered a man an opportunity to show his mettle, it was this.

"Sorry the lotus-eating existence had to come to an end," he said. "I believe you'll like this place all the same. It's corrupt but amusing, and it offers a wide range of pleasures to suit all tastes." He paused and fixed Ferguson with his own slightly watered-down version of the famous Sicilian stare. "It is also one of the cockpits of the modern world," he added.

"Nobody would ever believe it," Ferguson said. His glance had strayed to several thin Negroes—waist-deep in light that rippled from the corn-colored buildings—who were picking under the chairs after cigar ends. Seven men slept nearby on ornate park benches. Someone had rammed a carnation into the mouthpiece of the free phone by the cash register on the counter.

"This is the Berlin of the sixties," Bradley said. "The interests of the Western world are just as much at stake here as they were in Berlin—and our national interests enormously more so. This isn't four thousand miles away; it's in our backyard."

Ferguson looked up at him, wondering. While talking, Bradley had gone through a plate of giant prawns, shelling them with incredible speed and deftness. Now he held a fat, pink, crustacean body between thumb and forefinger and shook it almost threateningly under Ferguson's nose. "Currently the situation here is fraught with peril for what we hold dear, though I've yet to meet anyone who appreciates how real that peril is. Yesterday I was shown a sit-rep issued by our own information service actually asserting that the Reds were at the end of their tether. The true facts are that we have been losing this war. I say 'we' because it's as much our war as the Cubans'."

He thrust the prawn into his mouth and chewed hastily, almost with anger. Suddenly his eyes lost their focus. Groping in the breast pocket of his jacket, he took out a small microphone and murmured a few indistinguishable words into it. On the previous day when their conversation had been similarly interrupted, Bradley had explained, "I commit my thoughts to this little machine, which I carry everywhere I go. I've been working on a book for a number of years. It attempts—I repeat, attempts—not so much to compress the wisdom of the ages into a single volume, as to re-deploy that wisdom in modern terms for the service of mankind." Later he had shown Ferguson a suitcase containing thousands of pages of neatly typed manuscript. "Therein lies the remedy, Alistair. Make no mistake about it, there lies the answer to it all. Next year, God willing, it will be published and the world will never be quite the same again."

Ferguson recalled the whisperings of the past. A megalomaniac, it had been said of Bradley, with a personal cure for the ills of mankind. But someone who had committed the unforgivable sin of going over Bradley's head to make this point to a superior had met with a sharp rebuke and subsequent demotion. So what if a man showed that he believed in himself? Anyone had the right to do so. He would be judged by his work, and by that alone. Bradley was devoted to duty. He had always shown imagination plus commendable initiative, and he had never allowed considerations of any kind to deflect him from his purpose. Therefore he remained beyond the reach of his detractors, particularly those of Ferguson's low rating in the organization. Vegetating peacefully in Sicily, Ferguson had been almost forgotten until he had applied for permission to marry a local girl—an application which was instantly turned down. Since then he'd had the feeling of being kept on sufferance, and that one false move would put an end to his career.

"The main purpose of this meeting," Bradley was saying, "is to fill in the background for you of a recent occurrence that is of more importance than it probably appeared. Two days ago a man called Cobbold was assassinated on a beach near here. I expect you read about it."

"I have the clippings."

"Any theories?"

"The *Diario de la Marina* said he'd probably been knocked off by the Reds, so I naturally assumed that the government had decided to put him out of the way for some reason of their own."

"You were wrong. It was a gangster killing, and I'll explain what it was all about." Bradley settled himself on his chair, stripped another prawn and dropped the head, claws and shell into the mouth of a waiting dog. Two splendid *mulatas* passed, enclosed in the high corral of their titters. Ferguson looked after them, sighing inwardly.

"Spina is here," Bradley said.

"So I hear."

"Running his hundred-million-dollar dope empire. He's also putting local prostitution on a rational basis. Cobbold headed a team that's in hotels and casinos. The point of conflict is that Cobbold was certain that the Reds were going to win, and believed that he could make a deal with them. So what did he do? He made them a present of a million dollars' worth of arms. The Reds grabbed a port somewhere down in Oriente Province and held it long enough to bring a shipload in. That's when the long list of their successes started. Ten thousand Czech automatic weapons can make a lot of difference to a military stalemate."

"I hear they've reached Escambray."

"Thanks to our friend Cobbold. He was prepared to sell his country down the river in exchange for a chance to run this city the way he wanted. Don't imagine that Spina is any better. The only difference is that he knows only too well that if the rebels get in, he'll be out because they won't stand for junk. Hence the antagonism between the two men."

Bradley smiled carefully in preparation for what he was about to say. These days his overworked facial muscles were beginning to lose their elasticity, so that there was a moment of delay before his lips crawled back to cover the bold teeth. "The trouble is," he went on, "these people have their own obscure loyalties. It was in Spina's interests to put Cobbold out of action in any case, but he used to be in business with Cobbold's boss, Vincent Stevens. They're still buddies, so before Cobbold could be hit Stevens had to be persuaded that he was a rat. This was a problem until someone had the idea of putting it into Spina's head that Cobbold was trying to turn him in to the Narcotics Bureau. What was called for was a really big operation to grab one of the light planes he uses for flying junk into Florida—which, by the way, meant keeping an eye on about a hundred airstrips all over the state. As soon as we managed to nab a plane, Spina was told that Cobbold had supplied all the details of his routes to the narcs. Two or three days later a top enforcer arrived in Havana. Guess who?"

"Am I supposed to know any enforcers?"

"You certainly know *one*."

"You mean Riccione?"

"Richards these days. Mark Richards. Our old friend from Palermo. None other."

"Riccione, huh? So it looks like he was useful after all. You always thought he would be."

"I was certain of it. But this is still small stuff. One day Richards is going to do something really big. He's going to leave his mark on history. Believe me, Alistair, it's something I feel right here." Bradley patted his diaphragm with reverence. "I don't think of this as anything more than a trial run. There are bigger things to come—something of real significance for the peace and stability of our world."

"And Riccione actually killed Cobbold?"

"I wouldn't for one moment imagine in person. It's not in his line. But I suspect he arranged the thing. Suffice it to say that Cobbold died in mysterious circumstances of a gunshot wound two days after Richards arrived in Cuba. Probably Richards got together with Spina, and they set it up between them."

Ferguson found himself unable to feel any surprise. Since he had come to Cuba, life was beginning to lose a dimension. One could not maintain one's amazement at the incredible for more than a relatively short period. In the space of a few days his head had been crammed with violent fables which he already accepted in a way a child can accept a cruel fairy tale without being touched by it. Two weeks in this city had stripped assassination of its drama.

"What now remains to be seen," Bradley said,

"is whether with the demise of Cobbold the military situation will ease."

"It may be too late."

"Not necessarily, because millions of dollars of hot money are still pouring in from Stevens and from others who are following his lead. They're powerful and resourceful men, and with a fat stake in the country they aren't going to sit around twiddling their thumbs and watch it go to the wall. You must realize that I dislike Spina and all he stands for as much as I'm sure you do, but right now he's worth a squadron of bombers to our side."

"Are the Cubans going to let him stay? I mean when they're through with this rebellion?"

"What do you think? There's not a man with his name over a door in customs or the Ministry of the Interior who doesn't get a piece of the drug business. Before long, he's going to be a lot bigger than he is now. Vincent Stevens isn't a well man, and when he retires or dies Spina will either take over his business here on his own, or will come to some sort of partnership arrangement with his no-good son. In either case the result will be the same, because this kid will do whatever Spina tells him. Which means that next to the president, our friend will be the biggest man in the country."

"Isn't the FBI doing anything about him?"

"There isn't much they can do. He's just about invulnerable. I'm told that in a matter of hours you can build an airstrip in Florida good enough for a Beechcroft or a Cessna to land on. They can fly a cargo of junk out of here and crawl under the radar screen whenever they like. It's a situation the law enforcement agencies can't cope with. Look at it from their point of view. Even if they double or treble their force in Florida, they'd be doing it at the expense of other danger spots on the frontier, and the stuff would start pouring in from Mexico or Canada instead. It wouldn't make any difference one way or another in the long run."

"No, I suppose not," Ferguson said. "So the Cubans have to learn to live with Spina and like it."

"That's the way it looks," Bradley said. "Unless they fail to stop this rebellion—in which case it's curtains for all of us, Spina included."

"The air force was in action yesterday down near Escambray attacking marshaling yards and blowing up bridges. Just how far is Escambray from here?" Ferguson asked.

"No distance at all. They only have to win one big battle, and the whole front will collapse. What they don't tell you in the paper is the army ran away. The only thing between us and them is fifty old Sherman tanks. Once past them they could be with us in a couple of hours, in which case Cuba as we know it will be no more, and the U.S. will have a hostile power on its back doorstep." Weariness suddenly flooded Bradley's face. Pouches had appeared under his eyes, and the corners of his mouth were obscured by two melancholic folds of skin. "Cobbold had a lot to answer for," he said.

9

As before, they sat carefully separated on the plane. At the American Airlines counter at Idlewild, Mark bought a ticket for Indianapolis and gave it to Linda. It was four P.M.—a stagnant period for travel, with few passengers about. He was sorry to see her go. There was a nearby bar, withdrawn in its twilight from the cold radiance of the airport, and when he went in to check it carefully it seemed to be doing no business, so he beckoned to her to follow him. They sat for a moment together over a drink; then he kissed her and turned to go, and at that moment the one-in-ten-thousand chance happened, the coincidence of the kind that had victimized him in the past. A man and a woman came into the bar together. The man was a stranger, but Mark had seen the woman somewhere before. Their eyes met for an instant, both looked away, and Mark left to catch his own plane.

He was home by seven. He took Teresa in his arms.

"I thought you'd never get back. Why didn't you phone?"

"I tried every night, but it was hopeless. The phone service there is terrible."

"I've been awfully worried about you," she said. "Did you hear about poor Andrew Cobbold?"

"Yeah," he said. "Shocking. I was there when it happened. I'd spent a bit of time with him the day before."

"His wife's absolutely broken up. There's some talk of the company arranging a typically Italian funeral. She doesn't want anything to do with it."

"I don't blame her," Mark said. "Funerals like that are a thing of the past. He's dead and gone, poor guy; why spend all that money that does nobody any good? Give it to charity instead. Where are the kids?" he asked.

"In bed," she said. "I promised to take them to the circus tomorrow so they'd go to bed early. Let's us go to bed early too."

"I can't wait," he said.

They made love on the couch, and then on the floor. She knew the peasant coarseness that was the trademark of the traveling prostitutes of his boyhood always excited him, and she gave him as good an imitation as she could—legs spread instantly and without encouragement, manipulating him artfully according to the instructions given to peasant girls by their mothers.

"You're bigger than ever," she groaned.

"*E tu sei più stretta.*"

They passed routinely to the little perversions that had long been stripped by habit of their cherished guilt.

"*Vuoi metterlo dietro?*"

"*Sì.*"

"*Ai-i-i-ie!*"

He hardly noticed any more the little shriek and half sobs that were inseparable from the ritual.

As their fury increased, they slipped into the treasure house that vulgarity offered to lovers.

" 'Sta minchia," she said. "Where have you been putting it while you've been in Havana?"

"Nessuna parte."

"Dimmi. Dimmi. Tell me."

"I already told you."

"What does it matter? I don't care what you've been doing. Quanto è grossa, 'sta minchia."

At breakfast the next morning there was a new brusqueness in the air. The Sicilian peasant girl of the night before had become the crisp and self-assured young American woman with ideas.

"I didn't want to bother you last night," Teresa said, "but there are some funny rumors going around."

"Rumors?"

"About Andrew Cobbold. He made a will the day before he went away."

"Nothing odd about that."

"There was something in a letter he wrote to his wife. She got it the same day she heard he was dead. Reading between the lines, she said, she could tell that he knew his life was in danger."

"I suppose you could say anybody's life is in danger in Cuba right now. A lot of people are getting killed."

"He didn't give you the impression of being worried in any way?"

"By business, maybe, that's all."

"One newspaper said one thing and the other something quite different. I wish they'd make up their minds. I hate mysteries. Anyway the district attorney has the letter."

"I doubt if they'll ever discover the whole truth of what happened," Mark said. "Or if it's worthwhile trying to do so. Cuba's a funny place—not much in the way of law and order as we know it. Good thing I didn't fall for the idea of taking you and the kids on the trip."

"I'm beginning to believe it *was* a good thing."

In the brief silence that followed, he surveyed the view through the window that he'd always found too large. The lawns were a bright, chemical green again after the autumn rains. At the moment plane trees partially screened them from the road and offered a little privacy, but in another month, with the fall of the leaves there would be nothing to hold back the eye. He would have liked to build a high wall around the house. The Cuban experience had weakened him and left him with a feeling of nakedness and exposure. He remembered enviously the phrase that an Englishman's home was his castle, and recalled nostalgically the stone womb of Campamaro, built in such a way that the backs of the houses formed a single high wall, pierced only here and there near the top with windows too small for an intruder to crawl through. In Salisbury he felt exposed.

"I have news for you," Teresa said.

He was jarred back unpleasantly into the present. "What's that?"

"I've been asked to join the Citizens' Defense Committee that's just been formed."

"What's that? Not political, I hope."

"It's an offshoot of the Cristoforo Colombo Society," she said. "Composed of persons of Italian origin living in this town."

"What are you defending yourself from?"

"Racketeering and all forms of corruption. We have to prove that the Italian minority here are as good citizens as anybody else."

"And do we need to do this?"

"Yes, we do. We've employed a firm to make inquiries for us, and we've already found out that the Italian ethnic minority, amounting to about ten percent of the population, owns more than half the businesses in town."

"They worked for them," Mark said. The turn of the conversation reminded him of Don Vincente. He glanced at his watch; he was due there to make his report in less than an hour.

"Not all of them," she said. "Some of them just threw out the original owners and took over."

"In the distant past, perhaps," he said, "but times have changed."

"We're declaring war on all those burlesque shows and gambling storefronts on Dwight Street. McClaren of the *Examiner* is behind us. He's starting a newspaper campaign to coincide with what we're doing."

"You ought to look for someone else," Mark said. "McClaren's a nut. He won't do you any good. Don't think I don't sympathize, but McClaren is not the right guy."

"He's sincere, whatever else they say," Teresa said. "The committee had a meeting with him, and he's starting his series next Monday with a profile of Vincent Stevens, this town's so-called benefactor."

Mark's uneasiness was deepening. He felt in need of a long period in which he could be left in peace, out of reach of telephones behind thick walls, with only his friends, gathered from the past, within earshot. "I think you're making a mistake," he said.

"Why?"

"Because the piece is bound to be an attack on him, and Don Vincente happens to be the man who signs my salary check."

"So he can do no wrong?"

"He looked after us when we arrived here without a friend. I had no qualifications of any kind. Without Don Vincente, I couldn't have found a job as a waiter. What do you want me to say? How are we going to send Martin of Notre Dame when I'm driving a taxi?"

In her impatience, which came close to anger, Teresa was unrecognizable from the night before, and this moment of tension gave him a preview of what she would be like in the years to come. A masculinity she had picked up like an infection from the intelligent and purposeful women with whom she socialized seemed about to take over her expression. Watching her as she dressed in the slanting autumnal light that morning, he had been surprised to see that she was losing the fullness of her bosom and hips.

"Do you deny that he made his money in bootlegging?" she asked.

"Of course I don't," Mark said. "He was a kid with no prospects who wanted a piece of life, who had to fight for himself in any way he could. But these days are over and done with. I hope your friend McClaren has the good grace to mention that Don Vincente put up a quarter of a million dollars for the new wing of the hospital."

"Don't you see?" she said. "It's all a part of the front. He steals ten million, then gives a quarter of a million back to keep people quiet. This town is corrupt from top to bottom, and he's behind it all."

"This town is wide open because people want it that way. The mayor who was here before Grubschek tried to clean it up, so they got rid of him. If you don't like what's happening here, blame the people who put Grubschek in, not Don Vincente. The citizens of this town gave Grubschek the biggest majority anyone's ever received."

"Grubschek and that police captain, What's-his-name, are in Stevens' pocket."

"They're in everybody's pocket."

"Last fall when that horrible son of Stevens' ran a man down and killed him, he fixed it up with the police to get him off. What do you call that?"

"He wouldn't be a normal father if he didn't do what he could for his son."

"That's not what I call being a normal father," Teresa said. "Anyway, the *Examiner*'s going to ask for the case to be reopened, and with all the publicity, I'll bet it will be."

Mark looked at her with astonishment. In this mood she was ready to fight him. She was on the opposite side of the fence. It was a mistake to have come here, he thought. We should have stuck it out. Maybe we should have moved to Rome and hoped for the best. "Do me a favor," he said. "Drop it."

"You're in a funny mood."

"Maybe."

"What's the matter?"

There was no way of putting in English, nor in

Italian either—this sensation of fatal involvement, this eavesdropping on the whispered premonitions of instinct.

"*Sono seccato*. I've dried out." The expression could mean whatever the listener cared to put into it. Since he could not define his own disquiet, there was no way of conveying his feeling to Teresa. He changed the subject. "I had a letter from Paolo. He's in a spot. Someone fixed it so that the new Palermo road is going to by-pass the village, and they're putting pressure on him to sell out. His asthma's a lot worse. It looks like he's going to lose his Agip agency."

At times like these Mark always liked to think and talk about the life back home, in which he was no longer allowed a share. "They found copper on my cousin Rossi's land. I should have been there to congratulate him" . . . "The D.C.'s got in again at Caltanissetta. The candidate's a relation of ours on my mother's side by marriage. A second cousin's son-in-law" . . . "They've made a film about Messina."

"The bandit, you mean?"

"Sure, the bandit. It gave everybody a big laugh" . . . "San Stefano's getting a tourist hotel. Can you imagine—a dump like that?"

"Did Paolo say anything about your sister?" Teresa asked.

"Her husband's gone off to work in Germany. She's on her own with three young children."

"He shouldn't have done that."

"How could he help it? The factory closed, and half the town's on relief. I ought to be there. This is a time when Paolo needs me at his side, even if he doesn't say so. People put up with too much. They don't want to worry me with their troubles. The way I feel right now is that everything is falling to pieces."

"At least they still write to you," Teresa said. "I don't seem to get letters any more. It's six months since I heard from Mamma. She fell out with the grocer who used to write for her. She could be ill, and I'd never know."

"We should go back," he said, feeling as he made this declaration an aching restriction in his throat.

"You mean home? To Sicily?"

Did he read the alarm in her face? "Just that. We've left people there who can't get by. They need us and we need them. Here we're on our own."

He searched desperately for rational excuses to bolster the facts of sentiment and his intangible, inexplicable fears. "There's a tough gang of kids in this town. We'd have to send Martin away to boarding school soon, and neither of us wants that. As it is, he gets ribbed because he's Catholic."

"It has to be your decision," Teresa said. "But if we go, we can't wait any longer; we have to leave now."

"A lot of people go back," he said. "Half of them, at least. Maybe they stay here four or five years and put together a little money, then they go back."

"Single men you're talking about, not families. You don't uproot families like that. In another year we'll have put down too many roots."

She wants to stay, he thought. She's American already.

Even in the morning light Don Vincente's house in the woods seemed gloomy and sinister. Donna Carlotta, his wife, by now a victim of pathological meanness as well as religious mania, employed no one on a regular basis to look after the house. The curtains had been taken down to be washed and never replaced, the windows were misted with grime, and the October gales had strewn the drive with small branches. One of the priests Donna Carlotta always kept about the place admitted him in silence, then flapped away into the depths of the house. Don Vincente awaited him in the overstuffed Victorian room, more crabbed than ever by daylight. As if he had been taken by surprise, his head emerged from a white turtleneck sweater—an unwanted present from his wife—that was too young for him and made him look older than he actually was. He bumbled about slowly, stirring currents of dust in the air as he shifted the furniture to clear a space where they could sit in comfort.

When Mark showed him the cutting from the Havana *Post,* Don Vincente studied it, nodding with a faint clacking of his false teeth. "I read about it in the local paper," he said. "Published a pretty nice obituary. Nice thing for the widow to read, kind of dignified and restrained. They cut out a lot of the usual yackety-yak. So they got the guys who did it, huh?"

"The Havana cops move fast," Mark said. "They'll be tried by a military court. Conspiracy and homicide."

"I heard on the radio this morning that the murder weapon's been found under the floor in one of the guys' houses. You didn't fix that, did you?"

Mark shook his head.

"It must have been Salvatore," Don Vincente said. "I recognized the touch." His fingers made a small gesture of appreciation, and then a change of tone of voice signified that the matter was closed. Mark had not expected gratitude. Thanks were ruled out between men of honor. Like Arabs, Sicilians of the old school thanked God but never men.

"You heard I got trouble with McClaren," Don Vincente said. He squirmed a little as if he had just felt the bite of a flea.

"Teresa told me," Mark said.

"He wants to write about me in his paper. That's okay—let him go ahead and say anything he likes."

"Teresa said something about his planning to re-open that business about Victor's car crash last year," Mark said, knowing that it was in this aspect of McClaren's attack that the trouble lay.

"I was coming to that," Don Vincente said. "He can say anything he likes as long as he keeps away from my boy. That accident was an attempted frame-up by a guy I clashed with some years ago, and I wouldn't like to see Victor used on my account. There's nothing wrong with Vic that a little understanding won't put right, and I don't like to see him picked

on by anybody. Mark, I'd take it as a favor if you'd
go see McClaren and explain to him the way I feel.
I want you to do this for me because you're a diplomat
and know how to make a man change his mind without
having to kick his teeth in." He leaned forward to
clasp Mark's shoulders in a light embrace.

"You want me to go right away, Don Vincente?"

"Well, if this profile, or whatever they call it, is
gonna appear next week, we don't have too much
time to lose."

"I'll talk to him this morning," Mark said.

"You don't have to lean too heavy on him. It can
be settled in a friendly manner. It's always better.
He can have anything he likes as long as he leaves
Victor out of it."

"I'll talk to him along those lines."

Mark drove over to the *Examiner* which occupied
a cinderblock building, flanked by a white-framed
Gospel tabernacle and a liquor store, in a section of
town where prosperity had once flowed and then
ebbed. A religious fundamentalist, McClaren sometimes preached in the tabernacle, and had appeared
on television with a chorus of girls from Freemont
High School in surplices to demand a return to a
belief in hellfire and damnation. His motives in the
matter of the campaign to clean up the town were
mixed; he saw in it a remedy not only for the community's ills, but for his own newspaper's falling circulation. He was a big man, stiff and fragile-looking
with faded eyes, not old but with the creaking voice
of old age. Moving forward to offer Mark his hand,
he seemed to be balancing himself on artificial limbs.

"You don't know me," Mark said. "My name's
Richards. I'm from the Vincent Stevens organization, and if you can spare a moment I'd like to talk
to you about this profile on Mr. Stevens you're running next week."

"Sit down, Mr. Richards," McClaren said. "I suppose you've come to tell me you're taking your advertising away." Watching the man's big red, arthritic hands,

Mark detected a faint tremble. McClaren thrust them out of sight underneath his desk.

"As far as I know, there's no question at all of that. "That's not the way Mr. Stevens works. The idea was that he might be able to contribute in some way to help you to get all the facts right. He'd certainly be happy to cooperate if you felt it was helpful."

"Well, Mr. Richards, I'm not sure that's a good idea." A defiant sparkle appeared and was instantly rinsed away by McClaren's watery stare. "The *Examiner* publishes without fear or favor. It has to be that way. You wouldn't be about to suggest, for example, that I might be persuaded to leave anything out?"

The dry, churchy smell of the office tickled Mark's nose, and a sneeze took him by surprise. "I think I can safely say that I'm speaking for Mr. Stevens when I assure you that nothing is further from his mind. The way he sees this, there are a whole bunch of facts about his childhood, both in Sicily and here, which you couldn't possibly have access to. He wouldn't have any objection to sitting down with one of your reporters—perhaps with you yourself, if you like—and discussing any aspect of his life you might want to know more about. As a young boy newly arrived in this country, he was thrown by accident into the company of a pretty tough bunch of men—some of whom have since become household names."

"I guess he was," McClaren said. "Men like Maranzano and Dutch Shultz. The shame of this country between the wars."

"As everyone knows, Mr. Stevens was lucky enough to be able to break away from that environment. However, although never a part of the criminal world of those days, as luck would have it he had a ringside seat for certain big-scale operations. I would imagine that some of his experiences revealed by your newspaper for the first time might make fascinating material for your readers."

"I'm inclined to agree with you, Mr. Richards," McClaren said. "If we could offer new material of the kind you describe, people would certainly want to read it." His large loose face had tightened with calculation. "Such material is never easy to come by."

"And it would be the real thing. No hearsay—what went on behind the scenes. Mr. Stevens has some fascinating letters from prominent persons that he might agree to let you use. Without knowing much about the newspaper world, I would think an article of this kind could be syndicated nationally."

"It isn't beyond the bounds of possibility," McClaren said, "assuming all the material is fresh and authentic." His eyes seemed to have grown closer to his nose. "What sort of an inducement would Mr. Stevens expect to receive for the exclusive right to use this material? I presume he has some such inducement in mind."

"As a matter of fact, he has," Mark said. "It's a very small thing. He'd like to leave any mention of his son Victor out of the piece."

"Well, I might be able to do that under the circumstances," McClaren said. "I think I can safely say we could come to an agreement in that direction."

"Mr. Stevens is very attached to his son. Say something nice about that boy and you're his friend for life. Naturally enough, it works the other way too."

10

Since puberty, much of Victor's time had been devoted to a study of the science and practice of rape. He had committed the first of these assaults while still at Freemont High School. They had always been on the persons of the maids-of-all-work employed by his mother, and his strategy had been based on the house's favorable geography. The maid was always given the garret room in a wing isolated by gloomy staircases and corridors from the rest of the house,

and Victor's bedroom—also out of earshot of his
parents' sleeping quarters—commanded the approach
to this area. In his middle teens, Victor watched for
a chance to slip an overdose of crushed-up sleeping
pills into the girls' food, and then went to work at lei-
sure on their insensible bodies. He was on the whole a
shy, withdrawn boy and could gather little confidence
even with an unconscious victim. But he was also an
intelligent student of human physiology, and when unable to enter a virgin he had learned how to carry out
a slight operation with his penknife to make this possible. Later, with the growth of confidence and potency,
and losing his taste for sheer passivity, he developed
a new system in which he frightened girls into surrender
by hiding a small loudspeaker in the beams of their
bedroom and transmitting eerie sounds through it
from a tape recorder hidden in a cupboard outside.
Then, when he judged the softening-up process of
fear had gone far enough, he would tap on the door
and offer his protection. The maids were all Puerto
Ricans from poor immigrant families—sometimes
orphans—supplied by a Catholic aid society to ap-
plicants who could satisfy the most searching inquiries
into their respectability.

The current maid, a replacement of one who had
suddenly departed red-eyed but silent a month before,
was a fifteen-year-old named Elvira. A week after
her arrival, Elvira was awakened by strange noises
in her room. She pulled the bedclothes over her head
and lay there, heart pounding, for several minutes,
and then, in an interval of silence, got out of bed
to switch on the tiny lamp provided by Donna Carlotta.
Victor had thrown the switch on the fuse board cutting
off the current to that part of the house, and the room
remained in darkness. Suddenly something invisible
above her gurgled and whooped, and Elvira ran to
the door, pulled back the bolt and rushed out into
the passage, where Victor was waiting.

Unfortunately, on this occasion Victor, who was
easily affected by liquor, was recklessly drunk, and
in the struggle to overcome the spasms of the levator

muscle, he lost all fear of the consequences and exerted terrible violence. By the time the defloration was complete, he had torn not only the hymen but the posterior vaginal wall itself. Finally released, Elvira rushed naked and in agony down the stairs, hands clasped over her torn genitals, blood streaming through her fingers. Her cries brought Don Vincente, who, preferring not to call an ambulance, wrapped a blanket around the girl and drove her to the hospital himself. Once there, he showered hundred-dollar bills on everyone within sight.

The next day the bruised silence of the house was shattered by the arrival of Police Chief Henry Weissman, who mutely handed over to Don Vincente a set of photographs. Weissman had spent fifteen years on the beat before being promoted overnight, the year before, by the incoming mayor, George Grubschek. He was a man whose profession had slowly but decisively chiseled his face into a new shape: a soft oval that had turned into a square of muscle and bone, with deep grooves curved at the corners of the nose and extending to the mouth by the routines of rage imposed by his calling.

Don Vincente stared down at the curling, glossy prints: the close-ups, almost unrealistically sharp, of the bloody vagina; the lacerations; the scratches gouged by fingernails in belly and buttocks; the broken-halfmoons of tooth marks in the breasts. His mouth filled with saliva in which his tongue floated, and for a moment he found it impossible to speak and difficult to swallow. "Can the mayor handle this?" he finally asked.

Weissman shook his head. His unhappiness and embarrassment showed only faintly in a face designed as a barometer of anger. The slight sweet tang of whiskey on his breath reached Don Vincente and sickened him. "I don't think so. One of the medicos up at the hospital is sticking his neck out. If we don't move he'll call in the state police."

"What do you mean by move?"

Weissman shrugged his shoulders, his eyes weak and evasive.

"Who took these pictures?"

"The usual guy. He didn't know who was mixed up in this."

"Can you get the negatives?"

"Sure I can get the negatives, but it's going to look just the same when the state police photographer gets down there to take some more."

"Didn't someone make a deal to keep the state police out of this town?"

"In cases of petty infringement, yes. But this is a big thing, Mr. Stevens. You can go to the chair in some states for a thing like this. Any judge who saw these pictures would send your son away for ten years."

"Listen, Weissman, just who told you my son did it? My son didn't do this. This is some sort of frame-up." His fury rising, Don Vincente almost believed it. Victor had assaulted an underage girl—that he knew —but nothing could convince him that he had inflicted the injuries shown in these pictures. What were they after? What was to prevent them from taking any set of rape pictures out of the police files and using his present misfortune as an excuse for a shakedown? Don Vincente knew all about Weissman—in particular that he collected a weekly toll of five dollars from the earnings of every prostitute in Salisbury. He was the kind of man, however much he had been compelled to use him, that Don Vincente most disliked.

"Take those photographs and get out of here, Weissman," he said. "If my son happens to come up on a rap sometime and any photographs like this are shown to anybody, you're going to be back the next day right where you started—on the beat."

Don Vincente called Mayor Grubschek. "George, that horse's ass Weissman was over here with a bunch of photographs. Do you know what this is all about?"

"I heard something," Grubschek said. "It doesn't sound too good. Something about your son and an underage girl."

"He had a little trouble with a girl who's been working for us up here. Some kid from Puerto Rico.

You know how it is with kids. I hear they're all snorting smack these days. If she or her family feel they have anything to beef about, I'm ready to listen. Would you contact them? I'd like to leave this to you. I don't know about Weissman; there's something about that guy I don't like. Maybe he ought to be a patrolman again. I'd like you to contact this kid's family as soon as you can, George, and settle it with them in any way that strikes you as reasonable. Would you do that, and let me know what's happening?"

"I certainly will, Vincent. I'll call you back as soon as I have any news."

"And tell Weissman that if I hear anything more about those photographs, I'm going to personally burn his ass."

"I'll do that too." Grubschek had an afterthought. "Where is Victor right now?"

"He's gone out for a ride in his car," Don Vincente said. "This thing has him pretty worried. I told him to go out, get away and relax."

"It might be a good idea if he kept out of sight for the next few days," Grubschek said. "These people are upset, and maybe this girl has brothers. Some of these Puerto Ricans can be pretty hard-nosed."

Back in the twenties, Grubschek's father, a Polish immigrant, had been employed in the terrible bone-meal plant of the Chicago stockyards where his salary had been twenty-three dollars a week. His son owned a garment factory employing eighty workers, in which Don Vincente had a modest stake of 20,000 dollars. He lived in the biggest house on Champlain Avenue, owned a thirty-two-foot Bermuda sloop which he kept at the Cape, and expected in the full course of his term—with nearly three years to run—to make something approaching a million dollars out of kick-backs and from his iron control of the councilman at the head of the city planning department. He was a man whose energy made an athletic performance of the simplest physical activity—going up and down stairs, or even dressing and undressing. At this moment he was the victim of a dilemma. Rumor and his own finely tuned nose for success and failure suggested that Don Vincente might be a spent force in Salisbury. He was reported to be selling his local interests as fast as he could and transferring the capital overseas, while the men who fronted for concealed owners of the clubs on Dwight Street privately admitted that they no longer took their orders from the Don. On the other hand, there was no telling how much Don Vincente's power over the electoral machine remained, and Grubschek suspected that if he failed the town's most prominent citizen in this emergency, his chances of reelection would be slight.

The Casals family lived at the top of a tenement on 43rd Street, the man with his wife and two young children occupying a single room containing two mattresses on the floor, three chairs, a chest of drawers, a cooking stove and an assortment of broken toys. When Grubschek started to explain the reason for his visit, Casals hastily got rid of his family and dragged a ruptured armchair into position for Grubschek to sit down. The mayor was surprised to find Casals so young—a man with an unlined face, intelligent eyes and an enormously high forehead, tufted with premature gray hair. It was the last of the warm days of autumn; the torpid air sandwiched between the high buildings, and the shrieks of the children at play in an enclosed courtyard below, magnified by the city's acoustics into the cries of savage hunters. A brown curtain hung aslant, like a drying fisherman's net, over a third of the bleary window. The air had been indelibly overprinted with the odor of food cooked in the cheapest semirefined olive oil, a reek with overtones of excrement.

"I'm talking to you not so much as man to man," Grubschek said, "but as father to father. I have five of my own." He laughed in a deep, hollow voice cultivated at a voice-production center. "And a sixth on the way."

Casals listened, a grave, intent expression on his face. So far he had said nothing. A frequent gesture of cupping his hand to his mouth, as if in preparation for a fit of coughing, hinted at a background of ill health.

"The fact that I'm here as mayor," Grubschek said, "expresses the civic concern felt in our town over this unfortunate matter, apart from any question of the horror and grief of the people most closely concerned."

Casals' sincere eyes watched Grubschek across the knuckles of his fist, raised once again to his mouth. He dropped his hand. "I'm sorry, I didn't hear the name," he said softly.

For Chrissake, Grubschek asked himself, doesn't he understand what the hell I'm talking about? "The name is Grubschek. Mayor George Grubschek," he said. "I'd appreciate it if you called me George."

"Roberto Casals," the Puerto Rican said. He jumped up to bow and sat down again.

"Before we go any further I want you to understand that I'm not here to put pressure on you in any way, Roberto," Grubschek said. "You could make a big thing of this; there's no denying it. On the other hand you may not wish to. A lot depends on you, and I'm sure you're the kind of man who's going to think twice, or maybe three times, before he decides on a line of action that may have not altogether pleasant repercussions. Am I right?"

Casals nodded slowly, then covered his mouth again.

"First and foremost," Grubschek said, "we ought to consider the interests of your little girl. We ought to try and forget our personal feelings and put her first. What did you say her name was?"

"Elvira."

"Elvira. My, that's a beautiful name. I have three daughters of my own. Well, now just imagine if this case came to trial and this little girl was compelled to testify—as she would be—We have to consider, first and foremost, what the psychological effect might be. Make no mistake, Roberto, it would be a terrible ordeal for any young girl to undergo."

"I don't want Elvira to suffer any more than she already has," Casals said.

"Of course you don't; what father worthy of the name would? Let me try to give you some idea of the experience she'd have to face. She'd have to go into that box and describe what had happened to her in every detail—maybe several times over, and in front of a whole bunch of strangers—newspapermen, and people who happened to be there out of curiosity, just because they had dirty minds."

"She'd have to do that?"

"I'm afraid she would. And she'd be cross-examined. Have you ever heard anybody cross-examined? It can be very traumatic. Some of these counsels for the defense adopt bullying tactics—the idea being to fluster a witness into contradicting himself and making a liar of him. Imagine a young girl from a nice family background being subjected to this kind of thing—all this argument in public over the physical details of what was alleged to have taken place."

"Alleged, Mr. Grubschek?"

"Merely a legal term, Roberto. No reflection of any kind. Any offense is said to be alleged until it's proved. A legal nicety. Now let's look at this from another point of view. The chances are that even if Elvira were exposed to this terrible ordeal, it would be to no purpose. Three rape cases out of four are thrown out. The reason, my lawyer friends tell me, is that there's a legal presumption that any strong and healthy young woman ought to be able to defend her honor against an average male who is unassisted in any way. If she's knocked on the head or half strangled, that's a different matter. Otherwise an element of doubt is always present, and I gather that most juries are very loath to convict."

There was a puckering at the corners of the mouth on the young-old face that confronted Grubschek. Spicks, Grubschek knew, wept easily, and he feared tears. Beyond the limp curtain a movement in the building opposite caught his eye. A polished black head had appeared at each of the three windows in sight. "Mr. Grubschek, what do you think I have to do?" Casals asked.

"What you have to do, Roberto? Well, nothing

very difficult, I can assure you. As I see it, what we both want is to cause as little unnecessary pain as we have to. In a way this poor young man is to be pitied as much as he's to be blamed, because he's going to have to walk around with this terrible thing on his conscience for the rest of his life. But it's his parents whom I'm really concerned about. The father and mother happen to be two of the most wonderful people I know. Dragging their good name through the mud isn't going to do Elvira or anyone else any good. Try to put yourself in Mr. Stevens' place. This kind of publicity is going to finish him off. They punish the innocent along with the guilty, I always say. What I'm aiming to do is get you two together. These are really lovely people, and—this is strictly between ourselves—I happen to know that Mr. Stevens, who is the father, would give a great deal to be given a chance to make what amends he can."

But was this guy taking it in? That was the thing. There was none of the animosity that Grubschek had feared; nor could he believe that Casals was simply lying low and waiting to see how much he could take him for. He was coming to the conclusion that Casals was just dumb—which was a pity, because he might turn out to be too dumb to know which side his bread was buttered on. Only the Puerto Rican's eyes were alert in a face numbed with resignation. What a place to live in, Grubschek thought. He hadn't realized that living conditions like this still existed. A limp tangle of music from phonographs and radios, mixed with the distant yelping of children, drifted in on the stagnant air, and the hollow spaces of the building gurgled and rumbled like an empty stomach behind the thin partition walls.

"Our cities are too large," Grubschek said. The horror of his surroundings had given him an idea. "Something ought to be done about you people. Your children are entitled to breathing space like any other kids. And to be able to play in safety—green fields and growing things. Look here, Roberto, let's quit shadow-boxing. Mr. Stevens wants to look after you. You lost your job through ill health, and he can fix you up with a better one tomorrow. While he's about it, he'd find you and your family a place to live where you'd be able to fill your lungs with God's fresh air. How's that sound to you?" He paused to correct an over-cheerful expression and replace it with one of proper solemnity. "Also we have to think about Elvira. Mr. Stevens would want to put something into a banking account—a few thousand bucks to take care of her future, to start a dowry for her."

The door of the apartment opened a crack, and Grubschek saw Mrs. Casals in the opening. She peered through at them with the shyness of an animal, her young, smudged face engraved with the anxieties of poverty. It seemed extraordinary that she could be old enough to have a rapable daughter.

"Please come in and join us, madam," he called to her. "I'm sure you know why I'm here. Roberto and I are getting together to try to settle this unhappy business like a couple of sensible human beings, and we'd very much appreciate any help you can give us as Elvira's mother."

Mrs. Casals came in reluctantly, as if freeing herself from invisible cords that had bound her down on the landing. She closed the door and stood with her back to it, in preparation for escape.

"I represent Mr. Stevens, the young boy's father," Grubschek said. "Insofar as any compensation can be made for what your daughter has suffered, he's prepared to make it."

Mrs. Casals, her eyes cast down, muttered something in Spanish to her husband.

"What does she say?" Grubschek asked.

"She wishes to know if Mr. Stevens' son would agree to marry Elvira," Casals said.

Grubschek could see by the man's expression that he realized how unrealistic his wife's suggestion was. "I'm afraid we all consider Mr. Stevens' son a little immature to take on the responsibilities of marriage," he said. "What Mr. Stevens has in mind, as I've explained to your husband, is the payment of a very considerable sum—besides which he'd fix Roberto up with a job and possibly find you more attractive living quarters."

"But for this you wish me to do something in return, Mr. Grubschek?" Casals asked. Moving toward his wife, he took her gently by the arm, opened the door, pushed her through and closed it again.

"Hardly anything at all, Roberto. It couldn't be easier. Some goddam doctor is at the back of all this. I wish I understood his motives, and I suggest that you tell him to keep his nose out of your affairs. Apart from that I'd like Elvira to withdraw any statement she made to the police. Just that. Simply that. Nothing more." He spread his hands with a conjurer's smile.

"I'm sorry, Mr. Grubschek. I'm doing my best to understand. What is meant, 'to withdraw her statement'?" His face was changing, the empty spaces below the eyes filling with some new emotion, an excitement that Grubschek could not identify.

Grubschek explained in his gentlest manner. "To put it in plain English, Roberto, she'd have to say she consented to whatever took place. There's no problem for her; the police are used to people changing their minds. They were just having a romp together and it turned that way, and she didn't say no—because she was so innocent, if you like, she didn't know what it was all about. Or she could even say she made the original statement because she was afraid of what her father would have to say. I leave it to you. Maybe you can think of something better."

As Casals rose and took two steps toward him, some instinct brought Grubschek to his feet. As he stood, a great spread of magenta light splashed over his eyes and a car door slammed in his head. Sound was instantly cut off as soft hands cupped his ears, filling them with a ringing vacuum. He fell back into the chair with such violence that he bounced. All the objects in the room, including Casals' face with its slow, analytical eyes, were locked in that static whirl of drunkenness that precedes vomiting. A tooth spat through his fluttering lips and hung for an instant on a thread of bloody spittle before falling into his lap. There was no room in his mind for anything but utter surprise. "Why d'ja do that?" he said. "Why d'ja do that?"

A week later the young doctor who had first examined Elvira and had subsequently interested himself in her case was called to the office of the chairman of the management committee of the City Hospital. His superior came quickly to the point. "John, I know how you feel about this Casals affair, but I don't think it's a good idea to turn it into some sort of personal crusade. From your own point of view, it's inadvisable because you can lay yourself open to the charge of publicity-seeking. Besides—and I'm going to be absolutely frank—you could be damaging the interests of the hospital."

The chairman waited for the young gynecologist's comment, but there was none. He wanted to end the conversation quickly but couldn't think of a way of doing so.

"Stevens is the most generous patron this hospital ever had or is likely to have," he went on finally, speaking with exaggerated firmness. "We need to reequip the x-ray department this year, and I was very much hoping to be able to turn to him again."

"I see, sir."

"Not only that, but I have more than a suspicion that the police might be very happy to let this thing drop. The Casals girl has been very incoherent in the accounts she has given them, and I'm told that there *are* inconsistencies. My feeling is that if they come to you again, all well and good, but if they don't I'd be inclined to let it slide, and by all means keep away from the press. Nobody can tell me that these matters aren't better settled out of court, and to put yourself in the position of sabotaging such a settlement seems to be a disservice to all concerned."

Tight-mouthed, the young gynecologist felt obliged to agree. To have stood up to the chairman would have meant his dismissal from the hospital, but he would have had to go all the same, and though his career might suffer no permanent damage the incident would do nothing to help it. The medical profession was stiff-necked and conservative, and inclined to show a lack of sympathy for young men of prickly independence.

As it turned out, there was no further compromising contact with the state police, whose Captain Wilbur Hart—also considered a young man with a promising future—came home one day to find his wife unwrapping a parcel that turned out to contain a mink coat. There was no indication of its sender, though Hart had a pretty good idea who he was, and this deprived him of a chance to demonstrate his reputed incorruptibility by sending it back. The Casals family remained obdurate in their poverty and pride, and after it was announced in the *Examiner* that the police had dropped their case against Victor Stevens, there seemed to be no point in trying to win Casals over.

It was immediately after this that Victor received the first of several letters containing threats on his life: a crude and illiterate affair with drawings that might have been done by a child of two stiff-limbed little manikins beating and stabbing a third. Don Vincente took the letters seriously. Friends having a nodding acquaintance with the underworld scene in New York and New Jersey told him of the emergence of Puerto Rican criminal gangs rivaling in ferocity—even in organization—the Sicilians of the Unione Siciliana of a generation back. It was considered not impossible that the Casals, determined on vengeance, might have taken their case to one of these. Don Vincente faced the difficult task of keeping his son safely at home until the trouble seemed past.

Seduced briefly at the time of the publication of Don Vincente's profile, the *Examiner* was forced by sheer weight of public opinion—as evidenced in its plummeting circulation—to change its position again. With this swing of the pendulum all the wickedness committed by lesser citizens, of which Don Vincente was completely innocent, were now laid to his charge. Ranting incoherently about Sodom and Gomorrah from his Sunday pulpit, McClaren went into efficient action every Monday, ordering his reporters into the gambling dens, bookie joints and brothels of Salisbury in search of penitent whores and reformed crooked gamblers who might be ready to enlist in the new crusade and give evidence of the corruption of the town's rulers. He uncovered many instances of intimidation, concealing as much as he could from his readers the fact that the majority of these had taken place in the distant past. Small businessmen had had their lives made unbearable until they sold out to more powerful rivals. In particular a garage that had resisted an enforced sale had been devastated by the explosion of a gasoline pump, and when a trucking outfit persisted in remaining independent, wheels had fallen off its vehicles three times in a single week. These revelations made startling reading and increased circulation temporarily by a thousand or so copies, but though few people noticed, it was old stuff forgotten ten years before.

Still inflamed by these disclosures, "Citizen Commandos" went into action in the streets. Most of these were middle-aged Methodist or Lutheran ladies, though one squad of younger women was led by Teresa. They picketed a number of establishments of ill-repute, shouted slogans, distributed 12,000 texts, broke one window, threw ink on the dress of a Gray Lady on her way to charity, believing her to be the madam of a brothel, presented a petition at City Hall calling for the mayor's resignation—and finally went home.

Weeks passed. The young gynecologist had been able to turn his back on the recent unpleasantnesses and was properly absorbed in his career. Grubschek, whose expensive tastes kept him continually under financial stress, worried off and on about the low trade-in price on his boat against a new forty-footer ordered for the next season. Mrs. Wilbur Hart tried on her mink coat many times but never dared wear it in public. McClaren unearthed more and more civic scandals in his search for circulation. Damaged by the campaign, Don Vincente released his hold on his few remaining interests in Salisbury. His real estate company changed hands, though Mark stayed on with it as the manager of a business enfeebled by loss of contact with City Hall. Don Vincente and Donna Carlotta maintained their belief in the essential goodness of their son. The Casals, man and wife, sometimes wept like spics over the fate of their daughter who, back from the hospital, dressed in funereal black and kept out of sight.

For Mark things had worsened. His mother's silence was explained by an illness caused by a tumor, and the letter received from her doctor was vague about the prospects of a complete recovery after the inevitable operation. Paolo wrote briefly to announce the loss of his Agip agency. Letters to his sister remained unanswered, and a prepaid telegram to the *sindaco* of San Gregorio, Catania, where she and her husband lived, gleaned the news that she had gone off with a traveling salesman in cutlery from Torino, taking the children with her. The *sindaco* had been unable to trace her whereabouts. In the interim a big mining company had succeeded in swindling his cousin Rossi out of any copper found on his land.

These people need me, he told himself, and here I am—cut off. The first commandment of a man of honor was total involvement, at whatever cost to himself, in the welfare of his family and friends. In the only interview ever given for publication, Don C., the Sicilian head of the Society, had recently stated, for all the world to know: "I live to serve others. This is the whole purpose of my existence." In this he was absolutely sincere. Don Vincente's present troubles bound Mark more closely to him, and Don Vincente's family substituted for his own, now almost completely deprived of his protection.

Within a month, Mark received news of his mother's death. The despair of his mourning was increased by the fact that recent events had cast a deepening shadow between him and Teresa.

"You mean to tell me that you really believe this attack never took place?" she asked, her face set once again in its new mask of angry, masculine intelligence.

"It all depends on what you mean by attack. I was talking to Weissman at the club. She probably gave him some encouragement, even if she got more than she asked for."

"He's been doing this kind of thing for years, and has always gotten away with it."

"What makes you think that?"

"Everybody says so."

"The fact that everybody says so doesn't impress me. This boy's an Italian like us. A lot of people living in this town are still ready to believe anything bad about an Italian. Just like that campaign the *Examiner*'s running. Stevens is Italian, so he gets the blame for everything any hoodlum ever did in this city."

"You can tell he's a psychopath just by looking at him."

"You may be able to, but I can't. I happen to know Victor pretty well. Half his trouble is that his parents had him late in life. He suffers from overprotection, and he has no confidence. Handle him right and you'll find he responds."

"You're going to defend him whatever happens. What's the point of talking about it?"

"If I defend him, it's because I believe he's worth defending."

"He's no better than a gangster. Did you know that he's tied up with Spina?"

"Spina?"

"Yes, Spina, the famous dope king, your friend from back in Sicily. The man who fixed it for us to come here. Victor Stevens went to Nassau to meet him last year."

"That's news to me," Mark said. "Where did you pick up that piece of information?"

"From Hannah Cobbold."

"You mean Cobbold's wife—widow, I should say." Mark was astonished. The second of the commandments by which Cobbold had been expected to regulate his life enjoined secrecy and silence, above all in the presence of women. "I didn't even realize he was married," he said, "until you told me the other day."

"He kept her in the background," Teresa said. "She's Jewish. Some second-generation Italians are like that, even the ones who went to college. She'd like to have a word with you, by the way, when you have time."

"With me? What for?" Only a woman who had lived with him for ten years could have discerned the concern and irritation in the calm of his voice.

"It's about Andrew. She's looking for a firm of private detectives who'd be willing to investigate the circumstances of his death, and she thought you might be able to suggest one."

Even before Teresa spoke, he had known what was coming. This little featureless nothing of a Jewish girl from the background of Cobbold's life had moved into the open, charged with conviction about the timelessness of justice and the law. Now she would go to work patiently, tirelessly, prepared for every frustration and discouragement separating her from her goal. Why ask *him* for a detective agency? Everybody knew who they were and where to find them. This was Hannah Cobbold's way of serving notice that she was watching him.

"Private eyes aren't in my line," he said. "She's wasting her money, but what's wrong with Pinkerton's? Tell her she'll find them in the phone book."

11

Victor stayed away from his old haunts and spent most of his time at home until the threatening letters ceased to arrive and the mysterious phone calls, possibly designed to check on his whereabouts, were no longer made. The twelfth of December was his twentieth birthday. Don Vincente had given him a new maroon Thunderbird, to replace the one he had wrecked just before the Elvira episode, and in the early afternoon Victor set out with a friend, Johnny Ventura, who played guitar in a rock group, to drive to a restaurant called Le Dauphin near Lake Mashapaug about fifty miles away.

They left the Massachusetts Turnpike at Sturbridge for the Wilbur Cross Highway. It was a splendid day in early winter: clean farmland spread under a crystal sky; precise buildings, planed and painted like well-made toys for the landscape of a millionaire's child; pockets of frost growing like gray moss in the shadows, where it waited to push forward its frontiers again as soon as night fell. Le Dauphin, a farmhouse in the restrained local style, its stocky charm impaired by additions in sallow brick, was up a dirt road off Route 197 after Nipmuck State Forest. It was favored by young artists from Worcester and Springfield, who in exchange for free meals had covered its walls with their largely undecipherable pictures.

Victor and Johnny, who had stopped twice for drinks en route, arrived at the restaurant shortly before three, by which time most of the lunch trade was over. The restaurant had booths along one wall, and a thirty-foot bar opposite. The booths were still full, so they sat at a table in the front. The specialty was steak broiled over charcoal, and a cook in a chef's hat came to take their order and went back to work in the blue haze over the grill at the end of the room. They were served drinks by a girl in a Hungarian peasant costume. Rock music played loudly. They drank beer, followed by vodka martinis, and Victor was just finishing his second when four small dark men came in and sat down at the next table. "That's him," one of the men said behind his hand to the others.

All Victor noticed about the men was that in some way they didn't fit into the surroundings. They were too small, too quiet, and they formed too compact a group. The young artists and their hangers-on, who came here because the food was cheap and it was possible to eat on credit, were stamped with a certain conformity of appearance and manner that these men lacked. They were like waiters on their day off, stripped of the confidence and authority of their profession. The waitress took an order for drinks from their spokesman, who addressed her with a deference she was unaccustomed to and apologized with a nervous smile for the time his friends were taking to make up their minds. He was facing Victor, who looked away and then back, feeling rather than seeing on the edge of his vision that the man's eyes remained fixed on him. The man smiled, as if at an old acquaintance.

Victor delved into his memory for a recollection of this face of neat, compressed features, small eyes and dark, tufted hair growing across the forehead to within an inch of the eyebrows. He drew a blank. Johnny wanted to argue the merits of a Red Sox game they'd seen together that summer. When the waitress came by, Victor put his hand out in such a way that she was obliged to brush his hand with her thigh. He felt compelled to turn his head again; the man's eyes were still on him, and he was still smiling. He mouthed a word, but an upsurge of random chatter and rock music from a nearby hatch dropped a curtain of noise between them. Puzzled, Victor leaned toward the man, waiting for the hubbub to subside.

"Motherfucker," the man said, still smiling. Or it seemed that this was what he said.

"Whaddaya say?" Victor said. Perhaps he hadn't heard right, or maybe the man was drunk.

"Motherfucker," the man said again, this time with unmistakable clarity.

Victor got up, unsteady from the three beers and four martinis, his face burning. This was an occasion when he would have been happy to be able to turn on the famous look that had been more valuable to his father as a weapon of defense in his early career than any revolver could have been. But Don Vincente's stare reflected a belief in himself that he had been unable to pass on to any of his sons. In such situations, Victor fell back on bluster.

Silence had spread to every corner of the room. The jukebox was mute, and all heads were turned.

"In case anybody wants to know," said the man,

"this is Mr. Victor Stevens. *The* Mr. Victor Stevens. You've all heard about him. When he's not screwing his old lady, he's having himself a hand gallop."

"But right now it looks like maybe he has a mind to make a fuss or something," one of the other men said. He pushed his glass back, put his hands on the table and hoisted himself to his feet. Johnny was whispering, "Let's get outta here," and the two college graduates who occasionally acted as bouncers on Saturday nights—which were often lively—but otherwise worked in the kitchen, appeared at Victor's side and took him by each arm.

"Didja hear that guy insult me?" Victor asked.

"We heard him, Mr. Stevens, and we're going to have to ask him and his party to leave too. But we feel that you and your friend should leave first purely in your own interest."

"Let go of my arm. I gotta pay my check."

"Anything you've been served here is with the manager's compliments. Now let's go, shall we, Mr. Stevens? The sooner you and your friend get away from here, the less chance there is of someone getting hurt."

Victor and Johnny left, got into the Thunderbird and drove down the dirt road, heading for the highway. Johnny thought he knew a shortcut, but the road only led to a farm and they had to turn around; no sooner were they back at the intersection than they were overtaken by a Skylark with the four men in it, and forced to the side. When Victor saw them climb out, each of them carrying a pick handle, he threw open his door and began to run back toward the restaurant, with the four in chase. There were two miles to go, and he had a small start on his pursuers, but after the weeks spent mostly sitting in front of the television drinking beer, he was in poor shape and knew he would never make it. He ran on because there was nothing else to do, but the four men steadily drew closer. To his right there was a neglected apple orchard of gnarled and cankered trees, and he smashed through the low hedge, hoping to find somewhere to hide. But the tree trunks were spindly and far apart, and there was no cover among their leafless branches.

When the first man had almost caught up with him, he dodged around a tree and doubled back, maneuvering wildly like a trapped stag surrounded by dogs, and with as little intelligent forethought. Finally they had him cornered, his back to a tree, mouth wide open to suck in air, saliva on his chin. They were in no hurry, still fighting to get their breath, grinning at each other, and a little uncertain as to how the next act would begin.

The oncoming of night had drawn the life out of the landscape and invested it with a terrible loneliness. Shutters of cloud were falling through a drained sky. Sea gulls that had flown inland up the Five Mile River to the ponds around Webster were soaring coastward. Delivered into the hands of the Puerto Ricans, Victor saw the red flash of his car distantly through a hedge, but Johnny Ventura, trotting brokenly up the dirt road to find help at Le Dauphin, with still a good mile to go, was out of sight. Shadows lay in all the hollows of the land, and the faces of the small men who had cornered him had yellowed in the waning light. Their mood now seemed one of awkwardness, almost of embarrassment. Victor's fear-drugged brain groped for the words that might soften, the excuse that would shelter him, the bribe that could buy deferment, from the sentence about to be executed.

But all he could find to say was, "Listen, fellers, I couldn't help it."

The Puerto Rican leader, who had smiled so insistently but was now grave, seemed to consider the plea, frowning and fidgeting. He stood his ground, legs planted well apart, his club in both hands, while restlessness began to spread among the others.

"*Anda,* let's go," one of them said. Though eager for action, he was a shy man who looked away. Up to that moment they had made a desultory street-corner group, held together with nothing to say, waiting for someone to make the first move to break it up.

"How about taking the car, fellers?" Victor asked, his voice husky and eager, but hopeless.

The shy Puerto Rican's eyes were on his boots.

"Mr. Stevens, it's you we want, not your shit-eating car."

"*Mátalo,*" said another voice. "*Por qué estamos esperando?*"

They were arguing in low voices as if in fear of eavesdroppers and gesticulating with their pick handles. Who was to start, seemed to be the question. "*Tú primero.*" "*No, tú.*" It was the Puerto Rican who no longer smiled who struck the first hesitant, ineffectual, half-hearted blow, like a parent called in to chastise a beloved child. Victor parried it with his right arm, but at that moment the shy Puerto Rican moved in, swung his club around his head and struck with all his force. The blow broke Victor's jaw in two places. It was followed by a swallow's wing of movement slicing up through juddering mists to end as a hammer stroke on his right cheekbone. He felt the bone crunch like glass, and as the eye fell out of alignment his world sprang apart, breaking into double images of grim faces and raised arms. His pulse had become a slow metronome ticking in his ears. He knelt, supporting himself on his one undamaged arm, prevented from lying down by the conviction that asserted itself through his pain that if he did so it would be for the last time. He would have prayed if he could have remembered the words of any prayer; since he could not, he called for his mother. The final blow crushed several ribs and sent a splinter of bone through one lung, which collapsed. Then he could no longer speak, though his mouth, frothing with the brilliantly scarlet blood bubbling from his lung, still struggled to form the word *Mamma*. Like a bull dying in the ring, he lost control of his rectal and bladder sphincters.

"Holy shit, he's pissed himself," one of the Puerto Ricans said. "*Carai.*"

As Victor toppled over on his side in a pool spreading from the crotch of his trousers onto the frosted grass, the little men started back in silence to their car.

Victor spent three months in the hospital, passing through several of the seven ages of man, from a mewing and puking infant to a premature senility—from which, as lesions healed and nerves regenerated, he emerged to a tremulous convalescence.

Don Vincente confided his predicament to Mark. "The poor guy just sits around all day. Half the time he's asleep, and when he has these dreams he wets himself. He don't seem to want to talk to anybody."

Don Vincente had not plainly said, "Do me a favor," but it was what he meant, and Mark felt obliged to accede to the unspoken plea with what grace he could muster.

"Why did he have to come here?" Teresa asked.

"Because this happens to be the best place to look after him. In any case, I made the offer. I knew it was expected of me. It was the least I could do."

"How long is he going to stay?"

"As long as he wants to."

"It's bad for the children."

"No," he said, "it's not bad for them. It's good for them. He plays as much as he can with them. They like him."

"The way he stares at me gives me the creeps."

"He only stares because he can't help it. It's going to be another six months before he can shut that damaged eye of his."

"Whenever I look at him, I think of the horrible things he did to that girl," Teresa said.

"He didn't do any horrible things to anybody," Mark said. "The case against him was dropped, wasn't it?"

"Because the police were bribed."

"Why do you say that? Three rape cases out of four are thrown out because they don't stand up. They're thrown out because the rape never took place."

"As a father, would you consider leaving Lucy in the house alone with him?"

"Of course I would."

"What I can't understand," Teresa said, "is that quite apart from doing something for someone who may have helped you once, you actually seem to *like* him. Just what *is* the attraction?"

"He has character," Mark said.

This typically Sicilian commendation exasperated her. "Would you mind telling me exactly what you mean by that?"

"Yes. He doesn't whine. He's loyal. He's on his way to being a man."

"A man of honor. Like you."

"It's the way I'd like to be."

"A man of honor respects women," she said.

"*He* respects women."

Teresa gave up. "We're never alone these days," she said. "I hate having a stranger in the house."

"As he gets better he'll go out more and you'll see less of him. In the meantime I hope you'll do your best to make him feel at home."

The precautions Mark had insisted on taking infuriated Teresa. A firm specializing in security systems had been called in to install a burglar alarm, and at their recommendation the first-floor windows at the back of the house had been barred and a steel plate bolted to the back door, now secured by a padlocked iron bar in addition to the ordinary lock. At night powerful lamps illuminated the lawns at the front and rear of the house.

"The neighbors—" she started to complain.

"To hell with them," he said calmly.

Mark bought a pump gun, which he kept in a cupboard in their bedroom. Wherever Victor went, he accompanied him. There were daily visits to the City Hospital for manipulation of the fingers of Victor's left hand, and to a clinic where a psychiatrist did battle with Victor's loss of memory and obsessional fears.

The two men got on well. Victor showed himself grateful for what was being done for him, and separation from his family improved him in every way. He struggled hopelessly to make Teresa accept him, staggering eagerly about the garden performing the odd jobs that she found for him to do. He played endlessly with the children, built them a crude rabbit hutch, taught the dog tricks, and spent many hours quietly cutting pictures of cars out of magazines and sticking them into scrapbooks. In certain ways his appearance had improved. The spoiled child's face had suddenly become manly. There was a stiff dignity in his expression, in the lids of the damaged eye struggling to blink and in the muscles at the mouth's corners learning to smile again. The jaw injuries he had suffered caused him to speak in a slurred voice, but the doctors claimed that time would put this right. No sign remained of the impetigo of adolescence, and where he had once been inclined to bluster, he was now quiet-spoken.

It seemed to Mark that Victor showed no interest in the female sex. Moreover, he suffered from paranoia, believing himself to be followed constantly, and Mark had some difficulty in convincing him that the doctor who massaged and twisted the carpal scaphoid of his left hand in an attempt to restore his grip was not an assassin in disguise.

One day, while she was making his bed, Teresa found a short-nosed .38 Police Special under the pillow. "What do you expect after what he's been through?" Mark said. "Of course he packs a gun."

"I don't think I can stand much more of this," she said. Her voice quavered, close to hysteria. "The day is coming when you'll have to decide whether he goes or I go."

Mark gave her a stern look, then relented. "He's due for another checkup at the hospital next week. I'll make a deal with you. I'm not prepared to throw him out, but if the doctor says it's okay, I'll try to get him away somewhere for a few weeks' vacation. If he wants to come back, that's up to him, but at least it will give you a break."

Part

Three

1

One splendid day in the winter of 1959, the rebels marched into Havana. The takeover of the city was carried out so calmly, even nonchalantly, that the citizens hardly realized what was happening. One day the president's ferocious, trigger-happy police were to be seen swaggering everywhere, and the next they had gone, replaced by thousands of polite little peasants in uniform, who aside from drinking up Havana's entire stock of Coca-Cola within twenty-four hours perpetrated no excesses of any kind. Planes had been lined up at the end of the runway at Rancho Boyaros Airport to carry the president, his close friends and the leading members of his government into exile, and these were allowed to take off. On the whole there was joy and relief at the way things had turned out. Restaurants and cafés were as full as ever, and tables at night clubs had to be booked a day in advance. People went about shaking hands with perfect strangers and congratulating them on being alive. The best-natured and least venal prostitutes in the world were kept as busy as ever, and a few of the most generous even gave their services free of charge in celebration of the first day of the revolution's triumph. Tourists continued to pour in by plane and ship, and to gamble as legally as ever in the casinos. An average of one hundred per night drank themselves unconscious, were picked up by the new urban welfare

196

squads, looked after, given black coffee and respectfully returned to their hotels. Foreign visitors as well
as natives were invited to join in games of marbles
played by peasant soldiers from the backwoods who
were enraptured by the facilities for this popular village
sport on Havana's smooth, beautifully tessellated
pavements.

The bland and tolerant public image cultivated by
the new Cuban government did not surprise Salvatore Spina; nor was he in any doubt of the firmness
of purpose behind the handshakes and smiles. A man
who had always been better able than most to judge
which way the wind was blowing, he had come in
the end to accept the certainty of the rebels' success,
and only the speed of the government's collapse caught
him unawares.

Even then his extraordinary and proverbial luck
stood him in good stead. The day before the fall
of Havana the *S.S. Golfo Di Policastro* from Naples
steamed into port bringing him the largest single consignment of heroin ever to reach the Western world.
Spina had bought ninety percent of the entire Turkish
opium production for a whole year, and, avoiding
the use of the traditional French middleman and the
laboratory facilities in Marseilles, had processed the
morphine base in an old bus garage in the Porta Nuova
suburb of Palermo. The *Golfo Di Policastro* was carrying 250 kilos in seven plain, strong fiber suitcases
in the charge of the ship's first officer, which would
offer its own brief but beguiling alternative to pain,
sorrow, hunger, lust, loneliness and fear to at least
five million customers at a total street cost of 130
million dollars.

When Spina boarded the ship shortly after dawn,
the chief of customs trotting up the gangplank at
his side, he could hear the pop of rifle fire in the
eastern suburbs as the last of the government troops
took wild and nervous aim at anything that moved
before throwing their guns away and hitching lifts
homeward. Spina drank a *capucino* with the first officer, who was a cousin four times removed, thanked

him and relieved him of the seven suitcases; then he, the chief of customs and several deck hands carried the suitcases down to Spina's Cadillac waiting on the wharf.

On that bland, tropical morning of rattling winches, gulls screaming after ships' waste, the clank of church bells and shots coming nearer, a world was about to end for Spina. In his mind's eye he saw the chief of customs dressed in the gray pajamas of a long-term prisoner on the Isle of Pines. The night before he had telephoned the governor at the island penitentiary and arranged for Bonachea Leon to be transferred to the political wing, and for his name and documentation to be exchanged with that of a prisoner held without trial under some all-embracing charge as a security risk to the regime that was about to collapse. In return, the governor was to be paid in hospitality or cash in Miami, but Spina's sixth sense in such matters assured him that with his reputation for brutality, the man would never survive to collect his reward.

Weeks passed and all went well. Happy for any excuse to celebrate, Havana busied itself with celebration. Spina was on the streets with the rest of the citizenry, waving a flag whenever one was pushed into his hand, and always ready to stop and embrace any bearded young soldier he bumped into. He had little else to do but relax and enjoy himself, because the new goverment, apparently so happy-go-lucky at first, proved surprisingly efficient when it came to imposing security checks at ports and airfields, and heroin shipments to the United States had to be suspended while new ways and means of beating the system were devised. Almost all of Spina's contacts were now in prison, and a handful had already faced a firing squad in the dry moat under the inner wall of the Cabana fortress, positioned so that their last view of life on earth would embrace the colossal floodlit Christ dominating the profile of the structure.

For a month the seven suitcases were kept in a safe in Spina's office. Foreigners had remained exempt from the minor harassments suffered by Cuban nationals, but once again his instinct assured him that sooner or later things would get worse: bank safes would be opened, premises searched and investigations made into the motives of affluent foreigners who stayed on in the country without any obvious means of support. In an attempt to avoid attracting attention, he started a small business of exporting alligator skins to a dummy company in the States.

The idea of a suitable place for his heroin came to Spina one evening while he was looking out his window across the Columbus Cemetery. It was a small-scale city, with thirteen avenues crossed by seventeen streets: a magnificent ghetto of the dead in which the families of the rich and powerful were laid to rest in sumptuous vaults—often miniature versions of the splendid villas they had occupied in their lifetimes. In Havana the cult of the dead was hardly less strong than in Egypt under the Pharaohs. A number of vaults were supplied with expensive imported furniture and such comforts as television sets, and in a few air conditioning and electrically operated elevators had even been installed. Nor was the cemetery deserted like cemeteries elsewhere; the Cubans spent a good deal of time visiting their graves, and the well-lit streets were thronged, particularly on weekends and holidays, by cheerful crowds who, having deposited their fresh flowers, found this a pleasant place for an evening stroll and were in no particular hurry to leave.

The next day Spina visited the cemetery and discovered that though most of the vaults were well-kept and showed signs of having been freshly painted in recent years, a few seemed abandoned and even derelict. He made inquiries with the chief caretaker, who confirmed that some vaults had not been visited for decades, and added that these presented an embarrassment because they had been purchased outright and there was little that could be done to prevent them from becoming an eyesore. They were eager for such abandoned vaults to be taken over and refurbished, and were delighted to put Spina in touch with an agent. He soon tracked down an aged and bedridden woman in a provincial town who had inherited a vault from some distant relative whose name she could no longer remember, and which she was happy to sell. The deal was clinched on the spot. Spina took over the key, and shortly afterwards his ownership was inscribed in the cemetery's register under the name of Arturo de Baeza. Eight coffins of adults and eleven of children were found in the vault, and for a small fee the cemetery officials arranged for them to be dumped into the common ossuary. Spina ordered an extensive renovation of the building, both external and internal, and when it was completed three new coffins were brought bearing brass plates with the names Luisa, Simón and Pedro de Baeza, along with the heroin, which was contained in packing cases marked for furniture. Spina in person spent some hours transferring the heroin into the coffins, and then in manhandling them into three of the recesses in which the original coffins had rested.

The years that had transformed Don Vincente from a middle-aged American into an aging Sicilian made his voice hardly recognizable during the long-distance phone call Spina received the following day. Gone was the Mulberry Bend accent of old; croaking feebly at the end of a bad line, Don Vincente seemed about to relapse into dialect. "I got bad news about Victor. He got pounced on way back in December."

"For Chrissake, Vin. I never heard that. What happened?"

"He had a run-in with a bunch of Puerto Rican hoods. They knocked him around with pick handles. The poor kid spent two months in an intensive-care unit. He still has the wiring in his jaw."

"*Madonna troia!* Did you say Puerto Ricans?"

"That's right. I swear on the mourning of my sister, who died a virgin . . ."

Spina listened patiently while Don Vincente completed his oath to be avenged. "What can we do, Vin? What can we do? They got the organization these days. You make a big fuss, they're gonna burn your house."

Suddenly Spina, a cheerful man, felt sad and old.

He could hardly believe the day had actually come when a son of the once most feared Sicilian on the Eastern seaboard could get himself in a jam with a bunch of spics, with nobody there to lift a finger to save or avenge him. "Is the kid at home with you now?" he asked.

Don Vincente's voice echoed thin and senile through the static. "He went to stay with Mark Richards and his wife. Riccione, I mean—the guy you sent over to me. You won't believe me when I tell you why. Someone—I won't go into who—gave these Puerto Rican hoods the contract for the hit, and when they heard that Victor didn't croak after all, they sent a letter to say they'd be waiting for him as soon as he got out of the hospital. We figured he'd be safer downtown with Richards to look after him than up here in the woods with us."

"Holy shit! That's a terrible story, Vin. I never thought I'd live to see the day when a bunch of immigrants could start pushing us around."

"I can look after myself, Salva, as you well know, but I can't afford to take any chances with Vic. They didn't only bust his face in; it's his brain. He talks like he's an old man of eighty. The way it was explained to me, he's got fluid inside his skull. He can't stand without falling over. They had a coupla nurses at his bedside night and day keeping him alive with a drip in his arm and tubes up his nose for the first two weeks. When they took the bandages off and let me see him, I thought there was some mistake. 'You sure this is my son?' I said. All he could do was to babble at me. I cried like a kid."

"That must have been a terrible experience. I wish I could help out in some way, Vin."

"As a matter of fact, I'm hoping you can. Victor has been staying down at the Richards', but my gut tells me that the situation isn't as bright as it could be. Richards is a great guy, but the wife is hard to bear, and she hasn't exactly taken a shine to the kid."

"Whyncha send him down to me for a month or two, Vin? Maybe Richards could come along. Vic could lie around in the sun here and take it easy and get back his strength. Also they tell me they don't like Puerto Ricans much in this country."

"I was hoping you'd say that, Salva. Maybe I'll take you up on it. As soon as he's okay to travel, huh? Just for a month or two. Keep him out of harm's way."

"Victor's a bright kid," Spina said. "Sometimes I wonder if you know how bright that boy is. It'll be a pleasure to have him around."

Victor arrived three days later in the care of Mark Richards, to be settled by Spina out of harm's way on a dude ranch owned by a Cuban friend in Pinar del Rio. Here he slept late, practiced his pistol shooting on scavenging buzzards, took in a movie or cockfight in the evening, and surprised the management by ignoring the pretty unattached girls encouraged to frequent the bar and public rooms. In the calm, relaxing tropical climate he began a quick recovery. After a few days, he made friends with the owner of a garage in the nearest village who allowed him to spend some of his spare time doing minor servicing jobs on his customers' cars.

Mark took a room in the Sevilla, and a few hours after his arrival Spina called him to his office, overlooking the cemetery. As he took Spina's hand, he felt a tingling current travel from the point of contact into his forearm. "Don Salvatore," he said.

"Cut out the 'Don,'" Spina said. He reached up to embrace Mark's shoulders. "Nice of you to get down here so fast, Mark. What do you think about Vic?"

"He's going to be okay," Mark said.

"Sure he is. And let me tell you something else. He needed that beating, and it's gonna to do him a lot of good. I took a beating when I was his age. Eleven bones broken, and I was all the better for it. You know something? I learned some philosophy that way, and we can all do with as much as we can get of that." Spina's nut-brown face creased in a smile as he remembered with pride and affection the occasion when he had been pitched out of a car into a vacant lot and left for dead. The scars had healed and the agony had long been forgotten, but the episode had inoculated him with a bitter capacity for resistance which had never failed him since. "How do you think he'll turn out?" he asked.

"Okay," Mark said again.

"Okay, for Chrissake," Spina said. "Do you have to talk like an American all the time? I want to know what you really think."

Obediently, Mark switched his thinking processes into Italian to consider Victor's character, then translated his conclusions into English. "He has the old man's brains, and eventually he's going to be a good organizer. I'd as soon have him in back of me as anyone I know. He's quit being a blowhard, but he still lacks self-control. That's something he has to learn."

"You've told me all I need to know," Spina said. "That's how I figure him too. He could be useful to have around. I hear your wife didn't enjoy having him in your home. What's the matter with Teresa these days? Don Vincente seems to think you and she may be having difficulties."

"Some things we don't see eye to eye about," Mark said.

"Pity. She was a sweet kid. I remember her the way she was when I saw you off at Genova that time. Nice, and kind of shy."

"She still is, but we have a problem living where we do. Teresa wants to fit in, and she tries too hard."

"It's the change in climate," Spina said. "Salisbury is too cold in winter. Women can't take it; they have trouble with their female organs. Donna Carlotta used to be the same. She gave Don Vincente a terrible time until she got religion."

"Can you imagine my wife joining a citizens' defense committee?" Mark said. "Going around with a bunch of Jewish girls to hold protest meetings and picket City Hall?"

An expression of true compassion filtered through the finely reticulated skin of Spina's features. A friend's shame was his own. "You oughta get her out of there and go some other place," he said.

"Salisbury's where I work," Mark said. "I have a house around my neck that's too big for us. The bills have to be paid."

"You could do better, and don't tell me you couldn't," Spina said. "My information is that Don Vincente's practically retired. Why should you stay in Salisbury? You could pull out, take Teresa someplace she'd be happier, and do better for yourself at the same time."

"Maybe I will if the opportunity shows up."

"Great. That's what I wanted to hear. You got the opportunity right now. I want you to work for me. I need a *persona di fiducia*." He crossed the floor and grabbed Mark by the shoulders again. Mark rose, arm half out, unable to decide whether he was expected to return Spina's hug. "I want us to go into business together—you and me," Spina said. He made it sound like a command.

Mark looked down into the small, wizened face and felt the small paws on his shoulders. He smiled his embarrassment.

"As soon as the bearded man goes," Spina said, "we'd be all set to run this city between us. It's a great place." He gestured through the window at the white towers and skyscrapers against the distant sea, and the gaudy tombs of their immediate environment. Just below them, a party had arrived with flutes and guitars to serenade the dead. "The big money's going to flow again. I want to bring Victor in on this; that's why I wanted to hear what you thought of him. Maybe we could fix up a deal with Don Vincente to turn those hotels over to him. A year from now that kid could be the biggest casino operator in Cuba."

"Where would I come into this?" Mark asked.

"I need to have someone around I can trust. Not just a hard limb—a guy with brains and imagination who could deal with the really big problems when they come up. Mark, I have a big thing going down here. I guess you already know what my line of business is."

"I seem to have heard something."

Spina's thin high cackle sounded like the caw of a distant crow. "Still the old *diplomatico,* huh? I'm in junk and you know it, and I guess you've always known it. What I want to know is how you feel about it."

"They tell me I'm old-fashioned," Mark said.

"I've heard that too. What's the objection?"

Mark searched for a justification of what was now beginning to appear to him as a foolish personal prejudice. "Where I came from, junk was out. It's no more than that." He felt himself weakened, threatened with a loss of standing in Spina's eyes. "I worked for Don Vincente, and he didn't want his people to fool with it. What he said went."

"The world's changed," Spina said. "Nowadays half this continent blows pot, eats mesc or shoots up with smack. All I do is satisfy an existing demand. The situation is strictly the way it was in prohibition days. If we don't give these people what they're looking for, someone else will. Anyway, do you give a shit what happens to them?"

It was an opportunity to recover lost ground. Mark gave no more thought to what happened to drug addicts than he did to the inhabitants of Venus, if they existed. "Why should I?" he asked firmly.

"Where you and I came from people were too goddam smart to use dope. If these animals want to kill themselves, do we need to worry? I didn't create the market; it was there."

"I guess you're right," Mark said. Drug takers were fools, and he felt the same aversion for fools as others might feel for lawbreakers. Whatever their punishment, they earned it.

"Whaddaya say, then?"

"I'd have to rearrange my life. Give me a few days to think about it."

Spina nodded his understanding, but Mark felt the weight of his will power. The aging Capo Mafia now projected a mysterious force, like one of those professional illusionists who came to beguile the mountain villagers of Caltanissetta on the feast day of the Three Kings; those uncouth and insignificant men in near rags bent the minds of their audiences to their will, drugged them with absurd hope and dazzled them with visions of phoenixes and angels that vanished with the dawn.

"Take all the time you want," Spina said. "Right now things are quiet and I can get by, but maybe I'm going to need you soon, and when the moment comes I'd like to feel I can call on you."

Mark nodded. Nothing was more certain, he knew, than that when the call came he would be compelled to answer it.

2

Mark left Spina's office for an appointment at the new Ministry of National Reconstruction where he would discuss the future of Don Vincente's hotel interests with an official of the office dealing with sequestered foreign property. At this stage legal nationalization was not complete, and the foreign capitalists who remained in Havana were doing all they could by arguments, appeals and delays to postpone the final calamity, in the belief that when and if the new regime toppled, those businesses that had not been transferred to the state could be smoothly restarted without legal complications over change of ownership. Like any other representative of foreign investments, Mark was prepared to clutch at straws of hope; there was nothing to be lost. He had a couple of spare days in the city, and he might as well use his time in a way which could ultimately benefit his old employer.

As soon as he had gone, Spina locked up for the day, took a taxi to the top of the Prado, where he dismissed it and turned into the Calle Animas, his favorite street in the world. He walked slowly in the warm, spiced air under a twittering ceiling of unseen birds that were never allowed by the noise of Havana to sleep. The Cuban crowd, out for their evening stroll, reminded him of the chorus of a musical which at any moment would break into a song-and-dance number. He was woven into a pattern of beautiful women who discussed among themselves the day's events in eloquent mime and scented the air with their flesh. Fans fluttered softly above the mosiac pavement of the street, and a filigree of shadows stirred like foliage as the streetlamps, suspended on chains, moved in the breeze.

Spina was on his way to the Buena Sombra, the town's leading *maison de rendezvous* which had fallen on lean times, and which he had picked up at a bargain price. He had been driven by cold economics to make drugs his livelihood, but his natural bent was toward anything to do with the female sex. He loved the company of women, and on the whole women responded to his admiration and liked him in return. The easiest way to involve himself in the lives of as many women as possible was by organized prostitution, in which, by his standards, there was little money but huge enjoyment.

In this field, Havana offered exceptional opportunities. The supply of beautiful but needy women was abundant, and the market limitless, but the organization was primitive. Havana's brothels were so situated that a tourist had to be blind drunk before he could be dragged inside to face their lavatory tiling, the sinister crones who took their money, and the whiff of antiseptic and stale towels. Cubans of the lower class went to these places, and at times of peak traffic when lines formed, would be called upon by the old woman in charge to prepare themselves with their hands for what was to come.

These dismal facilities left the rich potential tourist market untapped, and it was to this that Spina was applying his genius. He took over six establishments, got rid of the tiles, suppressed the sound of flushed cisterns and installed dim, comfortable American bars, complete with pleasant hostesses perched on stools sipping colored water. They charged customers five times what they had paid before, but they no

longer wriggled from under them to reach for the
douche can when the buzzer operated by the hag
downstairs sounded the end of the allotted fifteen
minutes.

Statistics by agents employed in a survey convinced
Spina of the vast potentialities of the call girl system.
He was staggered to be informed by men who knew
the local flesh trade inside out that an estimated fifty
percent of the nubile female population of Havana
were ready, on occasion, to sell themselves for sums
as low as five dollars, and that nobody thought anything
of it. The practice, he was told, was widespread among
normally respectable housewives when their husbands
were out of work and money was tight, and among
badly paid shopgirls, cleaners and laundresses, to
whom sums of this kind were irresistible windfalls.

Hence, in his spare time, just as another man might
have occupied himself with some relaxing hobby like
carpentry or breeding orchids, Spina had begun the
organization of this eager material, compiling a central catalog from which addresses, phone numbers,
physical statistics and photographs were made available to contacts working on commission in every
hotel. Ninety percent of these ladies were colored—
referred to affectionately by Spina as "caramel ass"
—but some customers preferred and were ready to
pay for whites, and it was to meet this demand that he
acquired the Buena Sombra. Ruled over by a cul-
tured and aristocratic old lady, it offered as its specialty white girls from the depressed middle class,
but now it had been hard hit by the times and the
fact that many rich Cubans mistrusted the intentions of
the new government and were beginning to leave
the country.

The entrance to the Buena Sombra was unimposing,
a narrow doorway between a shoeshop and a bank.
Spina pressed the bell and was let in by a maid, a
lively mulatto child with eyes too big for her face.
She went to announce him and Spina called after
her, "Hey, you, Big-Eyes, come back here. Speak
English? What's your name?"

"Dolores, sir. At your service."

"At your service, huh? That's nice. How old are you?"

"Thirteen, sir."

Spina used two fingers to pluck a five-dollar bill out of the breast pocket of his many-pleated Cuban shirt and gave it to her. To his delight, she curtsied.

"Someone has you pretty well trained, Dolores. Okay, go tell the señora I'm here."

The place cried out for a new broom, he thought. The house had been built around a patio, and it was dark and old-fashioned, with too many tarnished mirrors and oil paintings on torn canvas. Attracted by the splash of the fountain in the center of the patio, he noted that even the goldfish circulating sluggishly in the basin had a bleached, elderly look about them. Too many coats of arms and too little life, light and music. The old madam, supposedly the granddaughter of a general, a witch with a yellow wig and a million powder-clogged wrinkles, had turned the reception room, which should have been cheerful and reassuring to the visitor, into a cavern full of her broken furniture. The worst thing about the house had been the señora's twelve tomcats. Spina had a phobia about cats, disliking even the sleek and well-fed pets to be found in most American homes, and the Cuban breed—skinny, long-legged with prominent testicles, tiny evil faces, and given to bald patches where the fur refused to grow over diseased or damaged skin—filled him with active disgust. At their first meeting he made his aversion plain. "The cats are out, señora."

"Señor Spina, they're my family. It will be hard to let them go."

Spina pressed his handkerchief to his nose. "I have to say this plainly. The place stinks. You can keep birds. Buy yourself a dog if you like. If you want to keep your cats, you'll have to take them some other place."

"Very well, Señor Spina." She was offended, but it couldn't be helped. She had the reputation of being honest and a good business woman, but she had to be shown who was boss.

"I'm prepared to give this a whirl, señora, if things are done my way. Throw the cats out in the street where they belong, and have someone give the house a good cleaning, then leave the windows open. I'll stop by in a day or two and see how things are going."

This time there were no cats in sight, and he was ready to talk about his plans.

"Times have changed," he said to the señora after she had greeted him and offered him coffee, "and we have to move with them. Your figures are down again this month. We have to do something to drum up more business."

"The house has its reputation to consider," she said. "Our clientele is conservative. Too drastic changes might be resented."

Spina sniffed the air. "What's that I smell?"

"Perfumed spray, Señor Spina. I had the house cleaned as you instructed. The spray was to remove any stale odors."

"I thought I could still smell cats," he said. "Now to get back to the matter of the clientele, señora. What you have to realize is that the aristocracy of this island is dying out. How many customers, for example, have you had today?"

"Monday is never a good day. However, we were honored by a visit from the Marqués de Santa Anna." Pronouncing the name, the señora dropped her voice to a reverent hush.

"And how long did the Marqués stay?"

"He was with us for the best part of the afternoon."

"May I ask what charge was made for the visit?"

She explained gently, "We do not speak of it as a charge. A guest may leave whatever he thinks fit." She lifted his coffee cup to straighten the finely decorated cambric doily it rested upon.

"That's half the trouble. How much did the guest think fit to leave in this case?"

"Twenty-five dollars."

"By the standards of the past a lot of money," he said. "In these days nothing. Some of the best-heeled tourists in the world come to this island. In the time your girl put in with Santa Anna, she could have entertained three or four of them." He chose his words carefully, doing his best to avoid offense. He was a man who smiled continually, even when a bearer of bad news.

The señora controlled herself with a small, desolate movement of the hand, as if waving away smoke; none of the revulsion she felt at the vulgarity of Spina's timetable showed through the screen of wrinkles. "I'm afraid that the young lady who was with the Marqués would not have consented, as you put it, to entertain three or four tourists in an afternoon."

"Excuse me, señora, I don't understand." Faced with a situation quite new to his experience, Spina checked an urge to burst into laughter. "Is this a sporting house or isn't it?"

"All the girls on our books have the elegance and style that are attractive to a man of breeding," she said.

"Can I see a picture of the one the Marqués goes for?"

"Certainly." She took a photograph from the pile that clients made their selection from.

To Spina there was something familiar about it. "Have I seen this one before?"

"No, Señor Spina."

It was a soft-focus, high-key portrait of a kind that had been out of fashion for twenty years. Set against a background of radiant mist, the face could have been that of a movie actress back in the thirties —Alice Faye, perhaps.

"A very deserving girl," the señora said, "with a tragic history. She lost her husband in the revolution. Put up against a wall and shot summarily. It's happened to so many. She speaks perfect English."

"Is this all you keep in the way of pictures?" he asked. "Don't the people who come here expect to see something in the buff?"

The señora's mouth, a lifeless hole in her mask of lizard skin, trembled, but she said nothing.

"I'd like to talk to this girl," Spina said. "Tell her to come around. Maybe we can read some poetry together." This face from the past interested him.

"I'll telephone her and see if she's free," the señora said. "This may be an inconvenient time; if not, she'll be here in half an hour."

"Okay. Now let's talk about the future. As I've already indicated, everything here is going to be changed. I'm going to pull this dump apart and put it together again. The Buena Sombra is going to have a face lift—music, a nice bar with hostesses, a dance floor, a welcoming atmosphere. Maybe the Marqués won't go for it by the time we've finished, but the tourists from the cruise ships will beat a path to this door. I'm going to have to see all the girls on your list and give them the once-over personally to make sure they're suitable for the kind of setup I have in mind. If I decide to take them on, there's only one thing they have to remember—that they're professionals. They're in this for a living, and they have a job to do, just like anyone else."

The señora listened, staring down at her stiff, arthritic fingers. "And how do I fit into this new scheme of things, Señor Spina?"

"Just like I said. Maybe we can work together. I hope we can, and if so, all well and good. If not—well, I don't have to tell you . . ."

She nodded in silent submission. A single tear rolled over a lid and was immediately absorbed in the fissured terrain of wrinkles.

"If you stay on, you'll have to get used to being in the background," Spina said. "Maybe I can fix up an office for you upstairs. We'll be needing this room. You'd have to store all this junk someplace else."

Spina's encounter with Maria de Mora, the star attraction of the Buena Sombra, was not a success. Though still vigorous and sexually active at fifty-five, his appetites craved more and more the stimulation of youth, and Maria, who in the flesh bore little resemblance to her nostalgic portrait, was no longer as young as she had been. She was thin and stiff, with fine, passionless features, grief-ridden eyes and a face full of distant thoughts. The engorgement in the blood vessels of Spina's loins subsided as he faced this reality. He took Maria's arm, which was as rigid as a plaster of Paris cast, to steer her toward the room indicated, with the señora smiling terribly and clucking her encouragement in the rear.

The room reminded him of the best bedroom in a fourth-rate hotel in New Orleans: a fourposter, massive, contorted furniture, gloom-soaked surfaces and an odor under the thin disguise of perfumed aerosol that was almost certainly tomcat. Maria, hands in lap and brooding with withdrawn eyes, sat on the edge of the bed. When the little maid, Dolores, with skipping steps and bold young breasts brought them thimblefuls of coffee and saffron cakes, Spina pinched her cheek and patted her bottom as she left.

He did his best to break the ice with Maria. "You're a pretty girl. Nice hair, nice eyes. How old are you?"

"Twenty-six."

"The señora told me you lost your husband."

"He was killed in the revolution."

"That's too bad. I guess it makes life hard for you. Any family?"

"Only my mother." Her eyes were resolutely averted and his questions were answered flatly, almost with resentment.

"Listen, Maria," Spina said, "I happen to own this joint, but right now you can consider me as just another customer who was shown your picture and liked what he saw. Go ahead and treat me like one."

There was no sign on her sorrowing profile that she had heard. He had the impression that if he'd taken her arm and yanked it out straight it would have stayed in that position.

"The señora tells me this is the second time you've been asked for today." He let his hand drop on her knee.

She reacted immediately, as if in self-defense. "I do not come here often. The person I saw today was an old friend. We chose to meet here because it is convenient for us." She spoke through her teeth with little movement of the lips.

"Lady," he said, "I'm a customer who wants to go

to bed with you. I'm some guy with money to blow who was sent here by a good friend in the purser's office of a cruise ship that just got into port. I'm in Bethlehem Steel with a wife and family at home. I've never stepped out before, but now I'm in the market for a little romance before it's too late. What I need is the encouragement of a warm and affectionate woman. Even if I depress the hell out of you, you gotta find some way not to show it."

"You want me to take my clothes off?" she said.

"Hell, yes, Maria, or I want you to encourage me to do it for you. As it is, you have me feeling nervous. I get the impression that if I lay a hand on you I'm gonna get slapped down."

She rose, her face like an ivory carving, turned away, and began to pull off her dress and slip in series of awkward disjointed postures. When nothing but pants and bra remained she hunched herself defensively, like a swimmer facing a plunge into a cold sea. Studying her body with connoisseurship, Spina sensed that it had been rarely displayed. If those buttocks had been caressed, it had been in the dark. There was a ghostliness to the skin, and when he took her in his arms and parted her thighs, her sex seemed to shrink away like the sensitive mouth of a sea anemone from the probing of his finger. What the hell do some of these classy Cubans do when they get into bed? he asked himself. Living in the past. A hundred years back.

Ten minutes later, Spina confronted the señora again.

"You didn't want to stay with her?"

"No," he said, "and I doubt whether anybody else would have except the Marqués."

"Señor Spina, please tell me what was wrong."

"The room stank," he said. "It stank of cat so bad that I wanted to gag."

"I can't understand it," she said. "It was washed out most thoroughly."

"Some goddam tomcat left its trademark all over the legs of the furniture. Besides which, your friend was a lady, and ladies don't fit into this business.

What's needed is a willingness to work, plus a little show of enthusiasm, even if you don't feel it."

"Señor Spina, I'll call someone else. A very sweet girl, much younger than Maria. I could have her around in ten minutes."

"That's okay," he said. "One experience like that is enough for today. I wouldn't want to risk another."

"This is different. Something you'll never forget. Are you still staying at the Sevilla? I'll send her to your hotel."

"Some other time, maybe."

She'll have to go, he thought, and I may as well tell her now. He was considering the best way to break the news to her when something moved in the clutter of furniture around his legs and a huge gray cat sprang into his lap. He jumped to his feet with a screech of horror. The cat hung on by its claws for a moment, then dropped to the ground, and Spina kicked it across the room. He showed his fury in a terrible smiling calm. "Okay, señora," he said, "I guess that's it."

She knew she was finished, and now she added hatred to the contempt she had previously felt for him. Brushed away as she tried to accompany him to the door, she slumped back in her chair and watched his quick, stealthy fumble with Dolores' body as the little maid let him out. It was at the sight of this that a plan for revenge was hatched in her mind.

Spina turned his face to the night, the milk-soft air, the cigar ends crushed on the mosaic pavement, the buildings carved in tusk, the gay, multicolored advertisements for soft drinks and cigarettes. The city had composed itself for its mighty encounter with its dreams, every beggar like a sentry at his post, a defeated army of lottery-ticket vendors drifting homeward under the banners of their unsold tickets, and the men who waited to occupy the chairs, padlocked and abandoned by the bootblacks, already in possession and asleep.

A man of organization, Spina had come to admire and love the order and finely adjusted sense of time of this filigree civilization. Havana offered its pleasures to him like a basket of choice fruit. The insurgents had come intending to demolish the symmetry of its arrangement, but he believed that whatever damage they did would be temporary, and in the long run they would be defeated. All he had to do was use his head, lie low, offer a ready and genial compliance to authority and keep out of trouble. In the end the sweet life would return, and when it did Cuba would belong not to those who had shed their blood to win it back, but to the syndicates, with himself at their head. As he saw it, the momentary cooling of the climate was not a bad thing; already it had frightened away the small-time mobsters from Florida who were now in the mood to sell out their interests to men of his own caliber who saw themselves staying the course.

He saw light at the end of the tunnel. In a quick trip to Turkey he had recently secured an option on the greater part of the country's opium production for the next three years, and he was about to extend his operations to the Far East, with his contacts now busy among the tribesmen of Laos and northern Burma. The belief, always at the back of his mind, that sooner or later he would take over Don Vincente's hotel and casino empire in Cuba had become more concrete with the calamity suffered by Victor. Spina knew that Victor hero-worshiped him, and by Don Vincente's account he would be even more ready to submit to guidance in the future than in the past.

He was happy also to have sealed, as he believed, an unspoken bond with Mark Richards. He had sensed in Mark the need to devote his service to a man he admired—a need equaled only by Spina's for inflexible loyalty of such a man as Richards. He saw Mark as eventually taking charge of all the details of the organization he proposed to build, leaving himself free to devote his energies to the great coups that lay ahead. In case of difficulty with the U.S.

government, the mysterious Bradley could be called in. Spina had never been able to understand just who Bradley was, but even if he was not prepared to accept the frequent hints that Bradley had the President's ear, there was no mistaking the reality of his power. Someday, Spina knew, Bradley would present his bill for the favors already rendered.

The last newspaper sellers with the last of the evening editions were on all the street corners. He bought the English-language *Post,* but thrust it into his pocket without even troubling to read the headlines, and was therefore unaware that on this day the new government had announced its determination to crack down on vice. In the Prado he paused a moment to shake hands with a brace of bowlegged little soldiers, returning on late leave from a Coca-Cola orgy. A squad of militia girls in green uniforms whom he had seen drilling earlier in the day, presenting and ordering arms, marching and counter-marching, boobs bouncing, to the orders of a coal-black sergeant, were now climbing onto a bus to be taken home. It was another sign of the times—the bad times. But they would pass.

Spina had taken over the suite in the Sevilla previously tenanted by Cobbold, and the moment he pushed through the hotel's swing doors he noted that in the passage of a single day things had got a little worse. A vast oil painting of a ship called the *Marie Celeste,* shown with the Morro Castle in the background, had been taken down and replaced with a propaganda poster about illiteracy, and in the past twenty-four hours half the hotel's gambling room had been screened off and filled with desks and a blackboard, in readiness for the staff to receive lessons in mathematics. A pretty girl handed him a leaflet inviting him to help in the nation's coffee-picking drive, for which no reward was offered other than praise, and he smiled and bowed. Though an abstemious man, Spina enjoyed brandy before turning in, and he went into the bar and ordered a Rémy Martin. The bar was full of bearded officers with silver bullets worn on chains around their necks. They were an affable collection, and as always he shook hands with them and bought a drink for anyone who would accept. Then he went to bed.

It was twelve-thirty, and he was on the point of ringing down for a laundress when there was a knock on his door and Dolores was there with the room boy. She showed not the slightest signs of shyness. A great kid, he thought, willing and affectionate. He felt fatherly toward her, but not for long. He knew barely a dozen words of Spanish, but as far as he could make out from the few he could understand, together with her lively mime, she was a present from the señora. Crafty old witch, he thought; as if that's going to do her any good.

But when the Public Morality Squad arrived shortly after, he knew that the old señora had won after all. A young inspectress told Dolores to get her clothes on, and carried her off to a rehabilitation center where she would remain for a year. Spina was given half an hour to get his portable possessions together, and then was escorted by two policemen to the airport.

Cool and resolute in any emergency, Spina was a man whose sang-froid rarely left him. The only person who might have been able to save him, he believed, was Bradley, but when he called the number Bradley had given him, Ferguson answered the phone and told him curtly that Bradley was out of the country. "I'll be in Nassau," Spina said. "Ask him to call me at the Cumberland House." Ferguson hung up.

The two policemen stayed with him for the next six hours in the airport departure lounge. They breakfasted together in an amicable fashion, the two men anxious to practice their English on an American, eagerly noting down new words and phrases. At nine A.M. the plane took off.

It was a setback, but Spina was not discouraged. Whereas before he had been prepared to go along with the regime and wait until somebody else pushed it over, he was now personally committed to its overthrow. He had five million dollars salted away in a bank in Nassau in preparation for any unforeseen emergency.

3

After a few days in the Bahamas, Spina moved down to Antigua, a quiet and orderly island devoted to the American tourist and his dollar. Here, a week later, Victor joined him.

They took rooms in the Galleon Bay Hotel Casino, where Spina could relax in an atmosphere that was as close to that of his beloved Cuba as he had ever found. The Casino was run according to the accepted Cuban pattern, with a variety of rigged games; woman dealers working with marked cards at the blackjack tables, mercury-loaded dice, "mechanics" to set up and control the various operations, prostitutes imported from New England, camouflaged as bored daughters of the rich, and cool-off men—specialists in the psychology of loss—who could calm a victim and send him home to Great Neck dazed but still smiling. Spina, a compulsive player who knew all the angles of crooked gambling, lost money in rigged games in exactly the same, effortless way as any hypnotized tycoon who had been induced to come on a "junket," and he was happily played for a sucker by more than one of the prostitutes brought in to admire brave losers and encourage them further along the road to ruin.

The weeks passed pleasantly. He lived on shellfish and raw eggs in brandy to keep up his vigor, was able to entertain a harlot most nights, and lost a thousand dollars a day at the tables. Daily he swam a few strokes for health's sake in the tepid sea, and exposed his skin, now wrinkled like the bark of an old crab apple, to the beneficent sun. He hired a 160-ton schooner with a crew of nine drunken Dutchmen, and kept it in English Harbour. Every other night he gave a party for the girls off duty at the Casino, and any sampling of what was locally known as beach pussy that happened to catch his eye. Offered a choice of sleeping companions that would have excited a pasha, Victor remained indifferent.

Spina was alarmed at this. "What happened, Vic? You still got both your balls?"

"I feel kind of tired all the time, that's all. Give me another coupla weeks and I'll be okay."

And it was obvious that Victor was improving. Every day the jumpiness and paranoia shrank. He no longer complained that people nudged each other and stared when he came into a room. The ticking in his head that he'd had to listen to for so many months had stopped, and the double vision had gone. His slurred speech had sharpened, the trembling had left his hands, and it was only when he was tired that any evidence of a limp still showed.

Plagued with loneliness, Spina felt real affection for Victor, a liking based not so much on observation as on intuition, which he believed never let him down. To be in a man's company for five minutes was all he needed to accept or reject him. He would never have been able to articulate what it was about Victor that appealed to him, but dimly in his animal-instinct way he sensed strength behind the weakness of Victor's presence, a capacity for loyalty and an iron determination.

"What do you want to do today, Vic?" he would ask.

The answer was usually the same. "Do you want to play cards or something, Salva?"

"Hell, no. Everything in that dump is in the bag. I'm tired of being suckered by those shysters."

"Maybe we could go for a ride in the boat, then."

This was Victor's idea of pleasure. They would wake up the captain, tell him to collect the crew from the bar of the Admiral's Inn, and then sail the yacht a few miles up the coast. Often they would attract a school of dolphins, and they would sit in chairs in the stern taking pot shots at them with Victor's .38 Police Special. Spina was a bad shot and rarely made a hit, but usually sudden streamers of blood flowing away in the water behind the leaping and cavorting animals showed that Victor's bullet had struck home.

The improvement in Victor's condition continued, and was marked by an encouraging growth of restlessness.

"Salva, I'd like to do something to earn my keep. Maybe I could work for you. Couldn't we set up a game someplace and skim off some of the sucker money?"

"What you see here is nothing," Spina said. "This is a small operation, strictly a grind. These guys are busting their asses to pull down a few thousand a week. You have to think in millions. Take it easy, Vic. Our time will come."

"I'd like to get started on something. The way I feel these days I could take on anything."

"Be patient," Spina said. "Relax. I already told you, you and me are going into business together as soon as the setup over in Cuba changes. I might as well tell you that it looks like we got a third partner—none other than our old friend Mark Richards."

"You're kidding."

"No shit, Victor baby. This is on the level. I talked to him about a proposition the other day. We gotta tie up one or two details, but it looks like he's gonna say yes. Whaddaya say?"

"That's the greatest news ever. Mark's one helluva guy. Listen, Salva, he's positively the greatest."

"He's the best man I know to have in back of you when things get tough."

"You know something, Mark doesn't talk too much. You don't hear him shooting off his mouth, but he sure gets things done. The action's there."

"Even more than you realize, Victor boy, even more than you realize. The way I have it planned, in a month or two you and me and Mark are going back to Cuba again, and we're gonna clean up."

"As soon as the bearded man goes, huh?"

"As soon as the bearded man is out. We'll be aboard the first plane bound for Havana to leave this island. And let me tell you, Victor boy, we're going to reorganize that city. What you've seen here is for the birds. Las Vegas won't have anything on Havana when we get through organizing it."

"I don't see how I'm gonna be much help to you, Salva, but I'll sure do my best."

"I know, and we'll be a great team together. But what I'm telling you is that you have to take it easy for a while longer, because we gotta be sure you're okay before we hit the big time down there."

"I'm okay now," Victor said. "I've never felt better."

"I'll believe that when I see you going after the tail," Spina said. "How about a trip on the boat this afternoon?"

"Sure thing. Let's go and knock off a few dolphins."

The yacht trip that day was marked by a small adventure. Recently, Spina had been taking, along with the sandwiches, a pretty, vapid colored girl who had worked as a stewardess and gotten as far as the preliminaries of the Miss World contest the previous year. One of the Dutch crew, a young man from Leyden who was number two in the engine room, had fallen idealistically in love with what he saw as this captive of white slavers, and had been drunk for a week.

While the yacht was moving out to sea, Spina in his chair was enjoying the beauty of English Harbour and in an absent fashion was caressing the rump of the girl, who had just brought him a lime squash. A clutter of footsteps distracted him, as the infatuated Dutchman appeared at the top of the companionway, slobbering with rage and brandishing a beer bottle.

"Hey, you. Dirty dago man. Take your hands off dat girl."

Spina stopped looking at the view, and turned his head slightly to observe the Dutchman's weaving approach. The girl tried to slip away, and he grabbed her firmly by the arm.

"Didja hear what I said, mister?"

The Dutchman came on, raising the bottle over his head, and Spina sat quietly and watched him with curiosity. When only three yards separated the men, Victor stepped between them. The Dutchman made a feeble pretense of a swipe at Victor's head, then his arm dropped. Victor looked at him in silence, hands still in his pockets, and the sailor backed away.

"Looks like you picked up some of your old man's style after all," Spina said casually later.

Because of the wind and tide, it was not a good day for dolphins, but in the end a live target presented itself in the shape of a booby that came flapping down out of the fleecy sky to alight on the mast. Spina, who had the gun at this moment, leveled it, screwed up his left eye, fired and damaged a wing, and the bird tumbled from its perch and fell into the sea. It paddled away trailing the broken wing and Spina handed the gun to Victor, who killed it with a perfect shot high in the breast at twenty yards. A piece of down was snatched away by the breeze as the booby's trim, swanlike shape collapsed in a mound of waterlogged feathers. Spina laughed with delight.

Later that afternoon, roused from a deck-chair nap, he went in search of Victor and found him in his unlocked cabin with the beauty queen, who darted naked into the wardrobe. He was overjoyed. Nothing could have proved with more certainty that Victor was restored to normality.

The next morning an expected emissary from Bradley in Cuba arrived, and after a long discussion Spina agreed to a remarkable deal.

"You'll be performing a patriotic service, Mr. Spina," Ferguson said. "What value do you put on the goods in question?"

"In Cuba, d'ya mean, where they are right now? Hell, that's anybody's guess. Delivered in the U.S., you could say ten million dollars to the trade in a quick sale."

"Of which you'd be willing to donate half—that is, five million—to the Save Cuba campaign funds."

"That's what I said. If Mr. Bradley gave me his guarantee. I'm as interested as he is in saving Cuba. Your friends could buy themselves a few jets with that kind of money."

"Let's hope they can," Ferguson said.

"I need Bradley's help to get this stuff out. It's no good to me where it is."

"I'm quite sure that Mr. Bradley will be able to help." He countered Spina's genial, tooth-revealing grin with the quiet half-smile that had become a habit, and which reminded Bradley of a baby troubled with wind. So this was what lay at the kernel of evil, Ferguson thought. This amiable, wizened man praised by so many people who had been close to him for his generosity, his capacity for friendship, the mildness and courtesy with which he habitually treated his inferiors, his courage, the stoicism with which he faced adversity.

Ferguson was now a follower of Hinayanist Buddhism of the Little Vehicle, where he had taken refuge when no longer able to live in peace with the betrayals and deceits of his profession. He had become a vegetarian who slept on a plank, and in benign consideration for life in all its forms would not even allow his servant to use an anti-fly spray in his flat. In a few months' time it was his unannounced intention to leave the Agency and begin a peregrination through those countries of the Far East that still conserved the faith in its pure form: Burma, Laos, Ceylon. Before he did so he proposed to make a special contribution to the welfare of humanity, but since all his training had been in the methods of secrecy and subterfuge, his plan would have to be carried out in the only way his qualifications had prepared him for. Employing whatever guile, duplicity, ruse or trick the occasion might demand, Ferguson was prepared to disrupt this alliance between Spina and his chief.

Spina was not quite sure what to make of Ferguson, but it was quite clear that he was not on the make. The man refused everything: food, drink, a pressing invitation to stay a few days and experience the lavish hospitality of the Galleon Bay Hotel Casino. "This joint draws the broads like flies," Spina said. "They're nutty about the mob guys who fix the games. If you're interested, it's all on the house. White, caramel-ass—it's all the same. If you see anything you like, all you have to do is crook your finger and mention my name."

"I'd be most happy to take you up on that," Ferguson said, "were time not so pressing." The limitless toleration enjoyed by the discipline of the Middle Way ruled out feeling, much less showing contempt. Ferguson had trained himself to feel nothing but compassion for such men as Bradley and Spina, trapped in the predicament of a cruel dharma, whose souls were destined to be reincarnated in some low animal form such as slugs or sewer rats. "At any other time, I'd have been happy," he added politely.

"Make it next time you come over," Spina said. "I'm sure you'll be back before long."

"I sincerely hope so, Mr. Spina."

"And I'm to take it that the deal's on."

"Most assuredly," Ferguson said. "I will now report back forthwith to Mr. Bradley, and I've no doubt at all that he'll set the wheels in motion. If there are any minor details that need attending to, we'll be in touch."

"It's been nice knowing you, Ferguson," Spina said. "And don't forget, when you want a night of fun, you always have one waiting for you right here."

4

"I can hardly believe it," Bradley said. "So all went well."

"Couldn't have gone better," Ferguson said. "Let me pour you a drink. How about a nice fresh pineapple juice?"

"That will be fine."

"You must be out on your feet."

"Slightly punch-drunk, maybe, from sitting around in planes. It's good to be back in Havana, I still like this place."

Ferguson filled a glass with pineapple juice from a jug and handed it to him. Bradley was about to sip the juice when he noticed a small fly afloat on its surface and put the glass down. "Seem to be a lot of flies in this apartment."

"They're always a little trying at this time of year. I learn to live with them. The mosquitoes are a bit of a problem too. Come out in clouds in the evening."

"Unhygienic. Flies all over the place," Bradley said. "Don't you suffer from stomach trouble?"

"A little diarrhea once in a while," Ferguson said with a soft laugh. "Nothing to trouble about."

"To get back to the news," Bradley said, "it's the best in years. I begin to see the light at the end of the tunnel. It's been a long dark night. And how did you find the great Spina in the flesh? I remember you always wanted to meet him."

"He was ordinary," Ferguson said. "I'd always expected that kind of killer to look like one, but he didn't. He was just an ordinary little man caught in the snare of his own fleshly desires."

Bradley shot him an amused glance. "He's quite a guy for the girls, isn't he? Despite his advanced years. The important thing from our point of view is that his word is his bond. If he says five million,

226

that's what he means. The money will be paid as soon as we've done our part."

"Seems strange, doesn't it, that a criminal's word can apparently be more binding than that of the average law-abiding individual," Ferguson said.

"But so often it's the case. Men like Spina are very complex. However, so far so good. What I'd like to do now is toss the rest of this operation in your lap. The trouble is, I'm due back with the pool-room cowboys in Guatemala tomorrow. In the hope you'd be able to bring the deal off, I got all the preliminaries going here so that there won't be much to do. I made out the forms before you left, so all you have to do is to take them to customs. When you have clearance, you merely present yourself at the Columbus Cemetery, ask to see the *jefe,* who happens to be a personal friend of mine, and hand over the letter of authorization and the vault key. He'll look after the rest, and provide transport to the airport."

"You don't want me to check about the plane?"

"It isn't necessary. As a matter of fact, the less fussing around the better. You're finished as soon as you hand over the letter and the key."

"And we can be quite certain that customs will let the shipment go through as easily as that?"

"Why shouldn't they? There's no reason for suspicion. They have a regular two-way traffic in stiffs. We have about two million Cuban families in the States. Those people have a special attitude toward their dead, and nothing's more natural than to want to have their father's and mother's bodies dug up and transported when they feel settled down and aren't likely to go back. Cubans who move to Cuba from the States do the same thing. Customs won't open any old coffins."

"It doesn't sound as though we're doing too much for our five million."

"You're right," Bradley said, "but we're the only connection Spina has over here now. It has to be this or nothing. Also, he knows we won't double-cross him."

He was about to add more assurances as to the

simplicity and foolproof character of the operation when his eye was suddenly taken by a small movement on the floor near his left foot. Looking closer, he saw an enormous cockroach. He lifted his shoe and brought it down carefully, hoping to crush the insect without actually making a mess on the floor. It cracked under his sole, but with a desperate vitality under the broken armor-plating of its shell it scurried along, leaving a pink slobber on the tiles. Bradley's foot came down again, and this time there was a squelch. A couple of yards away another beetle, even more monstrously large, came into sight through the legs of the chair, and he jumped up and made for it.

"Could I possibly ask you not to, Ronald," Ferguson said.

Bradley laughed apologetically, then pursed his lips and sat down while the cockroach ambled past and disappeared under a settee. "Sorry," he said. "I was quite forgetting. It *was* Buddhism you took up, wasn't it?"

"Correct," Ferguson said.

"The trouble is, one always tends to expect some sort of robe and a shaven head. You don't look the part, Alistair. I notice you've even stopped wearing sandals."

"I don't feel it necessary to advertise my inward and spiritual state," Ferguson said. He had administered to himself a quick reproof for the flash of anger he had felt, and his face was once again composed and wearing the half-smile Bradley found so foolish.

"But being a Buddhist you wouldn't even kill a cockroach."

"No, you wouldn't," Ferguson said with compelling sincerity. "Because the cockroach you destroyed might well be, say, your grandfather in another incarnation."

Bradley checked an impulse to try to make a joke out of it. The man was absolutely serious.

"I felt sick when you did that just now," Ferguson said. "To me it was an interference with purpose—like throwing a wrench into a wonderfully intricate piece of machinery."

"It was very stupid of me," Bradley said. "I'm afraid I didn't realize. All of us in our different ways are groping toward the same distant ideal. Another man's religious views always interest me deeply. I'll go no further than that; they even excite me if they're sincerely held. Even if it so happens I don't share them myself. If I have any reservation, Alistair, as far as you're concerned, it's that as a result of your beliefs you don't eat enough for a kitten. You're all skin and bone."

Ferguson nodded his acceptance of the compliment. "I'm the correct weight for my height, maybe a pound or two less. Fasting clears the brain."

"And reduces the carnal appetites, huh?"

"To some extent, yes. Which is all to the good."

"Well, I'm sorry about the cockroach. So you're a practicing Buddhist, Alistair, and you won't take life in any form if you can help it. Do you know something? It all sounds kind of fantastic. I can hardly believe this now, but there used to be talk of grooming you to be the tough guy of the outfit. When I heard you were interested in Oriental techniques, I thought they meant something like karate."

"Methods of self-defense certainly provided an introduction to Eastern thought. I was interested in judo and ceremonial swordsmanship for a short time, but these were soon diverted into other paths. It seems to me to have been a natural process of development."

"Tell me, do you feel any difficulties in reconciling your personal convictions with your job?"

Ferguson gave earnest consideration to the question. "As of this moment, no. In the past, perhaps yes. I have to admit that I suffered from misgivings."

"Anyway, you've came to a satisfactory working arrangement with yourself."

"I think so. As far as anyone ever does."

"How did you manage it, Alistair?"

"It's too complicated and personal a thing to be able to explain. Muck exists everywhere on the phys-

ical plane. It isn't always possible to avoid contact
with it. The question is to avoid defilement."

Bradley laughed. "I'm not at all sure how I
should take that. Frankly, I'd be very worried if
your newly found religious attitude ever appeared
to be competing with your allegiance to your professional code, because if that were so, your only
course would be to resign. Our profession is one
that calls for commitment and its own kind of religious faith. A faith within a faith, as I sometimes
put it."

"I accept that," Ferguson said.

"What do you accept—that it would be necessary
to resign?"

"Yes."

"And can you assure me that you're prepared
without reservation of any kind, to go all the way
with this project of ours?"

Ferguson hesitated, and felt Bradley watching
him.

"Are you, Alistair?"

Lying diminished him as a person, placing him
further back on the long path through many lives to
the ultimate escape to perfection beyond the cycles
of reincarnation, but the moment required him to
accept the penalties. "I guess so," he said.

"All the way?"

"Yes."

"Good, that makes me feel a lot better. You've
reassured me."

5

Spina phoned Mark, probed and eventually broke
through his caution and reluctance. "Listen, Mark,
the kid acts rational, he walks straight, and he's
chasing tail again. I had him checked out by a medic
here and he gave us the green light. It's gonna help
him take this on. He needs action and responsibil-

ity, to feel he's doing something with his life. The only thing is, he shouldn't have to handle it on his own. Somebody has to be there to steer him along. I'd go myself, but you know the way it is. If we can pull this off and get the dough to our friends, we have it made. They're gonna be able to buy all the hardware they can use."

"What do you want me to do?" Mark said.

"I want you to meet him off the plane at Miami. He'll tell you where you're bound for after that. And remember, you have no problem. The fix is in. From the time the stuff leaves the island until you pick it up, everything's been taken care of. After that it's your baby. I can't tell you where delivery has to be made because I don't know. Vic will give you the number to call as soon as you're ready to move out. Nothing can go wrong with this, short of a one-in-a-million accident."

Mark's voice was flat and noncommittal. "Do I collect?"

"Nope. The money that will go to our mutual friend will be taken care of by bank transfer. The guys who take delivery will handle it. You have nothing to worry about. As soon as you've handed over the goods, you can go home. It's as simple as that."

"Okay," Mark said. "I'll be waiting for him when he gets off the plane. Is there anything else I should know?"

"Nothing that I can think of, except maybe for one small precaution you should take. Vic has stopped blowing off, so I know he's gonna be all right, but keep a lookout for his iron—just in case, huh? You know kids. He has a piece of machinery with him right now, and I'm gonna tell him to leave it behind, but I figure you can't be too careful. See that he doesn't try to pick up something in Miami or someplace while you're not looking. You never know."

"Leave it to me," Mark said. "I'll keep him under control."

"As soon as you went for that caramel-ass I told

myself we were in the clear," Spina said. "When a man can raise a gallop he isn't in too bad shape."

"I'm looking forward to a return engagement there when I get back," Victor said. He felt it wise to encourage Spina's belief in his restored virility. "I hope she's still around."

"She'll be around. She'll be right there waiting for you. We'll take the boat out the day you get back. I'm gonna have to get a little practice with that gun of yours while you're away."

"It's the way you hold it," Victor said, feeling modest pride in being able to offer advice to the great Spina on such a subject. "You can do anything with a Police Special if you hold it right. It has to be part of your arm. You point it like you were pointing your finger."

"Sure, I know it's the way you hold it," Spina said. "It's the way it fits your hand."

They were on their way to the airport, driving through All Saints, a village cluttered with trees that had escaped from the jungle, and the hulks of forgotten cars. At eighty miles an hour they struck a dog and hurled it through a garden fence. Victor hung on the edge of his seat as Spina righted a dry skid.

Spina had established the right balance between them. His skull's smile spread a little. "I guess a car's like a gun, Vic. You and the machine joined together, huh? Everything has to fit."

A bottleneck in Parham took them by surprise, and friezes of staring Negro faces closed in on them. A hen disintegrating, blotted the windshield with blood, and Spina set the sprayer and wipers working. "We're gonna get there too soon," he said, and eased off the throttle. Victor felt his muscles relax, and his fingers uncurled. In the last five minutes a throbbing had started in his temples.

"We have to talk a little," Spina said. "Mark is in trouble. Maybe he doesn't know it yet, and maybe he does. There's something you have to tell him which couldn't be mentioned when I called him yesterday. Tell him that I heard through the grape-

vine they're going to want to talk to him pretty soon
about that Cobbold thing. He'll know what I mean.
The story is, some broad is supposed to have blown
the whistle on him."

"Andrew Cobbold, you mean?"

"Sure, Andrew Cobbold. Who else? That punk
who worked for your old man. The story going
around is that they've been waiting to pounce on
him for some time."

"I always thought Mark rubbed Cobbold out."

"You have no right to think anything," Spina said.
"Nobody gave you the right to an opinion on this
subject. All you need to know is that the Feds have
become interested in the case. I don't understand
what's been holding them up until now. Maybe they're
gonna work a squeeze play on him. Tell him from
me that the best thing he can do is pull out. Tell him
that this is one more reason why we have to pull the
Cuba deal off, because they'd extradite him from
Cuba. One other thing—remember that whatever
Mark says goes. He's the boss."

"Sure thing, Sal."

Spina glanced skywards through the window. The
plane from Miami, sun-burnished behind telephone
wire and tattered foliage, trailed its carpet of pol-
lution as it came in to land. He waited, then spoke
again. "Any questions?"

"One thing," Victor said. "What's the idea of having to go all the way down to Sedge Bay to pick up
the coffins? Why couldn't they have flown them in
to some place like Biscayne or Fort Lauderdale that
you can get to without wearing out your ass having
to take a Greyhound bus? Seems kind of stupid to
have to haul them from one end of the state to
the other."

"They have their reasons," Spina said. "These men
who deal in junk are seeing ghosts these days. You
heard how the Narcotics Bureau put a tail on that
runner coming over from France last fall?"

"That was the New Jersey syndicate, wasn't it?"

"*This* is the New Jersey syndicate. They have a
branch office down in Florida. Right now three of

their buddies are serving eight to fifteen in Latuna.
You have to expect them to be careful. All you have
to do is book the hearse for Fort Pierce, then call
them and do whatever they tell you. Maybe you're
gonna have to change your route two or three times.
My guess is you will. What these guys will wanna do
is work out some system to make sure they're not
thrown to the lions because of a fuckup on your
part."

"There won't be any," Victor said.

"I hope there won't, Victor baby. For all our
sakes." Spina pushed down the accelerator. The
green lanes of Antigua had uncurled into a small
brown cone of desert, and on it the glittering Pan
American plane awaited its passengers.

6

A message to call Don Vincente was waiting for
Mark at Miami Airport.

"Thank God Teresa knew where I could reach
you. Listen, Marco, get a hold on yourself; I got bad
news. Your brother got hit yesterday. A certain person was just on the line from Palermo."

"Paolo," Mark said. "You mean Paolo was
killed?"

"Sure he was killed."

The instructions for the use of the telephone,
level with Mark's eyes, were suddenly rearranged in
absurd sentences, embedded in which stood out a
single, inconsequential Italian word: *timballo*. Timballo, he read. Drum. Why drum? The word vanished, leaving nothing but chaotic English. Don
Vincente's voice babbled and chirped in the depths of
space. Mark returned the instrument to his ear.

"Don Vincente, what happened? I don't understand."

"I said they wired his car and blew it up."

"You mean Paolo went up with the car?"

"He went up with the car," Don Vincente said with exaggerated clarity, an instant of irritation breaking through the solemnity of his voice. "They put a big charge in the trunk, and they were picking up bits of the car a hundred yards away."

"Maybe this could be a mistake. There were fifteen or twenty Ricciones in the place where we lived. Maybe it could have been meant for one of the others."

"It couldn't," Don Vincente said. "They went for your brother, the poor guy who ran the garage. He was hit this morning. If you want to know the time, it was just after seven. Your brother is dead. You gotta face it."

For a moment disbelief contrived to exist in Mark's mind simultaneously with the conviction that tragedy had struck him. Then disbelief collapsed. "He was a quiet guy," he said. "He was never in trouble."

"No. But somebody else we know was. They waited a long time."

"He didn't say anything? They couldn't get him a priest?"

"I told you three times—he was blown all over the street. He's gone. Nothing's gonna bring him back, Mark. This is something you gotta accept."

Mark felt the shock of amputation. A raw and bleeding violence had been done to his life. "He didn't suffer," he said to himself by way of self-assurance.

"What was that?"

"He was a fine man. I said he didn't suffer."

"Sure he didn't suffer. How could he? You're blown to bits, you don't suffer."

"Don Vincente. I'm sorry. I don't know what I'm supposed to say. You have to remember that Paolo looked after us when I was a kid after Papa died. I guess I'd feel better if I could have seen him again before he passed away."

"I know that, Mark. Listen, I got an idea. I checked, and I could fix it for you to go over for the funeral if you wanna."

"I have to go, whatever happens."

"Nothing would happen. Nothing could happen. I talked to this certain person about it, and he said it would be okay. They'll hold the ceremony up until you get there. You could go over for a day and then come back. People wouldn't notice you were there. It would be a truce. Someone would meet you and stick around to take care of you till you took off again. But if you stayed more than twenty-four hours, you'd come back in a box."

"I'll take the first plane I can get. And thank you for doing this for me."

"Nothing, Marco. You're a member of my family, and that went for your brother too. I got to do what I can. I'll get back to Palermo and let them know you'll be coming. How long do you figure it's gonna take you to get there from where you are now?"

"I don't know. It all depends on how soon I can make a connection. Maybe seventeen or eighteen hours. It couldn't be less."

"They'll be waiting for you," Don Vincente said.

An hour later Mark met Victor off the flight from Antigua and they found the airport Howard Johnson's and fitted themselves into an empty corner of the restaurant. Victor's handclasp had been firm and his walk was jaunty, but a ghost image of despair—as in a photographic double exposure—still showed beneath the practiced confidence of his expression.

"Jeeze, it's good to see you again, Mark."

"Good to see *you*. You're looking great."

"I'm feeling it." Victor grinned broadly. He had learned to smile to cover tension and embarrassment, but the smile was synthetic and a little wild.

"Good time in Antigua?"

"Wonderful. Sun, sea, dames, booze. Plenty of everything you wanted."

"I heard it was a very nice place," Mark said. "You have a nice tan."

In fact, all of Victor's skin that could be seen was splendidly bronzed, but in the depth of the suntan the small, pale shapes of scars were more noticeable than in the normal pallor of his complexion.

"The open-air life," Victor said. "That way it is down there, you quit worrying. You live for the day, I guess."

"Nice if you can get it," Mark said. "How's Salva these days?"

"Having himself a whale of a time. Lemme tell you something about Salva: that guy has stamina." The smile came and went, leaving a momentary aftermath of depression.

"You're right there," Mark said. By now he was in full possession of himself again, a monarch in command of an empire of calm. A waitress in Bavarian costume had come with their order, and he exchanged a friendly nod with her.

"What's the news of Teresa and the kids?"

"They're well."

"You got a coupla great kids there. They're more fun than a barrel of monkeys. I sure dug that stay in your home. Every minute of it."

"We enjoyed having you, Vic. The kids are always talking about you."

There was a moment of silence. The minute hand of the Quaker State Oil clock over Victor's head ticked up to 1:45. At 2:30 Mark would have to go.

"So here we are then," Victor said. "All set up to go places together. Ya know something, Mark? It's really great to be on this with you. Makes me feel I'm gonna be of some use for once in my life. When do we start?"

Mark tipped a level teaspoon of sugar into his coffee and stirred it thoughtfully. "There's been a change of plans," he said. "Sorry, Vic, but we have things to discuss."

Anxiety brought another level of intelligence to Victor's expression. "Jeeze, Mark. What happened?"

"I just heard my brother Paolo got hit."

"What? Your brother Paolo got hit? You're kidding."

"I'm afraid not. He got hit back in Sicily. I just got the news from your old man. They're going to bury him tomorrow, and I have to be there."

Bewildered, Victor searched Mark's face for a sign of emotion and found none. "For Chrissake, Mark. I don't get this. Your brother got hit and you've been sitting here talking to me like nothing was wrong. You actually telling me your brother Paolo is dead?"

"They blew him up in his car," Mark said. "I have to tell you more about this than I would have, because otherwise nothing's going to make sense to you. I was in trouble with some people back home. They waited ten years to settle things, the way they do. Since they couldn't get to me, they took him. For this reason I have to go back. I hate to do this to you, but you can see the way it is. It ought to have been me they'll be burying tomorrow; instead, it's him. I couldn't let him be put away in the earth without being there."

"Sure you couldn't, Mark. I wish I could tell you the way I feel about this, but I guess you know. I heard they don't come any better than Paolo. Teresa used to talk about him all the time. I guess she was as crazy about him as everyone else."

"We were very close," Mark said. "I don't want to say too much, but he was more like a father than a brother. You heard they kept him in a British camp for two years, and when they sent him back to us you could count his bones through the skin. The reason why he didn't marry was because he had to look after us. There wasn't enough food for a wife and kids as well."

"Teresa told me. She was wild about him."

"Everyone was," Mark said. "He was a very special person."

The face and form of his brother, clad until now in no more than a mild, shapeless benevolence, had taken on a new edge in death. In life he had been an insignificant man, but death in a vendetta killing had instantly rescued him from mediocrity. In Campamaro, too, his memory would now rank with those of men who had committed terrible crimes or performed great acts of charity. In the short span of folk recognition, his place was assured: *quella benedetta anima*—that blessed soul. A face, however foolish, that took on dignity, like that of a saint painted on the wall of a catacomb.

"To make the connection to Rome," Mark went on, "I have to take a plane out of here in half an hour. I hear from Salva you have everything lined up. You know what has to be done?"

"There's nothing to it," Victor said. "The arrangement was that we were to go down to Sedge Bay and pick up the stuff, in three coffins that have been shipped across to an undertaker there. Everything's been taken care of. A Greyhound leaves here every coupla hours for Sedge Bay. All we were supposed to do was pick up the coffins and hire a hearse to make the delivery. I got a number to ring from Sedge Bay as soon as we were ready to go."

"How much time have we got for this deal? I mean, could it wait until I made this trip home and got back here?"

"Salva says the delivery has to be made within three days."

"Good. I've been working on schedules and connections, and if everything goes okay, I can make it in two."

"Whaddaya want me to do, Mark?" Victor asked.

"I want you to check in at the airport hotel, stay right there and wait for me." He glanced up at the clock. "It's now two P.M. on Monday. Let's say that if I'm not back by Wednesday at four P.M. you'd better handle it alone. How do you feel about that?"

"I can do it, Mark. Leave it to me. There won't be any problem."

"I know that. You know I'd like to be with you, and I'm going to do all I can to make it back in time, but if I can't I know you won't let Salva and me down."

Minutes later Mark's flight was called. At the barrier they shook hands and embraced.

"Be seeing you," Mark said. "And remember, if I can't get back, stay cool. Whatever happens, don't blow your top. You have a good head, so use it all the time."

7

On the long Atlantic flight from New York to Rome, Mark came to a decision. He would watch for any opportunity created by this visit to negotiate a return to Sicily. Since his business connection with Don Vincente had petered out, life in New England offered few prospects. He had no special talent or liking for small-time wheeler-dealing in the real estate market, and he felt that his family was slowly disintegrating under the impact of its new way of life. Don Vincente had already probed for his reactions to the Cuba project, but his first enthusiasm had cooled.

"There's no future in Salisbury, Marco, even if we wanted to stay. Grubschek's not going to get himself reelected, and as soon as he goes that horse's neck Weissman is gonna be back hitting the beat. Not that either of those guys are any use to me. It has to be faced: when spic immigrants can come up here and hit us, times have changed. The question I'm coming to is, do you have any personal plans?"

"I can't say that I do."

"The way I feel, you oughta at least consider the Cuba deal. We know it's a sure-fire winner through that contact we have down there. I mean Bradley. I guess you know him better than I do. I did him a favor a few years ago, since when we've been stringing along together. I may as well tell you, he put the finger on Cobbold."

"Bradley gives me a rash," Mark said. "I have an instinctive feeling about him."

"He gives me a rash too, but he's useful. This new government is out on its feet, just waiting for somebody to knock it off. I took a dive for thirty million in Cuba, and now it begins to look like I might get some of it back."

"You'll get it all back. You have a lot of friends

working for you. Most of them you don't even know."

"So whyncha come in with us? Why don't we get the old combination started again?"

A moment of hope and enthusiasm had driven a little blood to the surface of Don Vincente's jaundiced cheeks, and the small, red-rimmed eyes glistened. "How about it, Marco? Whaddaya say?"

"I'd have to talk to Teresa about it, Don Vincente. We have problems with children and schools. I'm not sure how she'd feel about another change of scene. It sounds like a nice idea if she felt like making the move. You know the way it is: women are conservative."

"Well, anyway, think about it, Marco. If you wanna come, we'd like to have you. The offer's always open."

There was a bad connection at Rome, then a three hours' delayed takeoff, so it was ten A.M. on Tuesday before his plane touched down at Palermo.

Everything had changed. The years had severed him not only from familiar landscapes now obscured by vast new buildings, but from his countrymen themselves, whose appearances he had forgotten; men were smaller than they had been, and scuttled like crabs about the polished airport spaces; the women had faces of the kind that had once been serene, but now seemed to him empty and apathetic.

He was met by a small spic-and-span man with sun-cured skin and a black cheroot in the corner of his lipless mouth. He grabbed Mark's hand and shook it violently, and flecks of sunlight joggled under his eyes through the pink-tinted shades he wore.

"I'm Joe Fosca, glad to know you."

"Nice to meet you, Joe."

"It sure feels good to speak English again," Joe said.

"You been in the States?" Mark asked politely.

"D'ya know East Sixty-ninth Street? I had an apartment there for eight years. After that I ran the Italian lottery down in Brooklyn for a while. They threw me out the same time as Spina. We came over together. Right now I'm back in the sticks at Castelnuovo." He made a face. "I guess it pays the food bills."

A red Alfa Romeo waited in the airport parking lot. They got in and Fosca started the engine.

"What's the pitch?" Mark asked.

"I've been told to drive you to Campamaro, stay with you until the funeral's over and then bring you right back here."

"I want to go to Pioppo to see my mother-in-law," Mark said. "I also have relations at Caltanissetta and San Stefano I want to visit."

"No can do," Fosca said. "You'll be tailed all the time you're in the country, and if you don't do what you're told you'll be hit."

"Who do you take orders from? Somebody by the name of Gentile—or someone connected with the Gentile outfit?"

"I don't take orders from anyone. This is a friendly gesture on my part. I'm doing this as a service to you, like I hope you'd do one for me. Only thing is, I don't want to get caught in the cross fire if you spring any surprises."

"How about taking me to Don C.? It wouldn't be too far out of the way."

"He's in bed since yesterday with another heart attack. He couldn't see you."

"Do you know Tagliaferri?"

"I knew him. He died last June. You seem to be losing your connections. That's what happens when you go away."

"How about Crespi? I mean the man who got in on the D.C. ticket for Caltanissetta. He's a cousin of mine."

"Now you're talking. They say he's gonna be in the next cabinet. Trouble is, he's away in Rome most of the time."

"I need a suit of mourning," Mark said.

"Okay, we can stop off in the city on our way through."

They stopped at an off-the-peg tailor's in a street specializing in cheap clothing at the back of the

Church of Santa Maria Nuova. Only the working
classes in Palermo bought ready-made suits, and or-
dinarily they were cut in a fashion that gave the
wearer a humble, even cringing appearance. But
mourning garments were tailored with a certain swag-
ger. The most dignified occasions in the lives of the
poor were those connected to the circumstances of
death. With its tight waist, wide lapels and padded,
confident shoulders, Mark's jacket could have been
made for an admiral. He stared at his reflection in
the speckled mirror and realized that mourning suited
him. At his back, Fosca clucked encouragement and
approval. A small, silent man who had followed them
into the shop fingered the cheap ties on their revolving
stand and ignored the assistant who approached him.
When Mark and Fosca left, he dawdled by the stand
for a moment, then followed them.

A rising despair calmed Mark's thoughts. He remembered a telephone number he had written in his
notebook. "Is it okay to make a phone call?"

"Why not? As long as I'm around when you make
it."

They stopped at the bar next-door, and Mark
bought a *gettone* at the counter, went into the
phone box and dialed a Palermo number. A woman
answered.

"C'è l'Avvocato Crespi?"

Her tone reproved him. *"Vuol' parlare con l'Onorevole?"*

"L'Onorevole. Sì. Scusi tanto. Mi sono dimenticato."

A man spoke, impatience in his voice. *"Pronto. Chi
parla."*

"Giovanni, this is Marco. Your cousin Riccione.
I'm speaking English in case any of the phones
around here are bugged."

"Marco, how good to hear your voice. It's been
a long time, eh? All of ten years. When can we
meet?"

Mark found it hard to believe that he could be
speaking to the man who a decade before had been
a weedy, tongue-tied seminarist on the point of turning
his back on the church to go into law.

"Listen, Giovanni. I'm here on a flying visit, and it's a bit tricky. I'd like to see you. You know all about my brother Paolo's death. Maybe you'll be at the funeral, in which case I'll see you there, and I hope you'll be able to help."

"Marco, I don't know what to say. To say I'm sorry isn't enough. I read about Paolo, and it grieves me not to be able to pay my last respects. He was a fine man, and his loss is a personal tragedy. If only it had been any other day. Maybe you've heard that a lot of people got together at Caltanissetta and decided to elect me as their member, since which my life is no longer my own. Actually, it was a lucky break that you found me here. I only got in from Rome yesterday, and I have three meetings to address before I go back tomorrow."

"In that case you'll be kept busy. Yes, I see, it's out of the question."

"Most unfortunately so. I have a taxi waiting for me right now; otherwise I'd have suggested your coming over here."

"That's all right. I understand. You're a busy man."

"It's terrible to miss seeing you like this, Marco. Listen, how about stopping off in Rome on your way back? I'd be happy to put you up and show you around."

"I'm only here for the day. I have to take off for the States again tonight."

"It's a shame, Marco. However, there it is; I suppose there's nothing can be done. Anyway, you have my address. In Rome it's care of the Chamber of Deputies. So we'll just have to hope we'll be seeing each other very soon. Whatever I can do at any time, Marco. Remember; whatever I can do."

Back in the car, Fosca seemed to read his mind. "Looks like you lost your fix here. I can sympathize; I know what it's like. When I got back from the States I had about as much weight as the day I was born. *And* I didn't have to fight any Gentiles, either."

They were in the suburbs now, and Roccella

loomed ahead behind the black-and-silver cubes of the new factories. The roar of the Alfa Romeo's exhaust quieted to a mutter at the traffic lights, but was replaced by a piercing industrial outcry.

"I studied your case," Fosca said. "It interested me. The way I see it, you were a man building up a lot of support, but just failing to make out. As soon as you blew, the whole setup fell apart. A house of cards. Those two nice obliging fellows who used to work for you in Caltanissetta—Sardi and Lobrano, wasn't it? They didn't last a month. They're pushing up daisies. Matta did the smart thing and went over to Gentile. Giordano got framed and is serving a five-year stretch in the Ucciardone. All the protection went up in smoke. Don C. had to line up with the Gentile bunch to be able to fight off the competition us new boys were giving him."

"Did you ever know my brother?" Mark asked.

"I tanked up with gas at his filling station once or twice, but I don't recall seeing him. He was bound to be hit sooner or later because you weren't there. It's understandable. Seems he was never connected in any way. They could have made the hit whenever they wanted to."

"Who was it who took the contract?"

"Some Gentile headhunter. You'll know soon enough, but it won't do you any good. They don't have any civilization where we're going. They're living in the past."

As they turned into the Bagheria road, Mark looked back; from here Palermo was no more than worn-down teeth in the bone of the skyline. All the great changes had come in the towns; outside them nothing altered but the season. The landscape burned out by the sun was gray and grained like an old movie, and oxen pulled the plows that scraped the pockets of earth among the rocks. The peasants who peered at them from their village hovels seemed dazed by the calamity of work.

"Things are pretty quiet now," Fosca said. "We had a civil war for five years after I got back. Anyone returning from the States got a rough ride. Most of us got behind Johnny La Barbera, but after someone blew the La Barberas up we didn't have a prayer. Whoever it was certainly started a fashion. Nowadays every time anyone has to be hit he goes up in his car."

Something like bile was at the back of Mark's throat. He swallowed. "I guess that way they don't suffer," he said.

Campamaro was hardly to be recognized. Money made out of the shortages and mean little rackets of the postwar years had been invested in whatever ugliness the villagers could afford. In a fit of civil mania a square had been half built and then abandoned, trenched like a battlefield for drains that had never been installed, with four cement benches, a fountain full of green slime and a public urinal still unconnected to the water supply. The dingy bar where he had been honored to play dominoes with the old men had bought a jukebox, displayed a sign advertising Pepsi-Cola, and served the youth of a new generation. No faces were familiar. Along with the priest, Don Carlo Magna, the old men had been shut away out of sight to await death. The weak-in-the-head daughter Mark had been offered as a bride was now married, with several imbecile children of her own, and the promising young girls he had once hoped to possess had already put on the disguise of approaching middle age. It was difficult to decide which of the village shacks camouflaged now with raw cinder block had been the one into which he had been dragged to be humiliated and tortured by the Moors, and to which cabbage patches African bodies had contributed their beneficial humus. Only the mountains remained as he had remembered them, piled up like rock salt awaiting refinement, a crystalline gloss in their shadows under the anemic sky.

Paolo had built his garage next to their old house, and the explosion that had occurred when, having been called by telephone for a repair job, he had climbed into his truck and switched on the ignition, had produced freakish results. A basic tangle of metal, hardly identifiable between the burned-out gas pumps, had been augmented by a radiator, a pair of wheels, a bumper and a number plate recovered from backyards and roofs where they had been distributed by the force of the explosion. Against this was propped a wreath composed of some hundreds of yellowing arum lilies. The house had been scarred by flying metal and blackened by the fire. Its single first-floor window was shuttered, the balcony was decorated with palm fronds intertwined with crepe, and broad ribbons of black satin imprinted in white with Paolo's name had been fastened in the form of an enormous cross over the façade to give the impression of a house canceled out by mourning.

"Don C. gave the O.K. to go ahead and give him the best we could," Fosca said. "We got a teak coffin. It would have been nice if you could have seen him, but we had to close it up. I guess you know why."

Mark knew. In such tragedies where little or nothing remained of the victim, a firm of Palermo specialists would provide a wax dummy, and this, dressed in the dead man's best suit and with an enlargement made from a recent photograph stuck over its face, would go into the coffin. When this happened it was not usual to leave the lid off for the mourners to pay their last respects.

"We got about a thousand lilies and three screechers," Fosca said. "You can't find screechers any more these days. They won't come to places like this unless you go and pick them up in a classy automobile and feed them a three-course meal. We had to work our asses off to find some to come out here."

Mark got out of the car and looked around. Motionless hooded figures were at every window in the street, and ahead, at the limits of the village, the ancient Isotta Fraschini motor hearse waited in utter silence, together with the pallbearers and the three women Fosca had engaged to tear their clothes and wail. It was a drama of the kind that a villager could hardly hope to see enacted more than once or twice in his lifetime, and custom prescribed an exact ceremony in which a number of players performed their parts, and in which Mark played the lead role. The rule, he knew, was that a pretense must be made that the murdered man had died from natural causes, and the news that he had been the victim of a vendetta killing would only be announced at the end of the funeral oration delivered by one of the professional mourners.

The village notables crowded forward to press his hand and mutter their condolences. What had happened had conferred on him a terrible distinction. A bird-faced little priest monopolized him for a moment; to be followed by an intellectual young schoolmaster translucent with good will; the owner of a cement factory; a man of honor with features carved like a totem pole; and then an assortment of grocers and butchers who made up the middle class. For an instant, behind their faces he thought he glimpsed the face of the man who had followed him into the tailor's shop.

They filed into the house and took up their places around the coffin on its trestle, under its mound of wreaths. Even the house was unfamiliar; Paolo had added this room, and his savings had gone into stuffing it with cheap shining furniture. An early photograph looked down on the scene from a space between brash mirrors. Lilies on the verge of withering had filled the room with an almost animal odor, and with it mingled a stale smell of clothing kept in chests and only exposed to the fresh air on occasions like this.

The priest bleated a prayer in Latin, and then Maria La Scaduta, the leader of the professional mourners, began her oration. She was an epileptic with a man's face, pockmarked cheeks and a deep, baying voice, and was beginning to make a name for herself as a folk singer on Palermo television. No one understood what she had to say because she was reciting what was, in reality, an ancient funerary ode, bearing no relation to the circumstances of Paolo's life or the manner of his death. The words were archaic, mispronounced and distorted to the point of having no meaning, but though it was hardly more than a litany of gibberish, the audience responded to the cadences with their nerves.

By the time the moment came for the announcement that Paolo had been murdered, the mood was close to hysteria. La Scaduta, who had managed to forget the name of the assassin, had to be prompted in a whisper by a nearby mourner. Then she threw back her head and howled, *"Giuseppe Gentile. Era lui chi ha mandatu u sicariu."* Cries of horror and astonishment were heard on all sides. One of the supporting professional mourners let out a powerful wail and pretended to faint in the arms of the man of honor, while the other, groaning, carefully scratched her cheek, producing a single drop of blood. The small priest reached up to throw a consoling arm around Mark's shoulder and quoted a verse of resignation from the Book of Ecclesiastes. Then they all shuffled out into the street.

The old hearse had been backed into position, and the pallbearers brought out the coffin and slid it into position, then piled the roof of the vehicle with wreaths. Its driver, in tails worn with dark glasses, his black velour on his knees, started the engine and maneuvered the hearse into position behind the old leader of the fraternal order of San Rocco, who waited with his drum to lead the procession. He would be followed by the priest and acolytes carrying the saint's banner, and by boys sprinkling holy water.

At a signal from the priest the rattle of the drum began, the Isotta crashed into bottom gear and jerked forward, and the three wailing women following immediately behind the hearse started to writhe and shriek. Mark walked alone, followed by Fosca and the leading lights of Campamaro trudging through the dust six abreast. A long straggling tail of cement workers, who had been ordered by the local man of honor to attend, plus a sprinkling of sharecroppers and goatherds, brought up the rear.

Mark's eyes were fixed on the coffin covered with its purple velvet pall, from which hung down a black cord with a tassel. Nothing of his brother was being carried to the graveyard but a dummy in new silk underclothing worn under Paolo's best suit, and a blurred enlargement from a group photograph taken at a Rotarian outing seven years before. This everyone knew but regarded as unimportant, because in the folk beliefs that asserted themselves on such occasions the tassel on the black cord represented the dead man's soul, which at this very moment was present, and would be released only with the interment of the body. In a few minutes' time, when the moment came for the coffin to be lowered into the grave, the dramatic crisis of the funeral would present itself, for simply by taking this tassel in his hand in the presence of the crowd, without so much as a word or gesture, Mark would assume all the obligations of the vendetta. In these ways Campamaro had not moved into the age of Pepsi-Cola and the Gaggia espresso machine.

They trudged on, out of step with the tapping of San Rocco's drum toward the squat, flinty church at the end of the village. Women and children had clustered on all the rooftops; the churchbell clanked; the siren of the invisible cement factory hooted in melancholy respect; the professionals sobbed loudly and tore at their clothing. A profound and sacred moment was near. Last year, across the mountains at Bompensiere, a boy of fourteen had been egged on to take the fateful tassel in his hand, and six months later he had been blasted to death by a sawed-off shotgun fired from ambush.

At the churchyard gate the Isotta squeaked to a halt, the pallbearers lifted the coffin out, the procession re-formed and moved forward again, squeezed into the narrow, winding path between the graves. At the graveside, Mark found himself hemmed in. Still under its pall, the coffin had been lowered to the ground, the black cord with its tassel now coiled on it like a snake. They were all waiting for him in a silence broken only by the distant sounds of the women and children, who had left the rooftops and scuttled up the street toward the graveyard. They

were all waiting for him. They all demanded that
having come here he should do his part. The priest,
book in hand, eyes hollowed in a face that had
suddenly become skull-like, demanded it. Fosca, the
man of honor and all the village's petty officials and
shopkeepers expected it. The intellectual young
schoolteacher had shelved his progressive ideals and
required him to keep faith with the past. La Scaduta
and her two assistants had performed to the best
of their ability and counted on him to do no less.
The cement workers, the goatherds and the day la-
borers insisted that he should respect the tradition
in which they had all been born. He felt the weight
of their will power, the silent pressure of their determination. The effort to resist these currents of mass
suggestion, and the atavistic urge within himself to
seize the tassel and clench it for them all to see, had
started a trembling in his hands. He closed his eyes
and thought of his wife and children.

In the great bewildered silence the priest opened
his book and began.

Now all the faces that had been fixed so hopefully
on Mark were turned away. He knew that he had
cut himself off from Campamaro forever.

8

Thirty-six hours of intermittent fog at Idlewild had
produced ripples of traffic dislocation in half the ma-
jor airports of the world. Mark's only hope of
being back in Miami by four P.M. on Wednesday de-
pended on a succession of nearly perfect plane connections, but the incoming Alitalia from New York
was five hours late arriving in Rome, and on the
return journey, with Mark aboard, was diverted to
Boston. By the time he had disembarked and reached
a phone booth in the transit lounge, it was twenty
minutes too late to catch Victor, who had checked out

of the hotel and was already in a taxi on his way
to the Greyhound bus station.

It was nearly seven P.M. before Victor reached
Sedge Bay, after two changes. By this time he was
not feeling at his best. In the last hours in Miami
he had suffered the suspense of waiting for Mark
to return, and now a nervous weakness he had been
careful to avoid mentioning to either Spina or Mark
took the form of a nagging migraine. He went to
the station men's room, washed in cold water, crossed
to the bar for a quick drink, then braced himself to
face the town. It was a lively evening in early spring,
with the light draining slowly away into a glowing
green horizon, the town's illumination winking un-
steadily along the distant profiles of shore, and the
last speedboat cutting a brief white signature at the darkening entrance to the harbor.

Victor took a taxi to the establishment of an undertaker called Edwin Axe, down by the sea front.
Since he was the only undertaker in Sedge Bay,
Victor hoped that as soon as Mark returned from
Rome he would trace him through the telephone
directory and leave a message with the undertaker
announcing his time of arrival.

"I'm afraid it wouldn't have been possible for your
friend to reach us," Axe said. "We had a storm
yesterday that did something to our local lines."

"When are they going to be fixed?" Victor asked.
"This evening sometime?"

"Oh, I doubt that. Possibly tomorrow. Our basic
arrangements down here are very primitive. For some
strange reason, the telephone works perfectly well just
outside the town limits." Axe was a big, breezy,
talkative man with exceptionally mobile eyes in a
bovine face, who moved—perhaps under the influence of the sea's constant presence—with solidity and
premeditation, like a fisherman in thigh boots.

He was happy to talk about his business. "This
was once a fish refrigeration plant," he explained.
"We snapped it up as soon as it came on the market. Nobody goes fishing any more. The town sup-
plies most of our bread-and-butter business, but we

still get a surprising amount of transit traffic."

Victor squirmed in indecision. Should he wait a little longer, or start right away? Axe could have no idea of the true content of the coffins; still, he gave Victor a feeling of uneasiness. There was something repellent about a man who made his living out of corpses.

"We have quite a nice little connection with the Bahamas," Axe said with enthusiasm. "More folks who go there seem to pop off unexpectedly than in places where they lead less exciting lives. People use us because we're a lot cheaper than any of the funeral homes in the big cities. What business we did with Cuba was in the other direction, but now the traffic seems to be turning round. This is the second case this year where we've had a shipment to this country. Must be a sign of the times. So many Cubans are coming here. It's lucky for us that interment is not practiced there. By that I mean we are not faced with the problem of handling a coffin that's been buried for a long period in the earth, and therefore suffered deterioration."

They had left Axe's office to stroll a few yards to a lime-washed building that showed signs of recent renovation.

"Mind you," Axe said, "and with all due respect to Mr. Baeza, the Cubans don't know how to care for their dead. The normal practice is to rent a wall compartment for a certain number of years, after which, if payments lapse, the body is simply taken and dumped unceremoniously in what they term a *fosa común*. Most Americans would find this offensive. One finds it hard to reconcile such a practice with strong religious beliefs. Am I right?"

"Right," Victor said.

"Caskets are normally of the cheapest materials, and all too frequently they are too small for the body they must contain." His normally inert expression was suddenly transfigured with a grimace of fastidious horror. "Causing them to indulge in expedients which I can only leave to your imagination . . . Well, here we are."

He unlocked and opened a large polished wooden door, slid back an inside glass partition and switched on a powerful light. Victor found himself in what might have been a newly completed supermarket waiting for its stock. It contained a number of large, white-enameled bins of the kind used to contain deep-frozen food. In these the coffins were kept. There was a faint smell of perfumed aerosol.

"I think we'll find what we're looking for over in that corner," Axe said. "Ah yes, here we are. Three coffins from Cuba consigned, if I remember rightly, by a Mr. Ferguson. I'll get them out for you. Did you say that you had some sort of transportation arranged?"

"What I'd like to do is rent a hearse from you if that could be done."

"Sure, why not? To go where?"

"Fort Pierce. Mr. Baeza's planning to settle there. He wants to have his parents in the local cemetery."

"Understandably. Fort Pierce. That's a nice place. Lot of Cubans are buying property around that section right now. Personally, I find it rather humid, but it doesn't seem to bother our Cuban friends. They're used to it; their own climate is a humid one."

"I'd like to ride with the hearse if that's okay with you."

"Why not? It's a nice drive. You see more of the country than you do from the train, and very interesting it is. You'll be leaving tomorrow, I take it?"

Victor reached his decision. "I want to take off tonight."

"I'm not so sure that's going to be possible," Axe said. His lively eyes swiveled, and Victor imagined that there was curiosity in the glance he intercepted.

"The thing is, I'm pushed for time."

"We'd have a little problem in finding a driver as late in the day as this. Fort Pierce is a long way from here. I'm afraid it would mean double rate, even if we could persuade anyone to take it on." Axe looked up as if at a flock of passing birds. It was his way of showing embarrassment when he feared that the efficiency of his service might be called into question. "The people I'm obliged to employ," he said, "are most independent. The vocation seems to attract men who live in a rut."

"Twice the rate would be all right," Victor said. "Three times, if you like; the main thing is to get going."

Axe had dropped his eyes to meet his, and Victor searched his face for fresh signs of curiosity. "What should I tell your friend if he calls?" Axe said.

"Just tell him I've taken off," Victor said.

"Shall I tell him to contact you at Fort Pierce?"

"I guess so."

"Can I give him a number?"

"He'll know where I am."

"Very well," Axe said. "Personally, I'd have thought an early-morning start would suit your purpose equally well. I could probably put you up if you don't object to rather simple home comforts. I'd like to save you money."

Distracted by the thumping behind the eyes, Victor was becoming impatient. "Nice of you to offer, Mr. Axe, but I happen to have a lot on my plate tomorrow. I'd regard it as a great favor if you could pick up a driver from somewhere."

"Well, one can but try," Axe said. "If none of my people are amenable, there happens to be a car rental agency just down the road. If you can bear with me for a moment, I'll skip down and see if they can help us out."

He went off, leaving Victor to carry out a close inspection of the Baeza coffins. He examined the screw heads in the lid. There were no small, bright telltale scratches in the tarnished metal, no evidence of the recent use of a screwdriver.

Axe seemed to be gone a long while, and as the time stretched Victor's nerves tightened. After what could have been twenty minutes he returned, plodding across the floor, eyes rolling, a longshoreman on sticky sand.

"Well, it seems we're in luck after all. Very good man, as it happens. Reliable. Used him several times before in this kind of emergency. We were lucky to have caught him at home, and he'll be here in a moment. I'll get my secretary to get out the forms and type a receipt for you to sign."

The driver reminded Victor of a movie Sioux. He was a lean man of inherited deprivation, with tendons tugging at fleshless cheekbones and jaw, and a nose defined abruptly by his skull.

"How long is this going to take us?"

"Fort Pierce, mister? Which road d'ya want to take? Route 1 or the turnpike?"

"The turnpike."

"Most folks like to take 1. It's a nice drive up the coast. You get a good view of the sea."

"Not at night, you don't."

"We're gonna have a full moon. You can see the lights of the fishing boats on the water. Some of those little towns like Jupiter and Stuart sure are pretty by night. If you take 1 you're going to pass through Palm Beach."

"Make it the turnpike all the same."

"You wanna go by the turnpike, I guess you can figure on three hours and a half."

"Three hours and a half. For Chrissake, how far is it?"

"Hundred and forty miles, could be."

"And it's gonna take us three and a half hours?"

"All of. This old clunk is worn out; don't do more'n sixty. Mr. Axe don't like to spend any money on his hearses except to give them a lick of paint once in a while. Besides, the road from here as far as Kitts Hollow ain't too good. You don't hit 1 until after that."

"Let's get going, then."

"Whatever you say." The driver seemed put out, and the voice, like the melancholy face, was finely tuned to dissatisfaction.

The throbbing in Victor's temples was worse, and when he shifted his position on the uncomfortable seat he felt twinges in his bones where they had cracked and splintered under the impact of the clubs. He put it down to the sudden change of climate. They were already in the slipshod tropical outskirts of the town, where thin, fevered-looking men lounged in undershirts around rickety frame houses, and when the driver stopped to salute a friend, a clatter of bullfrogs and crickets came from water out of sight.

There was wet mud on the road. "Been raining a lot here?" Victor asked.

"It's the time of the year, mister."

"How far do we have to drive to find a phone that works?"

"They're repairing this section."

"Pull over to that bar," Victor said. "I have to make a call."

He went into the bar, ordered a shot of whiskey and a beer and dialed the Miami number on the pay phone. The number was busy, so Victor left the booth and went back to the door. Across the street two wooden houses leaned on each other under wind-stripped palms, and rain was spitting into a black puddle shaped like a map of South America. The Chrysler hearse sagging at the curb, its windows misted and an occasional trickle of rainwater coursing through the condensation on its flanks, was part of the landscape and could have stood there forever. He waited five minutes before trying the number again. This time a child's voice answered.

"This is Victor," he said. "Tell your daddy Victor wants to speak to him."

There was no reply, and he was afraid that the line had gone dead; then a man came on the line. "Who's this?"

"Victor. I was told to call you. I just got in."

"Where you calling from?"

"A pay phone in some bar."

"Do you have the delivery?"

"Yeah."

"Listen, let me speak to Richards."

"He's not here. He couldn't make it."

"Whaddaya mean he couldn't make it? We heard he was setting this up."

"He got delayed. Some family trouble he had to attend to."

"I don't like this. We were counting on Richards being in charge."

"I could have waited till he showed up, but I was told you wanted delivery within three days. You want me to wait till he shows?"

"No, come just as you are. So you're by yourself?"

"There's a driver."

"Somebody you know?"

"How could I? I never been here before in my life. He goes with the car."

"Uh huh. Well, listen; get his name and where he lives. Everything you can find out about him—his age, and what he looks like. The important thing is where he's from. We want to know all about him."

Victor put down the phone and was making for the door when the woman who had served him came out from behind a bead curtain. "Listen, don't tie up that phone too long. I got a coupla people here waiting to make calls."

He waved to her and went out to the hearse, where the driver sat collapsed, eyes shut, as though he had died of heart failure during the wait.

Victor grabbed his shoulder and shook it. "What's your name?"

The man opened his eyes and seemed to gather his wits with difficulty.

"I said what's your name?"

"Eddie."

"Eddie who?"

"Mister, does it matter?"

"I've just been talking to a friend who says he knows you."

"My name is Eddie Moreno." The driver made the announcement with a kind of quiet pride. "Moreno. In Spanish that means dark."

"Yeah, sure. And you live in Sedge Bay, huh?"

"I work in Sedge Bay. I live in New River Inlet. Ever heard of New River Inlet?"

"Nope."

"No, I reckon you never did. It's a small place. Before that I lived in Simon Drum. Ya know something? The way I figure it, your friend must have made a mistake." He grinned craftily, looking at Victor with his head tilted back along his long nose.

"I'll go tell him," Victor said. "He wanted to say hello."

The woman was standing by the phone, hands on hips, and he had to glare at her before she would go away. "Don't make it too long, mister, will you?" she whined.

"Name's Eddie Moreno," Victor said into the mouthpiece. "Lives in New River Inlet, and before that in Simon Drum. Age about thirty-five, weight about a hundred and forty. Could be some kind of Indian."

"All right, friend. We're gonna have to check on that, and it may take time. Call me back in an hour, but this time it's gonna be a different number. Write it down: Coppervale eight-eight-five-three. Stay on Route 107, but call back before you get to Kitts Hollow. We may want to redirect you."

"Okay, I'll call you back."

"One other thing. Tell me some more about Richards. What's his first name?"

"Mark. His friends call him Marco."

"What sort of a guy is he? What does he look like?"

"Mark's about thirty-five. Pretty short. Thin. Dark hair going gray at the sides. Sharp nose. Looks like George Raft in his first movies." Now they're checking up on me, he thought. They don't seem too happy.

"Happen to know where he was born?"

"Someplace near Caltanissetta. Anything else?"

"I guess not. You'd better get going."

Victor went outside, rattled the door of the hearse and got in. The driver started up and they rumbled off. Within minutes the last of Sedge Bay's outlying shacks were swallowed up in the gloomy palisade of trees lining the road.

"Slow down," Victor said.

"I thought you were in a hurry."

"I can't stand the way this thing sways. It's making me sick."

"You give the orders."

"Slow down some more. Keep it at thirty."

"Mister, I hafta tell you, at this rate we're gonna be all night."

"The longer this trip takes the more you get paid. Why should you worry?"

"You're wrong there. The pay's the same, no matter how long it takes. I got a wife to think about. She don't care for me staying out at night." He mumbled with vexation, chewing at his lips like an old man.

"What do they call this section?"

"All this is the Everglades. Right over there, if you could see it, is the beginning of the Big Cypress Swamp."

"It's kind of lonely, huh, Eddie? Not too much traffic on this road."

"All the traffic is earlier. Guys who work in the chemical plant going home to Clarksville and Stan Creek. They all went home an hour or two ago."

Victor felt a cramp take his left hand, the tendons and cartilage of which had been damaged by the first blow of the pick handle which he had warded off. He wrenched at the door to release a locked thumb. A tingling had started in his extremities as the circulation slowed in his fingers and toes. He tried to divert his attention from these symptoms, which his doctor had assured him had their origin, along with his migraine, as much in his mind as in his body, by lewd images of Spina's air hostess, with whom he had been prevented from having intercourse by a last-minute loss in potency. The distraction was unsuccessful; even in his imagination the girl's splendid and willing body escaped him.

"How long to Kitts Hollow?"

"At this rate, forty minutes."

"Go slower. I'm not feeling too good."

"It's the springing," the driver said. "It's too light for the body. We're carrying a coupla tons behind. D'ya want to stop for a minute?"

"No, go on," Victor said. The patterns of sour greens endlessly repeated in the headlights were having a hypnotic effect. He felt his head swim, and the onset of real nausea.

His distrust of the driver had deepened. "You do a lot of this driving around, Eddie?"

"Sure. I'm driving most of the time."

"Who for? Mr. Axe?"

"Nah, he only hires me once in a while. Sometimes I work for the Sedge Bay Timber Company. Or for Hertz in the tourist season."

"That a map you got there? Lemme see it. You must know this section pretty well, Eddie. Where do you go most of the time when you're driving around?"

"Naples, Arcadia, Canal Point, Punta Gorda. Almost any place you can name, I guess."

"For the timber company, huh?" Victor studied the fine detail of the map. "Know Lake Istokpoga, for instance?"

"Sure."

"How d'ya get there?"

"Along Highway 98. North of Lake Okeechobee."

"That's pretty convincing, Eddie. You certainly must spend a lot of time at the wheel."

"Any place you want to know how to get to in Florida, mister, I can tell you."

Victor's attention had been suddenly alerted by a small square of light that appeared on the windshield and immediately disappeared. He turned his head. The headlights of a car had swung into sight around a bend a hundred yards back.

"Speed up," he said to the driver.

The driver pushed the throttle down and the needle of the speedometer slowly crept up to sixty-five.

"That the best you can do?"

"That's the best, mister."

The lights behind them had dropped back, but not much.

"Okay, now slow down. Drop right down to twenty," Victor said.

The car behind slowed with them, then after a mile turned off to the left.

"That car behind us—where did it go?" Victor asked.

"Down to Jackson Pond, maybe. One or two guys from Jackson Pond work at the plant."

"Did you get the impression like I did that he was tailing us?"

"No. Why should he?"

"Why did he speed up and slow down when we did?"

"He wanted to stay with us. Could be he was using our lights on account of his generator had given out."

"Yeah, maybe it was just that; it could be. Just some guy with a crummy generator who didn't want to get lost in the woods. Listen, I have to call the man we're delivering these stiffs to and tell him we're gonna be late. How far is the nearest booth?"

"There's one where the gas station used to be just down the road. Unless they took it away when the place burned down."

Five minutes later they pulled up at the burned-out gas station. Jimson weed was growing knee-high among the blackened pumps, and railroad vine had converted what was left of the building into a ruin that could have been a century old.

The telephone still operated. It was 8:55. He waited until nine, then put in his dime and dialed the Coppervale number, but there was no reply.

"Number's busy," he explained to the driver. "We have to wait."

"There's another booth at Honey Mile."

"This one works. Let's play it safe."

"It's gonna be past midnight before we hit Fort Pierce," Eddie grumbled.

Victor kicked aside a spar of charred wood. "What happened to this place?"

"Guy went bankrupt and brought in a torch artist from Miami. By the time the fire department got here from Sedge Bay the place was in a teacup."

"What was the torch artist's name?" Victor asked.

"Foster. Benedict Foster."

"How do you know all these things, Eddie?" Victor asked. "How come you're so on the ball?"

"I read the newspapers same as anybody else."

"And you got a good memory, huh?"

Victor dialed Coppervale again, and this time the operator told him to put forty cents in the box when the phone was picked up.

The voice was the same as before. "Listen carefully, friend. I want to know where you are, but don't tell me the actual place. Just tell me roughly how many miles you are along that road you were taking the last time you called."

"About thirty."

"About thirty, huh? Well, now listen, do you have a map with you?"

"Sure."

"About five miles short of the town you're heading for, there's an intersection with a road going off to the left. Take it."

"Anything else?"

"Yeah. This guy you're with. We checked at both those places you mentioned, and nobody ever heard of him. What was the idea of bringing him, anyway? We thought you and Richards were coming alone."

"It couldn't be done any other way. You'll see for yourself."

"Any chance you got somebody on your tail?"

"I don't think so, but it's possible."

"Well, the first thing you have to do is find out for sure."

"How?"

"Just pull off the road somewhere and sit and watch for a while. Suppose you had to dump that clown you have with you—could you get here on your own?"

"I guess so."

"Well then, give him a going-over, and if it looks like anything smells, lose him."

"Okay, I'll do that."

"And call again in an hour. Henderson eight-four-three-one. Let us know how you make out. Maybe we'll send someone out to bring you in."

Ahead, the moon was rising behind the trees, and weak light began to separate the shapes in the car's interior. In a quick, stealthy fumble Victor took the .25 Beretta that, unbeknownst to Spina, he had bought in Antigua, out of his bag and slipped it under his shirt into his shoulder holster.

"Want to speed up yet?" Eddie asked.

"Just keep going like this. I have this sick feeling. The way this thing rolls on the bends hurts my stomach."

"Maybe you're tired, mister. Maybe you ought to try to grab some sleep."

"My mind's too active for that, Eddie. I got a lot on my mind. I been thinking about you. You're an Indian, aren't you?"

"My old man was," Eddie said. As a matter of habit, he half-grinned a wincing apology. "A Seminole. One of the Indians from around here."

"I've heard of them. Seminoles. Swamp Indians, huh? They put on a Seminole village attraction at Coral Gables when I was down there. You could photograph a woman giving her kid the tit for fifty cents. Did your old man live in New River Inlet too —or was it Simon Drum?"

"Simon Drum. They had two or three Indian families living there a few years back. We had to move out for the sake of the kids. Our youngest's a spastic. She couldn't get the treatment she needed, so we moved to the Inlet where we could take her in to Biscayne twice a week."

"How's she making out now?"

"Pretty good. They've made progress with this thing in the last few years."

"A spastic, huh? That's tough."

"As the doctor said, we had to give away five years of our lives. Special everything. The kid never had a day's schooling until last year. All the money had to go into putting her right. We have to think of her first all the time." An urgent whine had entered his voice; something had frightened him, Victor realized. He must have seen the gun, he thought.

"Well, that's certainly a hard-luck story, Eddie. You make it sound like you're quite a family man. I guess any man's dearest possession is his family. Something you don't want to be separated from any more than you can help, huh? Just one thing's bugging me about you and your sad history, Eddie, and I'd like to feel easy in my mind about it, so maybe you'd switch on the light and pass over your license."

The driver snapped on the interior light, took his license out of the breast pocket of his shirt and handed it over. Victor examined it. "The picture's a nice one, Eddie, but it gives your address here as Yeehaw Junction. How come?"

The man sucked in his cheeks and a smirk of ingratiation stiffened to a grimace. "I was there for three months at the time I took out the license, that's all."

"And you didn't bother to make the change when you moved to New River Inlet. Nothing unusual in that. Right now this family of yours are at the Inlet?"

"Right."

"But you told me you had to get home to your wife in Sedge Bay. You're getting me all mixed up, Eddie. I don't know what to think about these stories of yours that don't match up."

"That was just an excuse, mister. I wanted to get back early, and I said the first thing that came into my head."

"Well, that's natural enough. I'll buy that. Tell me one thing, though, Eddie. Satisfy my curiosity: how much are you being paid for this job?"

"To drive you to Fort Pierce?"

"If you like to put it that way. Yeah, let's call it that."

"Seventy-five. It's under the regular rate. Mr. Axe doesn't pay any extra for night work."

"Well, every little bit helps with the expenses you have to meet."

"It sure does."

"These lanes we've been passing off to the right —where do you suppose they go?"

"Maybe down to one of the rivers; I don't know. This section's full of rivers."

"Take the next one." Victor put his hand in his shirt and took a grip on the gun without drawing it.

"What *is* this?" Eddie asked.

"You'll see in a minute," Victor said. "Just do as I say."

Moreno swung the hearse into the next opening, and as he did so Victor leaned across and turned off the light switch. Trapped in the sudden gloom, the driver braked hard, then wrenched at the steering wheel to correct a skid in the dirt of the side road. They were on a narrowing downhill track, with saw palmetto and fern palms closing in on either side in compact tropical masses. Moreno slowed to walking speed and changed down to first gear.

"Stop here," Victor said.

The car slithered to a standstill.

"Get out."

Moreno seemed not to have heard. He kept his grip on the wheel with his right hand and fumbled for the glove compartment with the left.

When Victor drew the gun and pointed it at his chest, still looking straight ahead, Moreno raised both hands slowly, holding them level with his ears in a way that reminded Victor of a convert at a revivalist meeting. Victor leaned across to open the glove compartment and took out an old army-issue Colt automatic. "What's the hardware for?" he asked. "Expecting trouble?"

"I been stuck up twice already. Any driver who goes without a gun these days is plain crazy."

Victor waved the Beretta at him. "Let's go back

to the road, Eddie. I got a hunch that something interesting is going to happen."

Moreno got out and Victor gestured to him to go ahead. He was a small figure in the moonlight, with a boy's head on narrow, sloping shoulders. It was fifty yards back to the road, and when they reached it Victor shoved Moreno ahead of him into some low bushes. "Don't feel nervous about this, Eddie. Just keep your head down and cooperate, and everything's gonna be fine."

"Mister, I wish you'd tell me what this is all about."

"All in good time, Eddie, all in good time. We're gonna wait here awhile and see if by any chance something happens to confirm a suspicion I have that keeps growing stronger."

After five minutes, through the small nocturnal sounds in the thickets all around, Victor heard the creep of car tires on macadam. Seconds later a Buick, its headlights switched off, passed them slowly, heading for Kitts Hollow. The car crept past in the dappling of shadows, with a faint gobble of its exhaust, and within seconds its grays had been absorbed in the trees.

"Looks like another guy's battery gave out on him, huh, Eddie?" Victor said. "Okay, let's take a little walk together into the woods."

They walked back down the dirt road, Moreno always slightly ahead, their heels digging into the spongy, moss-carpeted earth, breathing in the black, balsamic odor of the Everglades. A coppery swamp moon had risen, revealing shapeless water among the trunks of pond cypress. Mist hung over it in thick patches like a dimpled quilt. Victor held the gun pointed at Moreno's back, his temples throbbing. Below them, the swamp hissed softly with insects like a distant escape of steam, and some herons bunched in the scrub unfolded their wings to scrabble among the branches, then settled down again.

"Quiet place," Victor said. "Be around here for a month without seeing anyone."

"House down there," Moreno said over his shoulder.

The ghost of an ancient porticoed building came into sight on a hillock over the water, and they walked toward it down the steep slope. A once gracious flight of steps, now husked and shredded by rot, led up to a porch reduced to gray ligaments of wood. A doorway, high and wide, contained no door, and the paintless window frames held no glass. Invisible in the shadows, a burrowing owl released its clear watery gurgle.

"There *was* a house," Victor said. "But not in my time. Or yours." He listened intently. The night was full of soft whistlings and the calls of nocturnal animals, and close by there was a rustling in the undergrowth. It made him uncomfortable. He had a horror of reptiles.

"There's a boat tied up," Moreno said. In these last minutes his voice, lifted by fear, had changed its pitch slightly, and he had become short of breath. He pushed the sweat out of the deep creases of his face with his fingertips. "Hunters come down here all the time, jacklighting for alligators."

"Not any more," Victor said. "Not in the Everglades. Even I know that. The only people who come to a dump like this are vacationers. In summer, not in March." He left Moreno for a moment to wander over to the boat, then returned. "Your boat's waterlogged and stove in. I figure that right now there's nobody within miles of where we're standing. We're on our own, Eddie. What do you suppose was the idea of that Buick tailing us back there?"

"Why should it have been tailing us, mister? For Chrissake, couldn't it have been a couple of guys with dames looking for somewhere to pull in?"

"With all the lights off?"

Moreno shrugged his shoulders.

"Want to know the way I figure it? The way I figure it, that was the same car that turned off back there down to Jackson Pond. Soon as we were out of sight he came back on the highway. With the moon up, he didn't have to use his lights any more. When I stopped to make that call, he stopped. He was back there waiting a couple of hundred yards away, but we couldn't see him."

"If that car *was* tailing us, mister, I don't know nothing about it."

"That's something we have to consider very seriously, Eddie. That's what we have to decide. Right now I'm gonna go through your pockets, so you just keep your hands up and let me see if there's anything more about you than meets the eye."

Moreno held his hands up and Victor went over to him and emptied his pockets, which yielded a few coins, a key ring, a torch and a bedraggled billfold. Victor shone the torch to examine the billfold's contents.

"Nothing very surprising here, Eddie. Two ten-dollar bills and three singles. One notice of insurance payment due sent to that Yeehaw Junction address of yours. One garage ticket. One receipt from the Immokalee Flamingo Motor Court for five ninety-five, and a religious pamphlet, *Prepare to Meet Thy God*. Know something? Everything about you— I mean that frayed shirt of yours, those pants with the patch in the knee, those boots just about falling off your feet and this stuff you carry around in your pocket—leaving aside what you tell me about yourself, gives me the impression that you're a pretty poor guy. Sure, you carry a gun—well, who doesn't these days? The picture I have of you is of a guy who busts his ass all day and half the night to be able to send home a few bucks regularly each week to his loving family on New River Inlet. I have to admit, Eddie, that the kind of man I go for is the one who puts his wife and kids first. That's what impresses me about you. But, Eddie, one little thing spoils this front of yours. Just who is Andy? I got a picture of a lovely young broad there who seems to know you. 'All my love, Eddie, to a wonderful guy,' she's written on it. 'And thanks for Reno. From Andy.' Thanks for Reno, huh? What were you doing in Reno, Nevada? You didn't tell me about that."

"I was a steerer for one of the clubs there."

"A coupla months or so ago, by the date of this picture. A steerer for a club in Reno, huh? That sure changes my image of your personality. Why didn't you tell me about Reno?"

"I guess I was scared."

"But of what, Eddie, of what? What's the matter with your breathing? You got to knock off chain-smoking those coffin nails. What were you so scared about?"

"Of the way you'd take it. Is it all right if I put my hands down?"

"No, just keep them up where they are. Let's talk about this beautiful young broad of yours. Some hooker. That looks to me like mink she's wearing. All my love to a wonderful guy. I bet you cut a swath out there. You in your tuxedo with that sweet little lady on your arm. Your old daddy back in Simon Drum would have been proud of you."

Suddenly Victor jammed the nose of his gun into Moreno's crotch. He let out a whimper like a dog.

"Listen, Eddie, that's where you keep your *colliones,* isn't it? I'll give you three seconds to talk, and then I'll blow them off. Just for a start. You're some sort of private dick, aren't you? One of the kind they write all those books about. Ever heard of the Mafia, Eddie? A lot of people will tell you it doesn't exist, but maybe that's what you're up against right now." He snapped off the safety catch. "Question number one, Eddie. Who are you working for—the Narcotics Bureau?"

"Get that gun out of my crotch, and I'll talk all you want."

Victor raised the gun. "Well?"

"I guess so. Well, sort of. I had to take the job because I was strapped for money. They throw something my way once in a while. They had a couple of special agents over from Miami waiting for you to show up, but they got into a car smash-up this afternoon. A couple more were on their way down from Melbourne; that's why Axe wanted you to stay the night. When you told him you wanted to take off right away, he had to pull me in because I happened to be the only guy on the spot with a private eye's license."

"So Axe was in on this."

"He had to be. The FBN had to tell him. They've had agents hanging around the place every day for the last two weeks. The shipment was held up in Cuba, for some reason. It only got in two days ago. They had a tip-off from Cuba, that it was coming."

"A tip-off from Cuba, huh? So that was what happened. Did they take all the stuff out and substitute bags of chalk or something?"

Moreno was recovering his breath and nerve, and seemed to go into details. "Nope. One of the guys handling the thing wanted to, but the others figured it wasn't a good idea. They wanted you to lead them to whoever was taking over the stuff, and they were afraid you might stop and check. They didn't think it was necessary. They had nothing to lose by not making the switch. They put a tail on you and they have prowl cars on every road between here and Miami. That hearse is conspicuous. I hate to tell you this, mister, but you aren't gonna get away."

Victor looked at him, weighing the possibilities and alternatives. By now there was a trace of impudence in Moreno's manner and expression, a rebirth of confidence. He seemed more relieved by the end of suspense than depressed by the predicament he was in. "Pretty soon that squad car is gonna decide they've lost you, and they'll put out a call for a roadblock at Kitts Hollow and then come back and take a look down all these side roads."

The sensation of being trapped was growing in Victor. He had been trapped before on that winter's day at Chipnuck and beaten almost to a pulp, and now it was happening again, and with this awareness he felt the onset of the fears and phobias which the psychiatrists had not quite succeeded in expelling forever. Why the hell wasn't Mark here when he really needed him? The ground at his feet moved; a pair of enormous copulating toads slithered past his boots on eight legs. He shuddered with disgust. "D'ya think they have snakes around here at night?" he asked irrelevantly.

"They come out at night. Cotton mouths and cane-brake rattlers. Buddy of mine died last fall from a bite. There's a kind of plague of them right now. They keep serum in the hospitals, but you gotta get to a hospital in time." There was a sly cheerfulness in Moreno's voice, as if the death of a buddy was entertaining.

"This is where it happened?"

"In this section. Five or ten miles away, maybe."

"Right here, you might say. What do they call this place?"

"Goose Flat."

"A plague of cotton mouths and canebrake rattlers. Jesus, no wonder nobody lives around here any more."

Being trapped had reactivated all the old symptoms. Signals from his body warned him again of damage incompletely healed; of nerves crushed in their casings, blocked-off veins, masses of inert scar tissue that fought the regeneration of the cells. *I was okay as long as I didn't have to worry about anything,* he thought. *Those punks sure marked me for life.* "Where's the nearest town of any kind over that way?" Victor gestured across the limp maze of water among the trees that now, in the full power of the tropical night, had begun to shimmer.

"The nearest town? Cooper Slough, I guess. Ten miles away as the crow flies. If you're thinking of taking off in that direction you hafta remember there's nothing but creeks full of pond cypress and alligators. You'd never come out alive."

"Not much of a proposition, huh, Eddie? Ya know something? I've never seen an alligator outside a zoo, and I never want to see one."

"I been in Brazil," Moreno said. "You ever heard

of the Mato Grosso? The Mato Grosso's got nothing on what's waiting for you out there. It would take one of those river-dozers the forest rangers use with equipment for cutting their way through the mangrove and cypress to get from here to Cooper Slough. Even if you made it, they'd be waiting for you. Listen, mister, why don't you give some thought to turning yourself in? Whatever you do, they're gonna pick you up sooner or later, and when they do they'll put you away for a long time. At this stage you still got a chance to make a deal. The way it is now, you're looking at eight to fifteen, minimum, but I'm gonna personally guarantee that if you surrender, you'll get half the regular sentence."

"Eight to fifteen, did you say?" Victor said. "Eight to fifteen's a long time, Eddie. That sure is a long time."

"You're a kid now. Christ, you'd be pushing middle age when you came out. If you want to make a deal, all you have to do is stop making things tough for people. Make it hard for them and they're bound to hit you with everything they got. This is the biggest haul of H anybody ever tried to bring into this country. If you get a judge who's rough, he's gonna bury you. He'll put you away until all your teeth fall out."

Victor dropped his left hand to his stomach, where pain had started to dart through his bowels. He knew it was an onset of nervous diarrhea, the most explosive and uncontrollable of all his old psychosomatic ailments. It felt as though a human hand had been plunged through the wall of his abdomen to twist at his entrails. Seen in a double version as his vision slipped out of register, Moreno was watching him with curiosity. His foolish, hangdog Indian face was now alert and intelligent. An idea flashed through Victor's anguish that should Moreno decide to rush him, nothing would happen if he pulled the trigger. Automatics were chancy and undependable. Maybe he's little, but he's as hard as nails, he thought. He knows all the tricks and I'm sick.

"Listen, Eddie," he said. "I hafta shit. Keep those hands up and don't move. Make the slightest move and I'll plug you." If I can hold him off while I shit, it's gonna be okay. If he's gonna try to take me, this is the time.

He unloosed his belt with his left hand and squatted, keeping the nose of the gun pointed at Moreno's navel. A tiny squirt of diarrhea did nothing to relieve his torment. He had lost all control of the muscles of the lower bowel, and could do nothing to help it expel its contents.

Softly haloed against the moon, Moreno stared down at him, contempt and derision on the threshold of his expression. The spasm passed. He realized that his next problem would be to speak without slurring his words and running them together.

"Not feeling too good, mister?" Moreno said. "Maybe something you ate."

"I'm okay," Victor said. "I've been wanting to shit ever since we left Sedge Bay." His sphincter gripped ground glass and fire, and he clenched his teeth to stop from groaning as a new pang began to grow and spread its roots to every part of his abdomen.

"You look pretty sick to me," Moreno said. "You look like something poisoned you."

Victor passed more diarrhea, the pain slackened and he could breathe again.

"Where did you say the trial would be?"

"I didn't say anything about a trial. You'd come up at Tallahassee for a federal offense."

"With a minimum of eight to fifteen."

"Or five to eight if there was a deal."

"Down here I guess they're not too fond of Guineas like me, any more than niggers or Indians. What's it like being an Indian in a place like this, Eddie? Not too great, huh?"

"You play ball with these people and they're okay whether you're a Guinea, an Indian or whatever. They hate to be hassled just like anybody else. When you're in a box, it don't make sense to make things hard for other folks. And you happen to be in a box, fella. Your only out is to turn yourself in. Cop a plea, do short time and forget about it."

Suddenly the fire in Victor's intestines went out, and with the passing of pain his brain cleared again. He got up, pulled up his pants and fastened his belt, the gun still trained on Moreno's solar plexus. He smiled happily. "I got a better idea, Eddie. I just decided I'm not going to turn myself in after all."

"You're making a great mistake, bud, that's all I can say."

"Like you said, we have the biggest haul of H ever brought into this country up there in that hearse. I've decided that I don't want to let it go. Why should I? I've never seen a better hiding place for a shipment of junk than these woods. All you and I have to do is carry those coffins to a nice safe place in the trees, pull a few ferns over the top of them, and there you are."

"They're gonna find it wherever you put it," Moreno said. His voice lost confidence with the swing of the pendulum.

"What makes you think that?"

"It stands to reason. They're gonna follow our tracks and then start looking around. Those coffins weigh a ton. They'll know they won't have to look far."

"Yeah, Eddie, I get your point. But there won't be any tracks. It won't take you and me five minutes to rub them out of this gravel. And there won't be any hearse. All I want you to do right now is just walk back to that hearse, keeping in mind that this gun is pointing at your spine, and do whatever you have to do to get those coffins unloaded."

Moreno turned around and started up the slope. Climbing into the driver's seat, he pressed the dash-board switch of the motor that opened the hearse's rear doors and sent the first coffin sliding out on its rollers. Five minutes later all three of them had been unloaded and dragged into a persimmon thicket at the side of the track. Bamboo vine in the persimmon bound the branches together, patching the smallest rent in the foliage with its big, heart-shaped leaves. Fireflies' needle-points of light pricked through the shadows of the thicket.

"Nobody's ever gonna find these coffins, Eddie, until we show them where they are."

"What are you planning on doing now, bud?" Moreno asked.

I've got to give him hope or he'll put up a fight, Victor thought. I have to convince him he has a chance. It has to go off without any fuss. He couldn't rely on his own strength; his double vision was back, accompanied by a persistent ringing in his head, and he was afraid that at any moment the cramps in his stomach might seize him again.

"I'm planning to dump this hearse."

"Where?"

"In the swamp down there. Where else?"

"The riverbed's way out. You only got two or three feet of water. What's the good of that?"

"Two or three feet of water and two or three feet of slime underneath. This clunk weighs like a railroad locomotive. It's going right down out of sight. All evidence that we've been here has to vanish, Eddie, and you personally have a big decision to make. I told you just now that boat was stove in. It isn't. We can bail it out and it will float. I'm about to offer you a chance to save your life. You know your way around these rivers. If you want to come in with me on this, you can come along. You want to play this the sensible way, you can even make yourself a bundle. This junk belongs to the biggest mob in the Southeast, and if I tell them you helped me look after it for them I'd expect them to show their gratitude in the usual way. Even if you do hit the big time in Reno once in a while, Eddie, I'll bet you could use a hundred grand for doing my friends a service."

"Why should I believe anything you tell me, bud? Whatever you say now, what's to stop you changing your mind as soon as you get out of that boat?"

"Eddie, you have to believe me because you don't

have any choice. I'm holding a gun on you. I'm figuring on getting away, and if you feel you've got to try and stop me, I'm gonna blow your head off. You're being offered a deal, so why not be smart and take it without arguing? Even if you put me in that courthouse in Tallahassee, you'd lose out in the end, because as soon as you'd testified the mob would send a couple of headhunters to lay in wait for you and finish you off."

"What's to stop you from knocking me off when we get wherever we're going?"

"Sentiment," Victor said. "I got sentiment like anybody else. I happen to have taken a liking to you, Eddie. You're a pretty smart guy; you know your way around. I have a feeling that if this works out right for us, we might get together. I mean, why should I want to whack you out?"

"You said a hundred grand?"

"That's right."

"I'd have to pull out of here until the heat was off. Where do you suppose I could go?"

"Mexico, Eddie. Maybe that broad in the mink would go along. They say Acapulco's a pretty nice place."

"Yeah, I guess it is."

"Meanwhile we have to do something about covering up the evidence around here, so why don't we make a start by smoothing out those tire tracks?"

Victor transferred the gun to his left hand to break away the dead branches that hung just off the track. He gave one to Moreno, and in a few minutes they had smoothed away the shallow ruts left when Moreno had braked to a standstill in the dirt.

Victor straightened himself, threw his branch away and looked down the track to where, at the water's edge, it plunged under the bog myrtle frosted by mist. "Steep, huh?" he said to Moreno. "How do you ever suppose the people living down there got up and down?"

"By mule cart," Moreno said. "All these houses

had mule carts in those days. A good team of mules can pull a cart up the side of a house."

"You know everything, Eddie. What do we use for oars when we get in that boat?"

"Pull a couple of boards off the house, shape them up a little and use them as paddles."

"How about all that mangrove and swamp cypress. We going to be able to get through?"

"If you know the way, you can do it. It's not too bad."

"In other words, you were exaggerating, Eddie."

"I might have been. You have to keep in the wide channels, that's all. It's common sense."

"Anyway, it looks like we're all set for our big adventure," Victor said. "All we have to do now is dump the crate. What we're gonna do is get in, get it started and jump."

"Or we could push it," Moreno said. "What's wrong with giving it a shove?"

"What's wrong with that is I have to be sure this crate really goes in under the surface. It has to be doing fifty when it hits the water. What you have to do is put it in second, turn the hand throttle wide open, drop the clutch and jump."

"What are you gonna do?"

"I'm gonna be right in there with you. I'll be at your side. We leave the doors open, and the moment she moves we jump."

"How about putting that gun away? If I trust you, you gotta trust me too."

"I will, Eddie, I'll put it away as soon as we're in that boat on our way to Cooper Slough. We're gonna be buddies on an equal footing, which is as it should be. We'll be heading for the big time, you and me, Eddie. Maybe they'll even ask you to join the mob."

Moreno was reluctant and suspicious, sensing the sickness, tension and submerged insanity in the man who confronted him. He stared up into the barrel of the gun, pointing now at his right eye, and tried to weigh the psychological pressures that produced the wild smile alternating with Victor's gritted teeth and wincing expression.

"Get in and get started, Eddie."

Moreno got into the driver's seat and started the engine, and Victor climbed in beside him.

"Got that door open, Eddie?"

"Sure."

"Okay, give her some more gas."

Moreno screwed open the throttle hand control another half-turn and the engine roared.

Victor braced himself, his right leg through the door. He held the gun close to Moreno's temple.

"Okay, Eddie, let her go."

The hearse gave a jump. Victor pressed the trigger and the gun leaped in his hand like a small trapped animal. The violent jerk of the car had deflected his aim. He saw a small black spot stamped in Moreno's profile at the hinge of the jawbone, and in the instant before will power and consciousness failed, Moreno dropped the wheel to throw himself sideways, and then Victor was pushing himself through the door, hitting the track with shoulder, rump and knees, rolling and picking himself up in time to see the hearse hit the swamp. The water spread wings on each side of it, like a great gray dove about to settle. Then a milky swirl closed over the hearse's roof, from which a second later there foamed a rush of bubbles. For a long time the bubbles formed and broke; then there were no more. A blister of water rose and deflated, and the whistling of tree-frogs, momentarily interrupted, resumed. Victor straightened himself, pushed the gun out of sight in the opening of his shirt and made for the cover of the thicket. All the fugitive's unreasoning fears pressed down on him. He had the sensation of being watched, along with an irrational conviction that in some way Moreno had managed to escape.

He let perhaps ten minutes go by, then began to tread softly among the leaves, picking his way from the cover of bush to bush, skirting the paper-white glare of moonlight, to the edge of the swamp.

Peering through the palmetto, he watched the water, unable to shake the conviction that sooner or later Moreno would appear, suffering from little more than loss of blood and exhaustion, to drag himself wearily ashore. Maybe that bullet only knocked a couple of teeth out, he thought. That guy may have been little, but he was tough. Chances are he got out of the car before it hit the water and is holing up somewhere, waiting for me to take off.

He listened again for the movement or sound that would warn him of Moreno's skulking presence, then, crouching, and like a man preparing an ambush among the underbrush, he skipped across to the ruined house. An opening in the wall offered a side entrance, and he slipped through. The Everglades jungle bursting in through the windows had taken over the first two rooms, and Moreno's flashlight revealed vines, tree fungus and bats among the exposed rafters. Victor was not prepared for the strange bareness of the third room, which had been cleaned. An oblong of moonlight lay across the swept floor, and at the edge of it stood a rocking chair with a broken back. A fishnet was propped in a corner, and a cupboard with its door hanging off contained an empty whiskey bottle and tins holding what might have been flour, sugar and salt. Four bricks where a hearth had once been enclosed the embers of a fire. The bricks were still warm, and the room reeked faintly of tobacco smoke. The feeling that he was being watched enveloped him again, so strongly this time that he backed to the wall and drew his gun. The house echoed with creaking sounds, and there was a sudden scuffling under the window. He tiptoed across to look out, but saw nothing but moon-whitened foliage and a corner of the swamp. Someone's been living here all along, he thought. Some hobo. Maybe he saw the whole thing and just took off. I have to get going.

The first thing was to find something he could make a paddle out of. The decayed cupboard seemed to offer the best possibility, and he ripped out a shelf. How am I gonna shape it, though? he thought. What am I gonna use for a knife? Maybe I should have taken the Indian along after all, and dumped him when we got to Cooper Slough. He had to get away. He went back through the rooms full of vines, and out into the moonlight again. He walked faster, and then he began to run toward the boat, the mud sucking at his boots. This surrender opened the stopcock to fear. Imagination merged with reality to pursue him with threatening sounds, movements and shapes; above all, he felt himself stalked by something that was both sub- and super-human in its malevolence—the very essence of death.

9

Mark had told Teresa that he expected to be away three or four days, but she showed no surprise or pleasure at his sudden reappearance, nor any concern for his dispirited condition.

"I thought you were still in Miami. What did Di Stefano want?"

"He wanted to tell me that my brother was dead," Mark said, his face averted.

Her indifference, worn carefully like an elaborate costume, was thrown into momentary disorder. Teresa had always had a soft spot for Paolo.

"*Madonna.*What happened?"

"A car accident. I flew back for the funeral."

She muttered incomprehensibly between whitened lips, but he waited in vain for the flood of disbelief and rage against the conquest of death, of which he knew she was capable.

"Where was he buried?" she asked in a small, quiet voice.

"Campamaro. In the grave with his father and mother."

"God rest his soul."

Beyond that there had been no questioning. Teresa appeared to regard the details of his stay in their home country as of no interest, and wanted no news of their friends.

"I tried to call you from Miami," he said. "There was no reply."

"I've been out a lot," she said. Suddenly he remembered that it was the children's midterm holiday, and that they had gone to stay with friends.

"Did Victor call?"

"Not while I've been here."

"He should have called Monday. I'm worried about him."

"If he heard my voice he'd probably have hung up. As a matter of fact, someone did."

Mark struggled against the barrier of her apparent indifference in an attempt to make her see how important the experience of his visit to Sicily had been to him, and how it had led him to the crossroads in his life. "There's nothing left there for me any more. Mamma and Paolo have gone. I may as well be realistic; I'm not likely to see or hear from my sister again. Crespi made it quite clear that he didn't want to see me . . . The other friends, too. No sign of any of them—they've given me up. It's finished as far as I'm concerned."

She had gone off into the kitchen, where he found her tinkering in a mechanical way with the dials of the new washing machine.

"I've often thought of going ahead and taking out citizenship papers. I guess there's no point in holding back any longer. I always had the idea at the back of my mind that maybe we'd go back someday. The way I feel about it now, the bond's no longer there."

"You should have taken out the papers long ago."

"I didn't feel sure, but now I do. The knot's been cut."

He tried again, battling against apathy and silence. "An offer's come up. We could pull out of this, go to Cuba and make a fresh start. How do you feel about it?"

Suddenly the indifference was shattered. She stared back at him with a fury that aged her by twenty years and disrupted all the proportions of her face. "For God's sake, don't talk to me about Cuba."

He gave up. "I don't think we're going to get anywhere with this discussion tonight. I'm tired, and maybe you are, too. Let's talk about it tomorrow."

The next day when he came home from the office, she received him tight-faced.

"Did Victor call, by any chance?" he asked.

"No, he didn't. A detective was here to see you today."

"A regular police detective?"

"No, a man from an agency."

"Did you see his license?"

"Should I have asked to?" she said. "He was very polite. A Mr. Smith, working for some firm in Boston."

"A private detective is bound to show his license," Mark said. "Otherwise how is anyone to know he's on the level? These guys have a way of pushing themselves in. What you have to remember is that you don't have to talk to them or let them into the house unless you want to. Did he say what he wanted?"

"Something about Cuba. As it happens, I'd be happy not to hear any more about that place. He left his card and said for you to call him."

"There's no reason why I should," Mark said. "If he shows up again, give him my office number, and if I'm not busy I'll talk to him. Anything else happen today?"

"Yes," Teresa said. "I saw Hannah."

"Hannah?"

"Hannah Cobbold."

"Yeah, I was forgetting. She got herself involved with some detective agency, didn't she? Maybe this fellow's visit had something to do with it."

"It could be," Teresa said. "Since it's about Cuba. Hannah's spent half the money Andrew left her on private investigators."

"With not too much to show for it, I imagine."

"Not until a few days ago, but there's been a breakthrough. She never believed that story they gave out about the way Andrew was killed, and now she's been proved right."

"You mean he wasn't knocked off by student revolutionaries?"

"No, he was either killed by an American, or by someone hired by an American. This agency sent a man to Cuba, and he was there for three months working on the case. The Cubans gave him all the help they could, and a lot of things came out. It was one of those typical mob killings."

"How do you tell a typical mob killing from any other kind?"

"The thought that goes into it, the preparation. The mob knows how to cover up its tracks. If they can find some way for an innocent person to take the rap, they do it. Any witness is liable to be killed. This time they shot a Cuban fisherman who saw what happened. No revolutionaries would have shot a poor fisherman."

Mark noticed the growing excitement in her manner and a new, hard edge to her voice. He felt that he was being stalked, driven toward a hidden trap. "How do you know about these things?" he asked.

"It was the same back at home. In Pioppo when I was a child, eighteen men were killed by the men of honor. They killed my uncle, and an innocent man was sent to prison for ten years."

"You never told me."

"I can keep things to myself just as well as you can. They killed my uncle because he started a lawsuit over some land, and a man who never harmed him or anybody else was sent to Procida. That was the way it always worked there, and that is the way it still works here—only here they call it the mob. So many men went to prison for murders they'd never done. Just like that student revolutionary they planted the gun on that was used to kill Andrew Cobbold. Only the men of honor would have thought of that."

"Being a woman, you only see half the picture,"

Mark said. "There are lots of things you can't possibly understand."

"As I've been told before so often," she said. Her cheeks were flushed with something like exultation. "But just because I've said nothing doesn't mean I didn't know what was going on. You wanted me to believe that story they put out about the way Andrew was killed, but I was never fooled by it. Andrew was killed because he came up against drug-pushers in Cuba."

"He's dead and gone, whichever way it was. Whatever they uncover, nothing's going to bring him back. He was the husband of someone who isn't even a close friend. Why should it matter so much?"

"It matters because I and my children happen to be involved."

"How can that be?" he asked, bracing himself and feeling the cold shadow of what was to come.

"A girl called Linda Watts was with Andrew when he was killed." A kind of malevolence had sharpened her face. He had never seen the expression before.

"What about her?" he said.

"The Cuban police say she may have been used as a decoy."

The feeling of remoteness he always experienced in moments of crisis overwhelmed him. The sensation of himself as an individual waned; soon he would see himself almost as a third person in this encounter.

"She was a stripper working in some cabaret right here in town. A hooker," she said, pronouncing the word carefully and uncertainly as if it was foreign. "She traveled to Cuba three days before Andrew's death, and left the day after."

"Why the drama? He was entitled to invite a girl friend down."

"She wasn't his girl friend. The Cuban police were able to account for practically every minute she spent while she was in Havana, and she wasn't sleeping with Cobbold. She gave a Boston address at the hotel she stayed at, and they've already traced the girl who shared an apartment with her before she came to Salisbury. After she left Havana she dropped out of sight for three months, and then she turned up in Boston to collect some things she'd left. She told her friend that some man had taken her on vacation to Cuba, and that she'd had a bad experience while she was there. Since then she's known to have changed her name, and they haven't been able to locate her. But now they say it's only a matter of days before they do." She was breathless after this rapid burst of words, waiting for him to speak.

"You still haven't told me where you come into this," he said.

"I come into it because you happen to be my husband. You took Linda Watts to Havana."

It was pointless and undignified to deny a fact that had certainly been checked and cross-checked by the meticulous firm from Boston. He kept silent, watching her face, where strange undercurrents of relief seemed to show under a shallow indignation.

"You may as well know. They found out you traveled to Cuba and back with her. The agency has shown Hannah a photograph of the three of you taken by a photographer in some nightspot. You were seen hugging her at Idlewild on the afternoon of the day you came back. Incidentally that piece of information didn't come from the agency. It was told to me by someone who thought I didn't deserve to be as happy as I was, and went out of their way to let me know long before all this blew up."

Mark examined the problem judiciously. "What you've told me," he explained gently, "doesn't throw any light on Andrew Cobbold's death. There was a girl with him when he was killed. I suppose that's news, but it doesn't seem to matter much. Why should she have been a decoy? If the police developed that theory from the fact that she ran off and changed her name, it's not enough. Girls like that are always in trouble; they're never short of reasons for wanting to drop out of circulation."

"The decoy theory is the police's, not mine. They

say they're certain that Andrew was murdered by an American, or by a gunman employed by an American, and that the girl acted as decoy. Whatever the truth is, we'll know as soon as they find the girl, and that's not far off."

"Have you talked to anyone about this? Anyone at all?"

"No," she said. "I've done all that could be expected of a good Sicilian wife. For the last time."

He stared into her face with a new curiosity. "It's hard to believe that you're the same woman I married," he said. For a moment the mask of a stranger had slipped over her face, as it had occasionally in the past. He realized now that the precious qualities of silence and acquiescence had been exhausted with her youth. In the last few years everything had changed so quickly and so totally. The children, once Sicilian, were now quite American—precociously independent, separated from them in an American way. As a family, they were being pried apart. In Sicily, he thought, we stayed together to fight the enemy outside, to keep it out of the home.

It was time to confess. "Whatever I've done, I've done for all of us, and there was nothing else to do but what I did."

"You've been a man of honor all your life," she said. She paused, startled by her own recklessness, almost as if in fear of a blow.

He stared at the new, unrecognizable face, shaking his head.

"The men of honor are like a monster," she said. "An *orco,* with twenty arms and ten heads. None of you has a separate life. You've never been free to live like other men. First it was Don C., then Vincente Di Stefano. Who will it be when Di Stefano goes? A man who carries out other men's orders. You're not allowed to think for yourself."

Coolly he wondered how she knew these things, how she had come by this deadly knowledge debarred by custom from women. Perhaps all the wives knew, after all; perhaps a womanly habit of pretense was as deeply ingrained as the secrecy of the men.

"I'm going to leave you" she said. "Not now, not immediately, because I haven't worked it all out, but as soon as we can settle things between us. I don't want a divorce, but if you do I'll take whatever steps are necessary so that you can be free. I'd like to find some sort of a job. They're advertising in the *Globe* for social workers. Perhaps I could work as a hospital trainee."

His calm was stoked by disbelief. Such a threat could never be put into action by a Catholic and a mother. "The children," he said. "What's going to happen to them?"

"We'll discuss that," Teresa said. "There's no hurry. Maybe Martin could go to Choate, if you could afford it. A convent school would be all right for Lucy."

"We never intended the children to go away to schools."

"We never foresaw that this would happen. As soon as Hannah Cobbold's people have finished their investigation, she'll hand the case over to the district attorney. When that happens the children ought to be where they can't see the local newspapers and have their friends bullying them about their father."

"I can keep my name out of this, whatever happens," Mark said.

"I doubt it. Even if the people in this town don't know what you are, they know you're tied up with Di Stefano. A case like this will be just what McClaren's been waiting for. He's going to crucify you."

He was leaving the room when she called him back. She was holding a letter in her hand. "I'm sorry," she said. "This letter came for you while you were away. Your office sent someone over with it. I forgot to give it to you yesterday."

He went into the next room, slit the envelope and took out the letter

Dear Mark,

Forgive me for troubling you, but it couldn't be avoided. At the time you seemed very convincing about a certain matter, but after a lot of thought I decided I couldn't accept your explanation. Last fall I heard that someone was wanting to talk to me, so I thought that I ought to move. Since coming here I've given my life new purpose by joining a religious community, and now a good man has asked me to marry him. Now I've learned that questions are being asked again. Mark, this is probably my last chance of happiness in life. The reason for this letter is to appeal to you to keep me out of whatever happens if you can. If you can't and worst comes to worst, I still believe in you and you know I'll be on your side.

L.

He pushed the letter into his pocket, then examined the back of the envelope, but the clean edges of the seal told him nothing. I wonder if she opened it, he thought. Anybody in her position would have, he supposed.

10

Still in Havana, Bradley lobbied remorselessly for action against the new left-wing government, badgering the White House incessantly to gain the President's ear for a plan of his own. In the end, Howard Springfield, a Secret Service man and reputedly a Presidential adviser, was sent to Cuba to deal with him.

Over the telephone, Bradley invited his visitor to meet him at the Miramar Beach Club. "Any taxi will take you there. We can have a swim if you feel like it, and a quiet chat about things."

The club, which had been Don Vincente's last

purchase in Havana, had recently been taken over by the government. Springfield, from a background of Oddfellows halls and small-town golf clubhouses, was astonished by its opulence—at the marble, the polished teakwood, the oil paintings, and the busts of the great sugar profiteers who had been past presidents and who gazed down serenely on Miramar's new patrons, half of whom were Negroes.

Springfield rented a bathing suit and towel, and left a message at the desk for Bradley that he would be on the beach. The tide had drawn back, leaving the sand, coarsely granular and almost as white as sugar, freckled with small jellyfish. The sea was still and slightly misted here and there, like a mirror just breathed upon. Inshore it was green, with lights leaping and curling under the surface, but the deeper water became inert and colorless, and a distant storm lay on the horizon like a bluish bruise. Pelicans were flying so low that they joined wingtips with their reflections in the water.

When Springfield waded in and swam a few strokes, schools of tiny silver fish darted just under the surface and nudged at his skin. The sensation was unpleasant, and the water too warm to refresh. He came out and lay down on the sand. A party of children under the care of a schoolmistress came out of the clubhouse, funneling their laughter into the bay. They began to lay out the foundations of an enormous sand castle, working from a plan unrolled on the sand and held in position with four stones. The mistress, swimsuited, her blond hair caught up in classic Greek style and splendidly elongated by the perspective, left them for a moment to kick crystal showers at the edge of the water.

Footsteps crunched on the soft sand behind him, and when he turned his head Bradley was standing above him, a club towel wrapped round his middle.

"Hello there, Howard."

"Good morning, *Mr*. Bradley."

"Glad you could make it," Bradley said. "Were you able to fix up a meeting for me with the President?"

"I was not."

"I understand he was at Palm Beach all last week," Bradley said.

"At this moment he's at Squaw Island."

"Do you think I could see him there?"

"Sorry, he's taking a vacation. In any case, he's arranged a meeting with Redpath, and I guess he'll be covering any points you want to make." It was three years since Springfield had worked under Bradley at the agency, and he still felt scarred by the experience. Now, removed though he was from the range of Bradley's power, he still found it difficult not to call him sir, and it seemed disrespectful to continue to lie stretched out on the sand and not get to his feet.

"That's very disappointing," Bradley said. "I was led to understand that a meeting would be arranged. Mr. Redpath was anxious for me to be able to put my views in person, since I happen to be the man on the spot."

Springfield did his best not to overreact, to be betrayed by his lack of self-confidence into outright brusqueness. "The President asked me to come down here," he said. "I have a paper bearing his signature and authorizing me to listen to any confidential matters you wish to raise."

"*You* have a paper bearing the President's signature," Bradley said. Somehow he managed to inject a contemptuous familiarity into the personal pronoun. It was the English equivalent of the French *tu*, used with servants, children or close friends outside the gradations of the social scale. Bradley's *you* made Springfield's possession of a signed note scribbled on an envelope a grotesque error of judgment on the President's part.

At this moment Springfield became aware of a desire to sneeze. It was an effect that confrontations with Bradley had always had on him in the past. The man is ridiculous, he told himself for the hundredth time, but his scorn had never quite erased his fear. "That's what I said," he told Bradley. He was determined to remain cool.

"You've been in intelligence long enough to know

that there are certain things for the President's ear alone. I've already declined to talk to the Chiefs of Staff."

"You can decline to talk to me if you like," Springfield said. "I was requested to make a point of seeing you and discussing anything you might wish to bring up. If you don't want to talk, it's entirely up to you."

Bradley squatted like an Arab at his side, gripping the sand firmly with his splayed, prehensile toes. Springfield felt his eye and the set half-smile containing both contempt and frustration.

"I take it you're one of the brilliant and dedicated young men who surround our new President, Howard?" Bradley said. "The next Augustan age, as the poem goes. It's hard to believe, isn't it?"

"From where you stand, I can imagine that," Springfield said.

"Tell me how do you get along with that bunch? You haven't taken up abstract painting, by any chance?"

The tickling in Springfield's nasal membranes increased. He would have blown his nose if he'd had a handkerchief. He turned his head in search of distraction. Out at sea a boat with a lateen sail of dark red was coming into port, and he tried to absorb himself in its progress.

"You didn't go to Harvard," Bradley said, "and so what? Unfortunately it's what counts in that set. Did they invite you to the Gridiron Club dinner this year?"

Springfield had not been invited to the Gridiron Club dinner. "If there's nothing particular you want to say, perhaps we could break this up," he said.

"Do you really like him as a man—the President, I mean?"

"Mr. Bradley, I'd prefer not to be asked questions of that kind. As far as you are concerned, I have no personal opinions."

"We worked together for three years," Bradley said. "I would have hoped to find some evidence of a little more rapport."

"Why don't we just go back to the locker room and I'll show you that piece of paper," Springfield said. "If you're not interested you can write 'Nothing doing' on it and then we can each go our own way." In a few minutes I'm going to tell the bastard to go to hell, he thought.

He shifted his position so that Bradley's profile was removed from his field of vision. By now the schoolchildren had finished their impressive sand castle, and it awaited the pretty teacher's inspection. She stood over them to discuss their work. In the past sand castles had been haphazard, but now they conformed to logic and order. Some pupils received commendation and others a gentle correction. The corner of a bastion was patted here, a shell added there. Finally a small national flag was tenderly unfurled and stuck on a turret. A calm scene. It was hard to believe, as Springfield had heard, that they were all sitting on a volcano.

Swiveling his body through an angle of ninety degrees, Bradley intruded on his sight again, making conciliatory hand movements, as if arranging flowers. "Actually, there's not a great deal to say. What I offer is a simple foolproof solution to a problem which must be weighing as heavily on our beloved President as on anybody else. I imagine you know what's been going on in Florida and Guatemala these days as well as I do."

"You mean that bunch of gin-mill cowboys you people have gotten together to take over this country? Yeah, I've heard—who hasn't?"

"It happens to be a project I'm not too happy about, in spite of Redpath's enthusiasm," Bradley said. "A lot of people could get killed. Even if all goes well, we can expect between two and ten thousand casualties."

"If all goes well."

"If it doesn't, it could be five times that number. As things stand, this is going to cost a hundred million dollars—fifty million a week for an estimated two weeks. But suppose it lasts six months. Or more? Besides which, what about the international repercussions? However often we tell people this show is being run by the Cubans, nobody's going to believe it isn't our war."

"So what's the foolproof solution?"

"A team of specialists we could send in to take out the man with the beard."

"I thought something like this was coming," Springfield said.

"I've given considerable study to it, and the situation's straightforward. You can take my word for it: there's no such thing as security here. It doesn't exist. The bearded man comes and goes as he pleases, and nobody gives it a thought. I've had my assistant keep a check on all his movements, and we've established a clear pattern. A specialist would have all the data he needed."

"And you have someone in mind for the job?"

"I have indeed. A perfectionist."

"I see," Springfield said. "Well, a number of things look wrong to me about this."

"Go on."

"What makes you think that if you take one man out you're going to topple the regime?"

"Because this is a one-man band. We believe we could make a deal with any successor. We've already had talks with a cabinet member who's told us that it's only the man with the beard who's holding them back."

"You said something about international repercussions," Springfield said. "Can you imagine what all these Latin American countries—who hate our guts as it is—are going to say?"

"There wouldn't be any problems. They might guess we'd had a hand in it, but they'd never know for sure. Taking one man out isn't quite the same thing as financing an invasion. Anyway, what's the Alliance for Progress all about? As soon as he's gone we could spread a little more money in the right places and have them eating out of our hand again."

Springfield scrambled to his feet. "That's what you wanted to talk about, is it?"

"That's the broad idea. If the President could give me an hour or so I'd be happy to fill him in on the details. When will you be seeing him?"

"I don't know," Springfield said. It was his moment of triumph and he savored it happily. He had never felt more relaxed. "What you've just told me wouldn't justify my breaking in on his vacation," he said. In this single sentence he wiped off all the old scores.

In complete command of the situation, he began to walk toward the clubhouse. Bradley tagged along at his side, suddenly defeated and subservient, reduced to expostulations to which Springfield hardly listened.

How have I handled this? Springfield asked himself. Just the way John, Lester or Bob would have played it, he hoped: with chilly calm, but no show of rancor.

When they reached the clubhouse door, Springfield stopped and turned to Bradley, smiling. "I hear they're still calling you Agency fellows Donovan's Dreamers," he said. "You know something? Times are changing, and we ought to change with them."

Still brooding on this reverse, Bradley flew to Guatemala, where he inspected a bedraggled contingent of exiles and mercenaries waiting to take part in the attack on Cuba, then returned with strengthened misgivings to Florida for an interview with his chief, Julius M. Redpath, Director of Special Operations, in his Palm Beach vacation home. It was the morning of the day of Victor's travails in the swamp.

"Well, I finally decided I had to see the President," Redpath said. "I suppose you succeeded in convincing me at last." He shook his head violently, either to emphasize what he had to say, or perhaps in a nervous spasm. He was a hypochondriac, a man hollowed out and aged by stress, from whom pessimism flowed like an electric current. "Let me say here and now, I don't feel—nor have I ever felt —that there is anything to be done with this man.

He was obviously determined to avoid a private meeting, and the impression I came away with was a wholly negative one. The only man he's prepared to listen to on the Cuban issue is Howard Springfield. Your suggestion, by the way, was turned down with some emphasis."

"Was I mentioned by name?"

"No, but Springfield referred to you indirectly and in an insulting manner. There was some reference to screwballs who hear voices. I'm sorry to say that the President laughed."

"I knew we were washed up when he sent Springfield in the first place."

Redpath sat miserably in a cane chair. He had attempted to disguise his flagging and sickly appearance in gay holiday attire, boldly striped Bermuda shorts and a flowered shirt, but it only underscored the atmosphere of dejection. In his youth he had taken over the leadership of the wild men of the organization, conducted flamboyant coups, fought secret wars and tricked and manipulated the malleable President of the day, confident that brilliant *faits accomplis* would excuse all—which they did. Under his shrunken and ailing exterior Redpath was still a buccaneer.

Mention of the current President, who, alas, was so far from being malleable, had stimulated a small, growling pain in the pit of his stomach. "Excuse me a moment," he said. He got up and went to a cupboard, poured a little white mixture from a bottle into a medicine glass and swallowed it down, wincing at the flavor of peppermint.

He sat down heavily again. "I fear, Ronald, that we no longer have anything to hope for from the White House, either as individuals or as an organization. Don't ask me to tell you how this information was obtained, but after I left the President he made no bones about expressing a totally hostile attitude to us. His actual words, as near as I recall, were, 'I made a mistake keeping Redpath on. Something's got to be done about the CIA. Bobby is wasted in the Justice Department. That's where he should be—if we decide to keep the Agency going. I sometimes wonder how Ike got by with that bunch of dogs yapping at his heels. McNamara is handling Defense and Rusk has done a lot with State, but no one's dealing with Redpath and the CIA—and that, gentlemen, is precisely what I propose to do.' Those were as near as doesn't matter a damn the President's actual words."

"It doesn't sound too promising, does it?" Bradley said.

"When the President saw fit to say that, he sounded the death knell of my hopes. But having excluded your simple solution for the problems of Cuba, I can't bring myself to believe that he's really committed to the alternative. However much he may pay lip service to the project, one senses a lack of enthusiasm. He says yes in a way that makes it sound like no. It's impossible to extract a firm promise from him. As things stand, we're short of men, money and arms. This thing could go off halfcocked, and if it did, it would be one of the worst disasters in our nation's history."

"The worst," Bradley said.

"Ronald, I want you to answer me straight from the shoulder: in your opinion, am I the kind of man to harbor delusions?"

"I wouldn't say so, Julius. No, most certainly not."

"Thank you," Redpath said. "That at least is reassuring, and I feel in need of reassurance." His eyelids flickered nervously, showing between them only the whites of the eyes, and he suddenly reached out to tear a sprig of foliage from a potted bougainvillaea and dangle it between his fingers. "I have a feeling that this nation of ours is being taken for a ride. Mysterious powers seem to me to be at work behind the scenes—non-democratic forces over which we have no control."

"As you know, those are my sentiments," Bradley said.

"It was expressed so well in that chapter you showed me from your book. By the way, what is the news on that front?"

"The publishers have it now. I hope they're going to rush it into print."

"It comes in the nick of time. It may well save our bacon, Ronald. If we fail on this Cuban enterprise, do you know what they'll do? They'll bury us."

"That is why we mustn't fail, and that's really why I came to see you today. I'm told we're short of funds again."

"We're short of everything. Not a single cent has been allocated since the last administration. Such funds as we have are under constant scrutiny."

"Have we passed the hat around?" Bradley asked.

"Several times," Redpath said. "But it's almost impossible to alert people to dangers that do not affect them directly. Several of our oilmen friends say they want time to think about it. One or two people with interests in Cuba—Di Stefano in particular —have been generous, but we're still broke."

"Would five million dollars help?"

"Five million dollars would be manna from heaven."

"I think I know where to get it. Remember Salvatore Spina?"

"Very well. It's a year or two since we met. He's a man one doesn't forget."

"He has a huge stake in Havana. I'm sure he'd do what he could."

"Five million, you say? I'm already wondering what to do with the money."

"We could buy seven B-26's, for instance."

"Are you joking?"

"I rarely joke when serious matters are at issue, Julius."

Redpath had suddenly undergone a physical change. The tightening muscles of his face had injected something bold and piratical into his expression. Color flowed into the gaunt cheeks, and a red spot appeared over each cheekbone, as though an inept make-up man had just daubed rouge on his face. "Where are they?" he asked with a firmness that was almost menacing.

"In cold storage at the Milonga military airfield in San José."

"And we could get them?"

"Why shouldn't we? The president and the defense minister run a racket. They've been trying to peddle them for years, but the market for bombers is very small."

"They can't resell war equipment supplied by our government without a license from the State Department, which would certainly want to know where they were going."

"The State Department needn't know about it. Everybody has old B-26's, and they all look the same. We have nine, don't we? This would bring our strength up to sixteen."

"Have you actually seen them?"

"With my own eyes. Seven beautiful B-26's." Bradley smirked with self-satisfaction. Suddenly he cupped both hands and dropped them to his crotch to execute the strangely obscene southern mime of a man weighing an enormous pair of testicles. It was a gesture meant to draw attention to the solidity and importance of any object or proposal, but was lost on Redpath who knew little of Mediterranean Europe.

"And you're saying that these people are in a position to dispose of national property and pocket the proceeds, just like that?"

"They sold a British frigate last year. It's kept them in funds until now. I haven't met the president, but I know the defense minister. He has fourteen sports cars, an executive jet, a helicopter and a big yacht. He runs through money fast. Five million dollars wouldn't go very far."

"Thank God for the corruptibility of Latin-American politicians," Redpath said.

The seven B-26 bombers which San José offered for sale to a discreet purchaser had never taken to the air since purchased five years before, and had stood in makeshift hangars with leaky roofs that provided little protection from the torrential summer rains. Some months previously, Bradley had taken an expert with him to inspect them. The price originally spoken of had been $200,000 a plane; now it was half a million. "We have been obliged to spend a good deal of money on them," explained the representative of the Ministry of Defense.

Bradley's expert shook his head. Rust and corrosion had penetrated wherever it could. The machine guns had been stolen, instruments stripped out, the tires were in poor shape, and nothing could persuade the bomb bays of three planes to open.

The defense minister had no objection to a U.S. firm overhauling the seven planes for a sum of $35,-000 per plane, to be paid by the eventual purchaser, and as a concession agreed that this cost might be considered a deposit deductible from the total price. The order was given for the work to go ahead.

Within three months the work had been completed, and Bradley was assured by his expert that the B-26's would fly. Then came the shattering news of the failure of Victor Di Stefano's mission, confirmed in a laconic telephone message from Spina himself. This meant that there would be no money to buy the planes.

In Miami, Redpath held out little hope of raising the cash elsewhere. "There isn't time," he said. "This thing is going to take place in a matter of days, and there's no way we can stop it."

"If we don't get these planes, we don't have a chance. Is there anything you can suggest?"

"I can give you a list of possibles," Redpath said, "but it's very late in the day. We should have appealed for our friends' financial support in the first place. Even an oilman doesn't keep millions of dollars under his bed."

Bradley made one desperate race against the clock around Texas, but the shrewd men who took his hand in their hard grips failed to take him seriously, and he came away with little but assurances of good will, sympathy and promises. From Houston, he flew to San José to throw himself on the mercy of his friend, the minister of defense, who embraced him warmly when they met but enormously regretted that credit could not be extended. The terms of cash on delivery would have to remain.

Redpath had flown to Guatemala, where preparations for the invasion were in their last stages. Bradley flew there from San José to report this reverse to his chief.

"I saw Ricardo Asturias," he said as they shook hands. "The B-26 deal is off."

Redpath showed no sign of surprise. "Frankly, I could never bring myself to believe it was on."

"The cash was not forthcoming, and Asturias and Company wouldn't agree to wait. Being men without faith, they have no faith in others."

"Of course not. That's understood," Redpath said.

"You realize we have Ferguson to thank for what's happened," Bradley said. "He was in league with our enemies. I've been very gullible. We're surrounded by spies."

"Trust no one," Redpath said. "Didn't I hear that he'd died in somewhat unusual circumstances? Somewhere in the Far East, wasn't it?"

"In Laos, actually," Bradley said. "He was traveling in a river boat that was attacked by insurgents. Fortunately he was the only casualty."

Despondency showed in Redpath's face like an onset of fever. "Of course, even if you had been able to produce the cash, they'd have found some excuse to call off the sale. I believe they are under orders —from you know whom. I'm convinced the President is preparing to betray us. Cuba is to be sacrificed, and all the other things we've fought for, Ronald, all the things we've fought for."

They were seated on the veranda of a farmhouse rented for the Director of Special Operations. Below, an Indian horseman on his way to the market town of Retaluleu rode past, dragging a capering bull calf on a rope. In the distance the perfect cone of the volcano of Santa Maria released a wisp of smoke, curled into a question mark. Wavering bugle calls came from the direction of the town, where the invasion forces were drilling out of sight.

"The legion of the doomed," Redpath said. "With inadequate air support, they'll be massacred on the beaches—if they ever do get ashore. What we are witnessing is sabotage in its most subtle and odious form. This is to be an engineered debacle, after which the President believes that he'll be allowed to turn his back on Cuba and everything it stands for."

"And international communism will have triumphed," Bradley said.

"Through its ability to establish a beachhead even in the White House itself. If I remember rightly, that is the central thesis of that book of yours."

"Above all in the White House. Beginning with Roosevelt and the New Deal."

"The eyes of the American public will be opened at last. When is it due to appear?"

"I'm afraid it won't be appearing," Bradley said. He smiled. "The allies of international communism have proved too much for me. It's been suppressed."

"Ronald, you don't mean that."

"It was done in the calmest, most diplomatic fashion. Sometimes one has to admire the way that they handle these situations. The publishers held the completed manuscript for as long as they dared, then simply asked to be excused from going ahead."

"Presumably they showed it to some member of the inner establishment."

"Undoubtedly. They offered no explanation other than that they felt the book lacked general appeal. I made no attempt to pursue the matter because I knew perfectly well that I would never be told what had really influenced their decision. My dear Julius, I've trained myself to be a realist. I'm a marked man, and so, I believe, are you. In Texas I heard that the Vice-President is going to be dumped in 1964. He's our last hope."

"My conviction," Redpath said, "is that the coming fiasco will provide the excuse to destroy us. Neither of us will survive the purge that lies ahead unless we're ready to contemplate extreme measures—not only in self-defense, but in the defense of our country."

"Extreme measures?" Bradley asked, exploring Redpath's dejected expression for a clue.

"Need I say more? Measures designed to confront an extreme emergency. Actions that might be unthinkable at any other time. I wonder if you have any inkling at all of the real purpose of my visit to Guatemala, Ronald? No, of course, you can't."

"My assumption was that you were here to do what you could to get the invasion off the ground."

"I am here," Redpath said, "to investigate a famous mystery: the assassination a few years back of President Castillo Armas." Suddenly he thrust out his jaw in a manner he believed to be Napoleonic, and waited in vain for Bradley's tribute of surprise. "Subjected to a dispassionate analysis," he said, "it was one of the most successful operations of its kind ever. It was quick, clean, and left no aftermath of public disquiet. A scapegoat was found, presented as mentally unstable, and quietly disposed of. The true motives behind the murder—which, of course, were political —never leaked out. If assassinations have to happen, this is how they should be carried out." He smiled in celebration of this triumph of death.

"I remember being taken in by the official version myself," Bradley said. "If anything, it was *too* smooth. That was the one thing that made me suspicious."

"Who do you suppose set the operation up?" Redpath asked. "I happen to know."

"One of our native crime syndicates, I would have guessed. It was executed in the Sicilian manner. My guess is that someone imported Mafia specialists who charged their fee and did a professional job." Bradley rubbed the palms of his hands together in a brisk gesture of finality.

"Your guess and my conclusions coincide," Redpath said. "Now, do you believe that you and I have anything to learn from this particular case that may be of value to us?"

His thin voice was enriched by insinuation, and while countering the stare of Redpath's eyes, suddenly alert in the dim mosaic of his features, Bradley speculated uneasily. "I'm not at all sure what you're getting at, Julius," he said.

"Why should we fence with each other? Let's put it this way. Are you personally willing to give up and be led like a sheep to the slaughter, or would you join me in a fight for the principles in which we believe? I'm anxious to be assured of your loyalty."

"Surely you could never have doubted it. Besides which, I have no intention of putting my head on the block," Bradley said.

"You have special contacts. You're the only one of us who has. I know you've always maintained that sooner or later an emergency might arise grave enough to compel us to turn to them. I believe that the moment has come. Do I make myself clear?"

"Abundantly," Bradley said. He found himself on his feet. Redpath had risen as well, and the two men clasped each other's hands. "I don't want to overdramatize," Redpath said, "but I have an extraordinary feeling that destiny is beckoning to us."

Bradley had the feeling too. His throat ached, as it sometimes did when he listened to great music.

"Our country awaits our action," Redpath said portentously.

Three days later a middle-aged Cuban air force officer, Captain Perez, in command of the military airfield at Havana, received a dawn phone call ordering him into action against an invasion force that had violated Cuban waters during the night. The captain, a brave but unemphatic man who had reached his position in the service purely through seniority, found himself in a quandary. It was the fifteenth of April, 1961. On the previous day, mysterious air attacks had been carried out against all the leading military airfields, in the course of which a quarter of the country's tiny air force had been put out of action, including the captain's nimble T-33 jet trainer, which was as good as any combat plane short of an outright fighter of the Mig-Mirage-Vampire class. This left him with only an old British Sea Fury which was

slow and cumbersome by comparison, and for which
Perez had no affection. Perez had never fired a shot
in anger, and neither of the two other pilots, Lieu-
tenants Ferrer and Mateos, who were available for
the mission, had any experience either.

Ferrer would fly a B-26 made largely from cannibalized spare parts, and with four instead of the
normal eight machine guns, and Mateos a second Sea
Fury. Perez, who had spent the night worrying, put
down the phone, drained his fourteenth cup of black
coffee since midnight, finished a letter to his wife
in which he gave instructions for the disposal of his
property and for his children's education, and went out
to take to the air.

Landings were reported at the Bahía de Cochinos,
and twenty minutes after takeoff the three planes
were over the bay. Perez saw that most of the invasion
fleet was at anchor a mile offshore, but that the largest of the transports, a Liberty ship with its decks
crowded with troops, had maneuvered to within a
hundred yards of the beach, and that landing craft
were leaving it. The scene from three thousand feet
was pacific, and what Perez did not know was that
debarkation had been much delayed in a climate of
panic and confusion, and that there had been a brisk
battle between the commandos from the ships and
parachutists on their own side who had been dropped
by the planes flying in from Central America. Following this debacle, one of the battalions aboard the
transport had refused to land.

Perez dropped one of his two 250-pound bombs,
missed by at least twenty yards, and sheered away,
his Sea Fury holed in several places by heavy
machine-gun fire. He decided that his best hope of
hitting the transport was to risk a low dive that might
tear the wings off the aged plane when he pulled it
out. At 1,200 feet, well under the ceiling of cannon
fire, blood vessels bursting in his sinuses, the plane's
nose held steady at 400 miles per hour and pointed
at the center of the deck crammed with stampeding
soldiers, he fired his four rockets. They struck amid-

ships, and almost immediately the ship began to heel over. On his second run he sank a small transport anchored out at sea, and used his cannon to scatter a procession of landing craft.

Mateos, who in Perez's opinion, suffered from defective vision and could never hit any target, however large, dropped a 500-pound bomb on the stern of the ship carrying all the expedition's communications equipment and its reserves of ammunition. It blew up and went to the bottom within minutes. "The biggest fluke in the history of aerial warfare," was Mateos' modest description of his feat, and though Perez secretly agreed with him, it was a fluke that ruled out any possibility of the invasion's success. For several days the men who had been put ashore fought a crippled, defensive battle, but those who looked on from behind the scenes knew that there was no hope for them. When the President, deceived, even disobeyed, was prevailed upon to permit a final bombing from Central America, it was only in the hope of making possible an evacuation of the beachhead. Even this bitter expedient failed because the difference in the international time clock had been overlooked, and the B-26's arrived over the beach exactly an hour earlier than the jets from a carrier that were to have given them support, and there they met their end.

Four days after the fiasco in the Bay of Pigs the last of the men who had been put ashore surrendered and were carried off to prison.

11

"Mark," said the voice, "this is Bradley. Yes, Ron Bradley, your old pal. That firm you used to work for gave me your number. I'm in town, and I have to see you. Listen, I was thinking of running over to that garage—Harrison's, isn't it, on 22nd Street? I've gotten the antique-car bug since I saw you last, and I hear they may have some parts for an old Cord I just picked up. It also sounds like a nice quiet place for a chat. Any chance of meeting you there in an hour's time?"

"You could have come here, but if you prefer it that way it's okay by me," Mark said. Bradley never seemed to grow up. Why all the stupid secrecy and playacting? Why not simply meet in any bar?

Salisbury's equivalent to the Parco della Favorita was a lane with a scrapyard on both sides, hidden from 22nd Street by low cliffs of cars waiting to be cannibalized or crushed in the hydraulic press. Here Bradley had parked a Porsche convertible, and he waylaid Mark on his way to the Harrison office and took his hand in a crushing grip. "Wonderful to see you again, Mark, after all this time. You're looking great. A lot thinner, I guess, but still pretty good."

A little more fat had accumulated on Bradley's cheekbones, and a white hair had appeared here and there in his eyebrows; otherwise there was no change. He was wearing the best-looking tweeds Mark had ever seen, but in a conservative English style that appeared flamboyant in Salisbury. They went over to sit in Bradley's car. Nearby a crane that reminded Mark of a praying mantis groped delicately among the disordered metal before fastening its metal jaws on a victim. A sharp-nosed trollish man, bald and pink, scanned them indifferently from its cabin, and a metal saw chirped over and over like a raucous tropical bird.

"I'm happy to see you again, Mark. I mean that; it's been a long time. I've made a point of stopping by in the hope of seeing you when I was in this area, but you've always been away. It was Havana last time, if I remember right. I notice you've been in the headlines a few times this year. I felt it as a kind of personal triumph when they decided to drop that homicide charge against you. As soon as the Watts girl dropped out of sight again, I knew they didn't have a chance. Even before they lost their key witness it was the shakiest case I've ever seen. What are you doing with yourself these days? Still in the real estate business?"

"I'm on my own, as a consultant," Mark said. "I

left the firm I was working for soon after Mr. Di Stefano gave up his interest in it."

"And how is Don Vincente? I haven't seen him in years either. A nice man, if ever there was one, a man I've always liked and admired. He's had a lot of bad breaks lately, from what I hear. Particularly with that son of his, Victor. I'm sincerely sorry for the poor guy. He loses all his money in Cuba and then this happens to his son. It's been one thing after another."

Mark waited, the tension doing its subtle, undermining work on his body. He remembered the Bradley cat-and-mouse technique of old.

"Victor took a bad beating, but he should be okay by now," he said. "When I last saw him he was looking good as ever."

"I wasn't referring to the beating," Bradley said. "Haven't you heard? They picked him up in Bonito Springs last week. He's in on a rap for murdering an agent of the Federal Bureau of Narcotics and for smuggling in the biggest single consignment of heroin ever brought into this country. My guess is he's going to the chair."

"That's bad news," Mark said. "I didn't know." He'd learned of Victor's capture thirty-six hours after it took place, but he wanted to hear the official version and judge how much Bradley had edited it for his benefit.

"It was pretty improbable, dramatic stuff," Bradley said, with a wide gesture that was circumscribed by the cramped spaces of the car. "Victor was carrying the H in a hearse. When they had him cornered he succeeded in hiding it, shot the agent and dumped the hearse in a swamp. They found some crazy hobo living in a shack down there who saw most of it. After that Victor hid out in the Everglades for a couple of weeks living on raw fish. By then he'd grown some sort of beard, so he came out of the swamp and took a job as a waiter in a fried-chicken restaurant, and that's where they picked him up."

"I heard they were looking for him, that's all, and that they'd found a lot of junk."

"He was very close to you, wasn't he?" Bradley said.

"I was sorry for him."

"He stayed with you for a month or two on Champlain Avenue, I'm told."

"We looked after him for a while after he got that beating. Whatever he did, in many ways he's a nice guy."

"It would do him a lot of good if they could find out where he put the heroin. And you too."

"Why me? All I know about this is what I read in the papers, and what you're telling me now."

"Mark, why don't we both quit stalling? We know and respect each other, and we're both grown men. I think I ought to tell you what this is all about without mincing words. You're in bad trouble."

"You're not telling me anything new."

"I'm not referring to the Cobbold affair alone; that's only part of it. I'll come straight to the point. The FBN is going to have you deported. They're going to send you back home."

"Quit bluffing, Bradley."

"I respect your intelligence too much to try. They *can* have you deported, and they will. Even apart from Cobbold and Linda Watts, you've been a close associate of a man who brought ten million dollars' worth of heroin into the country and knocked off one of their agents. Further, since you've been in the U.S. until a month or two ago, you've worked for another man recently described in the *Providence Journal,* and I quote, as 'one of the dark captains of the underworld.' "

Scorn showed in the depressed corners of Mark's mouth.

"Sure it's journalistic license," Bradley said, "and you and I aren't impressed, but it all tends to count in formulating a recommendation for deportation. Some say that you were Di Stefano's right arm. At this moment it's all that's needed. Anyone knows they can never make any charge they bring against you stick, but nothing's going to be easier than to deport you. I can never understand why, against all good sense as most people see it, so many of you fellows never bother to take out citizenship papers. All the Bureau has to do is make a case that you're an undesirable, and they're in the process of doing this! You're going to be a victim of the awakened public conscience over the rise in drug usage. So I very much regret to tell you that within two weeks you'll be on your way. If it's any consolation, you won't be alone. You'll be the third to go in a month. It's one of their periodic drives."

Mark, who had been working in a climate of patient austerity to rebuild some sort of future for himself, and to construct an anonymous life in some other city where eventually he hoped to persuade Teresa to return to him, was stunned by the weight of the blow. He knew that Bradley was not bluffing; it would have been pointless because the man knew that through his connections Mark would have little difficulty in checking the FBI's intentions.

"What's the deal?" he asked.

Bradley winced. "I wish we didn't have to think of it as a deal. You're an old comrade-in-arms of mine. I've led a lonely life in the service, and made few friends, but I always think of you as one of them. We've both hit a bad patch, Mark. You're in a terrible spot, and I've just been faced with the knowledge that my life's work has crumpled . . . We ought to consider helping each other. That's the way I'd like to look at it."

Mark fully understood that the showdown had come at last. For all Bradley's sentimental flimflam, the facts were as hard as facts always were. Deportation was the weapon of the moment, and he wholly accepted the fact that he was going to have to do something for Bradley. Back in Sicily he wouldn't last twenty-four hours, and Bradley probably knew that too. "Let's have it," Mark said. "Why beat around the bush?"

"Very well," Bradley said. "So be it. Have you ever heard of a man called Armas? Castillo Armas?"

"The name rings a bell," Mark said. "He was in the news a few years back, wasn't he?"

"In 1957, to be precise," Bradley said. "He was the president of Guatemala and was rubbed out for political reasons."

"Wasn't he knocked off by some whacky palace guard?"

"According to the story they put out," Bradley said. "The true facts are that it was a killing of a very special kind, carried out by what I prefer to call by its original name: the Mafia. Sorry to have used that word again, Mark; I know you used to find it offensive."

In the old days, Mark would have returned a stony glance. Now he smiled. "It's only that I associate it with the tabloids."

"Call a spade a spade, I always say. However, to proceed: as far as we can gather, the marksman was a Cuban who was serving a life sentence in prison somewhere. The prison governor used to make nice little sums on the side letting him out to do jobs like this."

It's a small world, Mark said to himself.

"Do you find that as fantastic as I do?" Bradley asked.

"Probably not," Mark said. "Latin America is like that."

"He was flown into the country and out again by a syndicate pilot."

"A Mafia pilot?" Mark said.

"If you insist." Bradley chuckled. "We are told that he was back in his cell within twelve hours." His enthusiasm grew, and he rolled his bulging eyes before going on. "It was a marvelous piece of organization. A political crank was used as a fall guy. They shot him and planted a diary on him that explained his motives and proved he was crazy. Everyone fell for it. The case wasn't even a six-day wonder."

"People believe what they are told," Mark said.

"Naturally there was some tidying up to be done afterwards. What do you call it? *Ripolitura,* isn't it?"

"*Ripulitura,*" Mark said. "With a *u.*"

"*Ripulitura.* Sorry. My Italian's getting rusty. It

wasn't too big an operation, but it was very thorough. Twenty or thirty people who could have known too much disappeared. There were a lot of car accidents, and at least one unexplained plane crash at about that time. Whoever set it up paid a lot of attention to detail."

"A craftsman, from what you say."

"Yes," said Bradley, "quite clearly an organizing genius in his way. The trouble is we have no way of finding the guy. That's why I've come to you. I believe you could learn more."

"What did you have in mind?" Mark asked.

"We want you to plan something along the same lines for us. Just what it is will come as a surprise. You can have twenty-four hours to think about it if you like."

The idea itself *was* a surprise, but with Mark all emotions produced their counterreaction. His mood of detachment set in.

"How about it?"

"I'm out of touch," Mark said. "I've been selling real estate for the past five years."

"We won't talk about that trip to Havana, but what about the years before that? I'm thinking of Messina, Sardi, Mancuso, Gentile, and the rest. And who had La Barbera whacked out?"

"What do you want me to say?"

"Mark, I'm probably the only Anglo-Saxon who ever had one foot inside the door of the Honored Society. I knew a lot of what went on."

"There were certain things I had to do, and I did them as efficiently as I could."

"In other words, you carried out the orders of your superiors, believing it to be your duty."

"You could call it that."

"Do you have any objection to telling me how Messina was killed? You don't have to go into the details; I know them. It's the strategy that interests me."

The past had become remote history, and Mark hardly ever thought of it any longer. He frowned a little in the effort to concentrate the sprawling epic of bloodshed and betrayal into a few unemphatic words. When he spoke, he did so slowly and thoughtfully as if discussing a mathematical problem and its solution. "The idea was to get him away from his friends to a place where he was on his own. In the mountains he had weight, but out of them he was nothing. As soon as he could be fooled into coming down from the mountains, he was finished. The death itself was nothing."

"How about Gentile?"

"It was the same thing. When he was surrounded by his people, no one could get near him. The man was crazy about goats. All they had to do was rig up a goat auction outside his own territory. The details were different, but the plan was more or less the same. The same thing applies to Cremona when he was taken out at Collo."

"But the Armas assassination presented a different kind of problem, as I see it," Bradley said.

"It was a political killing, wasn't it? So it's bound to be different. The difficulty there must have been to keep the people of Guatemala from getting wise. I'm only going by what you told me. That's where the fall guy came in."

"The ideal hit might be a combination of both methods," Bradley said.

"It could be unbeatable."

"I want you to do just that for us," Bradley said. "This is the operation I want set up. The marksman, the pilot, as much *ripulitura* as necessary. Craftsmanship, Mark, huh?"

"You're asking for the moon," Mark answered, but already he knew that there was no remedy but acquiescence.

"In return," Bradley went on as if he hadn't spoken, "I offer my guarantee that the FBN will cease to press for the deportation. Then that Watts girl could come out of hiding, which will kill the story going around that you've had her put to sleep. I'd sponsor your citizenship if you wanted. The main thing is, you'd be left in peace."

"Something else would have to be included in the deal."

"What's that, Mark? I thought I was being very generous."

"Victor Di Stefano. I wouldn't like to see him go to the chair."

"I'm not sure I can promise anything there."

"You'll have to. His father will have to come into this, and I can't go to him empty-handed."

"What would he expect? Eight to fifteen?"

"Five to eight," Mark said. "Maximum. He dotes on that boy."

"I can only say that I'll see what can be done. You know me, Mark. I've got a few connections, and I'm going to try very hard. When will you see Don Vincente?"

"As soon as I can."

"Good. You know something, Mark? I'm not much of a drinking man, but I wish we could have had a drink together to celebrate this. It's taken a long time."

"What's taken a long time?"

"It's taken a long time for us to get together again in a purposeful manner. Way back in Sicily fifteen years ago I knew that sooner or later there would be something that had to be done that only you could do, and I planned that we should be together. For your good, for my good, and for the good of the country. It's been a long time coming, but right now it seems that it's working out the way I figured it might."

Mark found a hint of insanity in the combination of Bradley's smile and stare. The man's turned into a nut case, he thought; some kind of psycho, maybe. "I don't get it," he said. "What do you mean you planned that we should be together?"

"I asked Don C. to send you to me in the States, and he did so. I had Don C. appointed mayor of his home town when we took over in Sicily. He wanted to repay me."

Mark drew in his breath and held it. Something in his imagination that had not yet expressed shape juggled with obscure intuitions and offered shadow solutions for unposed questions. He felt astonishment in so pure and intense a form that it barred all other emotion. Then calm settled like the anesthesia that sometimes accompanies a terrible wound.

He breathed out again. "And so Don C. turned me in to the Gentile outfit."

"Whatever the mechanics of the thing were, I have no idea, and I would certainly have resisted any suggestion of betraying you to your enemies. We both agreed that a young man with your unique talents could look forward to a brighter future in the new world than the old. In those days the prospects for both of us seemed pretty rosy, though to date it hasn't worked out as well as I'd hoped. Our working partnership is being resumed at a time when my life's work has been frustrated. My only ambition ever has been to be able to serve my country and better humanity, but you wouldn't understand that, would you?"

Gli anime, chi ti murt, May God punish your dead souls, Mark was muttering to himself without moving his lips. His ancestors, those hard men who had survived the centuries of despair, forbade the display of anger through which power was squandered, and enjoined reflection and self-control. All that mattered was to be allowed to stay in the United States, so that sentence could be passed on Bradley in the secret, internal court he would soon set up. If it was decided that Bradley must pay with his own blood for Paolo's, there was time. But the enemy must never be warned in advance by any sign of overt hostility.

"You're a man devoid of passion," Bradley was saying. "Perhaps the only human being I've ever known to be so. I can't think of anyone else who would sit there as you do, without moving a muscle of his face, after being told what I've just told you. Either you really have nerves of steel, or you don't experience emotion in the way that other people do. Which is it?"

Mark turned a bland face to him. "I've learned to be philosophical."

12

Dinner at the Di Stefanos' proved an orgy of gluttony
and grief. The aged Donna Carlotta, once a delicate
beauty from Castellammare Del Golfo but now re-
sembling a skinny old man in feminine attire, presided
over a table laden with greasy food which was constantly replenished by the latest Puerto Rican maid-
of-all-work. It was a family affair. A place had been
carefully set for the absent Victor, but the two priests
Mark had seen in the hallway casting their shadows
like bat's wings had not been invited to join them at
table. Donna Carlotta's skull-like features were heavily powdered, and rouge coated her cheekbones. She
wore a rust-colored dress fifteen years out of fashion,
bought second-hand, and talked incessantly in a
monkey-like chatter, between words snatching mouth-
fuls which she chewed angrily and swallowed with a
rolling of the eyes. The tips of her long, stringy fingers
were greasy from sly fumblings in her plate.

"As you can see, we're in despair," she said. *"Ridotti
alla disperazione.* My poor boy. If ever there was a
saint. Tell me, Marco, what they going to do to him?"

Don Vincente sat huddled over his plate, his eyes
the color of the saffron rice with which it was heaped.
He ate with difficulty, forcing himself to swallow only
because he believed it was good for him. He waved
a hand that was slowly turning into a claw, the fingers
curled as if around small coins. "Nothing's going to
happen to him, Mamma. He's going to get off. He'll
be okay."

"You say that, but you don't do nothing. You don't
do nothing for your son." At that moment the maid
returned with a tray of roast suckling pig in garlic
sauce, to add to the cooling tagliarini *in brodo,* stuffed
artichokes, chicken and veal already on the table,
and Donna Carlotta's eyes swiveled to follow its progress. "Take *porchetta,"* she said to Mark. "Please

don't make compliments. Here you're in your own house." She grabbed his plate for the second time and piled it high with a haunch and half a dozen ribs. Don Vincente looked away hastily. In the presence of food his wife became like an Arab. After she had helped herself to a shoulder and crammed a roll into her mouth, she remembered her misery again, and her eyes filled with tears.

"He was framed. My boy was framed," she said.

"Sure he was framed," Don Vincente said. "It was the biggest frame-up in history. This poor kid was naïve. I figured on a double play when they tried to pin that rap on him for rape. I made a bunch of enemies way back, and this is how they get to me."

"Our son wouldn't fool with junk," Donna Carlotta said. "We brought him up to be a good boy. Maybe nobody told you this, Marco, but he was going into the Church. Only his father didn't want it . . . *Ma Lei non mangia.* Why don't you eat nothing? Maybe you don't like *porchetta*. The chicken is good, take some chicken."

Don Vincente rinsed his mouth with inky Sicilian wine and shook his head. "You could say that horse's ass McClaren started all this, but there was somebody behind him bankrolling him, and who it was I'm going to find out."

"Our boy was as good as bread from the oven," Donna Carlotta said. "Incapable to hurt a fly. To say that he has shot and killed a man is a *sciocchezza*." A tear began to roll down each cheek. "Go on, eat," she said. *"Porca miseria,* excuse me, but you're too thin."

"When Mr. Truman visited this town, I was presented to him by the Dutch mayor we had in those days—what was his name?—and he shook me by the hand. I put the word around and Salisbury voted Democrat. I guess now maybe I made a mistake. Truman was okay, and Eisenhower too, but look what we got now, for Chrissake. Look what's happened to us. Who d'ya suppose this country's being run for nowadays? Lemme tell you the answer: for the niggers, the commies and the spics."

"What's that word they say he had?" Donna Carlotta asked. "I mean for a boy who wants to listen to God's word, and pass it on, when other kids are out playing ball games, or maybe playing hooky?"

"A vocation?" Mark suggested.

"A vocation. *Vocazione*. Sure, that's what I mean. You can't believe what a sweet boy that was. Marco, you're our best friend. Even if his father won't stir a finger for him, you have to do something to save him."

"You wanna hear what Truman said to me? Because I can remember the words, just the same as if it was yesterday. 'Mr. Di Stefano,' he said—this was before the time they all started calling me Stevens— 'Mr. Di Stefano, I value the unique contribution of the Italian community to the prosperity and the well-being of this nation. I've heard how the people talk about you in this town, and it certainly is a pleasure to make your acquaintance, and shake you by the hand.'"

"And so he should shake you by the hand," Donna Carlotta said. "Who put this town on its feet? Who fixed it so that not one single father of a family had to stand in the breadline? Who handed out a quarter of a million dollars to the City Hospital? Who gave dowries for twenty-two girls in the Three Mary's Orphanage?"

"I happened to have a nice cigar on me, and he took it and put it in his pocket," Don Vincente said. "That was a guy who knew how to make a friend."

"If you'll pardon me the expression, *siamo fottuti*," Donna Carlotta said. "Nobody raised a finger to stop the Reds taking away all we owned in Cuba. Who's going to find two hundred turkeys for the poor of this city next Christmas? Not McClaren, lemme tell you."

"That horse's ass," Don Vincente said. He took another mouthful of harsh wine, wincing at its flavor. "They've closed down everything. Thirty-two empty buildings on Dwight Street, and an unemployment rate of ten percent. I don't hafta tell you this, but if you want to place a bet you gotta drive into Cranston. You hear we got a coupla gangs of kids in the streets?

They'll break both your legs if you don't turn out your pockets and hand over your watch. All these young punks shoot themselves up with horse. Whaddaya call that—progress, democracy?"

"This town has become a jungle," Mark said. "Everybody knows that."

"This used to be a great place to live in," Don Vincente said. "D'ya know something? It was trouble-free. All the police had to do here was hand out parking tickets. You can thank McClaren for the way it is now."

"Quello stronzo," Donna Carlotta said. "He wants to clean his ass on our faces."

Don Vincente brushed the vulgarity aside. "Please don't say that, Mamma. Just call him shit . . . Lemme say this, Marco, I used to run this town. President Eisenhower sent me a signed picture of himself. I guess someone mentioned to him how much I contributed to his campaign."

Her eyes brimming with tears, Donna Carlotta was tugging at Mark's sleeve. "Do me a favor. At least try the *polpette.* You're going to ask me what's in those meatballs, and when I tell you, you won't believe me. Filet steak, onion and *prezzemolo*—nothing more. We don't use herbs in this house. I want you to taste them and tell me what you think."

"Listen, Mamma, for Chrissake leave the poor guy alone," Don Vincente said. "He can't eat no more than I can. He's got too much trouble on his plate."

"I'm sorry. I was forgetting. Excuse me. I thought maybe you didn't want to talk about it, Marco, but how are things going between you and Teresa? Something tells me you two are going to get back together again soon. Sure you are. We don't want to think too much about our own personal selfishness at a time like this. For the sake of the kids, Marco, for the sake of the kids."

After dinner Don Vincente led Mark off to the privacy of his room, where a television set of his own assembly flickered with greenish ghost images, and the canary, now baldheaded in its molt, still twit-

tered continually and showered its surroundings with
birdseed and sand. As Don Vincente reached out to
switch off a garbled commercial, Mark detected a
nervousness in his expression that was habitually slug-
gish and inert under its cast of melancholy.

"Let's have it. What happened?" Don Vincente
asked.

"So far, so good," Mark said. "Getting a line on
Leon was the biggest break ever. It turns out that
Salvatore pulled him out of that Cuban prison and
put him on the last plane to Miami before the
bearded man took over."

"Salva thinks ahead," Don Vincente said. "He always did. That's why he went right to the top."

"I told Bradley that I could find the guy, but that
I had to have time. He fixed it with the Bureau to
give me all the time I wanted."

"Looks like he's playing ball. I know he gives you
a rash, but right now we have no cause for complaint.
You heard that Victor got moved to Lewisburg? They
gave him a television, and he lives on steak and
eggs. They tell me the cons there sit around chewing
the fat in a rose garden most of the day. We got
another postponement of the hearing. All we need now
is to find a friend in Washington so that he can cop
a plea, do eighteen months and get out on parole."

"I took off for Miami thinking I could run Leon
down in a matter of days. Turns out there have a
million Cubans down there right now. It's chaos.
Without our friends to fall back on, I might as well
have gone home. It would be nice if you sent Malatesta
and that fellow Veneziano at Jacksonville some small
recognition for the work they put in. Between them
they must have spoken to about a thousand spic
refugees."

"It pays to be a friend and to have friends," Don
Vincente said. He was interrupted by a rooster that
staggered into the room and fell against his leg. It
was one of Donna Carlotta's pet cockerels; reared in
the matrimonial bed, and spending their subsequent
lives in house confinement, they were all crippled
with rickets. Don Vincente let out a whinny of

concern, picked up the bird, smoothed its feathers and set it on its feet.

"In the end we found his name on the list of one of the freedom committees they set up. It turned out that he'd taken off for Mexico months before. They picked him up in Miami on suspicion of burning a house down, and he flew the coop."

"A torch artist too, huh?"

"No, just a psycho. He kills and he burns houses down."

"Right now he's in a Mexican can, you said."

"A criminal lunatic asylum. He shot some Mexican kid as soon as he got across the frontier and was up on a murder rap, but they found him not fit to plead. Mexico has a very humane penal system."

"What a *carogna*," Don Vincente said. "How God can let them live." He spat accurately into a small brass spittoon, then wiped his mouth with the back of his hand. "And you believe you can talk them into springing this guy?"

"I've already done it. I went to Mexico City and saw our friend Pascuale. He fixed up a meeting with a guy in the prison service who is interested in raising a large sum for charity. It's going to cost a hundred grand, but Bradley will pick up the tab."

"Jeeze, Marco, that's wonderful. You mean you can get this guy out whenever you want?"

"With a few days' notice. He's going to stay right where he is, weaving baskets, until we want him. We can take him out for a couple of days, just like in Cuba. That way no one notices he's not there."

"What comes next?" Don Vincente asked.

"We have to find a pilot."

"No reason why we shouldn't use the same one."

"If we can find him."

"We can. I made a few inquiries while you were away," Don Vincente said. "The guy turns out to be none other than the famous Harry Morgan, who was used by Rossi of New Jersey in the Galdos snatch."

"I thought he was dead. Didn't he hang himself in his cell in the pen in Panama or someplace like that?"

"The Dominican Republic," Don Vincente said.

"He was going to be extradited, so he had to disappear. My information is that he's living there under a false name."

Mark remembered well the case of Harry Morgan and the kidnapping by plane of a distinguished refugee, who had been seized on a Manhattan street, drugged and spirited away, never to be seen again. The protests by action groups had been vociferous. McClaren's *Examiner* had added a few hundred copies to its circulation while the sensation lasted, and Teresa had joined a Save Galdos committee, formed some weeks after Galdos had been quietly buried.

"That was a terrible *sciocchezza*," Don Vincente said. "Twenty years ago Rossi would have come to me, and I would have said no. These days we don't have respect any more. What we have is egotists who cause trouble to their friends. Cleaning up after this Galdos operation was like a war. So many people got their heads blown off. Sure, Rossi's friends picked up the gambling concession in the Dominican Republic for doing it, but how about all the other poor bastards who were left holding the bag?"

"They tell me the Armas hit was better."

"Even it was bad. All these things are bad. Maybe they learned a little after what happened with Galdos. Two things I always told my people not to fool with —junk and politics. What we all need is a quiet life."

"Amen to that," Mark said.

"The story about Morgan," Don Vincente said, "is that Rossi's brother-in-law, Cardillo, now has the concession in Trujillo City. He looks after Morgan and keeps him out of trouble, and the guy does the odd job once in a while to earn his keep. I have to lay it out, Marco—I have no pull with Cardillo. Maybe I could have told him what to do a few years back." Behind their viscous film his eyes filled with sorrow. "I've lost a lotta weight, Marco. The word went around that I took a bath for thirty million in Cuba, and the respect kind of dried up." He groped for a way of describing his loss of face, but could only find an expression in the Sicilian dialect, which he translated. "I kinda felt my bones fall apart."

"You'll get the money back. We'll be back in Cuba before the year's out."

Don Vincente shook his head. "Listen, Marco, don't let anybody kid you. We aren't going back, and believe me, guys like Rossi and Cardillo know it as well as I do. That's why I have to tell you that if you want to use Morgan for this operation of Bradley's, there's nothing I personally can do for you. You'll have to go and see Cardillo yourself. All I can do is tell him to expect you, and that you're on the level."

"Thanks, Don Vincente. I'll go down there as soon as I can."

"And I want to see you as soon as you get back. Whatever you fix up with Cardillo, I have to know." Don Vincente's gaze had been drawn away to the screen of the television set, apparently searching its flickering depths for some clue to what the future might hold. "I got a feeling about this I don't like," he said at last. "For instance, I used to think we were keeping Bradley on ice for something maybe he could do for us. Now it looks like it's the other way around. I have to admit that he gives me the creeps. *Non è un cristiano*. If there's anything I hate, Marco, it's a mystery."

13

"Send us a picture of yourself, go to Trujillo City, stay at the Managua and you'll be contacted," was the advice Mark received when on Don Vincente's instructions he called a Cincinnati number.

A week later he arrived in the capital of the Dominican Republic, a strange and silent tropical land on which a dictatorship of thirty years' duration had imposed its somber peace. At the immigration desk a concealed camera photographed him while his passport was being stamped, his newspaper was confiscated, and the transistor radio he was carrying was impounded with the assurance that it would be returned to him when he left the country. From every wall the dictator stared down: a burly, thick-lipped man in a general's uniform with four rows of decorations; a yachtsman at the helm of the world's largest yacht; a statesman in full evening attire addressing his tame senate. He had come to power by an election in which he had polled more votes than there were voters, after which he had cold-bloodedly destroyed 30,000 of his political opponents, and was now said to pocket 75 percent of the national revenue.

Mark was astounded by the brilliantly lit but quite empty city streets, and by the servility of the taxi driver, who both saluted and bowed when he got into the cab, and again when they reached the Managua. There the captain and the bellboys also swept off their hats and bowed low. It was a country where those who fetched and carried were under strict orders to be polite to foreign visitors.

Mark checked in and waited, and for nearly twenty-four hours nothing happened. He killed the time as best he could by writing a long letter to Teresa imploring her to send more news of the children, and of herself. He swam in the hotel pool, bought and thumbed through the muscle and girlie magazines that were all the reading matter in English offered for sale by the cigar stand. No visitors were allowed to leave the city limits without a special police permit, and the only sights a taxi drive could provide were three churches and a derelict zoo. The town closed down at sunset.

At night the hotel became an oasis of noise in the silent desert of the city as gamblers poured into the casino and the dice and card games began. Mark sat in the bar waiting until all but one of the drinkers had gone off to play. At last the remaining customer called for his check, came over and sat down at Mark's table and held out a well-manicured hand. "You're Richards, aren't you? I'm Johnny Cardillo. I heard you might be down here."

Cardillo had inherited the kind of peasant face that

economized in flesh, with deeply set eyes, a meager nose and small, makeshift ears added as an after-thought. He was dressed in gray mohair, with a finicky conservatism that betrayed his race.

"You American or Italian, Richards?"

"Sicilian."

"From what part of Sicily?" Cardillo looked at him closely, as if suspicious of a boast.

"Campamaro. Near Caltanissetta."

"Do you happen to know Enna?"

"It's about fifteen miles from where I was born."

A cautious delight appeared in Cardillo's face and began to spread. "Well, whaddaya know. My father came from Enna, and the old lady was from Santa Caterina on the Caltanissetta road."

"My grandmother on my father's side used to live there. She ran the bakery. Died at ninety-four."

"In Santa Caterina? Well, it sure is a small world, Richards. Fancy meeting a guy from Caltanissetta in a dump like this. Some coincidence, paisano, huh? How long are you planning on staying in Trujillo City?"

"A couple of days, maybe. Not more."

"That's a pity, Richards. I don't often have the chance to bat the breeze with someone from the old country. You should stick around. We have a nice little thing going down here. I might even be able to cut you in. We had an operation going in Haiti before we moved down here. Know Haiti? Too many god-damn niggers around for the big spenders we used to bring down from Kansas City and St. Louis. This is white man's country. They keep the jigs in their place." He stubbed his cigarette out in an ashtray decorated, like all the others, with a small bust of the dictator. "El Benefactor," Cardillo said. "He's half jig himself. You may not like him—most people don't —but he sure keeps this country on its toes. You hafta face it, now that Cuba's gone, this guy's all that stands between us and Communism south of the Rio Grande."

Two visitors from the north with the standard faces of gamblers drifted in. "Hey, where's the game around here, fellas?" one called, and like a man herding sheep, Cardillo waved them toward the far door.

"Listen, Richards, I hear you want to meet Morgan," he said when they'd gone. "This can be arranged—otherwise we wouldn't have told you to come down—but we hafta talk a little. Were you planning to take him off our hands?"

"Only for a week or so. After that the idea was to send him back. At this stage we can't say that the contract's definitely going to be put out."

"Yeah. Well, if it is, we'd like you to take him away and lose him somewhere."

"I thought he made himself useful once in a while."

"He did, but those days are past. As you probably heard, we worked a squeeze play on him to take a contract in Guatemala, but since then he's no longer worth his keep. The time's come to kiss him goodbye. He's a nice, sincere kid. You can't help liking him. But he's been kept down here out of sight for three years, and he's so lonely he's going crazy. He wants to spill out his guts to everyone he sees. One of these days he's gonna come walking right in here where we're sitting and blow his cork to the first barroom glad-hander he meets. This guy is supposed to be dead, Richards. We spend half our time trying to keep him out of harm's way, but sooner or later he's gonna break loose, and when he does he'll be a terrible embarrassment."

"So you want to get him off your back."

"And I'd like your help to do it, paisano. I'd personally be happy to help you in any way I can, but I'd regard it as a great favor if you'd do this small thing for me in return. Listen, do you know that this character actually wrote to some broad back in the States telling her that he was alive after all, and asking her to come down here? She had to go in a car accident. That kind of trouble nobody wants."

"Couldn't you have taken care of him yourselves?" Mark asked.

"It would spoil the image. One of the local big shots—some air force general—has taken him under his wing. If Morgan happened to disappear, they'd know who'd done it. The last thing we want down here is any heat."

"When can I talk to him?"

"Right now, if you want. One thing, though: we'll do what we can to help, but if he doesn't want to take the contract you can't force him. You'll have to find some way to tempt the guy; it's your only hope."

"Does he like money?"

"Not as much as most of us. There's nothing he can do with it. He leads a kind of confined existence."

"But as a pilot he's as good as they say he is?"

"In a light plane, he's in a class of his own. He can fly in anywhere—and get out. Plus, he isn't afraid of anything. D'ya know something? He should have been a Sicilian. He should have been born somewhere like Enna where they'd have taught him to keep his trap shut."

Morgan lived in a beach cottage two miles up the coast, a bleak concrete cube with a barbed-wire fence around it and a small, drowsy soldier guarding the gate. Light from the glow over the city revealed lean dogs nuzzling for offal at the edge of the tide and a gray twinkle of bats against the cobalt depths of the sky. "Señor Lunt," Cardillo said. He gave the soldier a cigarette, and he let them through the gate and rang the bell. Before he'd had time to remove his finger from the buzzer the door opened, and a man dressed as an Eagle Scout stood there, puzzled and affable under the lamp.

"This is Harry Morgan," Cardillo said. "Harry, meet Mark Richards, a very good friend of mine. May we come in, Harry? I brought Mark along because he has a proposition to make to you which I personally believe you're going to find very interesting. He hasn't told me all the details, but the way it sounds to me it's the kind of opportunity that doesn't happen more than once in anybody's lifetime. I don't want to say any more than to assure you that Mark's a stand-up guy. Okay, Harry? Well, now I'm going to leave you two guys to talk a little and hightail it back to the Managua where I have reason to believe there's a poker game waiting for me. Mark, gimme a call when you're ready to come back, and I'll pick you up."

Morgan pulled out a small hard chair and Mark sat down uncomfortably. "Let me fix you a drink, Mr. Richards," Morgan said. "Too bad Mr. Cardillo couldn't stay. How about a rum and coke? The rum down here is pretty good—or else you get used to it. I could give you a bourbon if you like, but for my money whiskey doesn't taste so good in this heat. I'm supposed to have air conditioning here, but the plant broke down a month ago, and I guess they're waiting for spare parts. Everything has to be flown in; that's the problem. As long as we're on the subject of drinks, maybe I should warn you to stay away from the ice. The water isn't too good unless you remember to put sterilizing tablets in it." He gave a sleepy smile. "And most people forget."

Mark had been told that Morgan was thirty years old, but he looked twenty, and there was something about his soft, hypnotized voice that reminded him of that of a lighthouse keeper he had once known, a fourth or fifth cousin back in Sicily, whose tour of duty, out of all contact with humanity on a rock in the Tyrrhenian Sea, had been twelve unbroken months.

"Maybe it should be rum and coke, Harry, if we can't use the ice. Rum and coke will be fine."

Morgan went to the refrigerator for the drinks while Mark sized up the room. It was a seaside cottage to be found the world over, starkly furnished for rental to vacationers who would leave no imprint of their personality when they left. Three chairs of unpainted wood, a small crudely carpentered table, ceramic floor tiles whose sour colorings and greasy glaze tried to imitate linoleum, a Hong Kong print of a thatched cottage framed in plastic, a new line of cheap plates in the kitchenette and a few thick drinking glasses on the dresser.

"I oughta have a lemon somewhere, but I guess it's been thrown away. It's better with a slice of lemon. We only get them once a month in winter. The months with an *r* in them."

Morgan had returned with the drinks, head tilted away, eyes placid but absent, in a way that reminded Mark of a blind man who has trained himself to sense the presence of obstacles he can no longer see. He put the glasses down on the table and swept away a litter of sea shells spread over its surface.

"Just polishing up a few shells when you came by," he explained. "Sometimes it's a bit hard to know what to do with your time. Shell-collecting helps keep me going." Mark remembered that the lighthouse keeper had made fine lace. "The trouble is, they don't have too many kinds on these beaches, so I've had to branch out into color variations. I have a pretty nice collection of fossilized wood which you can see before you go. Right here where we're sitting there used to be a forest a few thousand years ago; then there was a change in the level of the ocean bed and the sea came in. The main thing is to keep the mind occupied."

"You don't get around too much these days, Harry, do you?"

"You could call me an eagle with clipped wings," Morgan said. He smiled with rueful modesty. "Well, maybe not an eagle. I figure you already know why I'm down here. You're a friend of Mr. Cardillo, so there can't be any harm in talking to you. You wouldn't exactly say I'm a prisoner, but I can't go out anywhere unless Mr. Cardillo or General Romero is with me, and they're both busy men. General Romero is interested in fossilized wood, but his English isn't too good. It's a situation in which a man has to develop resources, and I guess I get by. Mr. Cardillo took me to see a movie last week, but they only show pretty old ones in this country. Did you ever see Kirk Douglas and Lauren Bacall in *Young Man with a Horn?* I've seen it three times in all, back in the States and here. Anyway, it passes the time."

"Don't you read at all? I see they had *Playboy* and *Esquire* on the cigar stand at the Managua."

"Well, to tell you the truth I avoid looking at that kind of magazine because the way I live it doesn't seem a good idea to get overstimulated."

"I'd have thought Cardillo could fix you up. There doesn't seem to be any shortage of pussy around here."

Morgan's face was suddenly prim, the eyes censorious. "I wouldn't want to go with a girl unless we were at least engaged, Mr. Richards. I'm not an immoral man. I don't think I'd be able to go on being a good pilot if I were. There was a girl I was interested in back home, but she died in an accident. We had a happy relationship, and I get a kick out of knowing I've been able to remain faithful to her memory."

"And nobody looks after you at all, Harry? Doesn't anybody do the laundry and cook for you?"

"Oh, sure. I've got no cause for complaint there. A woman called Josefa comes in every day and cleans the place for me and does the washing. She'd cook, too, if I'd let her, but I don't go much for the local idea of what constitutes food. What I'd like to eat for every meal from now on until the end of my life would be chicken noodle soup, followed by strawberry shortcake, but maybe I feel that way because it's beyond my reach. If I ask Josefa to buy potatoes for me in the market, she shows up with sweet potatoes. I guess the problem of raw materials is insuperable. As it is, I practically live on eggs. The way I see it, it all depends on how you were raised. Let me show you something."

He pulled open a drawer in the table, took out a file stuffed with what seemed to be newspaper clippings, rummaged through them and handed one to Mark. It was a picture of Morgan at the age of fifteen, making a formal speech on the occasion of his promotion to Eagle Scout in Bethel, Vermont, in 1950. The uniform could have been the same one he was wearing now. "I was a pilot, soloing by the end of the next year," Morgan said.

Mark noted that as Bethel's first Eagle Scout, Morgan wore spectacles. "Do you still have eye trouble?" he asked.

"No. I don't have any trouble with my eyes."

"But you wear contacts, don't you?"

Morgan nodded. "I sure do, and that was what threw me. You could say that it put me where I am now." He made a face, and for an instant a blueprint of depression and defeat was drawn in the stolid optimism of his boyish face. "I was crazy about flying. Whatever happened, I had to fly somehow or other, and all the companies had this ruling about eyesight. I have the smallest correction they grind a lens for, but none of the companies cared. It was kind of ridiculous. I was all right to fly air taxis in Canada, where you have to take off and land on water and have to know about a thousand different lakes by sight. They don't have any navigational aids up there, and theory doesn't get you any place."

Outside, the scavenging dogs had started a fight over the pickings at the tide's edge, and presently a chase developed which took them yelping and whimpering out of earshot. A baleful silence settled again. How can this guy endure it? Mark asked himself; I wouldn't last a week. "How did you come to lose your license, Harry?"

"Flying junk in from Cuba, Mr. Richards. I had to do something. Up in Canada the freeze starts in October, and then you're grounded until May. There was no problem in Cuba until the Reds got there. We used to fly in and out of Rancho Boyeros Airport along with all the regular traffic, and then flip across to Florida under the radar screen. It was okay as long as you kept out of sight of Key West."

"Have you ever heard of a man called Spina? He was in that business."

"Nope, but I guess I only dealt with the small guys. I did about thirty trips until someone tipped off the FBN. The people I was working for must have come through for me in a big way, because I only got a suspended sentence, but I lost my license for illegal entry."

"Which meant that you were finished in the U.S."

"I was finished anywhere for legitimate employment. After that I went to work for a Mr. Williamson in Chiapas, Mexico. He used to specialize in taking old statues out of the jungle and selling them to museums and collectors. The Indians cut a strip with their machetes near some temple that Mr. Williamson found, and then burned it off, and I used to fly in whenever he had a load ready. The trick was to put your wheels down right at the beginning of the strip, because there were only thirty of forty yards to play with and you'd run into the bush at the other end if you didn't. Then you could sit around thinking about how you were going to take off loaded up with a coupla tons of stone idols, without ripping the tops off a few trees. I have to say, Mr. Richards, that really was flying. I could give it all I had." He grinned with almost babyish delight. "Those were the days. That was my kind of gambling. I'd still be there if the Mexicans hadn't caught up with Mr. Williamson. They sent him away for ten years."

"And after that it was the Galdos deal?"

"It had to be. I had to take anything that came my way, and Mr. Rossi befriended me. I should tell you right now that the deal was misrepresented to me. They told me this Galdos fellow had been involved in some big stealing, and that for some reason he couldn't be extradited. How was I to know they were going to massacre him when they got him back?"

"How *were* you to know, Harry? What did they pay you for it?"

"I don't remember."

"Are you kidding me?"

"No, really, Mr. Richards. It was a pretty large sum by my standards, but I don't remember how much. I went to Guatemala after that, and I don't remember how much they gave me for that, either. I don't need a great deal of money. The way I see it, the important thing in life is self-fulfillment. I guess we're really all the same. To do anything I undertake as well as I can—that's what matters to me. The money is of secondary importance."

"There's a hundred grand going for the trip I have in mind." Mark laughed. "But the way you feel, maybe I shouldn't even mention it as an inducement."

"Mr. Richards, what would I do with a hundred grand? I pay Josefa fifteen dollars a week. Maybe the food I eat costs me another twenty. This dump is rent-free. Mr. Cardillo said that you might want me to fly a plane somewhere for you, but even if you paid me a million I'd go right on being a poor man if there was nothing I could do with the money. Something tells me I'm going to stay here for the rest of my life."

"Supposing it could be fixed so that you could get away from the Dominican Republic?"

"That would be different."

"Because maybe that could be done. Nothing's impossible; maybe it could be part of the deal. The people I work for have a lot of pull. You'd be doing a big thing for them, and they'd like to offer you an attractive proposition. What's to stop them getting you a new pilot's license in the name of Lunt? Then you could move back to Canada."

"My face," Morgan said. "Too many people have seen this face in the newspapers. It may surprise you, but in a way Canada's a small place."

"You ever heard of plastic surgery, Harry? You could go into a clinic and come out a week later looking so different that your own mother wouldn't know you. If Canada doesn't seem far enough away, you could work in Australia as a bush pilot. Or I have a pretty strong hunch that my friends could fix you up with a regular airline flying freight in South America. How does that sound?"

"A regular airline. Gee! Do you really think that's a possibility?"

"You'd like that, would you, Harry? Something like Aeronaves do Brasil?"

"Would I like it? It's been my life's ambition."

Mark smiled involuntarily at the spectacle of so much enthusiasm. The creation of hope was a familiar ingredient of his task. Though no man of honor would have admitted to it, compassion joined with expediency in the preparation of a victim to meet his fate. By tradition the condemned man should never be allowed to suspect that his days were numbered, and he should die suddenly and happily—as, for example, Mr. Masseria had died by Spina's orders at a banquet in his honor at Scarpato's Restaurant in Coney Island, his stomach warmed by food and wine, and surrounded by smiling friends. Mark, who found himself unable to like many of his fellow men, liked Morgan, and admired his rare quality of stoicism. The kid was no whiner, and he made the best of things. He had little except rosy promises to offer Morgan, but he was ready to shower him with these.

"Do you suppose I'd be able to get back to the States sooner or later, Mr. Richards?"

"Sure, why not?"

"Within two or three years, maybe?"

"Well, let's say five at the outside. With that new face and a new identity. Wilbur J. Lunt of Rio de Janeiro. Brazil. How does that sound?"

"All my friends think I'm dead. Do you think there'd be some way of letting them know? I know it would have to be done discreetly."

"Eventually, maybe. Right now it would raise too many difficulties. Sooner or later we might be able to do that. I'd have to give it some thought."

"It sure would be great to get back to Canada for the summer flying. Canada's a great place in summer. You're up there with about a thousand miles of pine forest under you, and nothing in them but bears and elks. It gives you the feeling you own the place. I could count on flying in Canada next year, couldn't I, Mr. Richards?"

"No problem at all," Mark said. "Come next June you'll be up there sorting out those thousands of lakes that all look the same."

"Mr. Richards, this contract you want me to take: can you give me any idea what it involves?"

Mark shook his head. "I can't give you the details, Harry, because I don't know them myself. The reason I wanted to see you was to find out if you were interested in principle. All I can tell you at this stage is that it's likely to be another trip like the Guatemala one. If it ever happens, that is, because so far nothing's been finalized. This is just a preliminary discussion to see whether it's the kind of thing you'd like to do."

"Sure, I'd like to do it," Morgan said. "There's nothing I wouldn't take on to get away from here." His apologetic smile contained a trace of anxiety. "Please don't think I'm trying to pry into your private arrangement, Mr. Richards. All I'd want to know when you make up your mind would be the flying time involved, because if it's a long way we have to think about extra tanks. Please understand that it's only the technical details that interest me. Anything else is none of my affair. All you have to do when you're ready is to tell me how many miles we have to fly, and leave the rest to me."

14

Six months passed, during which, in the knowledge that Mark had found his men, Bradley laid his plans. A second fund-raising trip around Texas produced better results than the first. He made his appeals to men whose discretion equaled their wealth, and was able to transfer a quarter of a million dollars to a bank in Trujillo City on which Mark was empowered to draw. "We need a plane with a range of up to fifteen thousand miles," he wrote to Mark. "There should be provision for fitting extra fuel tanks." Mark arranged for the purchase of a twin-engined Beechcroft, and Morgan, overjoyed to be at the controls again, was soon startling the citizens of the Dominican Republic by wild aerobatic displays in the sky overhead.

Back in Salisbury, Mark had put his house on Champlain Avenue up for sale and moved into a downtown hotel. He was cautiously optimistic about the future. The frigidly polite notes with which Teresa had at first acknowledged money sent for the children's upkeep had been superseded by letters containing at least some news, to which Martin and Lucy added dutiful postscripts. Mark was working to tidy up his business affairs in Salisbury, and as soon as the threat of deportation was lifted he intended to move—perhaps to California, where he had contacts among the Italian wine-growing community. He hoped that eventually Teresa's resistance would break down, and that she would return to him in new surroundings where neither of them was known.

Awaiting trial in the Lewisburg penitentiary, notorious for its "Mafia Row," Victor lived on prime steak and put on weight. Regarded as a criminal with powerful connections, he was looked up to equally by the inmates and prison staff, and his acquittal was seen as certain if he ever came to trial. He had inherited the family mania for pets, and kept a cage of white rats and a talking myna with a strong Brooklyn accent in his cell. With time on his hands he wrote respectful and carefully phrased letters to Mark and Spina full of the trivialities of prison existence.

Sitting in Antigua and awaiting with slackening confidence his restoration to power in Cuba, Spina received a flying visit from Bradley. They strolled out to a quiet place on the beach.

"You're a man of action," Bradley said. "How can you stand this life?"

"I've got no option," Spina told him. "My luck ran thin."

"You still think you'll get back eventually?"

"Not while that guy who lucked his way into the hot seat back home is still around."

"That's what I have to talk to you about," Bradley said. "There's an operation in the works. You could walk away from all this and live again."

"Let's hear about it."

Bradley outlined the plan that was to change the American destiny and usher in the glorious millennium of justice and light.

"What made Richards come in on this?" Spina asked.

"I was able to be of help over that Cobbold affair, as well as do something for Victor Di Stefano.

He's very fond of that boy. It may have been his way of showing his gratitude."

The corners of Spina's mouth drew apart with a porcelain glimpse of teeth as he smiled. "You know something, Bradley? I like you—I always have. I wish I could put things the way you do. What are you going to do for me?"

"Get that deportation order rescinded, by way of a start."

"Tell me what I have to do for you."

"Handle the *ripulitura*," Bradley said.

"The what? Jeeze, do people still talk about *ripulituras*? Listen, how about speaking English?"

"I was referring to the mopping-up operation that must follow. I've always regarded it as your greatest specialty, ever since the occasion when Mr. Masseria departed from this world."

"How can I do anything when I'm stuck in this dump?"

Bradley stopped abruptly and the two men faced each other: Spina a smiling, dapper gnome, his gnarled skin matched by the driftwood littering the beach; Bradley twitching with the excitement that crackled like static in his nerves.

"I happen to have devoted some years to the study of your life history," Bradley said. "Maybe all I saw was the tip of the iceberg, but I believe I learned a lot."

"Go on," Spina said. "What did you learn?"

"I learned how men could be ruled," Bradley said. "You were the king. In terms of personal power you came next to the President of the United States."

Remembrance of things past subdued the mockery in Spina's face. "I guess I had a lot of friends," he said.

"What do you mean *had?* You still have. In every city in the States, and you know it. Thousands of members of the famous organization of yours would be very happy to do you a favor. You know that, too, don't you? Crook your finger, and they'd come running. Whatever tidying up there was to be done, they'd be glad to do it for you."

"They might, they might. I helped a few guys one time or another in different ways. There's still one or two who'd do a service for me."

Bradley felt himself on the threshold of success. "I don't say you'd want to stay in the States," he said, "but it would be nice to feel you could come and go as you please."

"It sure would be nice to visit some of the guys again," Spina said. "I kinda miss some of the old faces."

Back in Sicily, one fine autumn morning when Don C. was on his way to a home for the waifs of Palermo, laden with sweets and toys, he felt a sharp pain in the chest, followed by extreme dizziness. He stopped the car and climbed out to squat on a low roadside bank, where purple grapes dangled before his eyes under a darkening sky. As his chauffeur bent over him and put his ear to his mouth, Don C. was able to whisper, "How beautiful life is!" These were the last words of the aged man who for a full decade had been secret ruler of Sicily. His funeral was the most impressive of any commoner's since Garibaldi's and a squadron of motorcycle police had to be rushed from Palermo to control the traffic.

The news of Don C.'s death was broken to Mark by Don Vincente. "This changes everything. That's why I told you to come over. Don Giuseppe held the tassel at the funeral."

"Excuse me, but what difference does that make, Don Vincente?"

"It makes this difference: everybody thought Rocco Gentile was gonna be chosen, and he wasn't. Gentile would have had you whacked out if you'd shown your face there, but Giuseppe happens to be an old friend of mine. I used to play boccie with him when we were kids. If you still want to go back, I can fix it for you. You gotta face it, Marco, you aren't never going to be happy living in this place, and Cuba is out. Wyncha just make your mind to go back with Teresa and the family, and maybe settle down to raise pigs?"

"You think she'd agree to that?"

"Sure, she would; I've already talked to her. Boston doesn't seem to agree with her the way she thought it would, and blood's always thicker than water. If you want me to, I can talk to Giuseppe about this and he can see the Gentile outfit and straighten things out with them. Maybe you're gonna have to spend a little money in the way of *danaro di sangue*. The Gentiles got a few grandchildren around the place. Maybe Giuseppe could fix up a marriage for Amedeo or Lucia."

"I'm in bad with my people for not picking up the tassel when Paolo was hit."

"Give them a *befana* for the kids. Buy all the girls talking dolls and admiral's uniforms for the boys. Hand out a few hampers—couple bottles of Asti Spumante, a little prosciutto, mozzarella, and a few cans of things. I don't need to tell you. You know as well as I do the way these things are done. Believe me, they'll soon forget."

"How long do you figure all this might take?"

"You'll have to allow three months. Giuseppe will do this for me if I ask him, but I can't tell him I want results the day after tomorrow. What's it matter, anyway, if the FBN isn't in a hurry to deport you? Get this operation with Bradley out of the way and you can take off."

"It will be out of the way in a couple of weeks. We have it arranged to get Leon at twenty-four hours' notice, and Cardillo will send Morgan up as soon as we give him the green light. The big news is that Salva's agreed to come in on it."

"You need him. It sounds like it's gonna be the biggest hit ever, and you can use his experience."

"All we're waiting for now is the word from Bradley."

"Where did you say the meeting's gonna be?"

"Some place on the Mexican coast around Matamoros. There's a desert airstrip we can use near the frontier."

"Near what frontier?"

"The U.S."

"The U.S. frontier, huh? Does anything about this setup surprise you the way it does me?"

"Everything about it surprises me," Mark said.

"How much has Bradley let you know about what's cooking?"

"Nothing."

"So you don't have any idea of who's gonna be taken out."

"He figures it isn't necessary until the last moment. I'm just a foreman on the assembly line of this operation."

"And it couldn't be Cuba? This couldn't be a party for the bearded man?"

"The geography's all wrong," Mark said. "Why would we meet up in Matamoros to go to Cuba? You only have to look at the map."

"Yeah, you only have to look at the map."

"What does it matter? I'll know as soon as I see Salva," Mark said. "He has to do the cleaning up so that Bradley and his friends will come out of this smelling like roses. He can't be working in the dark."

"I've been thinking a lot about Bradley," Don Vincente said. "I still have this feeling in my gut that he and that outfit he works with, doing whatever they do, have been sitting back watching us for years. I figure that way back in Sicily he was watching you, like he's been watching you and me ever since. He wanted to learn all he could about how we operate."

"Well, he learned fast," Mark said. "I hear they're likely to drop that homicide charge against Victor since that crazy hobo disappeared."

Don Vincente nodded with wolfish glee. "He learned fast because we taught him all that our fathers and grandfathers taught us. Well, almost all, anyway. Just look at the way they went to work to find out how that Armas hit was set up. Thirty years ago guys like Bradley didn't exist. You know something, Marco? They saw the way our people ran Sicily behind the backs of the King or the Duce, or whoever was supposed to be running it, and they figured they might be able to make the same thing work for them here."

For Mark there was a warning in Don Vincente's summation.

"This could be the last time they want to fall back on us," the old man went on. "Maybe the way they see it, we've taught them all we can. I bet Bradley's brought us in to set up this hit, just to be on the safe side, because he knows we'll do it right. After this, he'll know all he wants to know when these things have to be done. Anyone he wants whacked out, he'll be able to do it himself."

15

They met at the Hamilton House, went straight up to the room Mark had booked and made love without preparation or preamble. As it had always been in the past, it was rough and urgent, and as satisfying as raw wine drunk in heat. She was wearing no under-clothing, just as before they came to Salisbury, and when he entered her she shrieked. She was tighter than he remembered.

"You felt like a virgin again," he told her afterwards.

"It's been a year," she said.

All the human perfumes of the past had returned, and the sharp and gritty sensualities that had gradually blunted and atrophied through the years and the world's distractions. Adventure had returned.

"What are we going to do now?" Teresa asked.

"Get the children back from school and move somewhere else," he said.

"Where?"

"California, maybe."

"I thought they were going to deport you."

"They won't now." He tried to think of some phrase of explanation that bore no taint of the past, but he couldn't. "The fix is in," he said finally.

"Why California?"

"It doesn't have to be California. It could be Phoenix or Kansas City or Chicago if you like."

"You mean places where you have connections?"

"Friends, or friends of friends," Mark said. "Don Vincente has connections in most of the big cities."

"Would we have to use them?" Teresa asked. "Couldn't we get by on our own?"

After the years they had spent together without explanations of any kind they came with difficulty now, even when he was prepared to give them. "When you're making a start in a fresh locality it helps," he said. What he was trying to convey in a sentence was the Sicilian peasant's fear—bred in his bones, to be carried with him until his dying day—of isolation in a hostile country. It was the fear, irrational as a terror of ghosts, that still sent the peasants of Campamaro, Agrigento and Caltanissetta scuttling homewards at nightfall to mountain villages built like fortresses, leaving the countryside to the phantoms of marauders who in reality had vanished from the scene fifty years or more before. In Sicily every man had taken the fear from his father and passed it on to his son, and each of them made what ties and alliances they could to protect themselves from a vengeful world.

"If California or the Midwest doesn't sound good to you," Mark said, "we could pull out altogether and go back to the people we know."

"You mean home?" she said.

He caught the eagerness in her voice. "In three months we could—if we wanted to. It might be the solution. Being deported is one thing; going because that's the way you want it is another."

"But you said you'd given up the idea of ever going back. You said you'd lost all your friends."

"That's the way it looked then. I'd had a bad break and I was depressed. There was some trouble I didn't tell you about, but now it's all going to be fixed up." He gave her a hug. "Between us, we have about a thousand cousins living on that island. All we have to do is go back and tell them who we are."

"I want to go back to Palermo and live in an apartment block with fifteen or twenty other families, and send the kids to play in the Parco della Favorita, and go to Mondello every Sunday and eat seafood like we used to."

"We could put the kids in the local school," Mark said. He had always believed that children should be kept at home. It was where Don Vincente had gone wrong; the two elder boys, Mario and Claudio, had been sent to boarding school, and when he had lost touch with them the rot had set in.

"Could we change our name back to Riccione?" Teresa asked. "I don't want to be Richards any more. It brought us nothing but bad luck. I want to be Riccione again."

"Sure we can change our name, and Martin will be Amedeo, and Lucy, Lucia. If we decide to go."

"I've made up my mind already," she said. She was full of enthusiasm, and suddenly he became aware that she had altered in every way. Her face had lost its solemn sterile intelligence, and a candor and clarity had returned, like a portrait cleaned of inept retouching and restored to its original freshness.

"How was Boston? Tell me the truth."

"It was miserable. I was just existing; it wasn't life. All I had to look forward to was seeing the children on weekends."

"You didn't take to hospital work?"

"I never had the chance to."

"But weren't you going to be trained for special work?"

"It never happened. The nearest I got to training as a social worker was filling out the form. I don't think they liked where I was born, and anyway I didn't have the qualifications. The only qualifications I ever had were when I lived in a ranch house in the best neighborhood of Salisbury. In Boston I shared a walk-up with a couple of waitresses in the Trattoria Fiorentina on Hanover Street. That's where I worked too."

"A waitress. Jesus. And yet you sent back the money I sent you."

"The first time, but not after that," Teresa said. "Anyway, in between the misery it was fine. It did me good. I got to know a little more about what life was all about. The girls were wonderful. They were two sisters from Catania, with three more sisters back home, and they were saving up for their sisters' dowries as well as their own. That's how it should be. That's the kind of thing I ought to have been doing instead of the silly life I lived in Salisbury."

"Did anybody find out about you and what you were doing in Boston?"

"They couldn't help finding out. Some reporter tracked me down and my picture was in the paper."

"That kind of guy should be shot."

"As it turned out, it didn't matter. The girls got a helluva kick out of it, and Mr. Agnelli, the owner, was so impressed that he offered me a better job. You'd have thought I was a movie actress."

"That stuff the papers printed was vomit," Mark said.

"The *Globe* was okay," she said. "Comparatively, anyway. I don't know what the *Examiner* had to say because as soon as I started reading it I felt sick."

"I suppose you know that McClaren accused me of having the Watts girl murdered."

Teresa stiffened. "I heard that too."

"I was supposed to have put her in cement and dropped her in the river."

"I didn't want to talk about it, or even think about it," Teresa said. "I knew it must be another of McClaren's lies."

"That was the one thing that really burned me up."

"Mark, I've never asked you many questions and I'm not going to start now. Just tell me one thing for the sake of my peace of mind: what really happened to her?"

"She was with a man who was a leading light in some religious sect. When the news broke, he asked them to make him a missionary and they got married and took off together. They're up with the Eskimos in Alaska, or someplace like that."

"You swear that?"

"On anything you like."

"Well, I'm not going to ask you to, because you don't lie to me. She was a beautiful girl, wasn't she? I don't believe she'd led the kind of life McClaren said she had."

"She hadn't. McClaren's kind spread dirt wherever they can. They've got a hack writer from one of the porno magazines who dishes out that kind of stuff to order. She did everything she knew how not to make it tough for me." He groped for words to express his gratitude, frustrated by the impoverishment of language. With Anglo-Saxon understatement, "okay" covered the whole spectrum of praise, and it didn't seem enough. *"Era una brava figluola,"* he said.

"Were you in love with her?" Teresa said, her voice suddenly faded and neutral. "I guess any man would have been."

He was astonished, and the sincerity of his surprise reassured her. "That would have been impossible."

"She was pretty, wasn't she? And you just said she was a good girl."

"But she was a hooker," Mark said. "Maybe she couldn't help it, but that's how it was. To love a hooker a man has to be sick."

"Why?"

Now he was confronted not only by a barrier of language, but by one of thought. His life, like Teresa's, was built on a prefabricated structure of assumption. He believed because he believed, and the more ancient, atavistic and irrational the belief, the stronger it was held. The flesh of a prostitute or of a woman whose virginity had been taken by another was tainted, and to love such a woman would have been a crime against himself.

"Why?" Teresa asked again.

"L'onore," he said. It was an answer that excluded further argument.

She nodded in acceptance, if not in agreement. *"Eh già, l'onore."* Suddenly she was completely happy and secure. *L'onore,* if nothing else, had protected her from defeat by the beauty of a strange woman. *Viva l'onore.*

"When can we go? When shall I tell them I'm quitting? I have to give a few days' notice."

The fact that she was not ready to leave immediately came as a relief. He had been afraid that she would insist on coming back to Salisbury with him there and then.

"I have a few things to settle up too," he said. "You know, it might be smart if you stayed on in Boston until we're ready to take off. We could give Salisbury a miss altogether, and maybe take the kids out of school and go down to Florida, or some place like that, and wait there until we were ready to go back home. Maybe you could plan on leaving in ten days, to be on the safe side. By that time I'll have everything fixed up and we can drive around to the schools, pick the kids up and be on our way."

"Can you imagine their faces? They've never stopped talking about you."

"Nothing ever came out at school, did it?" he asked.

"No, we were lucky there. Whatever they may have heard, nobody let on."

"I figure you won't lose any sleep if you never set eyes on Salisbury again."

"No," she said. "Not a wink. But where can I call you if anything comes up?"

She saw the change in his face, in the split second when his mind was elsewhere the voice of intuition whispered doubt.

"I just heard this morning that I have to be away for a few days. You won't be able to reach me, but I'll do my best to call you."

"Please tell me where you're going," Teresa said.

"I can't, because I don't know myself."

"You actually mean to tell me that you're going somewhere but don't know where? I was hoping that was over and done with."

"It's a service I'm doing for a friend," Mark said. He felt the necessity for evasion weaken him. "It's one of those things I can't explain." His pleading look implored her to ask no more. "After next week I'll be able to tell you anything you want," he said. "I'll be my own master again."

She turned away from him to hide her tears. "You're kidding yourself, but you can't kid me," she answered. "I realize now that's something you'll never be."

16

Spina picked Mark up at Matamoros Airport and they drove southwards through desert country under rain slanting from the clouds rolling above them like smoke.

"I managed to round up Lupo, Di Angelis and Cianfarani in Memphis," Mark said. "It took a lot of talking, but it was okay in the end. If they're prepared to cooperate, I guess the others will too."

"Young Lupo," Spina said. "I haven't seen him in years. He married my niece. Sure, he'll cooperate. He'll have to; I helped that guy make his bones."

"We have a fall guy ready," Mark said. "And a couple in reserve, just in case anything goes wrong."

"A nut case?"

"Just an average screwball. Joins movements. Writes stupid letters to politicians and plays around with guns. Bradley found him. He's had him on his payroll for one or two small jobs."

"Is he gonna leave a diary?" Spina asked.

"We hadn't thought of doing that. My hunch is we have to think of something new. The way Cardillo set up the Guatemala hit was okay for a small country, but we don't think this man ought to be gunned down on the spot. People should have a chance to see his picture in the newspapers, and get to know how wacky he is. It makes less of a mystery."

"You're absolutely right."

Spina braked gently. A bus lay on its side in yellow mud and water ahead, and he tried to spare its stranded passengers a further drenching from his tires.

"This thing is big," he went on as he eased by the wreck. "You have to study it from every angle. We have to arrange it so that all our friends are in the clear. Our job is to think ahead. I've never played chess, but they tell me that the thing is to cover all the moves."

"A few people down here in Mexico are going to know more about this than they ought to," Mark said.

"Yeah, and it's worse than you think. That friend of yours in the prison service turns out to have handed some of his loot over to a buddy, who found out what was going on. That makes more work. At least two of the screws in the nut house will have to be taken care of. Didja ever think how Leon is going to get here from Mexico City? Somebody's gonna have to bring him. That makes more complications. And what about the guy Cardillo sent with Morgan?"

"If he has to be taken out, we're never going to stop, and maybe Cardillo would object. He's a member."

"To do this right you got to plug all the holes. I got work for days in this country."

"It could be that our friends in the States are going to have plenty to keep themselves occupied for weeks."

"And you, I have to remind you," Spina said. "You too."

"That's not in the deal," Mark said. "I'm excused from the cleaning up."

"Right now I'd rather be in your shoes than mine. Where you're going they're all on our side. Even the cops. Bradley tells me they've actually got the police lined up, and I believe him. You'll get all the help you need. Listen, you mean to tell me that all you're expected to do is look over the arrangements and then tell them how the hit's to be set up?"

"And see that everything goes off according to plan. That's the contract I took."

"Why do they treat you like some fancy consultant?" Spina said. "You have all the breaks. It must be that Ivy League appearance of yours."

The adobe building by the airstrip came into sight through the rain. Until a year before, this had been a stop for a local line working on a shoestring with DC-3's, but with the crash of the last DC-3, silence had fallen. The building where the passengers and their luggage had been sheltered still flew the tatters of Coca-Cola and Bohemia beer advertisements like prayer flags in the wind. A few nondescript Mexicans, driven out of the sodden desert like fleas from the coat of a drowning dog, squatted in the shelter of its eaves, their faces stoic and impassive in the openings of shawls and blankets pulled around their heads. A hundred yards away Morgan's Beechcroft crouched among organ cactus, hardly distinguishable at first sight from the wreckage normally abandoned at the edge of such informal airfields.

"Think it will be able to take off in this weather?" Mark asked.

"Sure. You got all the visibility you need. That's all that matters."

"Let's hope you're right," Mark said. "How much does Morgan know?"

"He knows where he's going, that's all. He hasn't asked any questions. He'll stay with the plane."

"That guy's stayed fourteen years old all his life. You'd think he'd be worried about what was going to happen to him. Did Cardillo tell you he didn't want him back?"

"He said that. I'll have to think what to do with him when you're gone." The sound of Spina's laughter reminded Mark more and more of the cackle of a talking parrot.

Morgan was waiting in the stripped office at the back of the old ticket counter. He looked up from the comic book he was reading, still studious yet smiling slightly, but when he saw Mark he jumped to his feet, holding out his hand.

"Harry," Mark said. "Nice to see you again so soon."

"I hafta get something from the car," Spina said. "I'll be right back."

"Seems we're going on a little trip together, Harry," Mark said.

"It will be my pleasure, Mr. Richards," Morgan said. He stood at attention, trim and eager in his new zip jacket on which three cloth scout's proficiency badges had been sewn. "I don't know how to begin to thank you for what you've done for me," he said. "I can't believe I'm actually going to be a free man at last."

"Think nothing of it," Mark said. "I've been able to help you, and you're doing something for me."

"I'm itching to be under way," Morgan said. "Kind of excited, I guess. When were you figuring on taking off?"

"As soon as the other passenger shows up."

"Anybody I happen to know, by chance?"

"As a matter of fact, yes. Remember Bonachea Leon, the man you went to Guatemala with?"

Something shattered the youthfulness of Morgan's expression. "Only too well."

"Why do you say that? Don't you like him?"

"I don't think he's the kind of man anybody could like, Mr. Richards. I can put up with him if I have to, but the fact is he gives me the creeps. He reminds me of a character I saw in a horror movie once. No one wants to spend more time than they have to with a person who's abnormal."

"You'll have to put up with him for a while, Harry. How long is the flight going to take?"

"Five hours, Mr. Richards, give or take a half-hour. Right now we have a force three southwesterly that will be pushing us along, but it's going to die out pretty soon and we'll be losing some speed. But the extra tanks are fitted now, so there won't be any problem there."

He talked rapidly, releasing a torrent of words with the garrulousness of a lonely man. ". . . have to expect a bit of turbulence down in this area, but we'll be flying under the worst of it. We have to, anyway, on account of the radar screen. I'd like to give you a nice smooth trip if I can. This is a pretty nice plane; it rides turbulence better than a DC-7. We don't have to worry too much about the weather. September is a bad month down here, but as soon as you're through October you can sit back and relax. November is okay, when it doesn't rain, and December is really beautiful. It's a pity we aren't making this trip in December. I used to fly up this way sometimes bringing back the stuff I told you about that we got out of the jungle, and the scenery can be swell. It sure is a wonderful feeling to be back at the controls of a plane again. I guess we aren't going to see much today, but it should be a nice smooth trip."

Tires scrunched in the wet gravel outside, and a moment later Spina signaled from the doorway. "He's here."

"Excuse me for a second, Harry," Mark said. He followed Spina out into the shell of the waiting room and saw two men standing with their backs turned. One, small and slight, in army surplus trousers and a checkered shirt, he recognized as Bonachea Leon. The other was an older man, with a heavy body and short legs, wearing a green Eisenhower jacket. Both were bending over a paper packet done up with string, which the older man was untying without haste and with fingers that were exceptionally small and delicate. Lying on the bench beside the packet was a brown gun case.

"Who's the other guy?" Mark asked.

"The boyfriend, if you can imagine it," Spina said. "I just had a word with one of the screws. He won't go anywhere without him."

"I didn't get it."

"I told you, he has to have this guy with him wherever he goes. They're in love or something." Spina made an ugly expression of distaste.

"Is *he* a nut, too?"

"Sure he's a nut. He's in the package deal—no extra charge."

"What are we going to do?" Mark asked.

"What was the arrangement with your friend in Mexico City?"

"Just to send Leon, and I'd see that he got back.

Nothing was said about a second nut coming along."

"So now we got three screws and a driver out there who are getting straight back to tell all their friends and neighbors what they've seen here today, and one extra nut who has to be taken out—but when and where? Didn't Leon have a wife and kid he was crazy about?"

"They had to be left behind in Cuba," Mark said.

"Yeah, I remember. I guess he just has an affectionate disposition. The thing is, he won't go without the other guy, so it looks like we gotta take a big chance. Supposing these two nuts decide they don't want to go back to Mexico?"

"They'd be alone and on the run in a strange land. They have it pretty good where they are. The Mexicans are kind to screwballs. They'll go right back where they came from."

"We'll have to take the chance, and decide what to do when they get back," Spina said.

"It's too late to do anything else."

"Listen," Spina said, "the guys who brought them want to take off, and I'd like to get pictures of them, just to be on the safe side. How about keeping them batting the breeze for a minute or two while I get a couple of shots?"

A shivering little knot of guards in flimsy khaki stood with the driver of the van in the doorway against the gray palisade of rain. One of them with an enormous Pancho Villa mustache held the dangling cuffs used to handcuff Bonachea Leon and his friend together. Mark pulled out a hip flask and handed it around, and the men's pleasure showed in revelations of exquisite teeth. The flask passed from man to man, scrupulously wiped between sips with a perfectly laundered handkerchief, and was handed back. In the meanwhile Spina moved around inconspicuously, a Minox held to his eye.

"Perhaps we may go?" said the English-speaking guard. He and the others raised their hats and smiled again. "Your servant to command," the guard said, and backed away with the others into the rain as the driver raced to start the van.

Spina put the Minox away. "I have to get those shots to Pascuale tomorrow," he said. "Let's hope they come out. The light was bad."

They returned to Leon and his friend. The big man had now succeeded in untying the string around the package, which he opened slowly and methodically, revealing two bulky Mexican sandwiches of the kind made from rolls cut through the middle and thickly stuffed with sliced tomatoes, chopped peppers and meat. He picked one up with great delicacy between finger and thumb and handed it to Leon, who pushed an end into his mouth and began to chew quickly. The older man stood over him, smiling down indulgently, then suddenly rotated his hips obscenely like a Turkish belly dancer. He had a pendulous, bluish lower lip, and his cheeks were dusted with powder.

Leon, a little coloring from the tomato staining the thin hairs at the corner of his mouth, was suddenly aware that they were being observed. He smiled slyly, tore the sandwich in half and thrust the unchewed end in Mark's direction. It was obvious that he was delighted to see him again. "You wanna a piece of taco?" he said.

Mark shook his head.

"This is my friend Ernesto," Leon said. "My good friend for me."

The big man bowed. *"Encantado,"* he said.

"I have to photograph this guy too," Spina said. "Let's go over to the doorway where we got a little light to work with."

Mark jerked his head in the direction of the door, and the four men walked toward it. Spina took photographs, and instantly, as if he had touched a switch, the rain stopped and a misted sun appeared. In the periphery of Mark's vision, Morgan, jacket over his head, was skipping around the puddles on his way out to the plane. "Looks like we can take off," Mark said.

"Yeah, I guess this is it." A syrupy current of cajolery flowed in Spina's voice. "Listen, how about coming back this way and giving me a hand with what has to be done? Nobody's gonna miss you in Salisbury for a couple of days."

"Sorry, I have family problems to attend to," Mark said. "I'm planning on taking off for Delano right away. We have a friend with a vineyard. If we delay any longer we won't make the end of the grape harvest. The kids are going to get a big kick out of picking grapes."

"Grape-picking," Spina said. "That's something I haven't done in forty years. I used to get a big kick out of it myself." He gave in with good grace. "But maybe you'll be seeing me before you expect to. California sounds good to me. How long are you figuring on staying? If this thing goes off smoothly, I may be paying you a surprise visit out there before long. Better write down that address for me; you never know."

Morgan had reached the Beechcroft and climbed into the pilot's seat. A happy man again, he was whistling his favorite tune, "Ghost Rider in the Sky."

17

Lying among the bushes, Bonachea Leon fired four times at the figure in the car approaching below, waited for a second to interpret the writhings of his target, then jumped to his feet, ran back up the grassy knoll and climbed the fence. Mark tried to take the gun away from him with the intention of throwing it into the bushes, but he refused to be parted from it, dodging with angry, marmoset grimaces beyond reach, and then scrambling back through the parked cars toward the railroad tower under which the Ford had been parked. Ernesto threw the case under a bush and went after him, and Mark followed.

Cars were parked here by the hundreds, bumper to bumper, and Leon fled as nimble and rubbery as a monkey over bumpers and hoods. There were distant faces on the overpass, but otherwise not a single human being in sight. The motorcade had drained away the population of the city into the streets forming its route, leaving such places as this to pigeons, cats, and an extraordinary silence. Through a gap in the rows of cars Mark saw the Ford, distinguished by its coating of dried mud, and then, as he came nearer, by the GOLDWATER FOR PRESIDENT sticker on the windshield. Bradley's man Philips stood on the bumper watching for them, and Mark could see the horror on his face at the spectacle of Leon running toward him still holding the gun. Jumping down, he rushed at Leon and tore it out of his hands. He looked round distractedly for somewhere to shove the gun away out of sight, then tossed it through the window into the back of the car. He had lost his head, and rushed about in a wild, uncoordinated way. Ernesto was lagging somewhere in the tangle of cars, and Philips began to wave his arms and shout.

Now police sirens were wailing along Elm Street, and Mark could see the heads of running figures bobbing among the cars near where they had stood by the fence to wait for the motorcade's approach. Ernesto came up, fighting for breath, and fell into the Ford's back seat at Leon's side. Philips started the car, grinding the gears, turned with a screech of tires to the left and fled up the lane of cars, engine whining in low. The truck ahead had been placed across the end of the lane to block off the entry of more cars that might have boxed them in; seeing the Ford approaching, the driver started up and moved away to let them through.

Mark pulled at Philips' arm. "Slower, friend. Take it easy. The slower we go, the better it looks." Ahead, police in cars and on foot were beginning to infiltrate the area of the railroad yards from the Houston Street entrance, and in a minute they were stopped by an officer on a motorcycle. Philips showed his special pass and the officer started his siren, swung ahead of them and led them out into

Houston Street, keeping ahead of them all the way down to the viaduct, where he waved them on and turned back. There was little traffic on the road going out of town, and Philips eased the Ford into the fast lane over the viaduct, and then along Zamp Boulevard into Thornton Freeway and open country. His jaws were clamped together, and occasionally he swallowed with conscious effort. Ernesto's heavy breathing had subsided and the color was back in his cheeks. He spoke for the first time after an admiring glance at Leon, who was asleep. *"Era una maravilla,"* he said. "He was marvelous."

It was an hour's drive to Wright Field in Van Zendi County, and Philips held the Ford at eighty miles an hour most of the way. Leon continued to sleep, and Ernesto crooned in Spanish, then suddenly put his head out of the window to vomit a little. Mark daydreamed of a serene future. At the airfield Philips showed his pass at the gate and they drove onto the tarmac. The Beechcroft was parked by a hangar two hundred yards away, but there were no signs of Morgan. Wright Field, which handled freight, air taxis and a few charter flights looked strangely deserted. Freight aircraft stood among crates piled on fork lifts that either awaited shipping or had just been unloaded. An EMPU electrical starter had been abandoned by its crew. A man in uniform came from behind a pile of fertilizer in sacks and strolled toward them, playing with the chain of his whistle.

"Seen the pilot of this plane?" Mark called to him.

"Sure, he went over to the office. Be right back. What's the latest from Dallas?"

"We're from Austin. We just got in. Been on the road."

"You heard they got the President?"

"We heard something."

"They got his wife too. Maybe a coupla fellers traveling in the car with them, as well. Some crazy guy with a machine gun. I guess he had it coming to him. We're not grieving too much down here."

"Let's get over to the office," Mark said to Philips, "and see what that stupid sonofabitch is up to."

They drove across to the airfield staff entrance and Mark ran in. The first thing he saw was three men propping each other up, bottles of beer in their hands. Addled laughter, cheering and some raw-edged singing came through the door of a bar. As Mark entered, he saw a man dancing Mexican-style around his hat, which he had thrown on the floor. Somebody else put an arm round his shoulders and thrust a glass in his hand. A man with a big, beefy Texas face was embracing the barman. Another held up a poster showing the President's head, full-faced and in profile. WANTED FOR TREASON. THIS MAN IS WANTED FOR TREASONOUS ACTIVITIES AGAINST THE UNITED STATES, ran the headline below.

He ran out, followed by laughter like the screeching of tropical birds, and rushed from one empty office to another. Finally he saw Morgan swinging through the door of the men's rest room. Mark went up, took him by the shoulders and peered into his face. There were pink flushes under the boyish eyes, and his smile was slipping out of control.

"Where the hell have you been?" Mark said. "Who told you to leave the plane?"

Morgan's face sank to the level of Mark's chest as his knees flexed. A bubble of saliva formed at a corner of his mouth and was sucked back. He breathed out a gas of food curdled by raw spirits. "I stayed with it the way you said, until just now. I slept in it. Then some guys came over and asked me to have a drink with them. They were celebrating."

"And you went. How much did you have?"

"Two, I guess. Rye on the rocks. To celebrate with the fellas. Some guy said he'd keep an eye on the Beech." He rocked stiffly like a toy figure stabilized by the lead in its feet.

"You're as drunk as a monkey," Mark said. "Or maybe someone slipped you a Mickey Finn. Let's get out of here." He grabbed Morgan's arm to steady him, and rushed him out of the building. "Listen, what did you talk to those guys about? What did you tell them? Did you tell them anything about yourself or about us?"

"Nothing. Maybe I said we were headed for Houston, but that's all. I don't remember. If anybody asked me, I guess that's what I said."

"You told them that, huh? You put Little Rock in the airfield log, and then you tell them we're going to Houston! First of all you leave the plane, then you do a crazy thing like that. Do you think they're all as goddam stupid as you are? *Of course* someone is going to start asking what the hell happened here. *Of course* they're going to call Houston and have a reception committee waiting for us."

"Those guys weren't listening to anything. The President got shot and they were celebrating. They were happy, as if this was the best thing that'd ever happened to them. Somebody asks me where we're headed for because he's making conversation, and I tell him out of politeness. When you're having a drink with someone, that's the way it is."

"You idiot," Mark said. "The Feds will be waiting to talk to us at Houston—or anywhere else in this state. They'll put out a general call."

And there was at least a one-in-four chance, Mark reflected, that exactly this would happen. He stopped and turned Morgan around to face him. "Listen, are we carrying enough gas to cut out Houston and get to Matamoros in one hop?"

Morgan thought about it, his expression tightening as he grappled with the problems of distance, fuel and probable winds.

"Yeah," he said after a minute. "We can do it. If we cut across the Gulf instead of following the coast, we've got enough."

There was no safe alternative, Mark thought. His plan to leave Morgan and the others at Houston and pick up the first plane to New York would have to be dropped. What difference did it make if he returned with them to the airstrip near Matamoros?

Five or six hours, maybe. Whatever happens, he told himself, I'll still be in Boston tomorrow.

The delta of the Brazos River spread beneath them like the veined wing of a butterfly. In the first of the passenger seats, Mark sat behind and to the right of Morgan at the controls. Sober now and nibbling a candy bar, Morgan occasionally removed a hand from the stick to massage an area of his temple where dandruff had appeared under the thinning hair. Leon had fallen off to sleep again in the seat behind Mark, his expression of placid exhaustion sometimes broken by wincing smiles like a baby with the wind. Ernesto mouthed a Mexican ballad silently against the rumble of the plane's exhaust and the chatter of loose fittings coming from every part of the cabin. Whenever they hit an air pocket, he crossed himself. Houston was behind them, with the Gulf flowing darkly into sight. The sun vibrating behind the bleared cabin window prepared to drop behind the earth's curvature somewhere in the region of Corpus Christi, above which hot desert mists hung like blue smoke. Everything seemed to be going as planned. Passing over Houston, Morgan had reassured him, with a gesticulation toward the gauge and an uplifted thumb, that there was gas to spare.

It was the end of the mission, and for Mark the end of all such missions. Suddenly he found himself emptied, like a poet without inspiration. Some ingredient, some mysterious element in his bodily chemistry that hitherto had conferred on his nerves immunization from fear, was exhausted. The cold exhilaration he had felt in killing the Moors, and later when he had presided in person at the massacre of Messina's bandits, and later still when he had witnessed Cobbold's death, had left him. In Dallas he had been calm but spiritless, a man stripped of his vocation. It was the first sign of the rebellion from within. Something inside had collapsed; he was no longer himself.

Spina, waiting at the desert airstrip, would be

surprised and happy to see him again. He was basically a lonely man who needed the presence of a friend, of a man of his own kind, when he went about his work. It was to be expected that he would renew his persuasions, but Mark would reject them tactfully.

He was experiencing a new sensation of freedom, but with it, one of emptiness and decline. For twenty years he had been under a discipline more effective than that imposed by any army. He had been a shock trooper who marched, when called upon, unquestioningly at the orders of his superiors, bound to their cause by some inexplicable domination of the mind. Now he was leaderless because he had cut himself adrift. Thinking back, he realized that the turning point had come with the shocking knowledge that in return for a favor Don C. had been prepared to commit him to the service of Bradley and to exposing his family to a vendetta, thus bringing about the death of his brother. A god had miserably failed, but in withdrawing his trust he had lost not only faith in the dimly defined code for which he had always fought, but faith in himself as well.

Spina, too, was involved in the disillusionment. Both of them, Mark saw, had been reduced to mercenaries. What had been done had nothing to do with the code they had sworn to. It was a deal, a contract to be fulfilled on the cheapest terms. Spina's role was to be the silencing of many voices; the hiring of specialists in elimination wherever they might be required; the suborning of policemen, politicians and judges; the preparation of a great fraud on which national credence was to be built. Let him get on with it on his own. Something about the approaching *ripulitura* reminded Mark of a piece he had read in *The Reader's Digest* about the burial of a Pharaoh with his treasures, followed by the strangling of all those employed in the construction of the secret tomb by an executioner—who was then himself strangled. *Who was then himself strangled.*

His head fell on his chest. In two seconds he slipped

through a dream in which he telephoned Teresa. "I'm on my way. *Arrivo subito.*"

Her voice was far, far away, small and hollow and grief-clogged. *"Tu non arrivi mai. Addio."*

He awoke protesting and startled, his hand jiggling the receiver on a line that had gone dead. All the loose objects in the plane were tinkling harder, and Morgan turned his head and gestured at his seat belt.

As Mark fastened it, he saw a late evening sierra of clouds, pushing rosy peaks into the sky through the window ahead. The Beechcroft was climbing on full throttle with an organ-pipe baying of exhaust, and black fingers of an oil leak from an engine clutched toward him across a wing. Luminous cloud shapes as smooth and as pink as maiden's flesh bulged beneath them, but suddenly the sky's light was switched off and they dropped down and down through a foaming crater to crash on hard boards of air. Wrenched from his seat as his belt's fastenings broke, Ernesto hit the plane's roof among the upward cascade of luggage, and fell open-mouthed in the aisle. Leon sluiced vomit while Morgan, nonchalant and improved by the emergency, gathered the plane masterfully, banked on full throttle, probed the clouds for a soft spot and punched through into tranquil air. Beneath them the sea spread like a pavement of softly sparkling granite, and the Mexican coast was a pale wedge to the west in the gathering blues of night. "That's what flying's all about," Morgan called triumphantly, but nobody heard.

They were riding on silk and coming into Matamoros, which already showed them its speckling of lights. Mark had unclipped his safety belt to go to Ernesto's aid when a hidden device, no larger than a pocket watch, exploded in the plane's tail. It had been timed to do its work shortly after the refueling stop at Houston, for which, to be on the safe side, forty-five minutes had been allowed. With a further ten minutes' delay, much expertise and ingenuity would have been wasted. The sound of the explosion was hardly louder than that of a biscuit being snapped in Mark's ear. As the plane began to fall, he grabbed at the armrests and held on, believing at first that they were in another air pocket.

The gray sea rushed up to take them.